10 SHADES OF
SEDUCTION

10 SHADES OF
SEDUCTION

SARAH McCARTY
TIFFANY REISZ
ALISON TYLER
LISA RENEE JONES
PORTIA DA COSTA
SASKIA WALKER
ANNE CALHOUN
ALEGRA VERDE

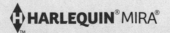
HARLEQUIN® MIRA®

Recycling programs
for this product may
not exist in your area.

ISBN-13: 978-0-7783-1703-6

10 SHADES OF SEDUCTION

HARLEQUIN®
www.Harlequin.com

CONTENTS

SUBMIT TO DESIRE
TIFFANY REISZ

"Another one bites the dust," Charlotte said, raising her glass. Two other glasses met it and the resulting clink sent Amaretto sour dripping over her fingers and onto the floor.

"Good riddance to bad boyfriends." London downed the last of her Fuzzy Navel and set the empty glass on the bar.

"I'll drink to that," Sasha said, sucking out the last drops of her Long Island Iced Tea.

Steele, the bartender, refilled her glass.

"That's the problem." Charlotte tucked a stray strand of red hair back into her straw cowboy hat. "Nick wasn't a bad boyfriend. He was…nice."

Sasha and London stared at her over the top of their drinks.

"You already dumped him, Char." London wadded up her napkin and tossed it at Steele. "Don't add insult to injury."

"You women are all the same." Steele set three shots up in front of them. "God forbid you date a guy who's nice to you."

"Nick *was* nice." Sasha picked up her shot. "And kind of hot. Nice isn't bad. Nice is just…boring."

"Boring," London agreed.

Charlotte sighed and gazed down into her drink.

Nick was nice. Too nice. So nice she wanted to kill him for it sometimes. Last week had been the last straw. She'd fallen asleep during sex. Missionary position. Five minutes of foreplay. Five minutes of thrusting. Ten minutes after of "I love everything about you." Just…like…always.

"Boring," Charlotte echoed as she looked up and met the eyes of a man walking through the bar. The man, whoever he was, looked to be in his mid-thirties and had shoulder-length dark hair and olive skin. From what Charlotte could tell, he wore a weird suit, kind of Victorian-looking, like something off a romance novel cover. And he wasn't walking so much as strolling, as if the crowded nightclub was a park in spring, and he was a country squire out on a pleasant Sunday ramble.

"Steele, who is that guy?" London asked.

Steele gave the three ladies a half-cocked smile.

"That is Kingsley Edge. And he is the opposite of boring. And if you three have any sense you'll stay away from him."

"What sense I had just took her panties off and lay down in front of him," Sasha said with a drunken giggle.

"God, he looks like a pirate." London ran her finger around the rim of her glass.

"I think he looks dangerous." Sasha shot the man her best come-over-here smile.

Charlotte sighed. Sasha and London had promised her a girls' night out to help cheer her up over yet another failed relationship. "No men" had been their promise. Only alcohol and dancing. Maybe it was time to get some real friends.

"He looks like he needs a haircut." Charlotte downed her shot in one bitter swallow.

"Hey, do your trick, Char. That'll get his attention," Sasha begged.

"I don't want to get his attention. He's a pimp." Charlotte had heard of Kingsley Edge. No one who haunted New York's nightlife hadn't. His respectable business interests included owning several of the city's top clubs. Rumors swirled about the man, however; rumors that he made the vast majority of his money pushing flesh and not cocktails.

Steele laughed and the three friends spun back around on their bar stools.

"Kingsley Edge is not a pimp." Steele poured Charlotte a fresh Amaretto sour. "Kingsley Edge is a talent scout."

"Talent scout?" Charlotte's eyes followed Kingsley Edge as he made his way through the club. Every few feet he'd pause and gaze at her through the crowd. "What sort of talent?"

"Maybe your talent." Steele winked at her. She'd worked at this club, *Le Cirque de Nuit,* a few years ago and had picked up a trick or two.

Sasha and London looked at Charlotte with pleading eyes. Steele held out a shot glass full of liquid paraffin. Once again Charlotte decided to make getting new friends a top priority. She was almost drunk. They were definitely drunk. And they were making her perform for them. Fine—if they insisted.

Charlotte sighed and took the shot glass. Sasha handed her a lighter.

Sasha and London clapped while they hopped off their stools and stood far away. Charlotte noticed that the commotion had not just gotten the attention of most of the nightclub patrons, but had alerted Kingsley Edge as well. He stood next to a column and leaned against it with one eyebrow raised.

Charlotte inhaled deeply, swigged the liquid paraffin, pursed her lips, flicked the lighter and pushed air out so hard her ears popped. A fireball blew out several feet in front of her and set everyone in the nightclub screaming and clapping.

She kept blowing even after the fire went out, knowing she had to exhale anything left in her mouth. Hopping off her bar stool, she gave a small bow before turning back to her drink. She'd already had five tonight. One for each nice boyfriend she'd dumped in the last five years.

Two hours later she lay on the floor in the VIP section. She heard two male voices talking above her. One sounded like Steele's. The other sounded almost melodic…deeply male and as intoxicating as all the alcohol she'd imbibed.

"It's last call, chief. What should I do with her?"

"I'll take care of *le petit dragon*."

"You sure about that?"

She was close to passing out but she remembered the laugh. A warm, low laugh, she felt it more than it heard it. It rolled down her body from her neck to her ankles.

"Quite sure," the voice said in an accent her addled mind recognized as French. "I like a woman with a little fire in her belly."

Charlotte woke up in the fetal position. Groaning, she opened her eyes and saw a pair of knee-high leather riding boots. The boots belonged to a pair of long legs crossed at the ankles and using her back as a footstool. Looking up she saw Kingsley Edge lounging on the VIP sofa with a dainty teacup and saucer in his hands. Sipping at his tea he smiled down at her.

"I hope you don't mind my saying this, *chérie*, but you need a new hobby."

It took her much longer than it should have to process his words.

"Hobby?" she asked. "Who are you?"

"You know who I am. And I know who you are." He

held up her driver's license and studied it with his dark eyes. "Charlotte Brand. Steele tells me your friends call you Char. Shameful. I'll call you Charlie, if you don't mind."

"I might mind."

"Twenty-seven years old," he said, still staring at her license. "A good age, Charlie."

"You're really going to call me Charlie?"

"*Oui.* I love women with men's names. It satisfies a certain deviant side to me."

"Is your boot on my back part of your deviant side?" Charlotte sat up, and Kingsley lifted his feet off her back with a graceful air.

"What can I say? When I see a beautiful woman so drunk she ends up passed out on the floor, I assume she's there because she wants to be walked all over."

"Nice guilt trip. I heard you were a pimp. Are you a priest, too?"

"*Non.* But I have a priest on speed dial if you need one," he said with a wicked grin on his sculpted lips. "Would you like to come home with me now, Charlie?"

"What are you going to do to me?" His face came into focus for the first time. She'd heard he was French...or half-French, something like that. He was rich and had half the judges and cops in town in his back pocket. She'd also heard he was handsome, but handsome didn't do justice to the man in front of her.

"Breakfast and a shower are in order. Perhaps then we can discuss a certain business opportunity."

The phrase *business opportunity* triggered a memory from last night. Steele said that Kingsley Edge wasn't a pimp but a talent scout. Talent scout—she had a feeling she knew exactly what this *business opportunity* might entail.

"The shower and breakfast might work. But I can save you the trouble—*no* to any business opportunities."

"You say that now…but wait until you try my pancakes."

He set his teacup and saucer down and held out his hand. What the hell was she getting herself into?

Charlotte reached out and put her hand into his. Wrapping his fingers around hers, he pulled her to her feet. Wobbling a little on her high heels, she put her hand on his chest to steady herself. He covered her hand with his and met her eyes.

"You're a beautiful woman." His dark-lashed eyes studied her face. "Even with scuff marks on your cheek."

Charlotte blushed and rubbed her face.

"Don't bother. We'll wash it off at my town house. Shall we, Charlie?"

"Okay, so you're going to call me Charlie. What do I call you?"

"Everyone calls me Kingsley or King. Or *Monsieur*. Take your pick."

"*Monsieur?*"

"*Mon père était français et j'ai servi dans la Légion étrangère française.*"

Charlotte blinked and tried to make out any of the words Kingsley had said. But none of it registered as anything but poetic nonsense.

"I said 'my father was French and I served in the French Foreign Legion.'"

Charlotte stared at Kingsley. French…riding boots…the suit…and he changed her name to Charlie.

"You're a little insane, aren't you, Kingsley?"

"*Oui*, and you're coming home with me." He flashed her a wicked grin.

"*Touché.*"

Kingsley strode off and Charlotte followed behind him. He paused as he passed the bar and picked up her cowboy hat, which someone had left there. He tossed it back to her.

"I'm giving it to you but don't think you're allowed to wear it in my presence."

"Why not?"

"Because you have the most beautiful claret-colored hair I've ever seen, and it's a crime to cover it."

Charlotte rolled her eyes.

"It's not real. Well, the hair's real, but not the color. I'm a hairstylist."

"I don't care if it's real. I wasn't born bilingual but that doesn't change the fact that it turns you on that I am. *Oui?*"

Kingsley spun on his heel to smile back at her. He raised his eyebrows and seemed to be waiting for her to answer.

"Okay, *oui*," she admitted.

"*J'accepte.*" Kingsley threw open the doors to the club.

Charlotte shielded her face as the morning sunlight beat down on her aching eyes. Once inside the back of Kingsley's car she noticed the lush leather interior and the old-world feel.

"Holy shit…is this a Rolls-Royce?"

Kingsley sat on the bench seat opposite her.

"She is. Not my favorite one, but she's fine for running errands."

"So am I an errand?" Charlie asked.

"I don't know." Kingsley gave her a long look that set the hairs on her arms standing up. "Are you running?"

Charlotte looked out the window and saw the city regulars on their way to work—men in power suits, women in severe dresses. And here she sat in a Rolls-Royce with one of the city's most notorious underground figures.

"Not yet."

Kingsley grinned.

"Good answer, Charlie. Here we are."

The Rolls pulled in front of an elegant black-and-white bricked town house that looked at least three stories high.

Kingsley left the car first and held out his hand for her. She tried to stay steady on her feet as he pulled her out. Kingsley steered her up two flights of stairs. A stunningly beautiful young woman delivered a file folder to him with a quick curtsy.

"You can shower while I read," Kingsley said.

"You're really going to make me take a shower?"

"I can give you a bath if you prefer."

"I wouldn't prefer," she said, not sure if she meant that.

Kingsley pushed open a set of intricately carved black double doors.

Never before had she seen a bedroom more erotic and inviting. She wished she knew more about architecture so she could properly describe it to her friends…if and when she ever made it out of here. She wanted to study the vaulted ceilings adorned with black-and-white paintings of lovers coupling in positions both pornographic and artistic. Or the hulking black marble fireplace on the lush oriental rugs that covered the black-and-white-tile floor.

But in truth only the bed held her attention. A huge four-poster behemoth, it captured both her attention and her imagination. She'd never seen sheets so red, like the color of fresh blood, or pillows so thick she thought she could drown in them and die happy.

"Nice bed," she said when Kingsley caught her staring. "It's really…big. King-size, I guess."

"Kingsley-size." He winked at her as he pointed at a door

across the room. "Bathroom in there. There is a bathrobe you can use while I have your clothes sent out."

Charlotte entered the bathroom and found it as luxurious as the bedroom. She locked the door behind her and looked in the mirror. Scuff marks had been only a slight exaggeration. A streak of black floor polish adorned her left cheek. It looked almost like a bruise. Her eyes were shaded with smudged and flaking eye makeup and her lipstick had worn halfway off from the alcohol and the paraffin. She turned on the steam shower and stepped inside. As she washed the club grime off she wondered what on earth Kingsley wanted with her before deciding she didn't really care.

She turned off the water and wrapped herself in the plushest towel she'd ever felt in her life. Squeezing the water out of her hair she pulled on the black silk bathrobe. With nothing on but the robe she emerged into the bedroom. Kingsley reclined in a chair with his feet propped up on an ottoman. He'd discarded his suit jacket and put on a pair of wire-rimmed glasses. With a cocktail in his hand he perused the file folder in his hand.

"Hypocrite." She nodded at his cocktail and tried to ignore how desirable he looked in his embroidered vest with his crisp white shirtsleeves rolled up to reveal muscular forearms and wrists.

"Everything in moderation, *ma chérie*. Except orgasms. Have a seat."

She didn't see anywhere to sit other than the bed and not wanting to seem too eager she sat on the floor. Kingsley gave her a strange look as she waited at his feet—a look both hungry and self-congratulatory.

Kingsley pulled out a sleek black cell phone. In rapid French he poured out what sounded like instructions and hung up.

"Pancakes forthcoming. Now this is all very interesting." He flipped another page in the file. "You had a four-point-oh at NYU before you dropped out your freshman year. *Pourquoi?*"

Charlotte sat up straighter.

"That file's about me?" she demanded.

"*Oui.* While I was waiting for you emerge from your Amaretto-sour coma, I had my secretary cull your records. You are a fascinating woman, Charlie."

"And you're such an asshole. I can't believe you're digging around my past."

"I intend to fuck you blind before you leave my home, Charlie. Is penetrating your past more intimate than penetrating your body?"

Charlotte closed her mouth and sat blushing on the floor as visions of Kingsley on top of her, inside her, raced through her mind.

"I think so," she finally answered.

"So do I, actually."

"That's a pretty old-fashioned view of sex," she said. "Especially for a pimp."

"I am not a pimp. My employees do not sell sex. If I'm anything, it would be an agent. Or—"

"A talent scout," she finished. "Yeah, Steele told me. So were you scouting for talent at the club last night?"

"I was. And found a fire-breather. Not a particularly useful talent but certainly interesting. As is this—your mother, she died when you were nineteen."

Charlotte swallowed. "Car accident. That's not interesting. Just horrible."

"Horrible, *très.* But you dropped out of school to raise your younger brother—that is interesting."

"Simon and my father do not get along. He was terrified at the prospect of living with my dad. We got a sympathetic judge, thank God."

Kingsley smiled at her over the top of his glasses.

"Your father is not a good man?"

Charlotte pulled the robe tighter around her. "He's strict, conservative. I stayed out an hour after curfew when I was sixteen. I was at the movies with a girlfriend and we got ice cream after. He assumed the worst and called me a slut, a whore, everything. He and mom divorced that year finally. I couldn't let Simon move in with him. Especially since—"

"Your brother is gay."

"Yeah, how did you know?"

"He interned with gay rights groups while in college and law school. You dropped out of university and started working so your gay brother wouldn't have to live with your conservative father. That's rather noble of you, Charlie."

Charlotte stared at the floor.

"My dad would have destroyed Simon. It wasn't noble. It was my only choice."

"It wasn't, but it's quite telling that you think that. Let's see," he said and flipped a few more pages. "You worked as a receptionist at a salon after you quit school and apprenticed there. You were a cocktail waitress at *Le Cirque de Nuit* a few nights a week as well. Must have been before I bought the club. I would have remembered a fire-breather."

"You got much better tips if you could do a stunt. The bartender there before Steele taught me the fire-breathing thing."

"Your brother is in law school now. Full scholarship, I see. There's no reason you can't go back to school."

"I'm a little too old. Besides, I like working. I've been out in the real world taking care of myself and Simon since I was nineteen. Don't think I can go back."

Kingsley closed the file and leaned forward. He started to open his mouth but a knock on the door interrupted.

"Entréz," he called out. The butler entered carrying a breakfast tray. He set it on the floor in front of Charlotte and quickly departed.

"So now you've had your shower and you are currently having your breakfast. Let's discuss the business opportunity you've already said no to."

"Discuss away," she said after her first delicious bite of pancake. "But it's still a no."

"Understandable." Kingsley stood up and removed his wire-rim glasses. "I'll talk. You eat."

"Happily."

Kingsley strolled leisurely about his bedroom.

"I told you I was no pimp and that's true. There is a sexual aspect to the work my employees do, but none of them have sexual intercourse for money. At least not on my time clock. The clients we serve are an unusual lot with unusual desires. If they wanted mere sex, they could get that from their husbands and wives, boyfriends and girlfriends. What they want from us is more complicated."

"You're talking about kink, right?"

Kingsley nodded. *"Oui.* Kink. Bondage, domination and sadomasochism. I said I was a talent agent. It wouldn't be far off the mark to also call myself a matchmaker. I have clients with specific desires, and I try to find a good match for those desires among my coterie. I have a client now—a wealthy businessman, not unattractive—who has found himself longing for a deeper connection than what he has experienced in his recent short-lived relationships. He prefers a beautiful woman somewhere between the age of twenty-five and thirty-five. No preference on race, height, or religion. Strong preference on intelligence—i.e. she must have it. And she must be very brave."

At his last word he turned around and looked down at her.

"A woman who breathes fire while drunk and comes to my home while sober is about as brave as this town has to offer. Wouldn't you agree, Charlie?"

Charlotte stared at him. She couldn't believe what he was asking her.

"Okay...I'm not saying yes or anything. I'm only asking out of curiosity—what exactly would this whole arrangement entail?"

"This particular client enjoys S and M on occasion but is more interested in absolute sexual dominance. He is particularly aroused by fear."

"So he's a rapist?"

"Hardly. Dominants in the lifestyle, as we call it, find submission erotic. Overpowering a woman and taking her by force is an act of assault and violence. A dominant desires his submissive trust him enough to allow him to take her even when she is afraid. Yes, he takes but she gives as well. And you, *ma chérie,* have all the makings of a world-class submissive."

"This is bizarre."

"Is it? Tell me, Charlie, those two blond Barbie dolls you were with last night—that was Sasha Walsh and London Faber, yes?"

"Yes. We met at the salon. I cut their hair."

"Their parents are worth roughly the state budget of Vermont. They are vapid and dull and spoiled. They are your opposites. Why do you spend time with them?"

"Rich people are easy to hang out with. They have all the money. They make all the decisions."

"And they left you alone passed out on the floor of my club. Anything could have happened to you—you could have been robbed, assaulted, raped...they are not your friends."

"I know. That's why I like hanging out with them. It's easier that way."

"Easier to be with people who don't care about you?"

"Easier to be with people I don't have to care about. I know—it's stupid."

"*Pas du tout*. It's understandable. Your mother died, you raised your brother and kept him safe from your father...."

Charlotte toyed with the pancake left on her plate.

"*Oui*," she agreed.

"At a young age you had to take on enormous responsibilities. What you must understand is that submissive women are not weak. They are often much stronger than the men who dominate them. They have to be strong and brave to submit without losing themselves. I believe you are both. And," he said, squatting down in front of her, "I think there's a part of you that would very much enjoy not being in control of everything for once."

Charlotte looked up at him. No one that handsome should also be that insightful.

"I've never done kink before," she finally said.

"I can teach you everything you need to know."

"You would teach me?"

Kingsley tapped her under her chin and grinned at her. Something in his smile made her stomach clench. "Is that such a terrible prospect?"

Charlotte stared at him. Never before had she seen a more

viscerally attractive man in her life. He seemed to read her reaction to him in her eyes.

The sane rational part of Charlotte's brain told her to get up and get out. Unfortunately every other part of her body and mind overruled her.

"Stand up," Kingsley ordered and Charlotte came to her feet.

He looked her up and down once before flashing her a dangerous smile. Raising his hand, he caressed her lips with the soft pad of his thumb while he reached out with his free hand and opened a drawer on the bedside table. From it he pulled a pair of handcuffs.

"Hey, no way in hell." Charlotte took a quick step back.

Kingsley said nothing as he slapped the cuffs onto his own left wrist.

"S'il vous plaît," he said and turned around, indicating he wanted her to cuff his hands behind his back.

Charlotte took the cuffs in her hand and nervously clapped them onto Kingsley's other wrist.

He turned around to face her.

"Do you feel safe with me now?" he asked.

Slowly she nodded. What could he really do to her with his hands cuffed, after all?

"Now," he said, "drop the robe."

Immediately Charlotte pulled the robe tighter around her body.

"Charlie...take off the robe. Now."

Something in Kingsley's voice, some hard edge of authority, spoke to something deep within her. Slowly she untied the cord and let the robe fall to the floor. Kingsley ran his eyes up and down her body with an appraising air as she stood naked and blushing before him.

He stepped forward and she fought the urge to step back. Instead she stood her ground as he made a circuit around her body.

"You have exquisite breasts," he said. "The perfect size to fit in the palm of a large hand. I'm sure other lovers have told you that."

One old boyfriend had said she had "great tits" but that had been the extent of it.

"Not in so many words."

"Pity. Also, lovely full hips. Well-rounded but with definition. Oh," he said pausing at her back. "You have a birthmark."

Every muscle in Charlotte's body tensed as Kingsley dropped to his knees behind her.

"Just a little one."

"It looks like—" Kingsley's voice dropped to a low whisper "—the Eiffel Tower."

Charlotte laughed but the laugh turned to a gasp when Kingsley's lips touched the birthmark that graced the back of her left hip. The heat from his mouth on her skin spread through her entire pelvic region and sunk deep into her stomach. Just as the gasp started to turn to a low moan, Kingsley stood back up again.

"Long legs but not excessively so. Not too thin. Beautiful Celtic skin. Exquisite Roman nose."

"Roman? Is that a synonym for hooked?"

"*Oui.* You, Charlie, will do nicely."

"Um…*merci?*" she said, remembering one other French word.

"*De rien.* Now tell me…would you care to stay with me? One month. Let me train you to be the perfect sexual submissive."

"I have a job, you know." She grabbed the robe and pulled it around her again.

"I'll pay you twice what you made in your best month last year. Cash. Of course."

"Of course." Charlotte swallowed. Good Lord, he really meant it. This drop-dead gorgeous rich weird Frenchman wanted her to stay with him for a month. And not just stay with him, he wanted to teach her how to submit sexually to some rich client of his. Insanity. And yet, the thought of walking away from this offer... No, not the offer, from Kingsley...

She couldn't quite bring herself to walk away from Kingsley.

"I'm not agreeing to anything," she finally said. "I haven't even met this guy."

"I won't ask you to agree to anything until you meet him. Nor will he agree to anything until he's met you. We'll spend the next few weeks in training. When you're ready, I'll arrange a meeting. If you like each other and decide to give a relationship a try, he'll pay me my rather exorbitant finder's fee and you and he can work out whatever financial arrangement best suits you both. Knowing him he'll offer you a room in his rather impressive home and the freedom to come and go as you please as long as you are at his disposal three to five evenings a week. He'll have a partner who is his sexual equal and you'll have someone who is quite happy to make most or all of the decisions so you, for once in your life, won't have to."

"My feminist friends would kill me."

"Those of us in the lifestyle are too busy having very good sex to worry about the gender wars. True, most submissives are women and most dominants are men. But I have several male submissives on my payroll, and I know every dominatrix in this town. I assure you the vast majority of my clients are men who want to be dominated by women. So you needn't worry

that you're giving up your right to vote or right to equal pay.
You're only giving up boring vanilla sex, and I promise you,
you won't miss it. Say yes, Charlie. We know you want to."

"Okay...yes. Fine. I want to."

"Beautiful, brave, and honest—I may have to keep you. You
can stay in the room next to mine. I'll send my secretary to see
you have everything you need. In the meantime, I'm afraid I
have to behave myself and get some actual work done today."

Charlotte took a slow, deep breath.

"Okay, I'll stay for a few days. Maybe a month. I've been
trying to take a vacation for two years."

Kingsley turned his head and smiled at her with a cocked
eyebrow.

"*Ma chérie*...this will be no vacation."

And then he laughed and something in that laugh caused
her toes to curl and dig into the rug under her feet. The laugh
rippled up her body and wrapped around her hips and dug
like fingers into her stomach.

"Right..." she said, suddenly very aware of her nakedness
under the bathrobe. Knowing Kingsley still had the handcuffs
on his wrists came as both a relief and a disappointment. "I
should go and let you get to work, I guess."

Charlotte started for the door but stopped before she leaving.

"I should probably take those off you," she said, remembering the handcuffs.

Gasping, Charlotte found herself with her back pressed to
the door and Kingsley's arms imprisoning her on either side.
The handcuffs dangled impotently off his right wrist.

"*Pas de problème*, Charlie. Anything that needs taking off...I
will do it."

At first fear alone kept Charlotte frozen to the door. She

sensed the iron strength in Kingsley's arms, in his body, that had her trapped in place. Kingsley pushed forward until his hips pressed into her hips, his chest into her breasts, and the fear turned to another feeling equally powerful but no less terrifying.

"Let me go," she whispered.

"*Non.* Not yet." Kingsley caressed the right side of her face with his fingertips. "You're here to learn. This is your first lesson. The man I'll train you for enjoys games like this…games of passion and fear. He will want you ready for him always. In the middle of the night he might wake you with his hunger. He may find you reading in the evening and without a word take your book from you and your clothes. You will try to pass him in the hallway, and he will stop you with his arms, turn you around, press you to the wall and force himself inside you. *Comprende?*"

Charlotte swallowed hard.

"So this is the lesson? Learning to keep my mouth shut while he does whatever he wants to me?"

Kingsley shook his head. He slid his hand from her face and down the front of her body. She inhaled as Kingsley cupped her left breast and gently kneaded her nipple with his thumb and forefinger.

"The lesson is that you must learn to speak when he does something you do not want him to do. Do you know what a safe word is, Charlie? We use them in my world."

"No…" she breathed as liquid need began to gather in her hips.

"It's a word, any word, that the two parties involved agree upon. It is the word that you must use to stop whatever is happening to you that you don't want."

"I can't say no?"

"No. For this man I will train you for," Kingsley said as he moved his hand lower over her quivering stomach, "the word *no* gasped in fear, in protest, will only stoke his passion further. It is a game, you see. The more you resist the more he will desire you. Say 'no' and he will carry on. Say 'stop' and he will not stop. Say 'don't' if you wish but he will do whatever he will do. Tell me to stop. I dare you."

Kingsley shifted his hand from her stomach to between her legs.

"Stop it," she whispered although she didn't mean it.

"Stop what? This?" Kingsley's middle finger slipped inside her. Closing her eyes tight, Charlotte thrust her hips out and into Kingsley's hand.

"Yes," she replied, panting the word. "Stop that."

"Should I stop this, too?" He pushed a second finger into her and began to move his hand, thrusting in and out of her with his fingers.

Charlotte nodded, unable to speak from the sheer pleasure of his touch.

She sensed Kingsley's mouth at her ear.

"Non," he said again. "I'm enjoying myself too much to stop. You feel exquisite inside. So warm, so wet…did you know if you touch right here—" Kingsley twisted his hand and pressed the tip of his finger hard and deep into a spot one inch inside her "—I can feel your pulse?"

"Kingsley…" His name was the only word Charlotte could push past her lips. He apparently took it as an encouragement because a third finger joined the second and Charlotte had to open her legs wider to take it.

"Now pretend for a moment that you aren't actually enjoying this as much as we both know you are," Kingsley said, making lazy circles with his hand inside her. "Shocking thought, *oui?*"

"Oui," Charlotte agreed. She truly couldn't remember the last time she'd felt anything so erotic. The expertise of his technique, the pressure, the movements were beyond pleasurable, but far more so was the power of the man who held her pressed to the door and refused to let her go even as she said "no" and "stop" and "don't."

"Let us say you really did want me to stop, but I love that word, love your protests, far too much to heed it. And we both know when you say 'stop' you don't really mean it. Not with me. So you should have a word that truly means stop and to that alone will I listen. That is your safe word. Do you understand?"

"I think so." Charlotte grasped his left forearm and held onto him as she felt her climax building. Hung over...scared... in a stranger's house...and yet she could scarcely breathe for her desire. "So what's my safe word?"

The muscles deep inside her tightened around Kingsley's hand. She felt a rush of wetness between her thighs.

"As you are my little redheaded fire-breather, your safe word should be 'dragon.' You must say it whenever you truly wish me to stop whatever I'm doing. No other word, no amount of struggling will do it."

Charlotte's breathing turned hard and heavy as Kingsley's hand moved faster and deeper into her. His thumb massaged her clitoris. Never before had she been with a man who knew how to manipulate a woman's body so well.

With his lips Kingsley traced a path from Charlotte's ear to her shoulder. Charlotte dug her fingernails into the fabric of his jacket.

"So if you truly wish me to stop what I'm doing, Charlie, you will say...?"

"Dragon."

Kingsley pulled his hand abruptly out of her body and took a step back. Charlotte nearly collapsed from the sudden shock of his departure as her vaginal muscles fluttered in protest.

"C'est ça," Kingsley said. "It's like magic."

Kingsley stepped forward, took her hand and kissed the back of it.

"Get settled in," he said. "I'm off to work now. No rest for the wicked."

Kingsley pulled her away from the door, opened it and strolled into the hall whistling a song she thought might have been the French national anthem.

Charlie closed her eyes and imagined fire shooting out of her mouth and burning Kingsley to the ground. She must have actually audibly hissed because Kingsley stopped whistling long enough to call back to her.

"Patience, Charlie. We have all month."

Charlotte spent the rest of the afternoon in the bedroom Kingsley had assigned to her, a bedroom nearly as luxurious as his own. His secretary came in and gathered information from her—emergency contacts, food preferences, even allergies.

"Allergies?" Charlotte had asked.

"Yes. Latex, for example?" Kingsley secretary answered with hardly a blink or a blush.

"Oh, God."

An hour after returning from her apartment with a month's worth of clothes and supplies, Charlotte tried to get some sleep but her mind wanted to wander down far too many dangerous paths. Kingsley Edge... The one and only Kingsley Edge.

She finally worked up the courage to call her younger brother and let him know a little of what was going on.

Simon sighed heavily, so heavily Charlotte nearly laughed aloud.

"You sure about this, Char?" Simon asked.

"I like him."

"Do you like him because he rich and infamous or because you actually like him?"

Charlotte thought about the question, a perfectly valid one, for a few seconds before answering.

"Yes."

After getting Simon's blessing, or at least his promise to not call the police, Charlotte hung up and stared around the room still not quite believing she'd be spending the next month here. What would Kingsley do with her during her stay? Part of her was terrified at the prospect. Another much bigger part of her couldn't wait to find out.

Charlotte started as an envelope slipped in under her door. She picked it up and found a hand-written invitation.

Charlie—Present yourself at my bedroom door this evening at nine o'clock. Wear your finest. We shall attend a piano recital in the Music Room. Do not be late. The consequences will be both severe and enjoyable if you are.

Charlotte corrected herself. Invitation? No, this was a summons. And although she knew she should bristle at the order to present herself on time or be punished, she almost wanted to be late simply to force Kingsley to make good on his threat.

For a solid hour, Charlotte stood before the bathroom mirror primping for the recital. She did her makeup quickly and spent the rest of the time curling her waist-length hair into thick red waves. The fanciest dress she had was a little black number. Hopefully the effect of her hair would distract Kingsley from the simplicity of the dress.

At nine on the dot, Charlotte stood outside Kingsley's bedroom door waiting impatiently. She still barely knew the man. The more time that passed from their one long conversation this morning, the more she questioned her decision to stay with him for the month. This was crazy, right? Spending a month with a stranger? No one in her right mind would have agreed to his offer. Why was she doing this?

Kingsley opened the door.

Okay, that was why.

"Wow," she said when all other words failed her.

He wore a black suit with silver buttons on the black-and-silver embroidered vest. His riding boots had been polished to a near-reflective shine and had she looked down she would have seen her wide-eyed face staring back at her.

"You approve?" Kingsley asked, a slight smile at the corner of his sensual lips.

Charlotte slowly nodded. "Um…yes. You look…damn."

"And you, *ma chérie*, look enchanting." Kingsley took her hand and kissed the back of it. "Utterly exquisite." Raising her hand over her head, he spun her in a slow circle. "*Parfait*, Charlie."

"*Merci*," she said and curtsied. "The dress isn't much. But it's all I have that's semiformal."

Kingsley took her by the arm and they started down the hallway.

"It will look lovely on the floor by my bed."

Charlotte blushed and laughed.

"Is there any particular reason why you dress like it's the nineteenth century instead of the twenty-first?"

"There's only one reason that matters," he said as he escorted her down to the main level of his home. "Because I can."

Still on his arm he led her to the Music Room. Kingsley introduced her to his guests. Most of men sat on the chairs and the love seats. But although there was enough room for all, a few of the women sat on the floor at the feet of the men they'd come with. One woman, almost forty and stunningly beautiful, took an imperious seat on a chair and snapped her fingers. Her date, a young man of about thirty, sat at her feet. Charlotte looked down at Kingsley. He had a wicked gleam in his eyes and watched her. She sank to the floor and leaned back against his knee. He ran a hand possessively through her hair. Now she knew why no one asked her who she was or how she'd met Kingsley. All his guests were part of his kinky little community.

Charlotte adjusted herself and found the floor was actually quite comfortable. The carpeting was thick and lush and Kingsley's fingers in her hair and on her neck felt extraordinary—sensual and seductive and also relaxing. She could stay here all night.

A tall blond man entered to a smattering of applause and sat at the piano. Charlotte's eyes widened when she saw he was dressed like a priest. A beautiful young woman with black hair followed him and sat on the floor next to the piano bench. Once the applause ceased, the man began to play. Charlotte sat entranced by the breathtakingly handsome pianist and the woman who rested so contentedly at his feet.

Kingsley leaned forward and put his mouth at her ear.

"I know he's handsome as the devil, Charlie. And you're welcome to look all you want. But don't touch. That," he said, inclining his head toward the piano playing priest and the young woman, "is a love match."

"A love match?" she asked. "One of yours?"

"Oh, no. Destiny brought those two together. I had nothing to do with it. When destiny fails, that's when I get called."

"You should put that on your business cards," she joked.

Kingsley reached into his pocket and handed her a black business card embossed with silver lettering. "Kingsley Edge, CEO, Edge Enterprises. *When destiny fails…*" it read.

She covered her mouth to stop herself from laughing out loud as she looked up at Kingsley. He was smiling at her. But it wasn't a normal smile of mirth or pleasure, but a smile that sent her body temperature shooting up a few degrees.

Charlotte turned away and tried to let the music calm her down. But it was such passionate music played so skillfully that Charlotte felt it wanted to seduce her as much as Kingsley. And both were succeeding. By the time the recital ended Charlotte was so desperate for Kingsley that she pretended to stumble when standing just so she could lean her full weight against him. He pulled her close to him, and she inhaled his scent. He smelled warm and masculine and every nerve in her body sat on edge at his nearness. When he bade his guests a swift goodbye and escorted her back upstairs, she was nearly shaking with eagerness. They stopped at the door to her room.

"So he's really a priest?" she asked. "The pianist?"

"I told you I had a priest on speed dial. You really should learn to trust me."

"I'm trying. This is all new."

Kingsley laid his hand on her neck and rested his thumb at the hollow of her throat. "I will not hurt you, Charlie. Or, at least, I won't harm you," he said with a roguish grin. "Do you believe that? We won't get very far until you know that at the moment you are most afraid of me, it is the moment you have the least reason to be."

"Okay, I'll try not be afraid."

"You can be afraid all you want. Just don't let your fear stop you."

Charlotte inhaled. For whatever reason, she did trust him.

"Good girl," he said and took her hand. He kissed it slowly and let it go. "Good night, Charlie."

She stared at him as he strode toward his own bedroom.

Stunned that he'd left her, Charlotte entered her bedroom on feet of lead. Hurt and embarrassed she considered gathering her things and getting out of this madhouse. He'd spent all evening seducing her with every glance, every touch and every smile. And now he just sauntered off to bed, leaving her alone in her room.

She took a deep breath and remembered his words—*you really should learn to trust me*. Maybe this was a test. Maybe he was seeing if she would get pissed and try to leave.

Charlotte kicked off her shoes and enjoyed the sound of them bouncing hollowly off the wall. She'd give this weird place one more day. But she couldn't completely talk herself out of her disappointment and frustration. Kingsley knew she was more than ready and willing to go to bed with him. Maybe he got off on being a tease. Maybe when he finally did invite her to his room, she'd kiss his hand and walk off like he had.

In the bathroom she brushed her teeth and glanced at herself in the mirror. Kingsley called her beautiful but she never really thought she was. Pretty maybe, but not beautiful. But tonight with her hair flowing like red wine down her back, she knew she'd never looked better. But that hadn't been good enough for him. Angry, she strode back into the bedroom.

Charlotte froze when she sensed something behind her. Suddenly she couldn't move as two incredibly strong arms grabbed her and held her hard and fast in place with a hand covering her mouth. She threw all of her strength into her struggle to get loose but the harder she fought the harder he held her.

"Shh…" Kingsley's mouth was at her ear again. "It's only me."

Knowing it was Kingsley didn't do anything to calm her fears. She tried to pull away again but still he held her tight against him. She screamed against his hand. Barely a sound came out.

"Charlie, I know you're afraid right now. You are allowed to be afraid. I want you to be afraid." His voice was low and intimate. She pushed back against him, hoping to knock him off balance and get away. But he was too tall, too strong. She turned her head trying to scream, but his hand was a vise over her mouth. "In the lifestyle we all have a safe word. It's the word you say when you want the game to stop. Your safe word is 'dragon' since you're my little redheaded fire-breather. And the second I take my hand away you can say 'dragon' and I'll let you go. Or… Or you can choose to not fear your fear. Vanilla sex is all about trust. Rape is all about fear. In that place between fear and trust is where we live. Trust me, Charlie. Don't think that the fear means you have to stop."

Charlotte closed her eyes. She wrenched herself to the side but still she couldn't get free from him.

"I'm going to move my hand away from your mouth now. Say your safe word if you must. But before you do, ask yourself how you felt when I walked away from you tonight. Ask yourself how you will feel tomorrow if you walk away from me now."

Charlotte panted against his palm. He slowly took his hand

away from her mouth. She started to speak and then swallowed her words.

She heard Kingsley's smug laugh at her ear. "I have good taste in women, don't I?"

Charlie opened her mouth to argue but Kingsley pushed her hard and bent her over the bed. He took her arms and yanked them behind her back and held them pinned there. With one hand he held her wrists and with the other he reached underneath her dress. He ran his hand up the back of her thighs and slid it over her hips and into her panties.

"Your clit's swollen and you're soaking wet," he said as he examined her. She clenched her jaw but was too humiliated to say anything. His fingers skimmed across the outside of her body. She flinched as he ripped her flimsy panties off her with a quick tear. Now naked underneath her dress there was nothing between him and her. Kingsley used his knees to push her legs wider apart. His hand came back to her and she groaned as he slid a single finger inside her.

"Since the moment I saw you breathing fire at my club last night," Kingsley whispered as one finger became two, and two fingers turned to three inside her, "I knew I had to have you...to feel that fire inside you."

He pulled his hand roughly out of her and she lay scared and panting against the sheets.

"Don't move," he ordered. Closing her eyes, she dug her hands into the sheets and tried to breathe through her fears.

"It's adrenaline," Kingsley said as he opened a drawer and pulled something out, something that sounded like metal. She gasped as he took her wrists again and yanked them behind her back. "What you're feeling right now—it isn't fear. You aren't afraid of me. You've simply never been this excited before."

"God, you're arrogant," Charlotte growled as Kingsley slapped cold metal handcuffs onto each of her wrists.

"I'm not arrogant. I'm French." Kingsley forced her legs apart again as Charlotte tried to relax into the handcuffs. The weighty cold metal dug into her skin. She felt helpless, and hopeless. One word could get her out of this. All she had to do was say it and Kingsley would let her go. But she couldn't say it. Even scared and humiliated she couldn't deny that she wanted him, wanted this so much it scared her more than the handcuffs and the man who had taken possession of her body. "Now, Charlie, I'm going to put my cock in you in two seconds. If you have an objection to that, I would raise it right now."

Charlotte said nothing as hot tears of shame welled up in her eyes.

"I thought as much," he said and shoved inside her.

He was so big it almost hurt going in. She strained against the handcuffs and pressed her face into the bed as Kingsley thrust into her with strokes both hard and slow. Reaching around her hips he found her clitoris again. With an expert touch he teased it until Charlotte cried out. As her orgasm peaked and waned, Kingsley roughly turned her onto her back and pushed her legs open again.

Kingsley yanked her dress down and bared her breasts. His mouth dropped to her neck. He rained violent kisses across her chest and shoulders so roughly she knew she'd have bruises from his mouth tomorrow. He took both breasts in his hands and held them as he penetrated her again. She opened her legs wider and took him as deep into her as she could.

Bending over her, he met her eye to eye. "You tilt your hips high. You like deep penetration, don't you?" Charlotte turned her head and stared at the wall. But Kingsley grabbed her face again and forced her to look at him. "Answer me."

"Yes," she said. "I like it deep."

"Then by all means." Kingsley grabbed her knees and wrenched them up and over his shoulders. She arched back—each thrust seemed to pound at the base of her stomach.

Charlotte panted as Kingsley continued his assault on her. She hated how good it felt being taken like this, hated herself for liking the brutality so much. He manipulated her body like he owned it, touched her like her body was an open book he'd read and memorized. Turning her head, Charlotte pressed her face to her arm. As Kingsley kneaded her clitoris between his thumb and forefinger she came so hard that tears rolled out of the corners of her eyes.

Kingsley lowered her legs off his shoulders and covered her body with his. Instinctively Charlotte wrapped her legs around his waist as he continued to move in her. He bit her neck, her collarbone, kissed the hollow of her throat all while still moving in her.

"You like this," he said.

"Yes," she whispered as she flinched at a particularly hard thrust.

"Call me 'sir' when I'm inside you, Charlie."

"Yes, sir," she breathed, wanting to both kiss him and slap him the second her hands were free.

She kept waiting for him to be done with her. But there seemed to be no end to the pleasure he inflicted on her. He pushed and pushed until Charlotte felt her inner muscles start to tighten. Raising her hips, she took him deep into her again. She closed her eyes as another orgasm ripped through her. Finally Kingsley's movements grew harsher and faster. His fingers dug into the back of her neck. He held her still, forcing her to meet his eyes. With one last brutal thrust he came with his eyes open and locked onto hers.

Still inside her he moved her legs flat on her bed. Her body continued to pulse around his length as his cock pulsed inside her. He dipped his head and for the first time since meeting, kissed her.

She opened her mouth to his and his tongue slipped inside. His kiss—gentle and subtle—was the opposite of the sex. She wanted him to stay in her mouth and her body all night. Kingsley pulled back and smiled down at her.

"Took you long enough to kiss me, sir," she said, remembering his orders, remembering he was still inside her.

"You're a fire-breather, Charlie. You can't blame me for being wary of your mouth."

She laughed a little but winced as he pulled out of her sore body. She lay on her back, letting her heart slow its frenetic beating as he disappeared into the bathroom. She wondered what she looked like. Kingsley hadn't raped her but she probably looked like someone had. Her dress was torn and still bunched around her stomach. She could already tell she was covered in bruises from his hands and his mouth. Even inside she felt bruised from his merciless thrusts.

Kingsley emerged and stood by the bed. He looked immaculate in his suit. He's been fully dressed when he'd taken her. Only his feet were bare and he had abandoned his jacket. He reached into his pocket and pulled out the handcuff key and released her. She rolled up and tried to straighten her dress.

"What?" she asked as Kingsley stared at her.

"You look beautiful."

"I look like a rape victim." She wiped her eyes and a smudge of eyeliner came off on her fingers.

"You look like a woman who's been ravished and thoroughly enjoyed it."

"You scared the shit out of me grabbing me like that."

Kingsley sat on the bed next to her.

"You like being scared."

Charlie didn't answer. Kingsley took her by the chin again, this time gently. He caressed her bottom lip with his thumb. "You like being scared," he repeated. "You don't have to be afraid of your fear, Charlie. You're allowed to be afraid and like it."

"Normal people aren't supposed to like this stuff. Normal people aren't supposed to enjoy being thrown down, tied up and practically raped."

"My beautiful Charlie." Kingsley kissed her slowly. "Perhaps it's time to admit you aren't normal people."

Charlotte woke early the next morning. She put on the black bathrobe and found his bedroom door ajar but no King seemed to be in residence.

After eating breakfast in his opulent kitchen, she wandered back upstairs to shower and dress. When she stepped out of the shower, she found Kingsley standing there waiting with a towel.

"You're trying to kill me," she said as she snatched the towel out of his hands. "Give me a little warning, please, if you're going to shower-stalk me."

"You must learn to stay on your toes. Come here, Charlie. Let's see the damage, shall we?"

Charlotte stepped out of the shower. Kingsley stood in front of her and unwrapped her towel. Even though they'd had the most intense sex of her life last night, he hadn't actually seen her completely naked. Just standing there in front of him was embarrassing and awkward. He, of course, seemed slightly aroused and amused as always.

"How bad is it?"

"Terrible. I barely left a mark on you. We'll have to rectify that."

"What do you call these?"

She pointed to the bruises on her chest and shoulders.

"Just nibbles." Kingsley bit her wet neck.

"This isn't fair, you know." She wrapped her arms over her bare breasts. "I haven't gotten to see you naked yet."

"Women tend to fall in love with me when I take my clothes off."

"You're a narcissist. Come on—just a peek?"

Kingsley arched an eyebrow at her. "Very well. If you insist."

He strode from the bathroom. Grabbing her towel, Charlotte followed him into his bedroom.

She stood in the center of his room while he started to undress. Today's look was more Edwardian than Victorian. His jacket had five buttons and she watched with eager anticipation as he brusquely undid all of them. Tossing the jacket aside, he unknotted his tie and pulled his white shirt from his trousers. She gasped when he shed the shirt and stood barechested in front of her.

"Oh, my God." Charlotte covered her mouth in shock.

"You were warned."

She reached out and tentatively touched his chest. His body was what she imagined—lean and muscled and tan. But she never imagined this.

"How?" She looked up at his eyes.

"I was in the French Foreign Legion in my early twenties. Bullet wounds."

"You were shot?"

"Four times. Thankfully all were small-caliber and missed vital organs. Especially my favorite vital organ."

"Thank God." Charlotte tried to laugh but it wasn't easy staring at the four small holes that riddled Kingsley's stomach and chest. "Was this from a battle?"

"Two are from a skirmish. The other two are friendly fire."

"Friendly fire?"

Kingsley grinned at her. "Not terribly friendly, really. My CO found me with his wife."

Now Charlotte did laugh. "Then you deserved it."

"Hardly. That poor woman was begging to be tied up and defiled. Literally—she begged me."

"You've always been this bad?" she asked as she ran her hand up and down his bare chest.

"*Au contraire.* I've always been this good."

Kingsley took her by the wrists and led her to his bed. He opened the drawer of the bedside table and pulled out a length of rope.

"Have you ever been hit by a man, Charlie?" Kingsley asked as he pulled the towel off her and threw it aside.

"No. Dad yelled but he never hit."

"And your boyfriends? Never even spanked?"

She shook her head as her heart started racing. Was he going to actually hit her?

"Your lovers have been vanilla," Kingsley said. "That's a tragedy. Did you even enjoy fucking them?"

She shrugged her shoulders. "They were nice. I had orgasms. It wasn't terrible. Just—"

"Boring? Unfulfilling? Bourgeois?"

"All of that, I guess. Simon told me I was crazy to keep

dumping such great guys. He said he'd take them if I didn't want them."

Kingsley took Charlotte's wrists and tied them high to the bedpost. Water from her shower ran down her back and her legs all the way to her ankles. The water droplets itched and tickled but she couldn't reach down to wipe them off.

"You would have been crazy to stay with men who didn't understand you. Compromise is one thing. Denying your true self is another. Now…" He stood behind her. "I'm going to do something to you that is neither boring nor bourgeois. I'm going to flog you for five minutes. And if you make it through those five minutes without saying your safe word, I'll give you an orgasm. And then I will flog you for eight minutes. And then I will give you another orgasm. And so on and so on. I'll add three minutes to each beating. And the game only ends when you safe out."

"What if I don't safe out?"

"Then we'll be here for a very long time," he whispered into her ear. "Because there's nothing in the world I enjoy more than beating a beautiful woman and then bringing her to climax. Now where did I put that cat?"

"Cat? You have a cat?"

"Cat of nine tails, Charlie. Now be a good girl and just stay put while I find a few things."

Charlotte was fairly certain Kingsley knew exactly where everything was. He just wanted to leave her tied up naked and waiting, letting the anticipation scare her. She heard what sounded like a trunk opening and then she felt him standing behind her again. Something landed on the bed. It was brown leather with a six-inch handle and nine leather thongs. It didn't look terrifying. But it didn't look fun, either. Something else landed on the bed—a tube of lubricant. One more thud—a rather impressive-looking vibrator. She blinked as Kingsley brought his hand around and waved a stopwatch in front of her face.

"Five minutes." He set the alarm. "Ready?"

"Yes, sir."

"You're trying to get me to fuck you by calling me 'sir,' aren't you? It will work. But not yet."

Before she could say anything else, the flogger was off the bed and he'd landed the first blow on her back. She flinched at the sudden burning pain. It was shockingly sharp, but not unbearable. She breathed through her nose in short desperate bursts. She was determined to not to say her safe word. It wasn't so much that she wanted the orgasm. She wanted to prove to Kingsley she wasn't boring.

When she heard the chiming of the stopwatch alarm she sagged with relief. Kingsley pressed his bare chest into her burning back. The flogger landed on his bed again.

"Did you enjoy that, Charlie?"

"No," she said, still panting.

"Good. I hate beating masochists. They take the fun out of it by actually enjoying the pain."

"I'm letting you do this to me," she said between breaths. "I'm not a masochist?"

"Oh, no, Charlie. You're not a masochist. You're a slut."

"I am not—"

He hushed her before she could finish her angry protest.

"Charlie, in this house, the word *slut* is the highest compliment I can give. It means you are a person who owns her sexuality and is unafraid to experiment and open her mind and body to new experiences. I'm a slut, too."

"I've noticed."

"Now that you've had your pain, I suppose you'll be wanting your pleasure."

Kingsley reached out for the lubricant and opened the tube. He slid his hand between her legs and applied a generous dose to her labia. She shivered from the cold and the wet, but relished the pleasure his dexterous fingers were giving her.

"I know I was a little rough on you last night. But I can be merciful."

He took the vibrator and turned it on. He moved Charlotte's legs apart and slid it slowly into her. She inhaled as it went deep inside her. Her body slowly stretched to take it all in.

"This is merciful?" she asked.

"It's not as big as I am."

He moved it in and out of her slowly as his fingers found her clitoris and teased it. The vibrator did its work quickly. She cried out as her body spasmed around it and against Kingsley's hand. He pulled it out of her and laid it on the bed again.

"I'll give you another one in eight minutes," he whispered into her ear. Again he set the alarm on the stopwatch. Her body was still twitching with pleasure when the flogger struck her sore back. She concentrated on her waning pleasure and tried to ignore the growing pain.

She found that if she opened her back instead of clenching her muscles, the agony was flatter, less acute. Her head fell back. She stared up at the ceiling. After a few minutes she barely felt anything at all.

A chiming sound jarred her from her trance.

Kingsley picked up the vibrator again and pressed the tip against her clitoris. She gasped from the shock of pleasure. She'd never been with a man who understood how to manipulate a woman's body so well. The pressure on her clitoris was perfect. His fingers inside her found all her sensitive spots. He seemed far more concerned with her orgasms than his. She couldn't believe what she thinking. She was tied to a bedpost for a flogging and all she could think about was how good he made her feel.

Charlotte's orgasm spiked into her stomach and she almost wrenched her shoulder from how hard she flinched.

"If you can take eleven minutes of beating, then I'll fuck you again," Kingsley whispered into her ear. "How does that sound?"

"Very good."

Kingsley slapped her hard on her right thigh.

"I mean, very good, sir."

By now Charlotte knew how to handle this. She closed her eyes and let the pain roll over her and off her. In her mind she was somewhere else. In her mind she was untied and on her back with Kingsley on top of her and deep inside her and before she knew it, she heard the beeping of the stopwatch alarm again.

"Thank God," she said. Another minute and she would have given in.

"You're welcome."

Kingsley threw the flogger on the bed. Standing behind her he ran his hands up and down the front of her body. He stopped at her breasts. He teased her nipples until they were hard and sore. He kissed her neck and shoulder.

"Tell me the truth, Charlie. Have you ever been taken here?" He ran his hand over her bottom.

"You mean anal?" she asked. "Once."

"Did you like it?"

"Undecided."

"That's because you've never had it with me. Let's rectify that, shall we?"

She wasn't sure she wanted this, but she knew she didn't want to stop him, either. Her heart fluttered in fear. But she remembered Kingsley's admonitions and didn't let the fear stop her.

He took the lubricant again and applied it to her. She sighed at how good the cold wet liquid felt going into her. Kingsley took his time preparing her body. She tried to relax. As big as he was she would have to be very relaxed to take him inside her.

King pressed close to her. She closed her eyes when she felt him start to push into her. He grabbed her thigh and lifted it. She rested her knee on top of the bed. Slowly he entered her inch by inch. Last night he'd been shockingly brutal with her. Now he was nothing but careful. She shivered at how strangely good it felt to have him inside her this way. Kingsley moved in and out of her with gentle, careful thrusts.

With her eyes still closed she didn't notice that Kingsley had picked up the vibrator again. But when he started to push it inside her she opened her eyes in shock.

"Breathe, Charlie. You can take both."

He pushed the vibrator all the way into her as he continued his slow thrusts from behind.

"You've never been penetrated anally and vaginally at the same time before?" Kingsley asked.

"No…never."

"My poor girl. You were practically a virgin." She heard his smug laugh at her ear.

He continued to thrust into her. Charlotte moved her hips in rhythm with Kingsley's. She climaxed quickly around the vibrator. The sensations were so intense they were almost painful. After her second orgasm he finally pulled the vibrator out.

Kingsley gripped her by the hips and thrust faster. She was nearly insensate from the two intense orgasms he'd given her. She simply hung from her bonds as he fucked her.

She winced as his fingers tightened their hold. He pushed hard into her and came with a ragged breath.

He pulled out slowly. A minute later he came back to the bed. Charlie saw him reach for the flogger.

"Dragon," she said and he dropped it again.

He reached up and untied her and she collapsed back into his arms. He picked her up and laid her down. Kneeling on the floor next to the bed, he ran a hand through her still wet hair.

"Too much pain, *ma chérie*?" He didn't seem the least upset with her that she'd stopped him.

"No." She shook her head and smiled tiredly at him. The muscles inside her still fluttered. "Too much pleasure."

The next few weeks at Chez Kingsley, as he called his home, passed in a haze of sex and pain and more sex. Kingsley was a near limitless font of alternative sexual knowledge and experience. He'd introduced her to something new every day. One day it was nipple clamps. The next day spanking. He taught her to beg for his cock. Taught her to crawl for him. One day he dressed in leather pants and whipped her. The next day he put her in lingerie, tied her to his bed with silk scarves and violated her every orifice. Last weekend he'd even videotaped them having sex and made her watch it. Then he'd given her the only copy of the tape and let her decide what to do with it. Her first instinct was to destroy it.

She hadn't.

And every few days when she least suspected it, when she

was certain he was out of the house or in a meeting, he would sneak up on her, grab her, throw her against the wall or push her onto the floor or the bed and ravish her brutally. No matter how many times he did it, it always terrified her. No matter how many times he did, she always loved it.

Charlotte wasn't sure what he was doing to her tonight. He'd ordered her to wait naked in his bedroom in his huge chaise longue armchair. She leaned back into the plush fabric and closed her eyes. The chair was nearly the size of a love seat. He'd taken her a few times on it already. The chair arms were the perfect place for her legs to drape over as he thrust into her. She only had one more week here with Kingsley before she met the client he'd been training her for. She didn't think she'd be able to run off with this guy no matter how rich and "not unattractive" he was. Still…she also couldn't imagine leaving this place and returning entirely to her old life. Kingsley had marked her and not just with the bruises on her body.

She did miss work, however, and would be glad to go back to it. She'd cut everyone's hair in Kingsley's household except for Kingsley himself. He told her no one but his barber in France was allowed near his hair. She called him a coward and he'd punished her in wicked ways for the insult.

"You've got a lovely smile on your lips, Charlie. I'd love to know if I put it there."

Opening her eyes, she found Kingsley standing above her.

"I was thinking about what I'd do to your hair if you let me cut it. Your hot mess is very dashing, but I could make it even better."

"You come near me with your scissors, and I'll make sure you wake up with significantly less hair in the morning."

Charlotte laughed. He'd shaved her in the bath last night.

If he had no compunction about removing her most private hair, she knew he wouldn't hesitate to cut any other hair off.

"Fine. I'll leave your hair alone. But you keep telling me I have to trust you. When are you going to start trusting me a little?"

"I trust you quite a bit. Just not with my hair. But I'm glad you mention trust."

He held up a black scarf.

"Blindfold?" she guessed.

"Très bien, ma chérie."

Everything Kingsley had done to her, he'd done with her eyes open. The blindfold made her nervous; she could tell from the smile on his face that he was enjoying that fact.

He tied it around her eyes and the room went completely dark.

She started when Kingsley took her ankles and pushed her legs wide open and draped them over the arms of the chair. She heard him pull the ottoman close. She knew he was sitting on it in front of her exposed body. A month ago she would have been terrified and mortified. She was still a little terrified but Kingsley had taught her to be shameless. She was enjoying shameless. She hadn't even gone out drinking or clubbing since she met Kingsley. He was all the decadence she needed.

"Let's play a guessing game, Charlie. You guess all five right and you can do anything you want to me when the game is over."

"Anything?"

"Anything that isn't illegal. Or at least anything we won't get caught doing."

"What am I guessing?"

"You're guessing what object I'm putting inside you."

All her self-congratulatory anti-shame thoughts went out the window.

"You are going to stick stuff in me, and I have to guess what it is?"

"I think I just said that. Ready?"

"No," she said but didn't safe out. She'd quickly learned with Kingsley that "no" meant anything but "no" to him. Until she said "dragon" she was in.

She felt Kingsley's fingertips opening her up. And then something slightly flat pushed slowly into her. It had a round base that narrowed. She tried to imagine what it was. She felt something on it tickle her outer lips. Something soft like a bristles.

"Jesus, Kingsley. That's my best hairbrush. Do you know how expensive those things are?"

"Very good, *ma chérie*," he said and pulled it out of her. "Such a good hairbrush is surely washable. That is one out of five. Next," he said. The next object was cold and smooth and widened as it neared the top. She remembered dinner with Kingsley last night. It had been a party with several of Kingsley's hilariously perverted friends. He'd let her have one glass of wine. Halfway through dinner he'd caught her staring at him. Winking at her he emptied the rest of the wine bottle into his glass and raised the bottle in a toast to her.

"It's the wine bottle."

"You're a very smart little pussy, Charlie." She laughed as he pulled the bottle out of her.

She tensed a little when she felt his fingers again.

Whatever it was he was putting into her was metallic and heavy. And it was big. It had a flat bottom and grooved sides.

"Can I get a hint?" Charlotte asked.

"You'll find the answer very illuminating."

She laughed. "It's a flashlight?"

"Bien, *ma chérie*. Three out of five." He gently pulled the flashlight out of her. "The next one I'm quite certain you've had inside you before."

"Probably not. Never done the object thing."

"Are you sure about that?" Kingsley pushed her open with his fingers again. Again she felt cold smooth metal. But this object was different. It had two parts. She heard something move like the turning of a screw and she felt her vagina start to open up.

She took a hard breath. "You have your own speculum?"

"Of course. I love to play doctor. Especially with such a beautiful and patient patient."

She waited for him to close it and pull out. But he left it in her. She heard a click. "And the flashlight will do double duty for us."

Charlotte's heart pounded. Now she *was* mortified. She knew he was looking deep inside her.

Kingsley ran his hand up her stomach and stopped at her breasts. He pinched a nipple and her body responded with a hard contraction. Kingsley laughed. She knew he had seen the muscle contraction with his own eyes.

"That is four out of five. You only have one more and you win. I'm starting to get nervous."

"I'm the one naked, spread open and being violated here," she reminded him.

"Yes, you are. Therefore I'm expecting rather gruesome revenge from you." He didn't sound the least worried about the prospect.

He closed the speculum and gently withdrew it.

"Last one. If you don't get this one right, I'll be very dis- appointed in you, Charlie."

"Do your worst."

"I think I will."

She shivered when something soft brushed her inner thighs. She felt warm wetness again. Oh, yes, she knew what this was.

"Your tongue," she guessed and knew she was right. Kingsley pushed his tongue into her and out again. He kissed her inner lips with the same passion and dexterity he used to kiss her mouth. He sucked on her clitoris, ran his tongue up and down her. For what felt like an eternity his mouth devoured her. He pushed two fingers into her and with his tongue and hand brought her to a fierce climax. Her inner muscles rippled and shivered. Her back arched. She pushed her hips up and Kingsley's fingers went deep into her. The orgasm seemed to last forever. She sank into the chair as her climax faded and left her tired and panting. Kingsley's hand was at the back of her head. He untied the blindfold and she blinked when the light intruded. Kingsley gazed at her with a dangerous grin on his lips.

"My turn," he said.

She rolled forward and went down on her knees in front of the ottoman. She unbuttoned Kingsley's pants and took him in her mouth. For such an alpha male, King didn't demand oral pleasure very often. He'd once said that if she's already on her knees he would just fuck her doggy-style and give them both a good time. She couldn't argue with that logic. But now she could tell he was definitely in the mood. He leaned back on his hands and tilted his hips toward her. She paused long enough to reach up and unbutton his shirt as well. Running her hands over his hard muscled chest, she kissed his flat stomach before taking him with her mouth again. He was always so dominant, so in control of everything, that it gave her enormous satisfaction to hear him gasp and feel him flinch with the pleasure she was inflicting on him.

Kingsley reached out and slipped his fingers into her hair. He caressed the side of her face and her neck. It always amazed her how depraved he could seem one moment and how gentle and caring the next.

Charlotte took him deep in her mouth and sucked hard. She teased and caressed him with her tongue. Licked, stroked and did everything in her power to make him moan as helplessly as he made her. Finally Kingsley took a hard breath and came. After swallowing his semen with more pleasure than she would ever admit to, she leaned back to look at him. With his shirt pulled open all the way to his shoulders and his bullet-riddled chest and stomach on display, he was undoubtedly the most erotic man she'd ever met.

He buttoned his pants and stood up. He took Charlotte's hand and pulled her to her feet. He kissed her long and hard. She loved that she could still taste his saltiness on her tongue.

"You won the game, Charlie. Whatever will become of me?"

"You said I get to do anything to you I want?"

"Oh, yes. Put me in a dress and take pictures. Make me walk down the street naked. Shave my testicles with a straight razor. Do you need time to decide?"

"Oh, no. I already know what I want to make you do." Charlotte wrapped her arms around Kingsley's shoulders and ran her hands through his long unruly hair.

"Charlie, no." Kingsley's voice was hard as iron.

"You don't get to say 'no' if I don't get to say 'no.' You never told me your safe word. And, need I remind you, you said I got to do anything I wanted to you. I want to cut your hair."

"I'm getting a new dragon."

"Not a chance. I'm all yours for another week and you are having a haircut. Stop being a coward. I'm one of the best stylists in the city."

Kingsley exhaled and shook his head. "Steele was right. You are trouble."

"He lets me cut his hair."

"He also lets you breathe fire when you're drunk. His is not an example we should be following."

Charlotte looked at Kingsley and turned the corners of her mouth down.

"*Mon Dieu*, don't pout at me. I can't resist a beautiful woman pouting. I'll have to spank you and let you cut my hair."

"Spanking later. Haircut now. We'll do it in your bathroom."

Charlotte threw on her robe and ran to her bedroom. She gathered all her supplies and took them back to Kingsley's room. Standing in the bathroom, he looked as pathetic as a child who'd lost his dog.

"Shower," she ordered.

"Only if you join me."

Charlotte sighed and pulled off her robe again. She'd probably spent as much time naked in King's house as she had clothed. Kingsley took off his shirt and pants and stepped into his large steam shower. The glass box was so full of steam she could barely see him when she entered. She laughed as he grabbed her and dragged her to him. He kissed her under the water and lifted her up. He pressed her back to the tile wall and penetrated her.

She wrapped her arms and legs around him and pushed her hips into his. She loved how strong he was, loved how easily he could lift her and take her like she weighed nothing.

He drove into her as the water poured over them. She only

meant for them to get his hair wet so she could properly cut it. As she climaxed around his hard length she decided Kingsley was definitely her favorite client of all time.

Kingsley lowered her to the floor and turned her around. He pushed into her from behind. Resting her face against the wall, she relaxed into the wet heat as he buried himself deep inside her and came again. He pulled out and Charlie turned around.

"On your knees."

"Charlie, you devil." Kingsley dropped to the floor. He didn't seem to mind the position. Taking a fistful of shampoo she washed his hair. He kissed her stomach and hips as she lathered and rinsed his hair.

"None of that. You aren't going to fuck me until I forget what I'm doing. Up and out," she said. Kingsley stood up and left the shower. She followed and found a towel and her robe again while Kingsley pulled on his pants without bothering to dry off. God, he looked even better wet than dry. Running out to her bedroom she found a chair of just the right height. She brought it back, set it in the middle of the bathroom floor and pointed it to it.

Kingsley sat in it with obvious reluctance.

"I think I'd rather be back in *la Légion* getting shot at again."

"If you keep acting like a big baby, I will shoot you. I've never known a man so in love with his hair before."

"I'm in love with all of me. I'm a very lovable pervert."

"Well, you're going to be a very sexy pervert when I'm done with you. Now hold still."

She combed his hair and made a study of it. It was a good base haircut already, only too long. Clearly he hadn't gone to see his French barber in some time. She decided to cut it fairly short in the back and leave the top nice and wavy and purposefully disheveled looking.

He recoiled as she brought up her scissors.

"Big baby," she said again.

"The more you taunt me, the more you'll pay for it tomorrow."

"Your punishments are the most fun I've had in years. You're going to have to find a better threat."

"Any suggestions?"

Charlotte thought about it. She took her first snip of his hair. It fell in a wet clump to the floor. "I guess you could kick me out earlier than we talked about."

She saw Kingsley's face in the mirror turn. The mask of the playful pervert temporarily dropped.

"I will not kick you out, Charlie. This was a business arrangement, recall? You are here to learn and then meet my client."

She continued to snip away.

"I know. I'm not complaining. I've had the time of my life. I'll just, you know, miss you."

"I warned you that if you made me take my clothes off you'd fall in love with me."

"Don't get so cocky. I'm not in love with you. I just like you. A lot."

"You know, you may like my client even more than you like me."

"Is he less arrogant than you are?"

"Slightly."

"Then I probably won't."

Kingsley laughed and she continued her work on him in silence. When she was done with the back of his hair she moved to the front. She blocked his view of himself in the mirror as she snipped away at the sides and top of his rich brown hair. He had only a hint of a few gray hairs and no balding at all. Along with the arrogance gene, he'd gotten the great hair gene, too. She set her scissors aside and ran her hands through his hair over and over again, tousling it this way and that. She took a tiny dab of hair serum and ran it through his waves.

"Perfect." Charlotte stepped aside. She watched with anticipation as Kingsley studied himself in the mirror.

"My God," he said. "I'm even more handsome than I thought."

Charlotte slapped him on the bottom, and he pulled her into his arms. It was a very good haircut. He looked younger and even more roguish. In fact, he looked very French. *Très* even.

"Your revenge is complete. You won the game and got to play barber."

"Stylist," she corrected. "If I beg can I get to do one more thing tonight that you never let me do?"

"Beg away and we'll see how magnanimous I'm feeling."

"Can I sleep with you in your bed tonight?"

Kingsley sighed and kissed her on the forehead.

"Charlie, while I adore hurting you, I must admit I don't actually enjoy hurting you."

"It's okay. Thought I'd ask."

"You may stay with me tonight and every night until you leave," he said.

She grinned up at him. "Really?"

"*Oui.* Now take off your clothes and get into my bed. I need to start punishing you for all your insubordination."

"Yes, sir." She took off running to the bed. Kingsley came in after her and crawled on top of her.

"Admit it," she said as he opened her robe and kissed her nipples. "You like me, too."

"I do. A good barber is so hard to find."

On her last day at Chez Kingsley, Charlotte woke up alone in his big red bed. She was surprised he was up so early considering how late they'd stayed up playing and fucking last night.

Tired and lonely, Charlotte showered in Kingsley's bathroom and dressed. She returned to her own room and packed her things. She had a feeling she'd be back at her own apartment by tomorrow. She'd promised Kingsley she would keep an open mind about his client, whom she would meet tonight. Kingsley had told her very little about him. All she knew was that he was, as Kingsley said, "not unattractive," "wealthy," and was "longing for a deeper connection than his previous relationships." She didn't know how deeply she could connect with this guy when her heart ached at the thought of leaving Kingsley behind. But he'd trained her well. By now she was used to doing what King told her to do. She'd meet him. She'd give him a chance. And then she'd go back to her old life.

At least she'd have some very good memories.

At seven that evening Kingsley came to her door. His too-handsome face wore a somber expression that pained her to see. They kissed in silence before Kingsley pulled away and whispered, "Time to go."

Offering her his arm, he escorted her to his Rolls-Royce, and she cried against his shoulder on her way to the restaurant where his client waited.

The Rolls pulled in front and parked. Charlotte wiped her face and gave King a sad smile.

"I'm only doing this for you," she said.

"I know, *chérie*. But give him a chance. I think you're exactly what he's been looking for."

"Okay. I'll see you in six weeks though, right?" Charlotte straightened her hair and her dress.

He raised his eyebrow at her.

"Your next haircut," she reminded him.

He smiled. *"Bien sûr."*

Charlotte took a deep breath and walked into the restaurant. Old and elegant, it reeked of money, and she felt completely out of place. She gave her name to the maitre d', who escorted her to a private table in the corner of the restaurant. She didn't want to eat anything. She didn't even want a drink. She just wanted to run from the place and straight back into the arms of—

Staring down morosely at the floor, she saw her face reflected back at her from a pair of riding boots polished to a mirror shine.

Charlotte looked up and smiled at Kingsley's mysterious "client."

"Bonjour, monsieur."

★ ★ ★ ★ ★

SECOND TIME AROUND
PORTIA DA COSTA

What is it with him? Why is he looking at me like that?

I glance across the assembly hall, and he's staring at me as if I'm some hot chick he's just spotted in a bar. A total stranger, but one he fancies. He's undressing me with his eyes, the way men who know exactly what to do with a woman do. Men who know they can get away with it too.

I start to sweat. My heart flutters like a bird inside my rib cage. Down there, oh, God, in my crotch, I can feel myself getting hot and slippery and aching and tense.

I can't believe it. He's my ex-husband. I shouldn't feel like this.

A server hovers at my elbow with a tray of glasses and I grab a glass of sparkling plonk and take a long swallow from it. The wine's pleasant, but I barely taste it. Even the alcohol doesn't register, I'm so shaken...so...so aroused.

Get a grip, Willa. Stay in control. It's James and you're bound to feel a bit weird seeing him again after three years. But there's nothing to get in a tizz and go to pieces over.

Yes, that's right. It's just surprise. Nothing more. Physical signals a bit scrambled. Bound to happen when it's a man you've been intimate with.

But he never used to look at me like that, not even when we were first married. Or even when we were high school pupils here, boarders at exclusive Walton Wood College and two randy teenagers just crazy-mad for one another.

Perhaps I shouldn't have come here? School reunion, not my thing really. Everybody playing at one-upmanship, my career's better than your career, my marriage is better than your marriage, my kids are better than your kids.

Yes, stupid to come here when my marriage foundered and even the career I thought I wanted isn't turning out to be as spectacular as I'd hoped.

And I really don't like feeling out of control like this!

It's all James's fault. For being different. For being...new somehow.

Oh, hell, he's coming across again. What shall I do?

As my ex-husband weaves across the hall, amongst my former classmates and teachers, his blue eyes narrow and assess me. By the time he reaches me, he's covered every inch of my body, and he's retracing the journey, flicking back to hover explicitly at my breasts, at my crotch. Blushing harder than I ever did in school, I want to toss my head and look away, outraged. But I can't. I just can't. It's like he's hypnotized me.

My mouth drops open when he quirks his lips, lifts his drink to me in an insolent toast, then takes a long swallow in a way that makes my sex flutter as his Adam's apple works in his long tanned throat. Is he ever going to speak, or just keep on staring me down, making me hot?

"Enjoying yourself, Willa?"

"Yes...sort of. I'm not sure..."

I sound like an idiot. God, I'm never like this. What is he *doing* to me?

He takes another sip from his glass, eyeing me over it. "That's not like you, love. You always know what you feel. What you want."

The word *want* makes me shudder. Right down there again, in my pussy.

What the hell's happened to the man who was *my* James? He was my childhood sweetheart. We dated here at Walton Wood, and wed later, when we'd got our degrees, and had what I thought was the whole world at our feet. Now I feel as if some kind of Stepford Husband scenario has happened in reverse. And the mild-mannered, so often too-tired-to-fight-or-fuck man I married has turned into a dangerous stranger, a new breed of steely, threatening cyborg. Sort of like the Terminator, but with emotions. Lots of emotions, and most of them sexual confidence and charisma.

Opening my mouth to retort…something…anything…I snap it shut again when a group of circulating reunion guests pitch up beside us. It's all "Hello," "How are you?," "What are you doing these days?" between James and I, and the newcomers. Under other circumstances, I'd be interested, nosy even, genuinely wanting to know how people have fared, especially one of our teachers, the cute but quirky Mr. Laurence, who seems to have been in the wars, poor man, and now walks with a stick. He had us all laughing with a surprisingly funny math joke, and even though James seemed to be laughing along, when I glanced at him, he was smiling at me. Only at me. His eyes were steady, steel in the blue, and the way they speared into me made me tremble in my smart pumps, and a fresh rush of blood made my face and ears and chest turn rosy pink.

I'm sweating now, when I look at him, and I can't think straight. I thought I was over him that way. We grew apart. I can't still want him, now we've split...or can I?

And yet like a hunter, he's watching me, sizing me up. As the chat goes on, I try glaring at him, to make him stop, but he only gives me that smile, that goddamn smile!

"Drink, madam?"

The server, superefficient, is at my elbow with more drinks. I have to hand it to my old classmate Caitlyn, her catering firm's really organized this shindig to perfection. As I reach for more Chardonnay, I make a note to seek her out and congratulate her on a job well done. At least *her* future's turned out well, she's met her goals.

But just as my fingers almost make contact with a glass, a hand catches me by the wrist, gentle but unyielding. I know that touch, even after three years of not feeling it, and I forget about my former classmates, I forget about wine, I forget about everything. There's nothing in the world but the heat in those strong fingers, and a contact that's intimately familiar, yet totally new.

"Don't have another," James says very quietly, making me face him. His words don't carry beyond the air between him and me, and I realize our companions have drifted away, as if sensing our tension. "We need to get out of here," he goes on. "I think it's time we talked."

I feel like a whirlwind inside. How dare he? He doesn't have the right to order me around anymore. Not that he ever did. To my shame, it was me who always did the ordering, and far too damn much of it. I realize that now, but it doesn't stop old, hard-dying instincts from making me flare at him.

"I don't think we have anything to say, James," I say airily, while the whirlwind picks up speed inside me, emotions spinning round and round, fueled by the mad, unexpected hormones pumping and sluicing through me.

I want sex all of a sudden. Sex with my ex. It doesn't make sense, but that doesn't make the ache between my thighs less keen, the state of my nipples less peaked where they fight against the lace of my bra, suddenly too tight. The reunion party slips out of phase slightly and I see James naked again, in our shared bed, his thick cock risen and rampant.

The sex *was* good, I can never deny that. Always satisfying. Plenty of orgasms. Even though James forever avoided confrontation with me, and that in turn made me confused, annoyed, desperate to goad him, he was nothing if not strong, and enduring, between the sheets.

"Please, Willa, come on."

The words are old James, steady and nonconfrontational.

But the tone is new James, all unyielding, dark and deliciously threatening. My world shifts around me and I allow myself to be led.

Old classmates watch us as we cross the room.

And why not? New James doesn't *look* like old James either.

Gone is the conservative suit, the understated shirt and tie, and the floppy banker's hair. Now he's in black jeans and a leather jacket, with a black silk shirt beneath, stark, uncompromising and macho. His hair is short, a bit spiky in the front, and his face is bronzed and healthy looking, rugged. He looks every inch the outdoorsman he's become in the last three years, rather than the rather pale, harassed junior executive he was before we parted. Keeping track of him, I know his garden-design business is thriving. He's doing far, far better for himself now than in the kinds of jobs I pushed him into to further our status as a "golden couple."

He's golden in his own right now. It's in the way he walks

and in his gilded, sun-bleached hair. He doesn't need me anymore. He doesn't need my ambition for him. He never did.

"What do you want, James?"

I finally face up to him in the lobby. He's still holding my wrist, the grip light, but I can't seem to shake him off. I can't make myself *want* to shake him off. And how is it he seems taller now than he did? A grim thought needles me. Did my constant drive forward diminish him somehow? I have a horrible feeling it might have done. It seemed like the right thing at the time, but with hindsight, I can see that free of me, he's flourished. He's proud and strong and utterly male and sexy.

All I ever really wanted but was just too blind to see.

I open my mouth, to say I know not what, probably an attempt to be more amenable, perhaps show him that I'm trying to grow too. But he places the fingers of his free hand over my lips for a moment, and the touch of them makes me shake, literally shake.

James seems to note this. His fingertips smooth across my mouth, and insanely, I'm tempted to kiss them. Too late, he's drawn back.

"Well, I'm pretty sure I want to fuck you, Willa," he says conversationally, then he pauses, does a thing with his tongue around his lower lip that looks positively obscene, "but before that…well…you'll have to come with me and see, won't you?"

My world reels faster, harder.

"But, James," protests old me, still trying to shake loose, and trying to cling to some semblance of control and normality, even though I don't want it, I don't want it, I don't want it! "We can't just walk out on the party. People will talk."

James smiles, wide, his white teeth dazzling against his tan. He's relaxed, unfazed by the kind of crap that he used to just accept from me. He was always too weary of it to fight it then. But now he's like a dynamo, humming with energy.

"So let them."

He's still not letting go, and the Willa of old, who just won't quit, gears herself to struggle and assert herself. But then the rapid *tap, tap, tap* of high heels behind me makes me turn, anxious, intrigued, grasping at a moment of respite. Whoever it is, she's in a tearing hurry.

It's Caitlyn, the caterer, and she's dazzling-eyed and happy, a broad smile on her face. She looks literally illuminated. What's all that about?

"Where are you going, Caitlyn? Are you leaving the party already?" I ask, aware of James watching me, not her. "Is something going on?"

"Yes…yes, it is," she hurls over her shoulder, dashing for the open doors and the large chauffeured car I can see beyond it. "But I can't explain because I don't know what it is yet."

Suddenly, I want what she seems to have. An adventure, something sexy and new and mysterious. And I want it with my ex-husband, with James.

"Look, James, let's go and have a quiet chat somewhere. Drinks maybe, and a bit of dinner? The restaurant at my hotel is quite good. Then perhaps afterward…"

He looks at me, still smiling that devastating but secretive smile. The one that tells me my efforts to steer the situation are meaningless. He tugs lightly on my hand.

"Yes, let's go somewhere. But never mind drinks and bits of dinner. We need to get a few things straightened out first."

I'm totally disorientated. This is a man I've known for years, and yet he's a stranger. His touch makes me all wound up and twittery as if I'm with a movie star or some other celebrity, or just some man I've fancied for years and years but never actually met before.

I don't think I'm "me" at all, either.

For the first time in our relationship, I follow him silently. Almost meekly. He looks over his shoulder, and winks, his smile slow and knowing as he heads for the stairs.

At first I think we're heading for the dorms, empty now, out-of-term time, but within seconds I realize where we're going. It's the old music room, one of our favorite haunts from our time here. It was never used much, even back then, as they'd just refurbished a much larger room, with better acoustics, as a music laboratory.

It's small, shabby, with stained wooden paneling adorned by a selection of dog-eared posters. A few rows of chairs, some askew now, facing the wrong way. There's an air of forlorn neglect about the place, dim and dusty—but somehow, against the odds, a strange electricity too.

Without looking back, James strides across the room and throws himself down on one of the chairs, facing the back of the room. He nods amiably to a rather bad-tempered portrait of Beethoven on the rear wall. He appears totally relaxed on the hard old chair, and in tight denim, his thighs and crotch look astounding.

Good God, he's got an erection! Part of me can't believe it. But there's another part of me that was expecting it. I feel a shudder of response, between my legs, and suddenly I'm wetter than ever. If I shifted from foot to foot, I swear I'd squelch… and he'd hear it.

What's going on? What's going on? My heart thuds hard, and it's like there's a tightening band of iron around my chest.

"Don't stand over there, love. Come closer, where I can see you."

I jump, and stare around like a startled rabbit, realizing that I've been standing at the door as if waiting for permission to move farther into the room.

Me, wait for permission? My legs feel weak, they'll barely carry me, but I obey him and stride toward the haphazard line of chairs. I feel as if I'm floating, and my head's gone all light. Something very strange is happening to me, and I can barely look at James, much less meet his eyes.

When I make as if to move toward a chair, the one next to him, he goes, "Uh-uh..." and shakes his head. I do meet his eyes then, and they're fiery, electric blue, yet dark.

Battling an overwhelming urge to pant for breath, I just stand there in front of him, fiddling with my bag on its strap. His eyes narrow and he reaches out and waggles his fingers, indicating that I give it to him. When I do so, he sets it down, alongside his chair.

Why can't I speak? Why can't I move? It's as if he's controlling me with his eyes, and that slight smile playing around his lips. I can't believe the way my body is going crazy simply from a glance, a narrowing of his eyes, the tap of his fingertip on the side of his wooden chair seat. Oh, God, it's as if he's reached between my legs and begun to stroke me, slowly and tantalizingly. My clit throbs and aches, and my nipples are like hard little stones in my bra.

"I want you back, Willa." His voice is low and velvety, the rich tones of it confident now, assured. The last bit of old Willa opens her mouth to say something, some stupid protest she doesn't mean, but he arches his dark blond brows and almost, but not quite laughs at my inability to get out the words. I realize he's always known me better than I've known him.

"And I think you want me back too, don't you, love?"

Even though he wants me to speak now, I can't, but he nods as if he's heard the yes I can't manage to utter.

"I've learned a lot about myself while we've been apart. I've learned to accept parts of me I'd been suppressing," he continues, clasping his hands lightly in front of him, thumb of one resting in the palm of the other. They look sinewy and strong, hardened by work, yet capable of great delicacy. I want to kiss them, but the notion astonishes me, and I suppress a gasp, amazed at the bizarre, bizarre thoughts that are forming in my head. I see myself kneeling before him, pressing my lips to those beautiful hands, then allowing them to do anything they want with me. And still kneeling, I imagine opening his jeans and drawing out his cock, so I can suck and worship it.

I sway again. I actually sway. Inches.

"Do you want to sit down, Willa?" He says it softly, yet with weight, as if suggesting that by saying "yes, I do want to sit," I'll incur some penalty.

So I brace my knees, shake my head—and just stand there, aching, aching in every nerve and cell, and mostly between my legs, where my pussy is swimming wet.

I do not know what has happened to me. I do not know what has happened to James. But I know we're two new people, transformed forever.

"Good girl, good girl." He flexes his fingers and the small action is beautiful, evocative. "Yes, I've learned a lot about me…and a lot about you, too. About what you need."

My face must show my confusion, because he chuckles.

"You probably don't even know it yourself yet, but if you'll let me, I'll show you. If you're brave enough."

Like I had a chance. I'm suddenly helpless before him. And I like it.

I manage a nod this time. And I keep on nodding, like some penitent, anxious to please.

"Very well, then. Take off your panties."

What?

My mouth opens in one last dying gasp of the old me, wanting to question or protest, but he quells me with a level, old-fashioned look.

"Willa, take off your panties."

Quiet tones. That thrill.

My heels are high and I glance around, looking for support, then realize I'm to be offered none. Awkward, like some half-grown gazelle not sure of its ability to stay upright, I rummage up my skirt, tug my knickers down, and step out of them, teetering from one foot to the other, nearly toppling over as I catch one stiletto in the elastic at the last moment. But I manage to right myself, and then straighten up and just stand there, clutching a little bundle of white lace in my hands, not sure what to do with it.

"Hand them to me."

I step forward, fighting not to give in to vertigo and topple over. I feel yearning and confusion, and I feel so very, very horny that I can barely see straight. I'm right in front of him, all senses ramped up. He's giving off waves and waves of power that lap across the tender surfaces of my now-exposed pussy and excite it unbearably. He puts out a hand, waggles his fingers, and obediently I drop my panties into it. I feel even fainter as a waft of strong woman-smell drifts up from the fabric.

Oh, God, how long have I been so turned on? They're saturated with juice, stained dark, revealing. He crumples them in his long fingers, wafts them quickly in front of his face, his eyes closing a moment. Then he stuffs them into the pocket of his leather jacket and returns his attention to me, only me.

"Have you been with a man since me?"

Regret sluices through me, even though it shouldn't. We weren't married. I was lonely. I took a man home, a work colleague who seemed nice. Who *was* nice, but not James. We fooled around and it was okay, just okay. But I couldn't go through with it and fuck him when the moment came.

"You can answer, sweetheart. I'm not going to punish you." His eyes are level and inquisitive. I wonder why I seem to add the word *yet* to that last sentence. "I'll only punish you if you lie to me. If you deceive me."

Punish? Oh… Oh…

I'm very, very conscious that I'm standing here without my knickers and my husband is talking about punishing me. It seems strange and surreal to be doing so, but also right in a way I cannot seem to quantify. I love James. I always will. And even though I understand the reasons why we parted, I want that parting to be over. To *make* things right.

And it's right and good and exciting and fitting that my pussy should be naked, beneath my skirt, to suit his will.

"There was one guy…I didn't fuck him. But we…we kissed and played around a bit."

James tips his head to one side, eyeing me. That smile's back, flirting around his lips. Is he pleased I didn't fuck someone else, or pleased I allowed some liberties? I really can't tell.

"Did you let him touch you *there?*" he nods toward my crotch. "Between your legs?"

"Yes, sort of…but not much. I thought I wanted it, but when it came to it, I didn't."

He shakes his head slowly. "Now you're prevaricating, Willa. Keeping the full truth from me." Standing up suddenly, he's right in my face, looking down at me. "I don't mind if he played with your pussy. I just want you to be honest with me."

I open my mouth to answer, but his lips come down on mine, hard and fast and unequivocal. Gasping around his tongue, I let him take me with his mouth, possessive and hungry. I put my arms around his neck to hold myself up, to hold myself against him, and as he continues to subdue me with the kiss, I feel his hand on my bottom, working my skirt up quickly and efficiently.

When the cool air hits my bare skin, I start to struggle, unable to control the automatic urge to cover myself.

"Someone might come in!" I protest, trying to break the kiss, but he kisses harder, a hand on the back of my head, holding me, while his other cups my bottom cheek, squeezing and massaging it in a way that's delicious, delicious, delicious...rude but intensely arousing.

"Ah, Willa, Willa, Willa," he purrs when he eventually ends the kiss. "Always worrying what people will think, worrying what other people do." He's looking at me, talking to me in a normal way, but as he stares into my eyes, he's running his fingertips up and down into the cleft of my sex, teasing me, tickling me. "You mustn't do that, love. It only spoils things for you. Just relax, let things happen, cease to strive and fret." He's petting my perineum now, stroking it, his fingers sliding on my juices.

I let out a little whimper, unable to contain myself. I feel a thick rush of lubrication slither down the inside of my thigh, wetting my stocking top.

"See how much easier life is when you surrender to pleasure. When you stop forever wanting to do things, and change things, and just let things happen to you."

Gasping, I lean against him, still holding on for dear life.

My clit's pulsating with hungry need, but I can't reach down, can't touch myself. I haven't had permission. I must wait for him to give it, or for him to do me himself. All I can do is step from one foot to the other, as if that might surreptitiously stimulate me without him realizing it.

The minute I think that, though, he murmurs, "Tut-tut... I know what you're trying to do. And I haven't given permission. You have to earn your pleasure, my sweet. Give me something, so I'll give you something." He presses his mouth to the side of my face, breathing in deeply. "Much as I love you, my dear wife, it's not all about you anymore. It's about me too. What *I* want."

Far back in my mind, the old me clamors. I'm not his wife, not really. We're not together, and even if we are, we don't have that kind of relationship...or do we?

But I swallow hard, turn my head, breathe his breath. I don't want the old relationship anymore. I was never happy, not even when I was getting all my own way. Because beneath the superficial satisfaction I knew I was hurting him. And only he was brave enough to walk away from the mess I was making.

Walk away, so he could come back. A new man. The one I need and love.

In a tiny voice, I ask, "What do you want?" I know the answer, I think, but I'm scared, still scared. It's the ultimate loss of control, a true submission.

"Well, tonight, for starters. I'd like to see your beautiful breasts again...and your thighs...and your pussy." His fingers move devilishly, sliding forward, playing around my entrance, but not quite reaching my clit. "And then I think I'd like to spank your bottom. You need to learn to let go, my love. To give in. Cut loose." He slips a finger into my vagina, and it goes in to the first joint, coasting on my honey. "To let someone other than you control your senses and your body." He kisses me again, his lips cruising my throat as his finger hooks inside me, making me gasp. "Only then will you really and truly be in charge of what makes you happy."

It sounds like New Age mumbo jumbo, but beneath the words I see the wisdom. It makes age-old sense, and my ex-husband is primal. He's male and he's alpha and he's been that way all along. He just made concessions to me, out of love. In error, but because he cared.

And now, because he still cares, he's become himself again.

But I'm afraid. In a way I never have been before. "I'm scared," I admit, my voice barely more than a breath.

"Don't be," he whispers back, stroking my hair in a way that's gentle and sweet, while his other hand is rude and wicked between my legs. We stand there for long, long moments, him soothing me with small kisses and wordless whispers, while all the while, the finger inside me owns me. Eventually though, he slips it out, and with a last brush of his lips against my hair, he steps away from me. "Undress," he says quietly.

It's a command.

Heart lurching in my chest, I slide off my jacket and place it on the chair at my side. Everything seems unreal, yet hyperreal as if we're living it in high definition. The sounds of the buttons of my blouse sliding out of the buttonholes are so distinct they seem to reverberate, and the whisper of the cloth as I drop that on the chair rings in my ears too. I know that at any moment someone might find it necessary to revisit this old haunt, but still I unsnap the fastener on my bra, ready to remove it. Cupping myself through the lace, I hesitate. James quirks an eyebrow, his blue eyes steady. I swallow, breathe deeply, bracing myself, then let the garment slip off me, exposing my breasts.

"Stop."

My hands falter on the zip of my skirt and he steps close again, reaching out to fondle my breasts with both hands. He lifts them slightly, cradling them, as if assessing their weight and resilience. I have to close my eyes, the sensations are so intense, and I bite my lips, stopping the moans that spring to them as my pussy ripples, so excited.

"Look at me."

I toss my head, unable to look.

"Look at me," he repeats, voice still low and calm, yet full of heat. His eyes are full of heat too, when I meet them. And as they hold mine, he tweaks my nipples, lightly at first, then with more force, plucking and twisting and playing.

I'm a bottle of sparkling wine and he's shaking me. I'm ready to explode, to effervesce. My sex aches in a hard, grinding ache, and my clitoris seems to swell between my pussy lips, crying to be touched. And still he torments my nipples in a way that transcends both pleasure and pain, yet is both.

"Ah!" I gasp as he squashes them between finger and thumb, and when he glances downward, I realize I'm clasping myself between my legs, my hand squeezing and massaging through my skirt.

"Uh-oh, now you've done it!" he teases, still strumming my nipples. "That will cost you, Willa, my love." Dipping down, he takes a nipple into his mouth and sucks hard on it, sending me beside myself. Unable to control my actions, I rub myself hard, pressing on my clit through the fabric of my skirt, and it jumps suddenly, and hard, and I'm coming. My knees buckle as quick, unexpected pleasure ripples through my sex and my belly and my entire groin. I clench on nothing, the muscles working, working, working as I groan. But

James has me, holds me, keeping me aloft while I'm out of my body, yet more in it than I've ever, ever been.

After a few moments, I get it together again. I've climaxed, but it wasn't enough. It was just a taster orgasm. I want more and I want more of this strange new lovemaking James has shown me. As I feel him release me, I know he knows I'm ready.

"Skirt now, baby," he urges, but not before he presses a last little kiss on the very tip of my breast.

I unzip, slide my skirt down, step out of it, taking care not to catch my heels in the hem. I only have to reach for James's outstretched hand once throughout the process to keep my balance. And then I'm naked, but for my thigh-high stockings and elegant black pumps. I won't say it doesn't bother me that I'm so exposed in a public room, but somehow the danger, and the knowledge that anybody might come in and see my breasts and my crotch, only excites me more. In another world, I might have automatically kicked off my shoes too, but somehow, a sharp new instinct tells me that James prefers me with them on.

I stand, lifting my head as if presenting myself to him, and he walks in a circle around me, his blond head cocked to one side as if grading my posture, the firmness of my breasts, the smoothness of my bottom.

Should I bow my head? Be the perfect submissive? I decide not. I'm surrendering my will to James now, but I'm still me, still Willa, and he seems to like that. That delicious sexy smile plays around his lips, and as he returns to stand in front of me, looking into my eye, he winks and laughs as if acknowledging my choice and approving it.

Stepping close again, he holds me against him, one hand around my back, hugging me to his body, while the other one rests lightly on my backside. He presses his face to mine, breathing in deeply as he holds me. His erection is like a rod of iron in his jeans, jammed up against me, owning me with its size and might and hunger.

"I'm going to smack you now," he murmurs in my ear, and before I have time to react or respond, he fetches me a hard whack on my bottom cheek, right on its crown. It's such a shock that I cry out, but he jams his lips against mine, taking the sharp, high sound into his mouth. My bottom is afire instantaneously from the powerful stroke, but there's no time to absorb the degree of pain and tingling because he repeats the slap immediately, catching me perfectly on the spot he hit before.

Beyond the control of my mind, which suspects I should be still, my hips begin to circle and move, rubbing my needy crotch against James and massaging his erection with the curve of my belly. I flutter at him with my hands, then slide my arms up to lock them around his neck again.

"Be still," he purrs, his lips still on mine and his arm tightening around my back. His hand comes down hard on my rear, again and again and again as I hold on, cleaving to my rock.

I'm sobbing now, but he's still kissing me as he spanks my bottom. I part my thighs, trying to rub myself on one of his, and though he permits it, he smacks me harder. In retribution. My clit burns too, just like my bottom, aroused by the thought of different, greater pains and punishments. The target area is blazing now, a mass of furious heat that soaks through my entire groin, centering on my clitoris. He's starting to mix it up a bit, landing blows higher, lower, spreading the inferno. My head droops onto his neck, and my mouth settles against bare skin, just above his shirt. My lips open and I kiss him messily, wetly.

How can I like this? How does it arouse me so, even as I'm crying in the midst of my kisses? It hurts, it really hurts, but I can't stop myself writhing about, enticing and encouraging him.

"Do you like it?" he murmurs in my ear, catching me with a sharp, devious blow right on the underhang of my bottom.

"Yes! No! I don't know!" I gabble, working myself against him furiously. I want to clasp my fingers to my burning bottom, but I know if I let go my arms from around his neck I'll collapse. He'll catch me, of course, but I want to stay upright... to continue. He slaps again, the spank falling across the vent of my anus this time...and I go crazy. Orgasm swoops in from left field and I crush my pussy against the denim of his jeans, and the iron-hard muscle beneath. Great wrenching waves of pleasure seem to possess my very soul, they're so massive, so all-consuming, so much more intense in every way than any orgasm I've ever had before.

"James...James...James..." I sob, and he holds me against him, with both hands this time. One hand clasps my sorely spanked bottom cheek, stirring the inferno, feeding the flames of the pain, and of my pleasure. Tears stream down my face and wet his too as I kiss him again and again in strange gratitude.

I never realized what I wanted until he showed me.

He strokes the heat, tantalizes the tender flesh, delicately caresses the rose of my anus and the sensitive area of my perineum. My climax surges again, but it's a more peaceful wave now, gently cresting then gradually receding. I slump against him, unable to stand, unable to think, and for moments—or is it hours?—we hold on to each other, silent but for our breathing, still heavy, and the sobs and sniffs and whimpers I can't control. But I don't feel embarrassed or troubled that I can't contain myself. I feel liberated. Free and happy in a new and magic way.

"Thank you, my love," I whisper at last, able to speak.

"Thank *you*, Willa," he answers, kissing me again, even as his fingers curve lightly, teasing my soreness.

"But…but…" I want to quiz him, ask him if he wants me to do anything about the raging erection that's still boring into my belly through his jeans. But I know that in good time, he'll make his desires known to me.

"Don't fret, love…" he soothes, stroking my hair.

"I want to please you," I admit, then feel a new flush of heat rush through my body, "Because you pleased me."

He shrugs, dropping a kiss on my cheek. "Seems reasonable." He withdraws his hands and rests them on my shoulders, pushing down lightly.

It seems perfectly sweet and natural to drop to my knees. His eyes are like sapphires, lit from within as he looks down at me, and he fusses with my hair again as I grapple with his belt and button and zipper of his jeans.

He isn't wearing any underwear! My neat, conventional, tidy, buttoned-down James has left off his briefs, and I feel a new pang of delicious desire at that, such a wicked excitement. I almost swoon with perverse yearning as his beautiful cock springs out and bounces up, magnificently stiff. He laughs, macho man, pleased with himself, and why not. Cradling my head gently, he edges me toward his shiny, rosy, inviting glans. The skin is taut and wet, awash with luscious pre-come.

I part my lips and admit him, loving the way he stretches my mouth and doesn't hesitate, pushing in, making me take his heat and hardness. He holds me in place, thrusting. I know he could go deeper, he's a big man, but even though he's dominant, he's not cruel, not a beast. He possesses my mouth confidently but respects my limits. Just…

Me, I don't feel I *have* limits. I encourage him, grabbing his firm-muscled buttocks, squeezing and caressing, pressing the seam of his jeans against his cleft.

"Oh, Willa, Willa…God, I've missed you!" His hips jerk as I press and press. "I've wanted this so long…so long. I don't think I can hold on, love. I'm too excited. I'm going to come!"

Silently, I cry out to him to let loose, to come, to flood my mouth with his semen. He can't hear me, can he? But maybe he can, and I want him to know it's not an order, never that, just an invitation, extended happily, and with love. As if he has heard, his hips hammer, thrusting wildly now, the hard head of his cock butting at my tongue and the inside of my cheeks. But I don't gag, I'm so relaxed, so ready for him.

"Yes! Yes! Yes!" he shouts prosaically, but to me it's like music. A sweet song I've not heard for over three years. My tears fall again, happy and salt, as he comes, copiously and freely in my mouth.

Later, I don't know how much, he helps me to dress, handing me my clothes and offering his arm for me to lean on when I step into my shoes. We do this without many words, but they're not needed. It's as if all the distance between us during our marriage has collapsed and we're soul to soul, closer now than we've ever been.

Clattering through the foyer, I realize I'm going to go with him, wherever he wants me to go. It's been good to see old school friends, but my place is by James's side now. We nod to a few folks as we pass through, but we don't stop.

"I have a hotel room at the Greybridge," I offer cautiously, once we're out on the gravel. At one time, I'd have been bustling him into going there, organizing, controlling, but not now.

"Sounds great. I just came on spec. I didn't plan that far." He leans over and gives me a kiss. "Let's go there then. Good thinking, love." He reaches up and ruffles my hair like I'm a dutiful child who's done well.

I glow, *feeling* like a dutiful child who's done well.

"You wait here. I'll get my car. Did you drive here?"

I shake my head, and he nods approvingly before striding off in the direction of the staff car park. He'll only be a moment or two, but I'm already missing him. I console myself by surreptitiously pressing my hand against my bottom, and stirring the fading remnants of my pain, and my pleasure.

Smiling to myself, it's several seconds before I realize I'm not alone. There's a figure sitting on a bench, by the entrance. She's got a glass of wine and seems to be sitting in the twilight, deep in thought, her brow puckered. I think of my own recent epiphany, and sidle over. I won't push or pry, but she looks as if she might need a sounding board.

"Hello, Annette…how are you? Didn't see you in there… How have you been?"

Annette Fraser is pretty and slender with long dark red hair, a bit of a Pre-Raphaelite babe. In our sixth-form year, it was an open secret that she adored Mr. Laurence, who was the youngest and most handsome of our teachers back then. There were whispers and speculation that he liked her too, but he was always very correct, with no hint of impropriety.

"Same old, same old," she says with a sigh, sipping her drink.

My God, she still likes him! After all this time…

Without thinking, I grab her by the shoulder and squeeze. "Look, Annie, go for it! He's available now…he's not married. Maybe he's been waiting for you." I think about my man, also waiting, and as I do, I hear a growling engine approaching. "Don't hold back, love. You might miss out on something wonderful."

As a rather rakish and slightly battered old gray S Type pulls up, and from within, James pops the passenger door, I decide I'm never going to hold back either. I'll try anything, do anything…at his command.

I fling myself into the seat, and impulsively lean forward to kiss him. Then, as he laughs, and guns the car, I glance out and wave to Annette. She smiles back, abandons her glass… and then turns and walks smartly back into the building.

As we head out, I dearly hope *she* heads for Nicholas Laurence.

At the Greybridge, I'm all nerves and fluttering, knees like jelly and stomach all aquiver. While James is calm and in control, relaxed yet confident. Staying here together has all the mystique and erotic intensity of a weekend tryst, the sort that recently weds indulge in as an excuse for wall-to-wall sex in a location that's new to them.

Having eaten little of Caitlyn's delicious buffet at the reunion, we dine first. It's James's suggestion, and I agree. I know I need time out, although a part of me is just sizzling, aching and burning for him as I pick at the salmon en croûte and garden vegetables. I wriggle in my seat, trying to ignite the fires in my bottom again, but it seems he has the clever knack of spanking hard without leaving much enduring pain.

James narrows his eyes, and as they twinkle, I know he's sussed me out. "Want some more?" He's holding the wine bottle over my glass, but I know what he's really asking.

"Yes! Yes, please!" I gush, almost the schoolgirl again, and he pours me an inch of Chardonnay, which I bring to my lips and gulp down thirstily as he laughs.

"Greedy girl…" He leans forward and his voice is low and gravelly. "But that's all right. I'm feeling the need to spank you again, my love. And the need to play with you and touch your pussy and make you come."

As my jaw drops, he's suddenly on his feet, and moving round to my side of the table. "Let's go. We can always have room service later when we've finished."

The way he discreetly hustles me out of the restaurant takes my breath away, and I feel myself getting wetter and wetter and wetter as we walk to the lift. Traveling upward, he doesn't touch me, but his eyes are on me constantly, as if monitoring my readiness. As I move restlessly, his nostrils flare as if he can smell my arousal.

When the room door closes behind us, I don't know what to do. Me, who's *always* known what to do, and what I want. But I love the sense of uncertainty, the excitement of the un-known.

"Kneel on the bed, Willa, facing the bed head." His voice isn't cold or hard or bossy, just soft and shot through with real power. I hurry to obey, not stopping to ask if I should un-dress or anything. Clambering onto the bed, I feel my heart thud, thud, thudding in my chest, and the beat of it echoes between my legs.

He moves to stand beside the bed, next to me, and I feel so wound up, so agitated I can't even look at him. I just kneel up, eyes closed, my breath already coming in ragged gasps, and I jump a mile when he takes my jacket by the lapels and peels it off me, leaving me in my blouse and skirt. With a slow gentle stroke across my shoulders he calms me, then pushes down until I'm resting on my elbows, my back dished. My bottom is pushed up, presented to him, displayed with my skirt stretched tight across it.

"Forward, baby," he instructs, helping me by tossing aside the mounds of pillows and edging me into position. Automatically I grab on to the brass rails and he fondles my hair approvingly. A moment later he's fastening my wrists to the bed head with the silk sash of my kimono, which I laid across the duvet earlier.

Involuntarily, I moan, my sex aching already, and we've hardly yet begun.

"Shush, Willa, you must be quiet and good." He speaks with gentleness, but there's steel there, and power beneath the words.

Reaching beneath me, he pushes up my blouse in a bunch above my breasts, then reaches into the cups of my bra to ease them out of it. They feel swollen and heavy, aggravated by their own weight now they're freed from clothing and support. James's fingertips brush each nipple lightly and I have to bite my lips to keep myself from crying out.

Watching my face in profile, James sees this, and he touches my nipples again, more lingeringly this time. He takes one between his finger and thumb, delicately twisting and forcing the suppressed cry from me. Just the way he did back in the music room. He knows my vulnerabilities now, and he's exquisitely ruthless. He pinches again and I groan, shaking my hips.

"Would it be easier if I gagged you?"

Would what be easier? I don't know what "it" is. But the effort of keeping silent, of not being as "quiet and good" as he wants me to, is exhausting. I nod my head as he continues to beleaguer my nipples with little twists and squeezes.

"Good girl. That's a sensible choice," he whispers in my ear, bending over me and brushing a kiss against the back of my neck. A second later, he bounds from the bed and then returns with a soft silk scarf of mine that was draped across the back of a chair. His warm fingers part my lips, then my teeth, handling me like a stockman would a prize mare, and he slips the silk into my mouth, then ties the ends at the back of my head.

"Good…very good," he murmurs again, then folds back the panels of my shirt and tucks them into the waistband of my skirt so that my breasts in my pushed-down bra are more exposed. "Look!" He gestures to the large mirror to one side of the room, and I see myself.

I'm kneeling, bound and gagged with my breasts rudely exposed and my nipples erect and ruddy. But my eyes are like stars, wide and glittering with dark, dilated pupils. I look like a model in a fetish photo. A totem of submission, yet an object of strange beauty.

I moan again, behind my gag, excited anew by my own reflected image.

"I love you, Willa."

The words should seem ludicrous, incongruous in this situation, but they are perfectly apposite. I glance at James's reflection too, and his tanned face is aglow as if he too is in awe of my transformation. He's all power, all control, but the love is there in him.

And lust too. At his groin his erection is massive in his jeans. Moving over me again, his hands settle on my bottom, sliding the cloth of my skirt in circles over the skin and flesh beneath. A faint echo of my earlier spanking whispers in the muscles there, but it's slight, almost nothing. My heart lurches at the thought of what might very soon replace that. Between my legs, I feel more liquid ooze, warm and slippery.

James slides my skirt up, exposing my silky panties. One

hand curves around from the back, cupping my crotch and pressing the narrow strand of fabric between my thighs against my weeping pussy. Wetting his fingers as he dabs lightly at my clit and I groan again, free to now that the sound is muffled by yet more wet silk.

How can I get so excited? It's not the sex we had before. It's not the sex I've ever even thought of before. And yet it's real. It's true. And it's full of love. On James's part, and mine too. I want to pleasure him in these strange ways, as he pleasures me.

Making a low, masculine sound of approval, he pulls my knickers down to just above my knees. Then taking me by the thighs, he sets them apart, stretching the flimsy garment like a bridge. A great wave of my aroused odor rises up and envelops us.

"Gorgeous," growls James, breathing it in. He inserts two fingers into my pussy and I squeal behind my gag, it's so sudden and electrifying. My clit throbs and I beg silently for him to fondle it.

"Not yet, baby," he breathes into my ear as if he's read my mind. His fingers are still lodged inside me and he parts them to stretch and stimulate me.

I start to move frantically, shaking my hips apart to try to get some ease.

"Steady...steady..." He puts his free hand on the small of my back, pressing hard to keep me still while he plays around inside me. Tears of delicious, aching frustration form in my eyes. "I'm going to beat you now," he says with perfect, quiet gentleness. "It'll hurt quite a lot, but you'll thank me for it afterward."

I don't know whether he means I'll thank him for it because in some perverse way I'll like it, or whether me thanking him is just a part of the ritual. Maybe it's both. But I'll know soon, as he withdraws his fingers, steps from the bed and fetches my wooden hairbrush from where I've left it on the dressing table.

Then, with no further word, he begins to spank my bottom with it.

It hurts! Oh, God, how it hurts! He wasn't wrong about that. The spanks resonate hugely, throughout my body, like a solid bar of fire impacting on the tender skin of my bottom, smack, smack, smack. Relentless…I shout and I curse behind my gag. I start to hurl my hips about, not avoiding the blows, just reacting to them, translating their energy into movement.

Within moments, my entire bottom feels like molten lava, and my pussy is dripping and drooling, my honey trickling down my legs I'm so aroused. My clit feels as if it's swollen, enormous and throbbing. If I could just touch it, I know I'd come immediately.

But I *can't* touch it, and the sumptuous torment goes on and on. Flexing my back in a concave dip, I push my bottom up to entice and encourage my own punishment, and at the same time rub my nipples against the duvet. My love permits this, but the smacks get harder as a consequence. I wiggle like some kind of she-beast, widening my legs as much as I can within the hobble of my knickers. My tears are falling, but I feel glorified, exalted.

James agrees.

"Oh, Willa, you're magnificent," he gasps, voice rough with exertion. "You're a wonder, my love… Now I need to see you come!"

Abruptly, he stops spanking, but doesn't abandon the brush. Instead, he reverses his grip on it, and pushes the handle, warm from his hand, into my pussy. My channel clenches down hard, already rippling, and when he reaches beneath me, to stroke my clit, I break into pieces. Not literally of course, but in every other way that counts. Great, heart-stopping waves of the most intense pleasure I've ever known sweep through me. I seem to come in every cell, in every atom, as my pussy grabs at the handle. It seems to go on for hours and yet I know it's only moments.

"Oh, hell!" cries James, and then he's off the bed, leaving me with the brush still sticking out of me, and still coming, while he kicks off his boots, pulls a condom out of his pocket, then swiftly and efficiently shucks off his jeans and rolls on the rubber. A second later, the brush goes skidding across the carpet and his rampant cock replaces it inside me. When he shoves hard, and in desperation, I ascend again and soar to fine new heights of rapture. Especially when he reaches around and caresses me, the delicacy and precision of his fingers on my clitoris quite at odds with the ferocious grip he has on my hip, and the way his body batters against my tingling bottom.

Of course, pretty soon, it's all too much. Too much for me, as I collapse into a protoplasmic blob of overloaded nerves and orgasmic pleasure messages. Too much for him, as he shouts harshly and incoherently, and climaxes hard in a prolonged, jerking frenzy.

We lie in a heap for an indeterminate period, gasping and glowing and knowing, somehow, that we've finally come home even though this is just a simple hotel room.

Much later, we make love quietly and sweetly, and talk, just as quietly but facing many truths. He's changed, and I've changed, and the new people we've become seem to like each other much better, besides being more in love than ever.

"So where did you learn all this stuff?" I ask him, comfortable now in being able to do so.

"Oh, I knew about it all along, but somehow there never seemed to be the right time or the right moment to tell you about it." I feel sad, but he senses it, and cuddles me. "I should have… We could have wasted far less time."

"And *I* had other priorities all the time. Bloody jobs. Promotions. All that crap that I hate now." It feels good to admit that to myself as much as to James.

"Come and work for me instead. We're doing well, expanding, I could do with a top-notch office manager, and I can't think of anyone better for the job than you."

I think about it. Not sure. Perhaps I want everything to change.

"Or if you don't fancy that, you can always be a gardener's assistant and come out with me on jobs." He kisses my hair, and I have a feeling this might be the option he prefers. It seems weird to me, but it's a change, and a seed of real curiosity germinates. "It's physical…wheelbarrowing earth around, sweeping up leaves, planting out under my supervision."

We're lying like spoons, and he moves against me and brushes my sore bottom with his hip, his thigh…and his erection. I melt all over again, longing to be fucked.

"And I'm a hard taskmaster, Willa," he breathes against my skin, cupping my bottom cheek with his hand and making me squeak. "If you don't pull your weight, I might have to punish you. And you know what that leads to afterward, don't you?"

I'm moving against him now, stirring the fire in my punished buttocks and the desire between my legs. Boldly, my traveling hand reaches back and grasps his penis. I think vaguely about gardens and soil and sweeping and leaves, and as we start to make love again, I look forward to learning about them. From James.

Yes, this time around, I'll let my husband be the boss. Well, at least sometimes...

"We'll work it out, Willa," he purrs, and I feel him shake his head, then smile against my neck as he reads my mind.

★ ★ ★ ★ ★

TEMPTING THE NEW GUY
ALEGRA VERDE

*"Any magician worth his salt can escape from a locked cage or
a pair of handcuffs."*

          —Murphy, the theater owner *(The Perfect Poison)*

Clement Johns was a new account exec at Davies and Birch
Advertising. He was from the South, born in Memphis, and
he had a slow, dusky way of talking that sent shivers up my
spine every time he came up behind me and said my name.
Something he seemed to enjoy, because he did it at every opportunity. I'd be standing in the lunchroom, staring at the
microwave, waiting for my Cup-a-Soup and he'd come up
behind me. "Glory," he'd breathe on my neck, the word tickling the soft hairs at my nape. "A lovely name for a beautiful
woman," he'd say from behind me as I bent over the copier
tray to retrieve my copies. I said, "Thanks, that's sweet of
you," the first couple of times, but that seemed to encourage
him. So I started rolling my eyes at him whenever he tried to
catch my eye, and when he came up behind me, I'd get my
cup of soup or my copies or my supplies and make my way
around the pillar that he'd become.

He was a find. Not because he looked like Jude Law, with his straight-teethed smile, the boyish look of his slightly mussed fair hair and the glow that emanated from his gaze, but because there was a definite charm to his Southern purr and his confidence was backed by substance. After earning an MBA from Stanford, he'd gone out to L.A. and bounced around from agency to agency before he went home and started his own ad firm, which focused primarily on evaluating and purchasing internet ad space. He came to Davies and Birch with a solid client list and a technical manual he'd developed that identified primary venues and established criteria for judging their potential effectiveness. The firm had hired him in at substantial cost, given him a staff of two and a small corner suite of offices. It was a sound move. The clients were impressed with the expanded markets and the projected figures looked as though the firm's faith in Johns would be realized sooner than expected.

He and his crew were to take center stage at the morning staff meeting. Bruce Davies was, as usual, at the head of the long oval table and Lucas Birch at the foot. Johns was to present a list of up-and-coming sites with suggestions for how and by whom they might be best used. It was his first presentation to the staff at large. Claire, Davies's assistant-cum-secretary, had reserved three prime center seats for Johns and his staff. The two nerdy looking guys who worked with him were fresh out of CUNY. They took two of the seats and dutifully held the one between them for their leader. But Johns, instead of assuming his position of prominence, slid in next to me as I sat on the mini sofa that rested against the wall behind Davies.

"Glooory, Glooory," he whispered savoring the extra set of O's as he lowered himself beside me. I thought of that scene in *The Long Hot Summer.* He had stretched out the O's and crooned my name just like the randy group of teenaged boys had when they'd hidden in the bushes and called out "Euula, Euula." A giddy Eula in the guise of a pert Lee Remick had giggled from her perch on the veranda. Her husband, Tony Franciosa, who'd been sitting there with her and other members of the family, hadn't been tickled in the least by their antics. He'd gotten red in the face as he ran to the edge of the porch, shouting and threatening all manner of violence at the boys. "Gloory," Clement said again close to my ear. It tickled and I laughed. Clement grinned, maybe he meant to make the connection.

Davies turned and glanced briefly at the two of us before turning to begin the meeting.

"Been looking for you," Clement murmured as he leaned close to my ear, his warm breath whisking across my cheek.

I looked at him, eyebrows raised as if to say "I can't imagine why."

He grinned again and slipped a flier for an off-off-Broadway production of Tennessee Williams's *The Glass Menagerie* onto my lap.

"Tonight?" he said, for my ears only. "They so rarely do the old masters up here."

I raised my eyebrows.

"You and me," he said, touching my chest and then his with the tip of his finger.

It made me smile, but I didn't say anything one way or the other. Instead, I put a finger over my lips, urging him to be quiet before we drew any more attention. Bruce Davies glanced back at us again, before returning his attention to a status report from the accounting department. The report, which ended with a recommendation that a new set of limits and restrictions should be placed on company credit cards, finished to a chorus of groans as Davies nodded and said he'd consider the suggestions.

"Mr. Johns." Bruce spoke without turning around even slightly. "The floor is yours."

Clement stood and, smiling, began his report. However, when he found himself speaking to the back of Bruce's head, he moved to the center of the table and stood behind the chair that his two staffers still held vacant for him. He delivered the presentation with his usual aplomb, but when he was done, he came back to squeeze in next to me. "Well?" he wrote on the back of the flier, and handed it to me with a pen.

"You were fine," I wrote, feeling like we were in high school, passing notes.

"Not the presentation," he scribbled. "The play?"

I shook my head.

"Why?" he wrote.

"Busy," I mouthed.

"Doing what?" he wrote.

Of all the nerve. I gave him the high brow and turned my attention to Linda, the receptionist, an attractive older woman who was also charged with ordering supplies and managing repairs. She seemed to have a beef about people not signing guests in and with people expecting her to deliver their messages, when the system required that they pick them up from the desk. She was the last, and after Birch said a few words of encouragement, everyone began to file out of the room.

Bruce was instantly besieged by two account executives, so I took the opportunity to try to slip out. I made my way quickly around Johns as he bent to pick up his materials from the floor, but soon he was up and following me to the door. When I didn't slow down, he called after me. "Wait, Glory," he was saying from behind me when I heard Davies say, "Glory, I'd like to see you in my office." I turned back to Davies and nodded. Clement looked at Davies, then he looked at me. I turned and kept walking, but Clement followed me out the door and down the hall.

"Hey," he said, grabbing me by my upper arm.

I stopped and frowned up at him as I removed my arm from his grasp.

"Sorry," he said, and looked repentant. "I just wanted to say I'm one of the good guys. Truly." He nodded and grinned. "My momma taught me right. I'd just like to spend an evening in your company and I've got these tickets and..."

"I can't," I said, and felt kind of bad about it. He seemed so earnest, but I didn't want to encourage him. One in-house affair was more than enough.

Davies walked past us, one of the account execs still dangling on his arm like a piranha, teeth sunk so deep that it was unwilling to admit defeat. Bruce did not even glance our way.

"Okay," Clement said. "Too short a notice. But I won't be giving up. Persistence is a Southern virtue." He grinned that straight-teethed grin at me, his eyes bright in their sincerity, and I couldn't help but smile.

"Soon enough, you'll break and be glad you did."

I laughed, couldn't help it. He was arrogant, but he was also cute and funny.

"I gotta go," I said.

He nodded and swiped a curved finger under my chin before releasing me from his gaze.

Bruce was standing before the window, his back to me when I entered his office.

"Lock the door," he said. His voice was barely audible.

I did as he asked. He was asking, wasn't he?

He waited until I was seated in one of the two chairs that fronted his desk before saying, "You and Johns seemed to be getting along well."

"He's a friendly guy." I shrugged, feigning nonchalance, but I sensed that some kind of showdown was coming.

"And you? How friendly have you been?"

How was I supposed to respond to that? Obviously, he had something he needed to say.

"He's been here, what, two months and you and he are whispering and handing off notes like a couple of teenagers."

Obviously, he had eyes in the back of his head, but this agitation was out of character. He needed to get a grip. This was not something that should be discussed here, even with the door locked. I hated it when he got all possessive. I'd never really made any commitments to him, and I don't like being pushed. I pressed my lips together. The walls were too thin.

"It's bad enough that I have to suffer Alex Rodriquez, but at least he doesn't live in town, and he doesn't work for the firm."

"What's really wrong here?" I asked him.

He turned back to the window. He didn't say anything for a long time, so I stood up to go.

"I want to fuck you," he said to the window.

"Maybe we can meet after work," I said, turning toward the door. "Maybe I can arrange something." I tossed him a smile over my shoulder.

"Here. Now." The words were a short burst through his pursed lips.

"I don't like bringing this to the job."

"You did with Alex."

"That was once and it was before."

"Well, then you owe me a once, here."

"I don't owe you anything, Bruce," I said as I headed to the door that joined my office to his.

But he was there before me. "Glory, Glory," he was saying. "I didn't mean... I..." And he was reaching for me, his long powerful arms securing me, but I pushed at his chest.

"No," I said, "neither of us owes the other anything." My hands were pushing hard against him. He held me tighter and, lowering his head to mine, he tried to kiss me, but I turned my head from side to side, trying to avoid his mouth.

"It's just that—" he was saying, and I could feel his hardness against my stomach. His hands were at the back of my skirt, on my ass, cupping and squeezing the flesh of my cheeks through the cloth. Then he was tugging at the skirt and I could feel the fabric rising, the cool air on my thighs. I tried to push him away again, but he held me tighter, his upper arms a vise trapping mine. His mouth groped for and found mine, his tongue eager and aggressive.

"Stop it," I said, and shoved at him. "Not like this. Not here."

"I just want to feel you," he was saying as his fingers ducked beneath the thin line of my thong and ran down the crevice of my ass to sink into the heated flesh of my sex. "You are always wet for me," he was saying as he slipped his fingers between the folds, oblivious to anything other than his own needs. "You're so fucking sexy." His fingers slid deeper, coating themselves in my lubricant as he pressed the thick ridge of his penis deeper into my stomach, burrowing, as though seeking warmth.

"When we were in the meeting, all I could think about was the time you bound my arms to the headboard with one of your stockings. Then you rolled that cock ring down the length of my penis and I was afraid that you would just leave me there. You can be so cruel sometimes. But you climbed over me, straddled my head, pressed your wetness to my face and made me suck and lick at you until you came." He was breathing hard now and his cock twitched against my stomach.

"You shivered against my face. The lips of your sex were so hot and your spicy smell was everywhere. I pressed closer so that I could feel the vibrations and my nose dipped into you. I inhaled so hard it made me dizzy." A thick finger was circling my entrance. "As you came, your pussy beat against my mouth and your juices ran down my jaw and coated my lips. I wanted to swallow you whole."

I stilled, thinking that maybe if I didn't respond he'd understand that I didn't want this. Not here. But he was intent on arousing my desire so that he could confirm his claim on my body.

"In the boardroom, with Linda complaining about sign-in sheets, I was thinking about how wet you always get. I was so hard for you I barely heard what Birch was saying. All I could think about was dipping my hard fucking cock into your wet pussy." He said the words into my hair as though they were words of love rather than lust.

He was a grown man, not a teenager. He knew how to reel it in, and I was far from falling for that "I'll die if I don't get some" bit. If we were anywhere else, I would have struck out, loudly proclaimed my objections, and he would have been on his ass, writhing in pain. But we weren't anywhere else and I would never call him out here. He knew it, too. So he pressed his advantage, his hand on my breast now rubbing it through the silk of my blouse and then using his thumb to rouse the nipple.

His hands were rough and purposeful as he turned me about and pressed me against the wall, face-first. I let him. I would concede him this victory. He shoved my skirt up farther until it rode my waist like a belt and then he was shoving my thong aside. From behind me, his hand pressed between my legs, opening my stance as a finger slid up through the widening passage of my thighs, nudging its way through the slippery labia to tangle with my clitoris. The broad tip of his finger slipped up and around, engaging in a sort of gliding dance that ended in a wet kiss as its tip pressed the swelling nub. I shuddered, as he knew I would. His lips nipped at my neck; his tongue darted out, leaving a trail of damp tingles. Even through the growing haze of need, the sound of his zipper seemed to resonate throughout the room. The muscles of my pussy clenched in expectation.

The tip of his penis, a huge knob, pierced my opening as he gripped my right hip with one hand and my left shoulder with the other, securing my position. I leaned against the wall, hands splayed, all at once angry with him and with myself. I should have never become involved with this man. You don't shit where you eat. An adage well worth repeating.

As he pushed forward, my sex twitched, anticipating the hard length of him.

"Glory," he breathed as he thrust forward. I knew he was biting his lip as my heat consumed him. I knew that when he got it all in, the whole length of him, he would hold it there and just rock it back and forth to soak up the heat and the juices and then he would ride me hard. I knew what he liked and that was why he was afraid, afraid that I might start to like someone else and that I might decide not to come back. This whole bit was about him staking his claim, marking his territory. But my knowing this didn't stop me from pressing back so that I could take more of him in.

He was a big man. Every time I was with him, it was a

revelation, that he could fill me so completely. The walls of my sex clenched around him as he rasped forward, his fingers digging into my hip, his heavy sacks slapping against the backs of my thighs as he rammed himself into me with a conquering force until the heavy knob touched bottom. Then he pushed forward even more, even though there was nowhere else to go. A groan, low and long, accompanied the pressure.

He pulled back just a little, then thrust forward, as if he was testing the depth of my womb, as if he was trying to plant himself there and was burrowing himself a little nest. Then he was moving, the long draw back and the rasping thrust forward, the pace increasing as he did this over and over as I clenched around him. He was breathing hard. I couldn't breathe. My hands were slippery against the wall. I trembled and, stumbling, stepped forward in order to restore my balance. "No," he said, much too loudly, as both of his hands found my hips to draw me closer and secure my sex to his.

"Oh, fuck, Glory," he was saying, "Glory." His voice was an incessant whisper.

My pussy twitched and tingled and a low growl slipped from my throat as the rasp and tug quickened. I closed my eyes and let the current take me, the clean frisson like water lapping up my body caused my toes to curl in my shoes and my nipples to become stones. He was pounding at my backside and ramming himself deep and deeper until my pussy started to jump and clutch at him. A low whine came from somewhere deep in him as he started to come, a long swoosh and then in a series of jerking spurts that caused him to bounce against my backside, a supple brush and press of his groin against my nether cheeks.

Stumbling, he fell drunkenly forward before he could catch himself. His weight and momentum thrust me into the wall and I crashed, headfirst. The loudness of the thud startled me more than the pain of the contact.

After only a moment, he caught himself. Using the strength and length of his arms, he secured me to his chest apologizing for his clumsiness while just as clumsily patting my head as though looking for lumps. Or maybe he was trying to soothe me. Whatever his motivation, his heavy hands only increased my irritation.

"I'm fine," I said, separating myself from him as I made an attempt to straighten my clothes. "I'm going home," I added. The extent of the wrinkles in my skirt became more and more obvious as I smoothed it down over my hips. My blouse was a mass of creases, I could feel his seed slithering out of me, and the stickiness of our mingled juices clung to my inner thighs.

He nodded, having tugged his pants back into place. "I'm sorry," he said, ducking his head as though embarrassed.

No, he wasn't sorry. He might have been a little embarrassed at having to temporarily relinquish the impenetrable mask that he usually wore, but he wasn't sorry that he'd taken what he wanted. I'm sure he was thinking that he'd done what he had to do, marked his territory, the evidence of which was oozing out of me as I stood there.

I opened the door and slipped into my office, where I cleaned myself up as best I could with the wet wipes I kept in my bottom drawer. When I was done, I used my cell to call Clement on his.

"Eight o'clock?" I asked.

"Seven," he said, without missing a beat. "I'd like to pick you up, if that's okay?"

I gave him my address and went home to take a bath.

The play had been a little sad, but well acted and Clement seemed to be a fan of Tennessee Williams and Lillian

Hellman, the Southern playwrights, he called them. After the curtains closed and the applause died, we walked along the rain-dampened streets and debated the merits of the play we'd just seen. I felt like I was being regaled by a scholar, but in a really good way. He supplied insightful asides about the writer and similarities between this and his other plays, and he spoke with a shy intensity that soon gave way to his playful wit when he realized that I found the topic entertaining.

Over dessert and coffee at a diner near my apartment, he spoke about his brief stint as a theater major before he realized that he was more interested in the literature than the performance and that neither promised to be profitable. I told him about the time I played Blanche Dubois in an undergraduate production of *Streetcar* and we both fell over laughing when I gave him a taste of my Southern accent. He saw me home and secured a promise that I would see an upcoming college production of a Beth Henley play the following week. Then, standing two steps below me on my stoop, he pressed his lips to mine in a very warm, but chaste kiss. It was a date, like something out of a Thornton Wilder play, but we were very much alive.

I was in great spirits at work the next day. At first, Bruce was a little cautious toward me. Instead of calling me in to pick up a set of contracts that I was supposed to review, he grouped them with some letters Claire had to post and had her deliver them to me. When he couldn't stand the suspense anymore, he came to stand in the door between our offices, something that he rarely did, and asked me how far I'd gotten with my research on a prospective client. I handed him the file with a smile. He beamed with relief.

Clement was waiting for me in the lunchroom. He plucked

my Lean Cuisine out of my hand before I made it to the microwave.

"Let me take you out to lunch," he said, clasping my hand with his free one. His fingers stroked the palm of my hand as he tried to pull me closer.

"I've got a lot to do."

"We can make it a quick one. But you need to get out. We need to get out."

I laughed. "You need to get out. I've got work to do."

"Davies can get along without you for a few minutes. Dottie's has a fried catfish special that goes well with Corona."

"And you would know this because?"

"It's the same special she had last Friday."

He must have seen my will floundering, because he put my Lean Cuisine back in the freezer and turned back to me with, "My treat."

Dottie's was full. As Clement and I stood near the entrance, giving our eyes time to adjust to the darkness of its interior, Claire came up behind us.

"Hey." She smiled at Clement. To me, she said, "You usually eat in. I'm surprised to see you here."

I shrugged.

"Hey, there's a booth opening up," she shouted over the din as she brushed past me. "Come on."

Clement grabbed my hand and we followed her to the booth. The guys who were leaving threw some bills on the table and, before they could move away, Claire was sliding onto the bench, pushing empty bottles and baskets of leftover crusts and fries to the center. She scooted all the way to the edge as though making room for someone else. I slid onto the bench opposite her and Clement slid in next to me. She looked a little disappointed, but moved her purse to the space next to the wall as she slid back to the center of the bench.

A waiter came, counted the bills left by the booth's previous occupants before shoving them into his apron pocket, and then ferried their leftovers to a nearby dishpan that sat on what looked like a luggage rack.

"Something to drink," he asked when he finished wiping the table down.

"Miller Light," Claire chimed.

"A couple of Coronas," Clement said, indicating with a twist of his fingers that I was included in the order.

Claire looked at me as though a light had come on in her head.

"To eat?" the waiter asked.

Clement looked to Claire. She smiled at him. "A burger, no fries." He nodded and told the waiter that we were having the catfish special. "Fries?" he asked me. I shook my head no. The waiter left and Clement settled back, his shoulder leaning against mine. I pressed my lips together to keep from calling him out in front of Claire. These men with their need to flex their feathers were beginning to annoy me beyond endurance and this one had no reason whatsoever to make claims or assumptions. Didn't he know that Claire was taking notes? His actions, however, suggested that he was counting on it. I scooted over a bit to give him some room. He settled his right hand down next to my hip, his pinky pressed against my thigh. The waiter returned balancing bottles of beer and glasses on a round tray.

"What was all that noise yesterday when you were in Mr. Davies's office?" Claire asked as she poured her beer into a tall glass.

"When?" I asked, pretending ignorance as I sipped my beer from the bottle.

"Right after the morning meeting," she clarified. "You went in and a few minutes later there was like this crash and then a groan or maybe the groan came first. I went to see what happened. You know, to see if anyone had been hurt, but the door was locked."

I wondered whether she was that naive or whether she was just being a bitch.

"I don't know. I was only in there a minute."

"You must have heard it. Your office is right next to his."

I shook my head, shrugged, and took another sip.

"Well, anyway, he came out a few minutes later. Left for the day, said to forward all of his calls to his home phone. When I went into his office to make sure everything was okay, the only thing out of order was the empty rocks glass he'd left on his desk blotter."

"How long have you been Davies's assistant?" Clement asked Claire.

Thank God, because when Claire got a whiff of something she stayed with it like an old bird dog until she'd broken its neck, shook the life out of it and laid it at her master's feet. That made her a good partner when you had something to research, but when you wanted something to stay buried, you had to work hard to distract her.

"Nearly three years." She smiled at Clement.

"What's he really like?"

Claire grinned. She liked the attention. She liked Clement.

"He's wonderful when he's in a good mood, but he can be a bear at times."

"What makes him a bear?" Clement asked, sounding genuinely curious.

Claire smiled coyly, taking a demure sip from her glass of beer as she thought about her answer. I sat back and watched the two of them. I liked being on the sideline.

Claire was saying, "It's hard to say. The little things don't bother him. Sometimes he can be a teddy bear, but at other times nothing seems to please him."

"What sets him off?" Clement asked me.

"He likes things his way."

"Yeah," Claire agreed. "But you usually handle him so well. That's why I didn't know what to think yesterday. That crash. Then you left, and a few minutes later he comes striding past my desk."

Under the table, Clement rested his hand on my thigh. First, he patted it as though to placate or soothe me, but after the last pat, it remained a hot weight on my thigh. I scooted farther away from him, and with my free hand, brushed his hot hand off my leg. I did it slowly, but firmly, so that he would understand that its removal wasn't an accident. It didn't go far. The side of his hand still rested next to my hip. His little finger lay flush against the fabric of my skirt.

"He did seem a little agitated at the meeting," Clement mused.

I shrugged, assuming nonchalance. Now she had Clement speculating. I wish she would just let it go already.

"Sounded like somebody was trying to break a wild horse in there."

I could feel the heat rush up into my face.

Clement laughed, so I smiled. "Such colorful language. Where are you from, Claire?" he asked.

She ducked her head and blushed. "I'm from here, born and bred. I think it's a line from a movie. I watch a lot of movies."

Our food came and we talked about movies as we ate.

Claire liked romantic comedies—no surprise there—but I was surprised by her knowledge of the vintage divas Monroe, Stanwyck, Colbert, Lombard and even Norma Shearer. After indulging us for a few minutes, Clement steered the conversation to directors Kurosawa and Tarantino, two of his favorites. We ordered another round of beers and shared a basket of fries while we recounted our favorite scenes and shouted good-naturedly over one another when a detail was missed or someone's description ignited a related thought. It was fun. Clement, being the gentleman he is, insisted on paying the entire bill. I objected strenuously, but Claire's objection was weak at best and in the end, Clement handed over his Visa. We walked three abreast back to work, Claire animated, almost dancing at Clement's side.

Only fifteen minutes late, we slipped back to our respective desks. I had just pulled out a set of contracts and was scouring my desktop for my favorite fine-point red pen when Claire rushed into my office.

"Alex Rodriquez is in with Mr. Davies," she said, making this funny "eek" face. "They wanted you to go to lunch with them. I told them we just got back, but Mr. Davies wants to see you anyway."

I took a deep breath. "Thanks, Claire."

She nodded and gave me a sympathetic shrug, but before she pulled the door closed, she turned back with, "That Clement is really cute."

I smiled and nodded a yeah.

"Do you think he liked me?" she asked, hopeful.

"He seemed to enjoy the lunch," I said.

"Me, too." She smiled.

"You and he aren't—" she stammered.

"No." I shook my head. I wasn't sure whether it was a lie

or not, but with Davies acting like such an ass, it was probably best to keep Clement out of the mix.

"He's a nice guy." I added just because I thought I should say something else.

"He is," she agreed, and pulled the door closed.

I pulled out the mirror I kept in my pencil drawer, and checked my hair and make-up before heading through the adjoining door.

Alex stood when I entered.

"Glory," he said, extending his arms, his eyes alight. "They said you've already eaten. Maybe you could join us for a drink." He squeezed my hand and pressed his lips to my cheek.

"I've got a set of contracts on my desk that I promised to turn over to Legal by three."

"Bruce won't hold you to that. The client's needs come first, right, Bruce?"

Alex's ex-wife and business partner, Sophia, stood next to the set of decanters and glasses on the far wall. She held a pair of tongs over the ice bucket as though she was searching for the perfect ice cube. I pulled my hand out of Alex's grasp and crossed over to her, pressing my cheek against hers.

"Oh, for heaven's sake, Glory, you must come along. I don't want to eat alone with these two ex-jocks. You understand the product. And I must tell you about the new shoe designer we've just hired. These are his work." She pointed the tongs at her shoes and stepped away from the bar so that I might see them better. "A bit daring, but I love them."

She was a tiny blonde, whose genes, frequent spa treatments and flighty but very expensive little haircut, snipped away at least fifteen of her forty-five years. The shoes were a sling back with an open toe, covered in a jungle-print textured fabric that favored a deep green. They had a four-inch heel and a one-inch platform sole. They were cute and she wore them well.

"Nice," I said, and meant it.

She smiled, "I knew you'd appreciate them. You must come along. I've brought his design book." She gestured to a binder that sat in one of the upholstered chairs before pouring a dollop of scotch over the ice.

Bruce stood behind his desk. "Legal can wait," he spoke decisively. And then softening his tone slightly, he said, "Go on. Get your things."

Well, I guess that was that. The boss had spoken. Alex beamed and Sophia sipped her drink and looked at me with speculation, as though she actually expected me to contradict Bruce. I went back to my office, got my purse and jacket, and we headed out.

It wasn't as much fun as lunch, but it was pleasant and the new designer had talent. In front of Sophia, Alex behaved himself, more or less. He did try to feed me some of his Beef Wellington because it was "so tender and seasoned so well," and he "didn't like to see me sitting there with only wine when everyone else was eating." While dodging his fork, I explained again that I'd eaten earlier. Sophia grinned into her glass.

We talked about the campaign, the series of television spots that the firm had developed for their clothing line, the demographics of the shows selected, the success of the recent store opening and their plans for the furniture line.

"Johns, the new guy, is reviewing your current webpage. He's working up a list of internet sites and strategies for creating possible links and buying ad space," Bruce said to Alex, and then his eyes found mine. "Glory had lunch with him today." He skewered a bit of tomato and popped it into his mouth. "Did you get any insight into his plan? A preview?"

I smiled and shook my head. "No. It wasn't a working lunch."

He nodded and chewed.

"I guess you'll have to wait for the formal report," he said after swallowing.

Alex inclined his head briefly as if to say "No problem."

Sophia talked about her current passion, their newest shoe designer. She planned to feature his new line in the fall.

Alex said, "She's fucking obsessed with this guy. If he wasn't such a fairy, I'd swear they were fucking."

Taking the slap in stride, she smirked and said, "If he wasn't such a fairy, I would fuck him."

Knowing that the sniping could easily escalate into something more volatile, Bruce quickly turned the conversation back to the status of the ad campaign outlining the strategy for the company's fledgling furniture line. Taking Bruce's offering, Sophia gave him a smile and listened attentively, asking questions in the appropriate places. Alex sent me a smoldering look that I dodged by becoming an active participant in the ongoing conversation.

On our way out, Alex allowed Bruce and Sophia to precede us. I tried to speed up, but he caught me by placing a hand at my waist and pulling me backward. He nudged his nose around my ear as though he was trying to smell me. "We could meet at the hotel in about half an hour. I'm at the Roosevelt," he whispered as his teeth tugged at my earlobe. Unseen, I rolled my eyes. As if he ever stayed anywhere else. I held still, trying not to shove an elbow into his gut or initiate a struggle to free myself from his grip. I was not in the mood for this.

"I've got work," I mouthed, gently pulling out of his hold and moving toward the exit.

"After work?" he asked as he kept pace with my hurried stride.

By then we were standing in front of the restaurant as one of the sleek black town cars leased by the agency pulled up in front.

"You two can take this one," Bruce said to Alex and Sophia as he reached out to clasp my elbow and pull me back to his side. "You're both going in the same direction. Glory and I can ride back to work together."

The driver had come around and was opening the door for Sophia. Alex looked a little put out, but unless he wanted to air his business, he could do nothing but follow his partner as she slid into the cool darkness of the car.

The long black car slid easily into the throng of traffic and the second car pulled up in front of us. Bruce opened the car door. I climbed in and he slid in after me. As the car made its way out into traffic, Bruce told the driver to take him to his town house. I just sat back. I said nothing, because there wasn't anything to say. I was beginning to feel like an indentured whore who'd let out her vagina for the duration of her employment at Davies and Birch. What began as a little fun was becoming a duty.

Bruce didn't say anything, either. I couldn't help but glance at him, a quick cut of the eye. He sat close to his window, pretending a fascination with the yellow cabs and towering office buildings that glided by as we rode through town. I knew his heart was beating fast. He would be afraid that I would lash out at his presumption, afraid that I would deny him. I crossed my legs and let the short skirt ride up my thighs just enough so that he could see the black lace of my thigh-high stockings. His head tilted slightly so that he could look without turning toward me.

The car pulled up in front of his town house. He slid out and held the door for me. I walked up the short flight of stairs, while he gave instructions to the driver.

He opened the door and stepped back so that I could enter.

I looked back at him briefly, a question in my brow.

"Tonya has a half day today." He closed the door behind him.

Tonya, a woman in her late fifties who spoke with a heavy Eastern European accent, was an immaculate housekeeper. The living room, done in masculine but airy beige and burnished browns, looked as though she had vacuumed then polished every centimeter. Two long, plush sofas bracketed a large square cocktail table of gleaming and intricately paneled oak. I pulled a very expensive cashmere throw pillow from one of the sofas and plopped it onto the center of the table. Then I slid the straight black skirt of my suit up over my hips so that I could slip off my thong and he could get a glimpse of snatch and taut thigh. With my skirt still riding my hips, I turned my back to him under the guise of placing the pillow just so. I wanted to give him a clear view of my tight ass, its smooth, well-oiled skin and its high rounded lobes. I bent over, just a bit farther, to pull the pillow forward. My ass aimed at him, my dampening sex peeking at him from just beneath my ass. Then, with my back still toward him, I stood back to survey my handiwork. He, in turn, would have a moment to take in the effect of the dark lace that topped my thigh-high hose, to consider how stark it was against the paleness of my skin, how the pale flesh peeked out of the gauzy eyelets before giving way to the sleek length of long leg and the perfectly turned calves. The three-and-one-half-inch spike heels could always be counted on to do their part.

When I was satisfied that he'd gotten a good look, I sat, scooting onto the pillow as it lay near the edge of the sturdy table. Bruce, barely breathing, stood in the entryway watching. I emptied my small handbag onto the table next to me, found my lipstick, a bitchin' red, and opening my legs, proceeded to paint the lips of my vagina while he watched. I dabbed the long stick of creamy red color down and around my already moist labia, drawing it over the lips and along the thin line of perfectly waxed hair. His eyes grew dark and he moved to take off his suit coat.

"No," I said as I worked to perfect the line. "Leave it on."

He, of course, complied.

When I was done applying the lipstick, I widened my legs to admire my handiwork. Then, I put everything back into my handbag, zipped it up, and, finally, turned my attention to Bruce. He was sweating, droplets clearly visible on his forehead.

"Kiss me," I said, opening my legs to him.

He took two long steps toward me and dropped down between my legs. With his large hands caressing my thighs, he buried his face deep in my sex. He was good at this, his long thick tongue plunging and rasping between the lips and then dipping deep to circle my clitoris as though he'd happily found a ripe juicy melon with a pleasing and extremely addictive surprise. When his tongue slurped around my clitoris and then sucked at it gently, I could barely sit still, but he held me in place, his long fingers anchoring my hips. But when his tongue curled and began to thrust into my opening, even the strength of his fingers couldn't hold me still. My thighs began to tremble and clench around his head, and my fingers blindly sought and found his short thick locks of hair and pulled. Ignoring the pain, he continued the assault until my womb began to tighten and spasm. My thighs became a vise around his head, and I could see stars, even though my eyes were closed.

He held my backside with one hand as he moved up my body, his mouth burrowing beneath my jacket to open over the peak of a very sensitive nipple dampening the cloth that covered it. I could hear him fumbling with his zipper with his other hand.

"No," I said, and slid back, taking the pillow with me.

He looked up at me. Smears of red lipstick and shiny dampness covered his lips and his cheeks, and there was a longing so fierce in his eyes that a lesser woman would have given in.

"No," I said, and he leaned in to kiss me. I moved my face out of reach. "I don't want your kisses." I pushed him away.

He looked at me and then lowered his head as though he knew he'd been bad and was ready for whatever punishment I doled out.

"Go sit in that chair." I pointed to a straight-back chair that sat against the wall.

He did as he was told.

"Push your pants down around your ankles."

He complied and sat back down. Legs wide, his cock stood on full alert, a beacon that made the muscles of my pussy twitch. His hands gripped the arm rails of the chair.

I stood before him, and just because it was so tempting, I leaned in and sucked the tip of his cock. He groaned and lifted his hips. I stopped and pulled back. He held his breath.

I stood up and looked down at him.

"Did I ask for your help?" I asked.

He wet his lips and waited, hoping that I would resume.

Instead, I turned my back to him, slid my skirt farther up my hips and lowered my wet pussy onto his soldier-hard cock. He groaned and lifted to greet me, thrusting upward, hard, his eager flesh filling me completely.

"No," I said, looking over my shoulder at him. "I want to do this. You are just a tool. I will take what I want. I decide how much." I pressed down, the dampness of my thighs mingling with his. I clenched around him, stroking his cock as I rose. He groaned and his hands came up to grasp at my waist.

"Don't touch me. If you do, I'll leave." His breath was ragged; his cock so hard and hot I wanted to scream. I rotated my ass, the flesh of my cheeks and my pussy strumming and stroking him before I began to rise again, tugging his length up with me. His hands gripped the arm rails. I placed my hands on top of his and peeked at him over my shoulder, biting my lip as I clutched at him with my pussy.

His breath came hot and fast on my neck as his stomach tightened and his body surged toward mine. I leaned back and slid down, down, down and pressed my heated flesh against his groin as the muscles of my sex sucked at him. He thrust upward as though he couldn't help it; his eyes now glued to the rise and fall of my ass as he clutched the chair. I let him move because it felt so good. His flesh grew wider and became more rigid as he strained upward, each eager thrust seemed to find a narrower path.

To slow him down, I leaned back again and rocked back and forth, feeling all of him as his heat and hardness scorched and massaged my walls. My skin, my sex, my flesh were awash in sensation. He groaned and leaned toward me; his mouth pressed against my back. I shook him off, bucking against him.

The urge to ride him pulled at me and I was dragging my sex up and down, up and down, my finger gripping his forearms, until I couldn't stand it anymore. The tingling stars took me and I couldn't rise because of the throbbing, so I began to rock back and forth, back and forth, the speed increasing of its own will. He cried out, a hoarse roar, before he grabbed me, his hands at my waist, my hips, my buttocks, my breasts, his lips on my neck, my back.

"No," I said, shaking him off as I pulled away, the width of him still lodged deep inside of me. I squirmed off of him and stood, but he was still coming, thick spurts of sperms spilling over the sweaty sheen of his thighs and dripping onto the up-holstered seat of the chair and off the wooden edge onto the carpet. His eyes were closed and his teeth were buried deep in his lower lip.

"I said don't touch me," I ground out as I pulled my skirt down over my hips, gathered my handbag and made my way to the door. I heard him groan once more as I let myself out and pulled the front door closed behind me.

Clement stood in the doorway of my office, his forearm leaning against the lintel. "All work and no play…" he said, shaking his head. I smiled up at the grin he offered, and then scooted my chair back and stretched.

"Trying to catch up."

"I've come to rescue you from yourself." He held out his hand.

I grumbled for show, but I was ready for a break so I rose and slipped my hand into his. He led me just down the hall to his suite of offices, past the empty desks that belonged to his staff and into his office, which was larger than I thought it would be. It boasted a sizable view of the city, but there wasn't much in the way of furnishings: a desk with a thickly pad-ded leather chair and a couple of the black-and-blue visitors' chairs that graced most of the other offices. His desk, cleared of paperwork, now hosted a plaid throw. A couple of stemmed glasses, a bottle of wine and an assortment of cheeses, fruit, deli meats and baguettes were artfully arranged on high-end paper plates in its center.

"A picnic," he said, beaming down at me as he led me to one of the visitors' chairs before turning to close the door. "No ants, just good company." He patted his chest.

What could I say? "This is so thoughtful, Clement."

"So you'll stay?"

I gave him a "you thought otherwise" look and helped myself to a piece of cheese. He poured and handed me a glass of wine. It was tart and slightly sweet. Perfection. I leaned back and sipped and he took the seat across from me.

"You've been out of circulation the last couple of days. You come in and head straight for your office as though you don't want to see or be seen by anyone."

"The workload, you know." I slipped my shoes off and dug my toes into the carpet.

"You don't even nuke meals in the lunchroom anymore."

"I've been getting Claire to pick me up something on her way back from lunch."

"I know. She told me."

The grapes were sweet and seedless. I took another handful.

"So, why have you become so reclusive?" He sipped his wine and his eyes probed my face.

"No reason, really. Guess I been in a kind of funk."

He lifted my feet into his lap and began to massage my toes and the arch of first one foot and then the other. His fingers glided over the silky fabric of my hose as though searching until his smooth, hard thumb, finding a knot, would stop, and with an almost innate authority, dispense with the offending kink before moving on. I purred. He laughed.

"Where did you learn that?" I asked.

"I took a class."

"Time well spent."

He smiled. "*Miss Firecracker,* the Beth Henley play I told you about, is this weekend. Are we still on?"

"Yeah, sure. When?"

"Friday at eight."

There was a knock on the door, perfunctory at best, and then the door opened and Alex Rodriquez stood there, an imposing force that filled the space.

He looked down at the two of us, the half-eaten picnic spread across Clement's desk, my feet curled in his lap and he forced his lips to curve up into what I'm sure he thought was a smile.

"Claire said I'd find you here. I thought to take you out to lunch, but I see you've already eaten."

"Mr. Rodriquez," I said, and Clement looked at me as if to say "who?" His question was followed by a smirk as he sensed my annoyance.

I slipped my feet off of his lap and into my shoes. Then I stood consciously shedding the comfort Clement had provided and steeled myself.

"You haven't met Clement Johns. He's the one Mr. Davies told you about."

By then Clement was also standing.

"The internet man." Alex thrust out his hand and Clement, as though reluctant, shook it. "I look forward to seeing your proposal."

Then as though having put up with all the protocol he was willing to endure, Alex turned to me. "Look, Glory," he said as though Clement wasn't there. "I need to talk to you. Can we go somewhere?"

I wanted to say "No. I thought I was pretty clear on the phone last night." But instead, I said, "Sure, we can talk in my office." Then I turned to Clement and gave him a reassuring smile. "Thanks. This was just what I needed, a brief respite." He reached for my hand and squeezed it.

"Friday night then?" he asked.

"Friday night." I nodded in agreement.

Alex stepped back so that I could get through the door, just barely, and then he was following at my heels.

"What's with the pinhead?" Alex asked, before I could close the door of my office.

"What do you want, Alex?" I went toward my desk with the intention of taking my seat in order to assume a position of authority and thereby establish distance. Textbook strategy. I graduated magna cum laude, but I guess Alex didn't get the press release. Before I could reach my chair, he had my ass balancing on the edge of the desk, his legs between mine, and his hand was inching up my skirt. He pissed me off. All I could see was red.

"Back the fuck off, Alex," I said as I pressed the flat of my hands against his chest and held them there.

"It's always been good between us, Glory. Why would you want to cut something short that's only really just getting started?" His fingers inched up my thigh.

"I said back off." I spoke slowly and with lethal intent. He didn't know what I would do, but he heard the threat in my voice. And while Alex was used to getting his way, he was neither violent nor a rapist.

His hand stilled on my thigh. "Glory." He sighed, and then he stepped back.

I slid off the desk and adjusted my skirt.

"I thought you just needed to see how much I want you."

"I like you, too, Alex. You're a lot of fun. We were spontaneous together, but it was meant to be temporary, to be over before the tedium set in."

"Tedium. We're a long way from tedium. Is it the pinhead?"

"Clement." I laughed. "No, it is not the pinhead."

"What is it then?"

"I guess I just need some downtime."

"Downtime," he repeated. Then he looked at me with shuttered eyes. "Does that mean I can call you next time I'm in town?"

I laughed and shook my head. "That means that I'm trying to get my act together and I can't go flitting around with clients, having hot sex on my desk or on rainy afternoons in their hotel rooms."

"And the problem lies where?" he asked, taking my hand.

I let him. "Not with you. You just do what comes naturally."

"There's certainly nothing unnatural about you."

"I'll take that as a compliment," I said as he pressed his lips to my fingers.

"I just need to take a step back and figure out what I want."

"I could help you with that." His fingers still tugged at the tips of mine.

"No, you can't. You'd just keep me in a crazed fog of need."

"I like the sound of that."

"You would," I said, grinning at his playfulness. "But I need to try something else. Maybe I'll be celibate for a while."

"Scary, I don't think I've ever driven a woman to celibacy." He crooked an eye at me. "Besides, I don't think Davies would stand for it."

That stunned me. "Bruce? Did he say something?"

"I had my suspicions. The way he looked at you. His possessiveness. I wasn't sure, thought he was being protective at first." Then he grinned down at me. "But you've confirmed my hunch."

I laughed and punched him in his shoulder. He pretended pain and stepped back.

Releasing a breath, he leaned forward and kissed my cheek. *"Así es la vida,"* he whispered as he straightened. He headed toward the door and, before opening it, he turned back to me. "I like having you on my team, regardless." Then, pressing his lips into a tight smile, he let himself out.

The play was funny, poignant and sweet and so was the company. Afterward, Clement and I walked along the city streets for a while enjoying the night air and each other. He held my hand, his long fingers stroking mine, sending a shiver of warmth as the threads of conversation drifted along companionably. He grew up in a small town and played in the marching band. I was a big-city girl and excelled in athletics, swimming and track. His mom was a great cook; mine not so much. I invited him back to my place for coffee and to sample the lemon bars I bought religiously from an uptown bakery. They were the same ones my mother bought after a meet, whether we won or lost. He hailed a cab and in the confines of its backseat, which smelled oddly of hotdogs, mustard and onions, he kissed me. It was a smoldering, breathless kiss that smeared my lipstick and left my blouse undone nearly to the waist.

We dislodged ourselves enough for him to pay the driver

before scooting out of the car as a unit, his hand at my waist. We were still standing on the sidewalk when the cab drove away. He held me free and loose, his arms around me just enough to know that they were there, but not enough to feel confining. His mouth was warm and drew on mine in short breathless tugs, his tongue teasingly darting about, making me want to draw nearer. He chuckled, as though his plan was working, just before drawing me closer to feast.

"The lemon bars," I breathed into his mouth. "We'd better go in."

He nodded and let me lead him up the stairs and through the main entrance, a tall glass door that opened in a short hall. It was fortunate that my apartment was immediately to the right of the front door, because just as I slid the key in, he leaned in again. His lips found a particularly sensitive place on my neck, while one hand fondled my ass and another palmed my breast. I was wet and hot, my pussy swollen and straining against the cloth of my panties. So when he pressed me against the door, I welcomed the pressure of his hardness as it jabbed at my heat.

We stumbled in somehow, made it to the living room and fell into the carpeted space between the sofa and the cocktail table before we began tearing at each other's clothing. My hands tore at his shirt until they found the firmness of his chest, and the pebbled tips among the crisp hair. He moaned as my fingers followed the wispy trail of hair down his stomach. The button and zipper of his jeans were already undone, so I slipped my hand in through the waistband of his shorts to grasp his sex. It felt hot and sleek in the palm of my hand. I squeezed it and he nipped my lip, his breathing picking up speed. I squeezed him again and tugged. His mouth trailed down to pluck at my nipples as they peeked over of the loosened cups of my bra. I squirmed, the lips of my sex tingling as he tugged at my panties, drawing them down my legs and then yanking them off as they snagged on my strappy spike heels. Then he was climbing up, positioning himself between my legs, as he bunched his jeans and shorts together and shoved them down, freeing himself. I could feel the feverish sleekness of his penis slip and slide against my wetness, the lips of my sex puckered and eager. He slid in, the huge head nudging its way through the swollen flesh and creamy wetness. Opening to him, I lifted my thighs high around his hips, shuddering as his width splayed the swollen labia, single-mindedly shoving and squeezing its way into my trembling body.

He surged forward and I cried out. It felt so good, the weight of him on my belly, my breasts, the wet heat of his mouth on my neck and the pressure of him as he sank into me, filling every corner.

"Oh, fuck, Glory. You're so goddamn hot," he croaked as he drew back before ramming into me again. My thighs trembled against his hips and I could feel the muscles of his ass clinch as he moved inside me.

He rose up almost to his knees, his hands straddling my head as he dipped his head down to ravage my mouth before he began a slow dip and drag. His eyes closed, his mouth twisted as the pace increased, and each thrust gained greater force. I lifted to him, impatient, eager to be filled, relishing the rasp and drag that ignited my womb each time he sank into me. The wet sound and pungent smell of our loving filled the room. I held on, my teeth sinking into his shoulder as he smashed into me again, swiping through heavily engorged labia as his thickness rampaged its way to my center. The jolting rhythm sent shock waves to my clitoris. My fingers found his back, my nails sank into flesh and I cried out again as a series of trembling shivers lashed my body and caused me to tighten and vibrate around him.

"Ah, fuck, baby," he said through clenched teeth as his back arched and he sank deeper. "No, no, no," he said as he jerked against me and I could feel him coming, the long stream of semen surging forward like a flood.

His damp forehead rested against mine. "Our first time," he said. "Anticipation. I couldn't hold it."

I laughed. The vibrations caused him to tense; his sex still deep inside me slipped halfway out. "You did good. Really good."

"Thanks," he said, and ducked his forehead against mine. "You, too."

That's when the light came on.

"You left these in the door," Bruce said, dangling my keys by their Eeyore key ring.

Clement pulled out and sat leaning against the cocktail table, looking a little dazed and confused. He looked up at Bruce and then down at me. By then I had set my bra to rights and was buttoning my blouse.

"How'd you get in the main door?" I asked to gain time in order to gather my wits because his response didn't matter. He was in now and was really blowing my post-coital high.

"Your neighbor. She didn't think you would mind."

I was on my knees now, straightening and smoothing my skirt. Clement was zipping up.

"So," Bruce said as he moved toward the wingback chair across from us. He unbuttoned his suit coat and sat down. "Now that you've sampled the new guy, are you done?"

Having buttoned the few remaining buttons on his shirt, Clement had dragged his sport coat from under the table and was shrugging it on. He looked at me as though waiting to hear what I would say.

"Why are you here?" I asked Bruce.

Clement took a seat on the sofa.

"I wanted to see you," he said simply.

Okay, no artifice. He was going to play it straight.

"You shouldn't have come without calling." Stating the obvious, I know, but I had nothing else.

"I don't want to share anymore, Glory. Not with Alex or anyone," Bruce spoke pointedly, glancing in Clement's direction.

"There is no more Alex," I said, disgusted with this whole situation. I really liked Clement and now he was going to think I was a fucking whore, which is just what Bruce wanted him to think.

"Do you want me to go or do you want me to stay?" Clement asked. His voice sounded sad.

"I think you better go." I could barely look at him. I felt ashamed and angry.

"Are you sure?" he asked, still seated.

"Yeah, he and I...we need to talk."

I followed Clement down the short hall to the door.

"I really like you, Glory," he said as he pulled me into his arms and pressed his forehead to mine. "Don't let him bully you."

I nodded and a fucking tear rolled down my cheek.

"I'll call you tomorrow morning, okay."

I nodded.

"You don't have to do anything you don't want to do," he said as he dipped down, trying to see my eyes.

"I know." And it was true, sort of. The problem was I didn't really know what I wanted. I liked Clement and the idea of a normal relationship with a really great guy, but I liked Bruce, too—especially when he let me make the demands. What I didn't like was being put on the spot and feeling like I had no control.

I closed the door and padded back down the hall to Bruce, who stood waiting for me.

"So, are you done with him?"

"Yeah, I think so," I said, and let him slip his arms around me.

"Can I stay the night?" he asked, sounding almost repentant.

"Yeah." I leaned my head against his chest. "Come take a shower with me." I took his hand and led him to the bedroom, where we undressed and then climbed into the shower. He washed my body reverently as though cleansing me of past sins and preparing me for future ones. I thought of Audrey Hepburn in *The Nun's Story* when they cut off her hair. When he was done and we had rinsed ourselves thoroughly, he carried me to bed and made tender love to me well into the night. Afterward, he pulled me close, his arm across my waist and his leg across mine, and we fell asleep.

He had golf the next morning with a client, so he was up and out early. He called later and so did Clement, but I didn't answer the phone. I didn't answer it all weekend. I spent most of the time eating kettle corn, watching old movies and composing my resignation letter and a brief report outlining the disposition of the projects I'd been assigned.

On Monday morning, I went in to work at six, before anyone else got there. I cleaned out my desk and left the letter and report on Bruce's blotter. I figured I couldn't ever make it right again with Bruce because he wanted too much or with Clement because the idea of us had been sullied. So, I decided to start fresh.

★ ★ ★ ★ ★

GIVING IN
ALISON TYLER

"I can't afford the airfare."

"When will you have an opportunity like this again?"

"I can't even afford a fucking taxi to the airport!" I never thought I'd allow myself to fail in such a spectacular manner. At 34, I was below rock bottom. I'd hit silt. Unless a fairy godmother suddenly arrived in a flutter of translucent wings, I had no way to pay rent. I didn't even know where my next meal was coming from.

"El, I have miles."

"Miles?" Was that a man? Would Miles help *me?*

"*Airplane* miles. I'll cash them in. You know I don't like traveling alone."

I glanced around at my surroundings. The small bedroom belonged to a distant cousin—three times removed, by marriage not blood. The watered-down family connection hadn't cut me any slack. Coldhearted Joyce loved cats more than humans. I knew she would put me out on the street as easily as any other deadbeat tenant if I couldn't pay her rent money.

"I don't have any cash," I said, drawing a pattern with the

quarters on my dresser. I'd changed my last few bills into coins to make the money last longer. "I mean, I can hardly afford…" The tears came then, even though I'm known for never crying. "I can't afford New York anymore," I said, "and I can't afford to go back home." Not that there was anyone waiting for me. "My next apartment is a cardboard box under the bridge."

"I know what's going on with you, honey," Sasha said. "Don't worry."

"If you take me to Venice, I won't be able to pay for anything. Food. Gas. Tickets. Toilet paper."

"Uncle Stefan will take care of everything. He always does."

"Uncle Stefan?"

"He's the one with the place in Venice. Not really an uncle—an old family friend. He's invited me to bring a guest to come stay. You won't have to pay for a thing. I know you need to get out of the city. Let's get."

"What will I do with my stuff?"

I'd been pondering this question for the past few days. I knew I was going to have to move out of Joyce's place on the first. And unless I got lucky with a generous one-night stand who might let me crash on his sofa and bring along my few pitiful belongings, I'd run out of options. Forget Blanche DuBois and her "kindness of strangers." I needed the kindness of *anyone.*

"Box up your gear, and bring it to my place. You should have moved in with me when you first lost your job. We room well together."

Sasha and I had met in the college dorm. But I hadn't wanted her to know how close to the edge I'd gotten myself. I hadn't even been honest with myself.

"I'm booking the flight right now," she said. "I'll be over in an hour to help you move."

And that was my goodbye to the U.S. and my hello to Italy. Right when I needed saving.

Business class was sublime. Sasha and I floated on champagne all the way to Brussels, with my oldest friend describing the place where we'd be staying. "The villa has been in his family for generations," she explained. "One of those grand palazzos on a canal."

"What does he do?"

She smiled.

"Why are you smiling like that?"

"He doesn't really do anything. He doesn't have to." She sipped her champagne thoughtfully. "Or rather, he does whatever he wants to. With money like that, he can do as pleases." I didn't hear another word about Uncle Stefan, even during our layover or the final part of the journey to VCE in Venice. I conjured an image in my head: sixties, like her parents. Heavyset. I gave him a bald pate and a bit of gout.

Then I let the champagne take over and I fell asleep.

When we arrived in Venice, I felt as if I'd woken from a magical dream only to discover that the dream was real. I've had good dreams before—but never one that lasted when I opened my eyes. Sasha appeared as fresh as if she'd just emerged from a douche commercial. Even on no sleep, or after a drinking binge, she always has neatly coiffed Princess Grace blond hair and angel-perfect skin.

I, on the other hand, looked exactly like someone who had slept in my clothes—which I had. Sasha didn't say anything about my rumpled turtleneck and messy ringlets. But she pulled a sumptuous indigo velvet shawl from her woven leather messenger bag and wrapped the length around me, pinning the cloth effortlessly with a rhinestone broach. In seconds, I'd captured a little of her style. Sasha is so high-end, she rubs off on the people around her. Without a word, she twisted my black hair into a makeshift bun and used a silver barrette to hold the curls in place.

A man in a suit stood at our gate. He was bald and heavily muscled with a ginger-colored goatee. *Uncle Stefan*, I thought, feeling pleased with myself for having so easily imagined the man. Maybe he was younger and less paunchy than I'd guessed, but I had nailed his basic appearance.

"Lou!" squealed Sasha, confusing me as she embraced the man. "Ellis, this is Lou. He works for Stefan. Lou, this is Ellis."

Lou shook my hand, and I wondered if he could see the difference between the two of us. Sasha, effortless with her money. Me, a poor church mouse on scholarship.

"You're just as lovely as Sasha described," he said. His accent was distinctly Irish, and charming. I felt my cheeks go pink at his words. The scarf slid a little and I hitched the burnt-out velvet back onto my shoulders. If he could discern the fact that I was in the empty-pocket club, he didn't show the knowledge in his expression. He treated us equally, following us to the baggage claim, not appearing at all judgmental about my battered suitcase in comparison to Sasha's pristine luggage.

On the way to the villa, Lou and Sasha shared stories, talking about people they knew in common. Sasha had spent many summers in Italy. I stared out the window, wanting to pinch myself. Was this for real? But something in my head nagged at me. *Two weeks*. I had two weeks in Venice, and then I'd have to return to the nightmare that was my real life. To the Frigidaire box under the bridge.

Sasha seemed to sense my mood. She put one hand on top

of mine and squeezed. "Everything will work out," she said. "Relax."

I saw Lou put one hand on top of Sasha's thigh and squeeze.

"Relax," Sasha said again, softer.

The word must mean something different in Venice, I thought.

I don't know what time it was when we arrived. New York time? Italian time? All I knew was that I was the walking dead. In a blur, Lou and Sasha led me through the grand entrance to the villa. I saw a tree in the foyer covered all over with small squares of white paper. We stopped here, and Lou said, "There's a tradition."

"A tradition?" I echoed. I could hardly make my mouth work.

"Write a wish," Sasha said. "I'll hang the paper on a branch for you."

I gripped the pencil in my fist and scrawled something almost illegible on the square. Sasha smiled, and moved us on. I caught glimpses of mirrors, dreamy-looking sofas, hanging rugs. But my eyes couldn't focus. Sasha tucked me into a guest room and told me that my mind would be clearer in the morning. "You have both a champagne and travel hangover," she said. "Sleep it off."

"I haven't even met our host," I told her, feeling uncomfortable. I didn't want to behave impolitely from the start. Not to someone so generous as to take me in for free.

"He's a traveler, himself. He'll understand."

I stripped down to my T-shirt and boy briefs and climbed into the huge, welcoming bed. I'd been worrying for months, now. The weight of the heavy duvet lulled me. For the first time since I'd lost my last job, I felt safe. I was asleep in seconds.

But I didn't stay asleep for long.

At some point during the night, I woke, feeling scared and alone. Was I in Joyce's tiny, cat-smelly apartment? No. I'd never been in a bed this comfortable before. Had I landed a lover who'd taken me back to his place for a one-night fuck? No. The bed was empty except for me. Slowly, I remembered where I was, but I didn't feel tired anymore. The excitement built with each breath.

I was in Venice! How could I sleep?

My watch read 2:00 a.m. I climbed out of bed and reached into my suitcase for my Walkman, thinking that a little Peter Gabriel might lull me back to dreamland. But when I clicked the on button, my ancient machine refused to do more than whine and sputter. The batteries had given up their alkaline ghost. Maybe Sasha had extras. Did I dare to go creeping through a house I didn't know in order to find my friend?

Right then, I heard a noise that sounded like clapping. For a moment, I stayed still, trying to orient myself. I'd been rushed through the house to this guest room when we'd arrived. Sasha had promised me a full tour in the morning. I'd caught glimpses of canvases framed in gold, of porcelain vases taller than I was, of a central room tiled in black-and-white marble. But I didn't have any sense of where I was in the house.

The noise didn't stop, and I found myself compelled to investigate. Quietly, I tiptoed out of the bedroom. The scent of honeysuckle was in the air. Sasha's favorite perfume. I strode along the hallway, doing my best to be silent. The old place was creaky. I walked on my toes down the darkened hall. I could hear the noise getting louder, and I could also hear something else: the sound of a woman crying.

When I arrived at my friend's room, I planned to simply push on the door and walk in. But something caught my eye and I stopped. The door was open a crack. A shaft of dust-shimmered light fell on the hallway runner. I was standing on an antique rug in my bare feet. The fibers were well-worn, yet decadent at the same time. I noticed how deep and lush the colors were in the rug. Every thought in my head seemed to be moving in slow motion. Maybe I ought not to interrupt. Who was I to barge in?

Carefully, I pressed closer to the crack in the door.

What I saw was something shocking. Sasha was over a man's lap, and her lemon-yellow nightgown was pushed up to her slim hips. She didn't have on panties, and her long, lean legs flailed in the air. The man was spanking her naked ass with a hard-backed black hairbrush, and Sasha's feet were kicking with each blow.

After the initial shock of the scene wore off, I took a second to stare at the man punishing my best friend. He was one of the most handsome men I'd ever seen in real life. Dark hair, dark eyes, a stern expression on his face. Not angry so much as fully focused.

The concept of what I was witnessing did not immediately compute in my mind. I'd known Sasha since freshman year of college. We'd discussed many boyfriends, dating, lovers. Kink had rarely come up before. Was I dreaming? I bit my lip hard, hoping against hope I didn't wake up back in Joyce's humble Brooklyn digs.

No. I was still here. In Venice. Watching my best friend receive a bottom-blistering spanking. And from what I could see, I'd missed most of the show. Sasha's normally pale skin was cherry-hued.

"Lou's been waiting for you," the man said. "He wanted me to tell you that he'll be going here tonight."

He licked his finger and parted Sasha's rear cheeks. Gently, he touched her asshole. Sasha shivered. So did I.

Sasha was going to fuck Lou? The man looked like a bouncer outside one of the meaner New York clubs. I crossed my legs, but kept staring through the crack in the door.

"You're such a tease, girl. He's been waiting since December," the man continued, and now I watched, my mouth open, as he slowly started to push his finger into her hole. My pussy tightened as I continued to stare, as the man firmly began to finger-fuck her asshole. "And you're going to let him, aren't you?"

"Yes, sir." Her response was barely audible.

"Why?"

"Because I'm a dirty little slut, sir."

Shit. *Sasha* was a dirty little slut? My *friend* Sasha? This had never occurred to me before. The girl only dated the best-looking, wealthiest men on the market. She never slummed in Manhattan. Whenever we'd discussed sex over the years, I always got the feeling that she enjoyed the activity, but would prefer a few rounds of shopping at Bloomingdales.

Now, she was bent over a man's lap having her most intimate regions explored, and she was telling him and the polished antique hardwood floor that she was a slut? My heart couldn't have been pounding any harder.

"Of course," the man said, "I've been waiting, too."

I swallowed hard. Were they *both* going to fuck her? Where had Sasha taken me? What world had we arrived in? And why were my panties sopping wet at the center?

"Yes, Stefan," said Sasha, shocking me even further. This was Stefan? I'd assumed the man was another employee, perhaps the major domo of the Villa. He was nothing like what I'd expected. He seemed young—not quite our age, perhaps ten years older. He had thick, dark hair and the type of face you see in magazine cologne ads. Chiseled.

While I watched, he stopped touching Sasha. She moaned. I would have, too. "Ah, my girl likes to be played with, doesn't she? It's been too long since you last had a good hard cock up your ass, hasn't it?" Sasha made soft mewing noises of assent. The man flipped her around, then picked her up in his arms and brought her toward the other end of the room. Now, I could no longer see them. Fuck. I wanted to watch whatever was going to happen next. But how could I? With a sigh, I turned around, coming face-to-face with Lou.

I upgraded my mental status from *fuck* to *Holy Fuck*.

He appeared completely nonchalant, undisturbed by the fact that I was spying on his boss and my friend. "Did you require something, Miss Ellis?" he asked.

Had my thoughts been coming slowly before? They'd just hit a brick wall. No going forward. I stared at him, blinking, as if I'd forgotten how to speak. Lou took me by the hand and kindly led me down the hallway. He didn't say a word, didn't ask me what I thought I was doing—snooping on my friend and the host. He simply escorted me back down the hallway. I wanted to turn, to look over my shoulder, but unlike Lot's doomed wife, I found a sliver of willpower and clung to it.

When we reached the bedroom, Lou opened the door and waited. Was he going to follow me inside? Was he going to spank *me?* I walked into the room. The bedside lamp gave the room a golden glow. On my bed? A new iPod with headphones and a vibrator.

I looked toward the doorway. Lou was still standing there,

smiling. I opened my mouth to say something, but he simply bowed slightly and wished me a pleasant night.

Pleasant.

The word must mean something else in Venice, I thought.

In the morning, I hurried to Sasha's room. I wanted to talk to her, to ask her questions, to find out what was going on. Were she and Stefan lovers? Had she really been with Lou? What was the true reason she'd brought me with her on this trip? Why had she never told me about the goings-on at the villa before? But when I got to Sasha's, the room was empty. The bed was made with hotel preciseness. Carnival roses, which I knew were Sasha's favorites, bloomed in bright pinks and oranges in a vase on the bedside table. All of her clothes were hung neatly in the closet. The black, hardback brush she'd been spanked with the previous evening lay innocently on the bedside table. My stomach tightened at the sight.

Where was she?

I wandered down the stairs, listening. Would I stumble upon a scenario as decadent as the one I'd found the previous night? Or had I possibly imagined the punishment scene? I felt disjointed and disoriented.

When I entered the kitchen, a white-clad chef told me that the others were waiting for me on the veranda. She spoke English with a British accent, and she was pretty in a slightly smudged way. Her crisp shirt had one too many buttons open in the front, so that I could see a peep of her scarlet lace bra. Her eye makeup, shimmering charcoal around beautiful green eyes, seemed too dark for so early in the morning, blurred as if she hadn't bothered to take it off the previous night.

Outside, Sasha looked same as always. Except, on second glance I realized that was not entirely true. She was wearing her traveling clothes—a more dramatic version of what she usually wore in the city. Her hair was down and straight, instead of up and pinned, and her eyes looked more alive, aglow.

"We're sightseeing, Ellis," she said excitedly. "Right away. I want you to love Venice."

I wanted something else. I wanted to ask her what the fuck was going on. But I couldn't, because just then Lou joined us on the terrace. Had she screwed Lou the night before? Had the debauchery I'd witnessed in the wee hours continued—or even occurred?

"Come on," she said, grabbing one of my hands in hers. "We're starting at my favorite museum."

"What about Stefan?" I asked. I was surprised at how normal my voice sounded. "We haven't been properly introduced," I continued, wondering who did I think I was, the Queen of England? Clearly, Sasha had invited me into a fairy-tale land where dirty dreams came true, and I ought to enjoy the program.

"You'll meet him later," she assured me. "He's busy this morning."

Busy punishing other guests? Busy paddling his staff? The chef came outside and handed me a cup of coffee and a plate of crisp buttered French bread and artfully arranged fruit. I set the plate on the stone railing, and I gratefully devoured the exquisite breakfast. Why was I so worried? My alternate choice in life was nothing. That concept *Be Here Now?* I had no other options.

Maybe Sasha would tell me what had happened while we were out. I decided I wouldn't ask any questions. She might not even have known I had seen her. Could I confess to spying without coming across as a pervert? All of these questions flickered through my mind as Sasha led me out of the villa and we began to stroll through the streets.

I had been to Venice years before, with a group of students from my university. We'd raced through Italy—not staying in any one place for more than 24 hours. But I still remembered the overwhelming beauty of the Piazza San Marco, the feel of riding beneath the bridges in a *vaporetto*, the magic that is Venice.

Yet although I was seeing The Floating City again, and listening to Sasha describe the sights, I could not fully focus. She chattered happily at my side, telling me of her past visits, the dinner she'd had at a special restaurant, the flowers she'd bought at a stand. I nodded, as if I were part of the conversation—but every time I looked at her, I saw her over Stefan's lap. This was my best friend. Why could I not simply say that I'd had trouble sleeping the previous night, that I'd found myself outside her room, and see how she responded?

Because I couldn't.

We arrived at a museum, and Sasha walked us past the glorious bronze statue of an athletic man riding a horse. The man sported an erection any man—statue or human—would be proud of. I wanted to stop and look, to figure out how one might impale herself on that metal sex toy. Clearly, I had fucking on my brain. But Sasha kept us moving. In the gardens stood an olive tree, a wishing tree, Sasha said, like the one in Stefan's foyer.

"That's where he got the idea," she explained. I gazed at the paper-covered tree. "What did you wish for last night?" she asked as I stood there, staring blankly.

I wanted to tell her that she'd made my wish come true. She'd saved me, at least for a short period of time. I didn't know how to say the fears that threatened to bubble up out of me.

"Write it down," she insisted.

I looked at the paper. I wrote the same thing I had on the square she'd given me the night before.

I Wish I Never Had To Leave

We moved to the next exhibit, but my thoughts remained on the wish. I couldn't see much of anything else. I was more aware of the travelers around us, the sounds of different languages in the air, the way Sasha's hand felt on my arm, the desire to ask her about what had happened the previous night. I walked, as if through water, until finally she seemed to realize that she was the only one paying attention to the art.

"We'll get coffee," she said, and she brought me as if I were an invalid to a café on the canal, where I could look at her, or down at the diamond-glinting water, look at the charming little porcelain cup, or at the antique architecture all around us.

"Do you love it, Ellis?"

"The coffee?"

"Venice, silly."

I nodded. The fears were taking hold once more with a cold fist around my heart. Where would I go next? How would I survive? I felt guilty even being unable to put down the few coins for the espressos. There was nothing in my wallet except a lucky dollar that was stamped NO WAR. At least, that's what I'd thought, but when I fumbled with my battered wallet—in that habit people have of pretending they're going to pay for a check—I saw European notes filling the interior.

"Don't think so much," she said, when I tried to ask what was going on. Who had put the bills in my billfold? "I promise, everything is going to be okay."

Sasha had always lived life like this. With a confidence and an assuredness. I took a sip of the coffee, and I vowed to try, at least for the few weeks we'd be here, to be more like her. Including her kink.

When we returned to Uncle Stefan's, she suggested we nap before dinner. I slipped on the headphones of my new iPod and reached for the brand-new vibrator that had been thoughtfully left for me the previous night. So Sasha hadn't said a word about what her true relationship was to the men in the house. Maybe that would come out later. I hadn't told Sasha the true level of my miserable existence for months. Some things are difficult to share, even with the best of friends.

That didn't mean I simply slept. I pressed the new sex toy against my pussy and fantasized about the night before. I didn't close my eyes after coming twice, the toy still clutched in my sticky fingers.

Waking up was one of those surreal moments. I couldn't immediately tell from the light if it was dawn or dusk. At least I knew where I was. The bed was becoming more familiar— the room felt like my own. I thrust the vibrator under my pillow, slid into my old shoes and rubbed my eyes. In the mirror, I saw a girl I recognized, but different from what I normally looked like. My hair was loose, curls flowing. I was actually starting to appear relaxed. Transformation. Was that the true magic of Venice?

I took a moment to write in my travel journal. I didn't want to forget what we'd seen today, what I'd wished for. I wrote quickly, my handwriting dancing across the page, comforting in its familiarity even if what I was describing was entirely foreign. Then I set down the notebook, stood and stretched.

I'd find Sasha and talk to her, I decided.

But when I looked, she wasn't in her room. She wasn't in

the main living room or in the kitchen. I wandered through the halls seeing no one, hearing nothing. Finally, I found a door I hadn't seen before. I put my hand on the knob, and then I stopped. From within, I heard Lou's deep Irish brogue, although I could not make out his words. This must be his room, I decided. I swallowed over a lump in my throat, imagining what I might find if I opened the door. Was he fucking her the way Stefan had described? Had he bound her down, tormented her in the most delightfully decadent ways imaginable? My fantasies ran wild, but I couldn't muster the courage to turn the handle.

What if I walked into a scene like the one I'd witnessed the night before?

"Miss?" I looked and saw the chef coming toward me.

"Yes?"

"Sasha's retired for the evening," she said. "You'll have dinner with Stefan. Tell me what you like, and I'll bring you whatever you desire."

The way she spoke the words made me think she was talking about more than food. Whatever I desired? *What* did I desire?

I heard a loud groan from inside the room. I could tell that Sasha had made the noise, even if I'd never have expected so guttural a moan from her lips.

What did the chef mean...*retired for the evening?* I was reading into everything. But I hadn't yet asked Sasha about what her true relationship was to Lou and Stefan. Now, it looked like I wouldn't find out until the morning.

I shouldn't have been so pessimistic. I began to learn more about the villa at dinner. The table was set with candles and pretty pastel plates. Stefan sat opposite me. He looked casually cultured in his crisp white shirt, black jacket and emerald silk tie. I felt as I had felt so often lately: underdressed and under-done. I was wearing a black tank dress that I hoped looked elegant in its simplicity rather than simply simple.

I wished I had dressed better.

"What did you wish for?" he asked almost immediately as I'd had that thought.

I stuttered my answer. "What do you mean?"

"The tree…" He motioned to the one in the foyer. I real-ized what he was talking about and sighed. I didn't have to tell him about the clothes. Then I thought about what I'd writ-ten, and I wasn't sure if I should say that, either.

"You can tell me later," he said. "I'm pleased that we're having this chance to dine on our own."

The chef came in then and served us from a painted wooden tray—starting with caviar on small rounds of toasted bread. The plates were as stunning as the artwork we'd seen earlier in the day. I didn't want to disturb the arrangement, but I was hungry. Each bite was delicious. I'd been on rations for the past month. The closest I'd come to caviar was tuna salad on special.

Stefan smiled as he watched me eat. I'm sure my appetite showed on my face, even in the candlelight.

"What do you know about me?" he asked.

I knew he was wealthy, and that he didn't officially have to work. I knew he was handsome and that he had spanked my best friend. I knew he had good taste in clothes, décor and food, and that he had stuck his pointer up Sasha's asshole. What did he want me to say?

"This isn't the world I'm accustomed to," I ultimately man-aged to respond.

"What do you mean?"

"Elegance," I said, made slightly more confident by the wine. "You deserve elegance."

Again, I wished I were better dressed, wished I could behave the way Sasha did, so refined. She always seemed to know exactly what to say in any given situation. I've always been better with words on paper. "What do you know about me?" I decided to ask, because the way he was looking at me made me think he had already acquired certain knowledge.

Stefan smiled, and I instantly envisioned what kissing him would feel like. He looked so different this evening. My first glimpse had been of him spanking Sasha, and his face had been set and stern. Now he appeared relaxed and magnanimous. "I've known you for years," he said, and the surreal quality that seemed to follow me in this villa settled on my shoulders like one of Sasha's fancy scarves.

"I don't understand...."

"Ellis, I had an ulterior motive to inviting you to stay here."

I thought about the spanking and didn't lift another round of caviar toast. I would say my heart began to beat faster, but actually it was a different part of my anatomy that responded. When I reached for the glass of wine, my hand shook.

"I've been reading your words for the past fifteen years, and I am a fan."

"My words?" I asked the question before I could stop myself.

"Sasha's sent me your writing—the articles, the copy. You have a flow." The fact that he'd like my work—that made me blush. "I want you to write something for me."

"I'd love to," I said too quickly, before knowing what he wanted, what he could be asking.

He looked at me carefully. "I'm not ready to tell you the assignment yet, but I will soon."

The rest of the meal seemed to pass like a movie I was watching by not starring. We spoke, I know, about his life in Venice. About where I had grown up and the different careers I'd tried. I worked not to let him know about my failures— about how low I'd gotten myself right before the journey. He didn't ask pointed questions. But the whole time we spoke, all I could think of was *a job*. I might have a job. The box under the bridge seemed like a distant threat now, as if I'd managed somehow to knock the cardboard flat.

At the end of the meal, Stefan led me to my room. I felt like a girl coming home from the prom, wondering if her date was going to try for a kiss. I hoped he'd try, but he didn't.

That night, I heard the same sounds as I had the previous evening…clapping, or what I realized now was spanking. This time, I wasn't surprised; I was excited. I followed the noise, not nearly as nervous as I had been on the prior evening. I felt as if someone was calling out to me. I had to respond.

That didn't mean I stomped my way to Sasha's room. I still tiptoed, as quietly as possible. I wanted to watch. I didn't even question the desire in myself. I yearned to see everything, to hear each word.

At the door, I noticed the same sliver of light as I had on the previous night. I came closer, closer, and then peeked inside. There was Sasha. But this time, she was over Lou's lap. He had a paddle in his hand—one that looked like a fraternity paddle, wooden, with holes drilled through in a uniform pattern. The chef was off to one side, and she seemed to be speaking to Lou, directing him. I crossed my legs and watched.

No, she wasn't directing, she was assisting. She was holding a tray of different sex toys and a bottle of lubrication. She looked exactly the same to me as she had when offering me my meal earlier in the evening, setting items from the tray in front of me, pouring me a glass of wine. Except now, she was pouring K-Y between Sasha's cheeks and then offering a molded-glass butt plug to Lou.

Did Venice artists blow these types of glass artifacts? That would be a souvenir tour I'd be willing to attend. I stifled a giggle. Then felt a pair of arms around my waist. I stiffened. This was not Lou, making sure I didn't need anything. I turned to come face-to-face with Stefan, and my heart felt as if it had forgotten how to beat. He had his tie and jacket off now. His shirtsleeves were rolled to the elbows, and his collar was unbuttoned.

"Don't be alarmed," he said. "Come with me."

He took me to the room adjoining Sasha's. There was only one small light on in the far corner. I was surprised to see that the room was set up in almost the exact opposite of Sasha's. The mirror image. Oh, the *mirror*. Stefan took me closer, and now I saw that the mirror looked into Sasha's room.

"You like to watch," he said. "This will give you a better vantage point."

"I…"

"Don't worry, Ellis." He ran his fingers through my hair, then kissed me, once, on the lips, exactly as I'd fantasized about after dinner. I wanted more. I wanted him to take me to the bed and do all the things to me that Lou and the chef were doing to Sasha. But I couldn't find my voice. "Sit here. Watch. We'll talk in the morning."

I looked wildly around the room, and I saw that all of my belongings had been brought to this room while I'd slept. Stefan seemed to take note of my realization, because he said, "This is where you will sleep tonight." One more kiss. "I'll see you at breakfast."

People didn't behave like this in the real world, did they? Nothing even remotely like this had ever happened to me before. Not outside of the dirty fairy tales that I wrote for my own pleasure, ones that only Sasha had been privy to reading. I thought about that as I sat in front of the mirror. The stories I'd given her over the years were fairy tales set in modern times—filthy stories set in New York. Had she given the stories to Stefan? Is that what he'd meant when he said he liked my writing?

It was clear to me that he had read my words, as he walked into the room occupied by the chef and Lou. Because wasn't this one of my all-time fantasies? I watched as Stefan bent Sasha over the bed. She had that butt plug between her cheeks, and he rocked the base of it gently. I couldn't hear the sounds she made, but I could imagine. He removed the plug and then began to spank her once more. He was such a handsome dom, the way he stood, the way he moved. He punished my friend with hard, even strokes.

I started to touch my pussy as he spanked her. I couldn't stop myself. I put my feet up on the marble table in front of the mirror, parted my thighs and stroked my pussy through my bikini bottoms. I was dripping wet already.

Somewhere in my mind I realized that the table on which I'd placed my feet was undoubtedly a priceless antique. But I couldn't worry about that. I needed access. Sasha was taking the punishment well. She didn't flinch or try to get out of the way. That is, not until Stefan motioned to the chef that he wanted something. What? What was he reaching for?

I saw her hand him a thin-looking weapon and my stomach dropped. A crop? Sasha turned to look over her shoulder, and she started to stand. There was Lou, moving quickly, holding her in place by her wrists. I realized I wasn't breathing, and I sucked in a great breath of air as Stefan struck the first blow. Sasha definitely responded to this. Maybe the hand spanking had been more of a warm-up. She squirmed and flailed, but Lou held her in place. Stefan parted her legs, and touched her in between. I felt myself growing more aroused by the second. I was watching a dirty scenario starring players I knew, but I felt as if I were viewing an X-rated movie put on solely for my enjoyment. I'd never been part of anything like this before.

I thought of the stories I'd written over the years. The first time I'd given Sasha one to read, I'd been embarrassed. She'd never seemed that into sex before. She'd written me a note back drawing a picture of herself with the words *Me and My Halo*, letting me know then that although she might appear pristine and perfect, she had a slight deviant streak. But she'd never talked about putting any of the themes in my stories into play.

Apparently, she did.

Then the chef came into view, and I realized, I'd forgotten about her. She took Lou's position, not holding Sasha's wrists, but moving to her side, stroking her hair, kissing her. I wasn't going to last much longer, I realized. I climbed onto the marble table so I could get as close to the action as possible. What would they say if I joined them, I wondered? What would Stefan do if I walked out of my room and into Sasha's? Is that what they hoped for? Was this their genteel style of an engraved invitation?

For some reason, I couldn't. I sat there, watching as Lou stood behind Sasha, and I understood when he started fucking her. I could hear the sounds, but not the words he said. The cadence, like a lullaby of how he spoke to her. I saw Stefan leave, and I wondered if he would come to my room, if he would find me up on the table and scold me or stroke me or spank me.

But I remained alone, all night, watching Lou and the chef make love to Sasha until the light in that room went out and I was all by myself.

In the morning, I found Sasha in a transparent nightgown on the veranda, standing and looking out at the water. I could see through the filmy material that her ass was still red. This brought back instant memories of the night before. My pussy clenched. Once the debauchery had ended, I'd spent the remainder of the previous night fucking myself with the vibrator while listening to my favorite songs. The iPod had been preprogrammed with music I adored. Someone knew my music tastes better than Pandora.

Sasha was drinking from a champagne flute. She didn't turn to me until I reached her side. When she did, her face lit up.

"Did you sleep well, Ellis?"

I stared at her. Sleep? Was another day going to pass where we were not going to talk about what I'd seen? Were we going to pretend that this was some normal vacation, where we'd take a boat out to the glass factory and buy paperweights and overpriced knickknacks?

"I don't think she slept for more than twenty minutes."

The voice surprised me. I turned to address Stefan.

"How do you know that?" I asked before I could stop myself. Was it rude to challenge so generous a host?

"Because I watched you."

Without hesitation, I took Sasha's champagne glass from her and began to drink. I had to work not to chatter the rim of the glass against my teeth. Sasha was smiling at me. I'd never seen her look so peaceful before. Was someone going to tell me how he had watched me? Was there another two-way mirror in the bedroom? Were the guest rooms fitted with video cameras?

But nobody spoke. Stefan reached for Sasha and brought her close to him. While I stood there, drinking her champagne, he bent her over the stone railing and lifted the back of her nightgown, exposing her beautiful ass. I'd worked out with Sasha at the gym before—she brought me in with her as a guest, like a city mouse taking pity on a poor Nautilus-deprived country mouse. I knew how hard she sweated to keep her body in shape. Now, I knew why.

"Did you enjoy watching me punish her?" he asked.

I stared at my feet. I was wearing my last best pair of shoes. Even these were scuffed, and if you flipped them over, you'd see holes in the soles.

"The answer isn't on your knock-off patent-leather mules," he said.

"I know." I liked the way he spoke, the way he described my footwear.

"How did you react?" he asked next. "What were you thinking?" While I watched, he stroked Sasha's ass. I felt a catch in my throat. How I wanted him to do that to me. But people didn't behave like this. Not in the really real world.

"I don't know," I stammered.

"Then let's try it again so we can see."

Part of me wanted to run back to my room, to repack my bags, to get out of this place. I had never experienced anything like this before. I didn't know how to behave. The other part of me wanted to stay exactly where I was. Due to the fact that I truly had no place to go—this was the end of my rock-island line—I held my ground. Stefan seemed pleased.

"I'll spank her. You watch. Then you tell me how you feel."

I sucked in my breath. He let his hand connect with her naked ass. He didn't hit her hard, and I was aware that something in me wished he had. He smacked her again. Then he smiled at me. He was playing a game, giving her soft little love pats. I wanted to see him let loose. What was going on inside of me? I felt all twisted and bent. I wanted to watch a man who was practically a stranger punish my best friend.

"This is Venice," a voice said behind me. I turned and saw the chef with a bottle of champagne. She motioned to my glass and I held it out, waiting for the refill. I felt as if I hadn't drunk a sip. Not that my head was clear, but that my edge was still sharp. Nothing in my brain was fuzzy or hazy. I craved release.

"Thank you, Bonnie," Stefan said.

I drained the second glass while I tried to process the tableau in front of me.

"Do you like this, Ellis?" Stefan asked.

I wanted him to smack her, to give her a proper thrashing. He tapped her again. I felt like an animal, caged. "Am I doing something wrong?" he asked innocently. Anger flickered through me. He was fucking with me, and I didn't know how to respond.

"You're not spanking her the way you did before," I said.

"How did I spank her?"

Was he really asking me this? I wanted to be able to talk freely, but I realized that I never had. I'd always measured out my thoughts, considered my words. And where had that gotten me? Stefan seemed to understand what I was thinking.

"Here, things are different," he said. "You'll get used to the way we behave. I know you will. Relax. Enjoy yourself. And answer my question."

"That first night, you spanked her hard," I said, "so that I could hear the sound all the way to my bedroom."

"That was the point, wasn't it?"

Oh, so he'd been calling to me with the sounds of his hand on her ass. I felt my pussy spasm. I could not believe that I'd be able to get off again. Not after fucking myself with the vibrator for most of the night, falling into twitchy slumber, only to wake up in a state of lust-drenched hunger once more. Bonnie refilled my glass. I sipped and waited. What was the game we were playing now? What were the rules?

"Tell me precisely what you saw."

"You had her over your lap, and you were spanking her hard, and she was crying."

"Did you like that?"

I nodded, embarrassed to admit how much pleasure her pain had given me.

"What did watching do for you?"

"It made my…"

"Say it."

I sucked in my breath. "It made my pussy wet." I felt defiant as I spoke the words, tilting my chin at Stefan. I felt both powerful and insolent at the same time. If I were him, I'd have slapped my face. But he seemed decidedly proud I'd finally found my voice.

"What else did I do?"

"On the first night, you played with her…." I didn't want to describe what I'd seen, but the way Stefan was looking at me somehow drew the words from my lips. "You were playing with her asshole, telling her that Lou was going to fuck her there."

"Good girl," Stefan said, and I felt a strange flush of dignity swell over me. Bonnie took that moment to put an arm around my waist and kiss me, and I felt lost and shaky once more.

"You are my guest," Uncle Stefan said, breaking my reverie. "You are not responsible for doing any chores, paying for any food or entertainment. There is only one thing I expect of you." I stared at him. "You must answer when I ask you a question."

That seemed simple, didn't it? More than fair. Until he said, "How about you? Do you like to have your asshole fucked?"

I didn't want to answer that. Nobody had ever spoken like that to me in my entire life. Yes, I'd had boyfriends. But I'd had the kind of boyfriends I thought you were supposed to date. Nice, sweet, with good jobs—at least, they'd all been that way on the surface. But something had gone wrong every time. Not in the bedroom, not necessarily. I'd never meshed. I'd thought it was me. This is why I'd written my stories.

Sasha looked over her shoulder. I had never seen her like this before. She was letting a man touch her, control her, debase her. The heat in her eyes showed me that she liked the situation. I knew she could answer Uncle Stefan's question for me. I'd been honest with Sasha about all of my past relationships. She could have said, "No, Ellis has only dated men who like to do her missionary style, with all the lights out." But she kept quiet.

"No," I said, looking at my feet, at the marbled patio.

There was silence then, and I wondered if I'd done something wrong until I felt a hand on my shoulder. I looked up, surprised. The pretty chef was stroking my arm. She seemed to be trying to offer me comfort, or at least support.

I looked at our host. He was smiling. "Was that difficult for you?" I nodded. "It will get easier. I promise."

I couldn't hold my tongue. "What will?"

"Giving in."

The chef refilled my champagne glass once more as Sasha stood up and rearranged her nightgown. The gossamer fabric billowed around her when she moved. I watched as she gave me the tiniest smile and then headed back into the villa. Stefan came over to the chef and said something to her. She nodded. I watched as he followed Sasha. I could feel my heart starting to pound faster. All of this felt like a dream. Maybe I would wake up in my cousin's tiny apartment. I'd search for change in my drawers, in the bottom of my purse, knowing there was none to be found. I'd wonder whether I could slink back to one of my exes and beg for a few days on his futon. The nightmare of my life would make this fantasy dream fade away.

In the entryway to the villa, Stefan caught Sasha in his arms and kissed her.

Everything else felt like fairy-tale fluff, but the jealousy I felt watching Stefan kiss Sasha was real.

Bonnie pushed my hair out of my eyes. "You've been sad lately, haven't you?"

"Sad doesn't even begin to describe it," I told her, as I saw Stefan and Sasha continue on their way. Why not be honest? I had nothing to lose. Plus the champagne helped make the words easier to accept.

"Stefan wants me to take care of you," she said.

"Take care..."

"You'll see." She put her hand in mine and led me into the house. She didn't lead me upstairs to my room but down a hallway. I noticed the art on the walls—barely. I saw the rich furnishings, knew the wealth that went into decorating a place this posh. But the chef took me to a small room in the back. The bedroom was simply outfitted—a bed that nearly filled the space, a vase on the small dresser overflowing with sweet peas, their fragrance lighting up the room. White sheets. Silver handcuffs.

I looked at her.

"You don't have to do a thing," she said. "Let me."

"I've never been with a woman," I lied. Why wasn't I telling her the truth? I'd dabbled in college when I thought that's what you were supposed to do.

"Liar."

I stared at her.

"Sasha told us your past. I know who you are."

"Who am I?"

"You'll find out."

She started to undress me. I was so shocked by her words that I let her, let her position me on her bed on my stomach. Let her cuff my wrists over my head.

"What are you going to do?" I asked.

"Everything you've ever wanted."

My pussy was so wet that I was embarrassed. I knew I'd be making a puddle on her white sheets. "What do I want?" I asked into the pillow. The champagne seemed to have finally kicked in, and I felt lazy and slow. When Bonnie began to stroke her hands along my back, I sighed and arched my hips.

"You want me to spank your bare bottom. And then you want me to get between your legs and lick your sweet slit until you come. After that, you want me to tongue your asshole. You've never had that before, and you want to know what being rimmed properly feels like."

I groaned.

"Stefan is going to fuck you there. You know that, right? He is going to take your ass the way other men have fucked your pussy. He's big, so he's going to stretch you open. But not until you're ready. Not until you're begging."

I shut my eyes as she started to finger my pussy. Nobody had ever spoken to me like this before. I thought of my last boyfriend. The only kink in his makeup was the fact that he liked me to wear my shoes in bed: high heels, the one good pair I had. No man had ever talked as dirty as Bonnie was. She worked her fingers in and out of me, and then she brought her hand up and smacked my ass. I thought of the way Stefan had spanked Sasha—both in her room and out on the balcony. Where were they? What were they doing now?

She spanked me again, and I forgot to worry about Sasha.

"Have you been punished before?" she asked.

I shook my head.

"But you want to be, don't you?"

It was as if she knew about the books I kept hidden under my bed. Or I had kept hidden, when I'd had a bed of my own. Books I'd gotten rid of when I moved in with my cousin. I couldn't stand the thought of her finding my secret stash, so I'd put them, one by one, into recycling bins that I passed on the street.

"Yes," I said into the pillow.

"Tell me," Bonnie instructed.

Facing away from her made saying the words easier. "I've always wanted to be with a lover who was..." I didn't know how to describe what I desired.

"Who was..." Bonnie prompted, her hand landing another stinging blow on my ass.

"In charge," I said.

"Good girl." She sounded just like Stefan. Bonnie spanked harder and faster now, and I groaned again and arched my body on the mattress. In between smacks, she used her fingers as if to test for wetness, and I could feel my juices spreading.

"You're like a little lake," she said, "here between your thighs. I can't wait to taste you."

I shivered as she climbed onto the bed and moved my body so that I was half on my knees, a bastardized yoga position.

She squirmed beneath me, her mouth to my pussy, and then she began to trick her tongue in magical circles. "Oh, God," I moaned, "that feels so good." I wished I could say something more eloquent than that. Bonnie licked and sucked, and then suddenly she stopped. I pushed downward, unable to stop myself, wanting the sensation to continue, bucking my pussy against her mouth. She gripped my hips and held me firmly in place. Her tongue was out of reach.

"You have to earn your climax," she said.

"What," I panted, "what do you mean?"

"Ten strokes on your ass will equal the sweetest fucking climax you've ever felt."

What did that mean? Ten strokes of what?

She wriggled from between my legs and I watched, eyes huge and desperate, as she opened up the tiny closet. Within, I saw the tools and toys I'd fantasized about for years. She had paddles and crops, a whippet-thin cane, bondage devices. But Bonnie was a tease. Before I could focus on each one, Bonnie grabbed what she wanted and then shut the door. I wished I could spend hours looking at each of her possessions, running my fingers over the handles, inspecting every angle.

"This is a crop," she said, bringing the weapon in front of my eyes. I stared. She pushed me so that I was prone on the bed once more, wrists over my head. "This is going to hurt," she said next. I swallowed hard. I wanted to look away, but I was mesmerized. "I expect you to count for me. Ten strokes. Can you do that?"

I nodded.

"Good girl," she said again, sounding so much like Stefan I blinked at her. "We've been together a long, long time," she said with a smile, as if reading the thought as it passed through my mind.

I didn't know what to do next. Did I stare at her, push my head into the pillow, look at the wall, gaze at the flowers…? She struck the first blow, and the worries evaporated, replaced by a pure sensation of pain. I hadn't known what to expect. The burning of the stroke made me forget my job. I was to count. But I didn't. "That's one," Bonnie said for me.

"One," I echoed hollowly.

She struck a second time; I managed to squeak out a "two." I could not believe the intensity of the pain—but I also could not fully process the explosion of pleasure that followed each stroke. Bonnie landed number three. My pussy contracted with a force that surprised me. The pain was turning me on. There was no doubt.

"Four." I thought that I might actually come with no other stimulation. Bonnie was an expert. She lined the blows up neatly next to each other. She took a breath after five, and I felt her hands on my ass, stroking the places that hurt the most. I wanted her to…

Oh, she was. Kissing me. Kissing the welts. Touching my pussy as she licked the stripes of fire on my skin. "You're doing so well," she said softly, "better than I would have expected. And see how wet your slit is?" She dipped her fingers inside of me, brought the gloss she gathered up to my lips. She spread my own juices on my lips and then kissed them clean. "Like honey," she said.

I groaned. I was lost. She was hurting me, helping me, touching me so fucking sweetly that I didn't know which way was up.

"When I reach ten," she said, "I am going to lick your pussy until you come." She stood and struck the sixth blow. "And then," she continued, "I'm going to put on a strap-on, and fuck you until you come again." Oh, God, I wanted that. I wanted to feel her pound into me. She landed seven and eight quickly, and I bucked and writhed on the bed. She took the handle of the crop then, and she slowly, gently, slid the molded tip inside of me. I almost started to cry. I wanted to be fucked. It had been months since my last hook-up. I'd almost managed to forget how important sex could be.

She let me bask in the sensation of having that handle up inside me, and then she pulled it out and landed the ninth blow. I shuddered all over. I hadn't started crying. Bonnie seemed impressed. "You know the tenth is going to be the worst," she said, "it has to be. But in a way, that's the best, isn't it? You need this."

I did. Why? I don't know. But she spoke the truth. I wanted everything she was doing to me. I shut my eyes as she raised her arm up. I held myself entirely still. She slammed into me and said, "Ten," and then I heard the clatter as she dropped the crop, felt the bed shift as she moved me, flipping me onto my back, handcuff chain rattling, getting in between my legs and starting to suck my clit.

Yes, I've had lovers go down on me before. I haven't been with men so uptight they couldn't tongue a girl's snatch. But nobody had ever made me feel the way Bonnie did. She used her fingers to spread open my nether lips. She pinched my clit between her thumb and finger and I began to moan and beg. "Let me come. Please…" The way she touched me was taunting and rough, and then right when I could take no more, she changed to gentle and soft, so that I missed the way she'd manhandled me only seconds before.

"You don't know what you want," she said, and she was right. I didn't.

"Stop thinking," she said. "Don't concentrate. Don't try so hard. Let go."

She licked and sucked with such obvious pleasure that I couldn't feel embarrassed or concerned that I wasn't coming fast enough. Worries that I usually feel melted away until there was only her mouth and my pussy in my world. That's the size of what mattered.

I would have come anyway. But it was Stefan standing in the doorway, staring in at us, that took me over the edge.

How long had he been there? I didn't know. He leaned against the door frame, casually watching. I would have covered my eyes with my hands, but my wrists were still cuffed and useless. I thought of looking away, but his gaze held me firmly. Last night, I'd been the voyeur. This morning, I was the show.

Bonnie didn't seem aware of our audience. She kept her mouth between my thighs and plunged her tongue inside of me as I started to come. I couldn't stay quiet any longer. Even with Stefan watching, so intently, I moaned and sighed, my breathing coming faster as I reached climax. Bonnie let me ride out the waves of the orgasm, and then she reached for a key on a chain around her neck and set me free.

"No strap-on today, I guess," she said to me as she rubbed my wrists. "She's a sweet girl," she said to Stefan—letting me know that she knew he was standing there. "Look at this." She motioned and, mortified, I rolled over, so that she could show him the welts on my ass.

I heard his footsteps as he approached the bed. "Very nice," he said. I felt his warm hand on my skin. His hand moved lower, between my thighs, feeling how wet I was. He could have been checking produce in the market with how indifferently he caressed me. And then he ordered, "Get her dressed and send her to my room. I have something to talk to her about."

How odd, I thought, even in my hazy, postcoital state. Odd how he talked to Bonnie instead of me. But somehow I didn't mind. There was a formality to the tone of his voice, one that turned me on.

"You and I are close to the same size," Bonnie said, opening the second wardrobe in the room. "Do you want to choose something of mine?" I was surprised to see so many different dresses, opulent colors, gauzy fabrics. "I'm not only the chef," she explained in answer to my unspoken query. "Stefan likes to dress me different ways for this and that." Clearly. There were costumes of all sorts on the racks: drum majorette, schoolgirl skirt, headmistress attire.

She pulled out a cashmere turtleneck the color of ripe peaches and a flirty short skirt that looked as if it had been made of layers of translucent scarves. "These will look lovely on you."

I started dressing. The clothes were so rich, I wanted to take my time. I'd been accustomed over the past few years to try to dress expensively without actually having money. I was focused on how luxurious the fabrics felt against my skin, when she added, "Don't worry about wearing knickers."

The worry was instantaneous.

"His room is at the end of the hall that yours is on," she said. "He's waiting."

I slid into my shoes—the only part of the outfit that looked sad now—and walked down the long hall. I wondered where Sasha was, where Lou was, wondered what Stefan wanted to tell me. Tell. That wasn't the right word at all, was it? Should I feel bad that I'd been invited to Venice as a sex toy? I couldn't manage to feel unhappy about that at all. The attention made me feel beautiful, and when I glanced into a mirror, I saw a warmth to my cheeks, to my eyes, that had been missing for longer than I could remember. Fear can turn a person cold inside.

I climbed the stairs, headed down the hall I'd walked the previous evening. Stefan was waiting, sitting in a deep leather chair, sipping from a cut-crystal glass. I entered the room and then stood, not knowing what to do, where to go, how to act. His room was twice the size of the one I was staying in. I felt as I always did when I'd been summoned to yet another boss's office after yet another merger—one that meant my job was redundant.

He smiled at me, and I felt myself begin to melt. "You know, you are exactly as Sasha described," he said.

I didn't know how to respond. How had Sasha described me?

"Hungry," he said. "Get your jacket and meet me down-stairs. I'll take you out."

I hurried back to my room, wondering if my battered old jacket would make the outfit look cheap. The first thing I saw was a typewriter on the desk. I'd always preferred working on a typewriter—and my old one had been the first beloved material object I'd jettisoned when I'd lost my apartment. This was identical to mine, a Remington. I'd sold mine for $500—trading a piece of myself for money I needed. And here was the twin, with the colored glass keys in mint, turquoise, yellow and red. Sasha must have told Stefan. There was no other way he could know. I had an urge to sit at the desk and start writing, but Stefan called out for me. I turned to grab my coat from the bed where I'd left it, but the coat was gone.

On the mattress was a raspberry-hued woven shawl, like tapestry. I wrapped the shawl around my body the way I'd seen Sasha do, and then I caught site of the little box on the pillow. When I took off the lid, I saw a glittering rhinestone broach, obviously antique, perfect for pinning the fabric in place. I was about to snag a pair of knickers from the drawer in my dresser, when I heard Bonnie calling. "Stefan's ready, El. Come on!"

I hesitated another second, and then decided to go without.

"I'm so grateful," I said when I found Stefan waiting for me in the foyer.

"For what?"

"You don't know what it's been like," I said.

But he shrugged away my gratitude, with a simple *"Prego"* and then added, "You look lovely in the wrap."

I stammered, trying to find the right words. He'd given me too much to accept with a simple thank-you.

"You say, *'Grazie,'*" he said graciously, and I whispered the word as he took my hand. The touch of his skin on mine made me feel hot all over. If he noticed, he didn't comment.

Stefan led us through tiny winding streets to the open-air market. I'd been to farmer's markets before, of course, but I'd never seen anything as lush and colorful as this. Every piece of fruit looked perfect, as if plucked from a photo. There were bowls of the largest berries I'd ever seen—raspberries, blueberries, blackberries—bunches of chilies, purple grapes that looked so ripe they would burst when you barely touched their dusky skin. The voices of the shoppers and clerks made music to me, as I didn't understand the words. Stefan had a hand in mine, I felt to make sure I didn't get lost. But then he let go of my hand, and his palm caressed my ass through the filmy fabric of the skirt. I was reminded in a heartbeat that I was without underwear. I wondered if other people could tell.

In Italian, Stefan ordered several pieces of fruit for us— peaches, figs, cherries—and then we continued walking once more. I wanted to take in everything: the water, the boats, the colorful awnings, the painted buildings, the busy restaurants, bustling with tourists. Every location I admired appeared as elegantly quaint as a picture postcard.

Then Stefan led me down a tiny alley—so narrow I hadn't noticed the space between the buildings at first. "This way," he said. I followed him for several steps until he stopped and turned around. "Lift your skirt."

"What?"

"Show me."

I pulled the skirt up, a warm buzz rushing over me.

"Spread your lips."

Who was he? Who was I? I was the girl who reached down and opened my pussy up so he could see.

"So beautiful," he said. "Did Bonnie treat that well?"

"Yes."

"Then so will I." He bent on his knees, pressed his mouth to my pussy and began to lick from me. I couldn't believe he was doing this out in the open. Except we weren't in the open, were we? We were off on the tiniest side street I'd ever been in. I had my body pressed against the building as firmly as Stefan had his mouth pressed against me. I sighed and closed my eyes as he licked me harder, faster. Was he going to make me come here, where I could listen to the sounds of the city all around us?

No. He pushed back and told me to turn around.

I didn't move quickly enough. He spun me, so I was facing the cold wall. He stayed on his knees, his hands spreading my ass cheeks apart. I felt a wetness around my hole, and I thought for a moment that he was licking me there. I would have pulled away if I could have, but I was sandwiched between Stefan and stone. I could not remember ever feeling this aroused and ashamed before, the two emotions warring within me. Shame won out, as Stefan stood and whispered in my ear, "That was sweet peach juices I spread around your asshole."

I shivered.

"I'll lick them off from you later."

The shivers persisted. My whole body was trembling. "I'm going to fit you with a plug. A large one. You'll wear that while I fuck your slippery pussy. It will be your introduction to having two holes filled at once."

I sagged against him. No one had ever spoken to me like that before.

"Do you want to hear more?"

"Yes."

"I'll take you home now," he said, "and I'll tell you the rest."

The sunlight glinting on the water, the colorful mélange of people and the beauty of the city blurred together. I could not think or speak on the ride home. I was so wet and the need for climax was so large, that I felt as if I were lost in a half swoon. Stefan seemed completely unchanged, as cool as ever. He led me through the villa, and we did not see anyone else on the way.

In his room, he poured us each a drink from a cut-crystal decanter, and handed mine to me. I breathed in the scent of good whiskey.

"You seem more naive than most women your age. And you seem unhappy. Too sad for someone who has no real problems."

No real problems? Suddenly, everything I worried and feared came back in a rush. A physical rush. I pushed back against the wall so that I would have something to hold me up. "I have problems."

He shook his head. "No, you don't."

Up until now, Stefan had been nothing but gracious to me. He'd treated me as if he'd invited me personally, as if I were his guest. I felt nothing but special. My life was not supposed to look the way it did now. Venice might be sinking, but so slowly nobody noticed on a day-to-day basis. I, on the other hand, had sunk.

"Look at you," he said, standing and moving me so I was facing a mirror. For a flicker of time, I wondered if someone was watching me on the other side. Sasha? Lou? "Is this a woman with problems?" he asked both of us.

I started to get angry. "I have no job, no family, no one to turn to, nowhere to go." I did what I'd promised myself I wouldn't. I took a firm step out of this fairy-tale land and into reality. "When I leave here, there is nothing else. I land at whatever airport Sasha helps me get to, and then…nothing."

"Then why leave?"

I turned to face him. I didn't understand what he was saying, what he was suggesting. Apparently, my confusion showed on my face, because he smiled and cupped my chin in his hand. "I mentioned a job."

I nodded.

"But I was talking about more than some freelance gig, Ellis. I didn't invite you for two weeks," he said. "I invited you forever."

I had to sit down. I pulled away from him and looked around the room. I couldn't take his seat—it was so obviously his. So I sat on the bed, knowing as I did so that maybe this was not the best choice for me. But my brain wasn't working well. I wished I could have slowed the world down for a moment or two, so that I could catch up.

"I told you that I've read your writing," he said, "not only the copy for ads, but your real writing."

I'd guessed this, but I had to ask, "How?"

"When Sasha would visit for the summers, and you'd trade

letters, she always let me read yours. When you mailed her stories you were working on, she shared your words with me."

I flushed. Sasha was the only friend I'd ever allowed to see my work. I'd been embarrassed to share them with her, but she'd always been supportive. Even in the brain haze I felt, I had to ask, "You liked my stories?"

He went to a desk and opened the drawer, bringing out a folder. "I've kept every one," he said, riffling the papers so I could see. I remembered writing the different pieces, modern-day fairy tales set in New York. Sexy, saucy stories I'd been unable to show to anyone but Sasha.

"Your words captivated me," he said. "I need them, the way I need you."

"What do you mean?"

"I want you to write about this place." He spread his arms out.

"Your bedroom?"

"Smart-ass." He spoke the words with a smile. "You'll get a spanking for that. Later. I want you to write about our world here in Venice. What we do here. The way we live."

"We..." My mind was still on the spanking.

"Lou and I. Bonnie. Sasha when she comes to stay. Our summer guests and our winter guests. And you."

"Me."

He sat on the bed at my side and he took one of my hands in his. "I was hoping you would be as unique as your words, that you would fall in love with this place—and with me— and I would fall in love with you. And now I only have one question for you...."

I waited. My heart was racing. I knew the rule. When he asked a question, he expected an answer.

"Have you?"

"Have I?"

"Fallen in love."

I couldn't breathe. What was he asking me?

"You wrote in your journal that you never wanted to leave. Did you mean it?"

I didn't care that he'd read the diary. Aren't all diaries written at least subconsciously with the hopes and wishes that the words will be found and revealed?

"Yes," I said. "Yes, Stefan."

"And have you?"

I had nothing to lose. I had truth to gain. "Yes," I said. "I have."

He gripped me in his arms and he kissed me. Differently from the way he'd kissed me at the market. Sweeter and rougher at the same time. I felt as if I were one of the characters in the fairy tales I'd written over the years, except this wasn't make-believe. Was it?

"I want you to write about this. About how we behave. About what our life is like," he said. "All the ways we play, all the things we do."

"What do you do?" I had to ask. I thought I understood, but I needed him to explain.

"People are so caught up in what's normal. What's right and wrong. I don't live like that. I don't have to. Not anymore." He kissed me in between sentences, and each time he did, I felt light-headed. "I used to," he continued. "At least, I tried. I went to parties, the opera. I joined the society circles you're supposed to be a part of if you have money. And then I realized, if you have money, you don't have to be a part of anything you don't want to be."

I stared at him. He seemed to want me to understand.

"It's different here. You'll get used to the way we behave. If you want someone to tie you up in the middle of the night, then you come to me. If you'd rather have Bonnie eat you then you go to her. If you have a need—we will fill it. And we'll find out needs you never thought you had."

I sighed. This was too much like being read on the inside. Everything he was describing was everything I've always wanted.

"You'll write each word in that style of yours. This is important to me. Do you understand?"

I nodded.

"Like this," he said, and he startled me by pulling me over his lap, his hand resting on my ass. I sucked in my breath at the same moment that he let his hand land against my rear. "You're a smart-ass. That's not a bad thing." He spanked me hard, through my skirt—through Bonnie's skirt. "But being flippant here will get you a spanking." Each time his hand landed, I flinched, but I didn't try to get free. "You might be spanked in the middle of a dinner party, with everyone watching me bend you over the table." I swallowed hard, as he described the scene. "My friends know me, they know the way I act. They're generous and compassionate. They'll sit and watch as I punish you, and then they'll go on with their meal."

He stroked my rear between blows, and then he sat me up again.

"Do you like being punished?"

My thoughts were captivated by what he'd just described, but I managed to respond with a soft "Yes."

"Why, Ellis?"

I looked all over the room rather than look into his eyes. But then I remembered—without him having to remind me—the one rule. When he asked a question, I was to answer. "Because I don't have to think anymore."

"What do you mean?"

I stared at the floor. "I'm always worrying, wondering, wishing. When the sensation—that pain/pleasure mix—

overtakes me, all my thoughts disappear." I hoped he'd understand. "I feel erased, somehow. Or washed clean."

"Yes. Perfect."

He stood me up. He seemed to be studying me, as if he
wanted to learn my face by heart. "You look good in new
clothes," he said, "but tomorrow we'll get you your own.
Not Bonnie's. And new shoes, too. We have the best shoes
in Italy. You'll see."

"What will I do?" I asked him, as he was leading me to
the bed.

"What do you mean?"

"If I stay, if you really want me to stay…"

"I really want you to stay."

"What will I do?"

"You'll write, and you'll eat, and you'll fuck and you'll be
fucked."

I shivered.

"Do you like the way that sounds? Like one of your fairy
tales, except instead of New York, you'll be here, in Venice.
And instead of a story that's tied up in a neat bow at the end,
this one will be never-ending."

He had my clothes off and he was spreading me out on
the bed.

"Who will I fuck?" I had to ask the question.

"Me," he said, "or rather, I'll fuck you. And so will Bonnie.
She's got a nice, long strap-on that she likes to use."

"And Lou?"

"If you like. If you want him to."

"It's about what I want?"

"Your wishes," he said, "your pleasure." He was parting my
nether lips now and he pressed his face to my pussy. I could
hardly think, but I wanted to think. The sensation was odd,
as if I was fighting my own lust. I needed to concentrate, but

Stefan was making thoughts impossible. His tongue tricked in circles around my clit, and then he reached his hand up to my mouth.

"Lick my fingers," he said, "get them all wet for me."

I did as he said, and then I shut my eyes as he brought his hand beneath me and began working one finger into my asshole. I was dizzy from longing, and I didn't make a sound as he started to slowly finger-fuck my ass.

"You said you always worry...."

I moaned in response.

"You won't have to worry anymore."

He slid a second finger inside of me.

"You like that," he said.

"Oh, yes."

"Roll over."

I did what he said, and I raised my hips up for him. I wanted him to do it. I knew what he was after. Nobody had ever had me there.

Stefan said, "Look at what Bonnie's left us on the table."

I opened my eyes and stared at where he was pointing—a jar of olive oil, sweet and golden by the bed. I watched as he opened the bottle, and I felt the river as he poured the liquid between the cheeks of my ass.

"Spread yourself for me," he said. "Wide."

I reached back and parted my cheeks for him.

"Now, relax."

I tried, I sucked in a great breath of air, but I was tight and tense. Very slowly, Stefan pressed the head of his cock to my back door. I shuddered all over. He worked in the head. I had never felt anything like that before. Tears leaked from my eyes—but not because I wanted him to stop. The pleasure outweighed the pain instantly.

"You like this," he said, biting into the ridge of my shoulder as he thrust his cock inside of me.

Yes. In my head. *Yes, oh, yes*. Then out loud I said, "Yes, Stefan."

"Tell me."

"Tell you…" My voice trailed.

"Describe what you're feeling."

"Your cock is filling me, oh, God, you're filling me up."

"Where?"

"My ass."

"Say the whole sentence."

"Your cock—" I was panting "—is fucking my asshole."

He reached a hand under my body so he could play with my clit while he worked me.

"But it's different from having my pussy fucked."

"I like the way you say that."

"I can imagine what it would be like to be between two men."

"Yes."

"You in my ass, Lou fucking my pussy. I've never done anything like that before. I've thought about it, of course." The words were coming faster now. I don't know why. Maybe I was trying to talk at the speed in which he was fucking me. Or maybe he'd managed to unlock something inside of me that set the words free.

"I want that to happen," I said. "I want it all to happen."

"Such a dirty girl."

I'd made his voice catch. This gave me a rush of pure pleasure.

Pleasure. The word must mean something different in Venice, I thought.

At dinner, Sasha stared back and forth between us. She seemed to know. What a strange group we were, I thought.

Lou and Sasha were next to each other. Bonnie sat at one end of the table, eating rather than serving.

"You were right, Sasha," Stefan said. "Ellis is everything you said."

"Then you're staying?" she asked me. She sounded excited.

I nodded.

"Your wish came true?"

I looked at her. "All the other papers were blank," she said in response. "You'd see if you looked that the only wish written on the tree was yours."

It hadn't even occurred to me to look.

"I still have to go back home," she continued, "but not yet. And I'll be back to visit every few months."

"Sasha can't stay away for long," Stefan explained. "Lou misses her too much."

Lou moved closer and kissed my friend, and she sighed and leaned her head back. I saw marks on her throat from where his kisses and love bites had bruised her pale skin. I understood they were not holding back now. I was part of the group, so much so that when Sasha moved her chair back and slid under the table, so obviously giving Lou a blow job, I hardly flinched.

Bonnie left the table, and then returned with a tray of oysters. She, Stefan and I began to eat, Lou settling back and closing his eyes. He was handsome in his own way, I realized. Tough, yes, but with a sweet edge.

"Look," said Bonnie, excitedly, "I found a pearl."

Stefan looked at me. "So did I."

I couldn't eat after that. My nerves were still all jangly. I'd been living in fear for months, and suddenly that fear had been removed. My body didn't seem to know how to respond. Stefan watched me carefully from across the table.

"Are you finished?" he asked me.

I nodded.

"Then we'll retire," he said, coming around to my side of the table and pulling out my chair. He led me to his room, where I saw an incredible array of devices arranged on the bed.

There were clips with a chain running between, black leather cuffs, a velvet mask. "Tonight will be the two of us," Stefan said. "But on another night, you'll wear the mask, and you'll try to guess who's inside of you."

I looked at him, and I thought about what that meant. Stefan came closer and lifted my skirt. He dragged his fingertips between my pussy lips, coming up with the nectar that waited for him.

"Does that thought make you wet? Or are you wet because of what Sasha did at dinner?"

"Both."

He smiled. When he smiled, his whole face softened. He did not appear stern or intimidating, simply happy.

"Lie down on the bed, Ellis."

"What about the clothes?"

"I'll cut them off you."

"They're Bonnie's...."

"They're replaceable."

He bound me to the bed, cuffs on my wrists, leather thongs on my ankles. He put the mask over my eyes, and then he took cold, steel scissors and slowly slit the clothes off my body. I could imagine what I looked like in the tatters. Stefan moved with a purpose, but not with any sort of hurry. He attached clamps on my nipples and I arched and moaned. He parted my pussy lips and placed a clip on my clit, and the moans turned to begging, wordless but urgent.

Then he did nothing, and I stayed like that, for him to admire.

It was a battle, in some way, I realized. If I begged him to take off the clamps, would he? Could he wait me out? There was so much to learn, I realized. So much to understand about Stefan, what he wanted, what he liked.

"You're so fucking beautiful," he said.

I shook my head. I couldn't fathom what he was saying. I hadn't felt beautiful for a long time.

"I'm going to love doing you every way you can think of. Every location. On the bridges outside in the middle of the night. On a gondola. In the limo. On the balcony. In the shower." He was stroking me now with the palms of his hands as he spoke. "I will never run out of ways to make you come."

I breathed deeply, trying to stay still.

"Now, tell me what you want."

What did I want? I realized that I had everything I wanted. Even without the finale of climaxing, I was suspended in a state of bliss.

"Tell me, Ellis."

"I already have everything I could want," I said, knowing as I spoke the words, that they were true.

He laughed, and I wished I could see his face. "You're bound up tight. You can't move. Your nipples are pinched between clamps. Your clit must be on fire. How do you have everything?"

I was breathing harder by the second, although I tried to keep myself in check. "The worry is gone," I said. "I can take anything else."

He climbed on the bed then. I could feel his weight joining mine. He kissed me, and then pressed his body to mine. He'd stripped. I felt his naked chest on mine, his cock against my thigh. Quickly, he undid the clamp on my clit and sensation flooded through me. He thrust his cock hard inside my pussy, and I gripped onto him with my inner muscles. He tugged the chain between the nipple clamps, and I groaned and arched.

"So pretty," he said. "You have no idea. In the future, I'll take pictures. So you can see, so you can understand."

He thrust into me in a rhythm that felt divine. Even though he'd made me come so many times earlier, I could feel my body preparing, responding. We were well-suited, weren't we?

"I would read your stories," he said, "the ones Sasha sent me. I would jerk off as I heard your words echo in my head."

I clenched my eyes shut tight even under the blindfold.

"I never thought I'd find someone who would write out my fantasies without ever knowing me."

"I never thought I'd find someone who'd make mine come true," I said, and he slid his hand between our bodies, giving my clit the exact pressure it craved. "But then I did," I said, "and I found even more…."

"What have you found, Ellis?" he whispered in my ear as he came. "What have you found?" I was coming, too, but I still managed to say the words:

"My happily-ever-after."

The End

"Is your story finished?" Sasha asked, looking over my shoulder as I typed. She was wrapped only in a white sheet, her feet bare, her normally pristine appearance mussed and disheveled.

"No, it's only just beginning," I told her as I typed in *The End*. Because I understood that those two words meant something different in Venice.

★ ★ ★ ★ ★

WHAT SHE NEEDS
ANNE CALHOUN

When Jack calls at 6:00 p.m. on a Saturday and tells me to meet him in the bar at the Embassy Suites, I know two things: he wants to fuck me, and I will let him.

But because he knows my answer even before he calls, I make him wait. A little. I shower, locate my sexy underwear at the back of my drawer, put some effort into my makeup and hair. When I get in my car and drive downtown, the knowledge of what I'll soon be doing, and with whom, sharpens the colors visible through the windshield, the verdant leaves vivid against black-shingled roofs and a Wedgwood-blue sky.

As I walk through the lobby my stride must project a confidence I don't feel; either bravado or my sheath skirt and tight sleeveless blouse have drawn attention from a cluster of loosened-ties-no-jackets businessmen waiting by the front desk. I ignore their appraising looks, pretending engrossment in the brass railings, plush patterned carpet and abundant plants working to create a tasteful atmosphere. What I'm about to do could easily take place in a rundown motel next to the interstate. Jack, however, likes comfort and couldn't care less about the two-hundred-dollar room rate. The bar is at the back of the large atrium and the waterfall doesn't quite mask the click of my fuck-me heels against the tile floor. He knows making this walk by myself heightens my nerves and leaves me to do it anyway.

There is always that moment, standing in the doorway to the bar and looking for him, when I torment myself with the impossible. I imagine he's found someone equally willing and right at hand, that he's disappeared upstairs in the time it took me to prepare myself and come to him. But then I see him, a half-full glass of beer next to the Heineken bottle. Tonight he is wearing dark navy jeans and an olive cotton sweater, the sleeves pushed up to his elbows.

The sight of his forearms, tanned and dusted with blond hair, sends a shock of lust straight to my pussy.

The rest of him is nothing special. Muscles don't strain the seams of his sweater. Despite the absence of a ring, the other women in the bar don't eye him with obvious interest. He's of average height and build for a man, with sandy-blond hair. He doesn't look like a man who can make a woman lose her mind.

But he is. With a woman, on a bed stripped to the bottom sheet, when there is nothing else to do and nowhere else to be, he is gifted. That's why I'm here.

I stand next to him. He acknowledges my presence with a slow once-over, the kind that stays just this side of insolent. A nod indicates his approval.

"You want a drink first?" His voice, unlike his eyes, is smooth, calm. His eyes, however, are melting, dark chocolate.

I consider his offer, then indicate acceptance by boosting myself onto the seat next to his. When the bartender comes around he asks what he can get me.

"White wine," I say as he openly eyes me. I'm not wearing

a ring, either, and I know from experience that despite Jack's presence, I am fair game. Jack doesn't stake his claim in front of the bartender, but when he leaves to pour my wine, Jack leans to whisper in my ear.

"Nice blouse."

I tip my head slightly to indicate interest, but keep my eyes on the condensation sliding down the green beer bottle. I never use that color in my work. It's too recognizable.

"Undo one more button."

My breath stops in my throat at his command, but I lift one hand to the front of my blouse and flick open the button just above the swell of my breasts. This button keeps me from being slutty. Jack wants it undone. I obey him.

That's the rule. If I meet him, I do what he asks, when he asks. I'm free to decline his invitation. If I accept, I'll do what I'm told.

I always accept.

The bartender returns with my glass of white wine and a flirtatious smile on his face. I don't smile back. When he left my collarbone was visible, my appearance demure but appealing. Now he can see cleavage and the edge of the red lacy cups of my bra. His eyes flash to my chest, then over to Jack, who rests one arm on the back of my chair.

I don't need to look at Jack to know what his expression is. A grin too hard to be pleasant will tell the bartender he should look elsewhere for his night's entertainment. That doesn't stop the bartender from taking one last, long look before he moves away.

I drink my wine, the slow pound of my heart making me lightheaded long before the alcohol enters my bloodstream. We sit in silence as Jack finishes his beer. Small talk is not part of this ritual. I once asked him what he was thinking about while we sipped our drinks before going upstairs.

"Fucking you," he'd said.

He didn't ask what I was thinking about.

I replayed those two words, the tone of his voice when he said them, every day until he called me again. The next time I met him I shook my head when he asked if I wanted a drink. He escorted me to a room on the seventh floor and within five minutes of entering the hotel I was naked and under him. I wanted him badly that night. Tonight I want a glass of wine first, and Jack humors me.

I stretch it out, because the Chardonnay is decent. The cotton of his sweater almost but not quite touches the bare skin of my shoulder, his body heat evoking the possibility of his skin in contact with mine. Without meaning to I shift ever so slightly on my stool. The movement makes the edges of my blouse gap open, revealing my breast all the way to the front clasp of my bra.

Jack doesn't miss this little drama playing out mere inches from him. With two long swallows he finishes the rest of his beer, pulls a bill from his pocket and tosses it on the bar, then stands. He holds out one hand to me, palm up, a command, not an invitation.

"You're done."

With those words, I am. I slide my hand into his, the tips of his fingers cold and a little damp from the condensation on his glass. In my heels I'm an inch shorter than he is. My skirt clings to my curves from hips to knees, shortening my stride. He matches my pace as we leave the bar. There's no need to hurry.

Because we are not boyfriend and girlfriend, as we walk through the lobby his warm palm leaves mine to slide under my hair at the nape of my neck. As I walk I focus on the brass doors to the nearest elevator but feel strangers' stares pressing against my skin. Neither Jack nor I usually garner stares, but his hand under my hair, guiding me, broadcasts his primal intentions. People look, then glance away. I move docilely, my hands holding my dark brown clutch purse at my waist. The heat of his palm radiates through the tender skin at my nape, slipping down my spine to gather in my pussy. My panties are wet before the elevator door closes behind us.

He pushes the button for the third floor. Once, when our room was on the top floor he fucked me in this elevator, up against the doors, just eight measured strokes before the bell dinged and he stepped away. I felt each purposeful thrust from tip to base and back again. They left me soft and aching, unable to walk steadily without his hand at my waist. That night was all about little tastes, teasing me with a few thrusts, then pulling out to lick or suckle or caress, again and again, until I shamelessly begged him to fuck me.

Tonight, though, he simply leans back against the wall, arms folded across his chest, and looks at me. Opposite him and a little to his left, I see myself in the mirrored doors, my dark brown hair shoulder length and tousled, my eyes more vivid than usual, bright with excitement and longing. My eyes are the same color as his sweater, my lips parted above the dark rose of my blouse, my legs long and enticing in the tight brown skirt and high heels.

While he looks his fill, I think about all the different kinds of sex I've had. New love sex, when it lasts for hours and every movement is imbued with meaning and emotion. Relationship sex, that later stage when fucking is as much maintenance as it is pleasure. "Getting an oil change," while crude, is an apt analogy: it has to be done on a regular basis or the engine of your relationship breaks down.

Sex with Jack at the Embassy Suites is an adrenaline rush, one that peels away layer after layer of the film clouding my vision and turns me on to the point where my skin feels too tight, when I am quite literally out of my mind, awash on pulsing waves of pleasure.

I don't know what these nights mean to him. I've never asked. Although well acquainted with it, he's not here for my sparkling conversation.

The elevator doors open and with an expressionless face he indicates I should precede him. I put a little extra into my hips as I walk, knowing he is watching. After a moment I feel the heat of his body behind me and his large hand cups my bottom, part copping a feel and part guiding me to the right room.

He backs into the door as it's closing behind us, pulling me to him for the kiss I've been thinking about since he called. The first kiss of the night is always slow, intense, aching and, when his lips slide over mine, his mouth open, I let out a little gasp of longing. He doesn't kiss like a man desperate to fuck. He kisses like a man who knows I am his for the taking.

In these heels I don't have to tilt my head back to kiss him, nor does he have to bend all that far to capture my lower lip in his teeth. He has one arm wrapped around my waist, the other hand back on the nape of my neck. I palm his butt through the back pockets of his jeans, and while I wait to feel his tongue, I push against the erection straining at his zipper.

My reward for my eagerness is the slow slide of his tongue over mine. He likes me eager, but my willingness doesn't guarantee immediate response, let alone satisfaction. This knowledge makes me soft, pliant and so very, very hot. Without conscious thought I grind against him in time to the flickering licks. His fingers flex, then release, against the nape of my neck, and heat surges through me at this evidence of his desire.

Whatever loss of control I've wrested from him is momentary. His hands smooth down my back, over my bottom to my hips, where he tugs the tight fabric of my skirt up just enough to expose the lower curve of my ass. His fingernails scratch gently, once, twice. I shudder at the rough sensation, then he shimmies my lacy high-cut panties down to my upper thighs. One hand stays on my bottom while the other trails over my hip, through my trimmed curls, and into my cleft.

"Oh, Jesus," he whispers against my mouth.

I feel not one ounce of shame at how wet and swollen I am for him. My pussy lips spread easily and his fingers glide through my slick heat, up into my vagina. I muffle my cry against his neck, lick at the faintly salty skin just above his collar, feel his pulse pounding against my lips. He smells like Jack—like Heineken and summer sun, clean sweat and some indefinable male musk that is his alone.

His nose bumps my cheek as he turns his head; I open my eyes to see our reflection in the full-length mirror so thoughtfully placed by the door. I watch his hand move, slight shifts I feel inside me as well, as he presses the base of his thumb against my clit. My knees wobble in reaction to the sensation streaking through me. I am heat and light, wetness and aching desire, and right now the only thing keeping me on my feet is his firm hand on my bared ass.

He's going to get me off right here, in front of this mirror, against the hotel room door. Pulses of sharp heat zing ever faster from my clit to my nipples and back again, making my hips rock as I push, push, push against his hand. It's the most erotic thing I've ever seen, my red lacy panties stretched taut around my thighs, my skirt hiked up just above my mound, his tanned hand moving between my legs.

I brace my hands against his chest and let out a whimper at the sight, but he gentles me with a "shhhh" and then closes his teeth around my earlobe. A gasp huffs out of me at the pressure, the pain, so he bends his head and does it again, this time on the spot between my neck and shoulder. The fierce sting sends lightning arcing through my body, every nerve alive with electricity, and I come.

He holds me through it, his mouth open and wet just inside my collar, while I watch mirror-me shudder, open-mouthed, eyes half-closed, with each spasm around his fingers. Orgasm usually brings relief, a return to clarity, but not tonight. The ache subsides a bit, true, but the demand remains.

His tongue slides along my collarbone to the hollow of my throat, then up over my chin. He kisses me, his fingers moving again in time to his tongue in my mouth, and I moan.

"That wasn't enough," I whisper against his lips. They curve in response, but somehow I know it's not a smile, but the same fierce bared-teeth look he gave the bartender.

Slowly, achingly slowly, he pulls his fingers out of my body and unfastens the remaining buttons on my blouse.

"You want more?"

I hesitate, the taut expression on his face catching me off-guard.

"I'm waiting," he says, his voice a low, rough warning.

"Yes," I reply as he pushes my blouse off my shoulders and down my arms.

He considers my red lacy bra, and I know he's evaluating the visual pleasure of the boldly sexy lingerie versus my bared breasts. He doesn't continue the conversation, such as it is, while he unbuttons my skirt and reverses the progress it made, pushing it down over my bottom to pool on the carpet. In a move so surprising it hits me like a slap, he crouches at my feet and looks up at me while he pulls my panties back up my legs and returns them to their place on my hips.

The message is clear. I'm not getting fucked, at least for a while.

The tug of lace over my clit coupled with the slick pressure of his tongue up the midline of my body makes me shudder as he stands, back once more against the door. I'm still wearing my dark brown open-toe heels. My pale skin gleams in the setting sunlight streaming through the room's window, turning the lingerie into vermilion streaks on my skin.

He's fully dressed, the shadow on his jaw dull, raspy gold. When he looks into my eyes, his hand firmly cupping my chin, I see no sign of the man I know in his gaze.

"Earn it."

His words make my heart stop, then slam against my ribs before regaining rhythm. I know what he means. I reach under his sweater for his belt buckle, but he stops my hand.

"On your knees."

The command, no less authoritative for being almost soundless, slices into me like a cutting wheel along a sheet of glass. With a crack my mind splits, eradicating all thought from my brain.

I get on my knees, the industrial carpet leaving imprints in the skin. Heat flares in his eyes as he pulls his sweater over his head and drops it to the floor, then looks down to watch me unbuckle his belt, slide down his zipper. Forget men with guns or clenched fists; if there is an image more symbolic of male power and control than a man looking down on a woman kneeling in front him, I haven't seen it. His eyes flicker from my face to my image in the mirror and back again. I slide my palms into the waistband of his white cotton boxer briefs, the faint, familiar scent of detergent released by the heat of his body as I slide his shorts and jeans down just far enough to free his cock. As I do this he braces one forearm against the wall at shoulder height and threads the other hand into my hair. His thumb rubs over my temple. Our eyes meet. His are hard and fierce. Whatever he sees in mine makes him growl, "Fuck, yeah."

Earn it, he said, and earn it I will. The hot, dry skin stretched taut over his swollen cock brushes my cheek as I press a kiss into his lower belly, then his upper thigh, then his scrotum before I lean back and part my lips.

"Tongue first," he says.

My eyelids quiver and close helplessly before I drag them open again and use the flat of my tongue to paint his cock with broad strokes. I concentrate on the sensitive stretch right under the head, but neglect no portion of his rigid length. I lay my palms flat on his upper thighs. When the muscles there and in his abdomen tremble under my fingertips with each lick, I open my mouth and take him all the way to the back of my throat, the press and release of his fingers against the back of my skull setting the rhythm. As the pace quickens I look up at him, note his hand now fisted against the wall.

He guides my pace and makes it last, taking his pleasure from my lips and tongue, the warm, wet suction of my mouth, with a single-minded focus that makes me crazy with longing. Eventually, however, he rests his head on the rigid muscles in his forearm and, with a low groan, begins to thrust into my mouth. I back off just enough to keep from gagging, but the tightening fist in my hair keeps me close. In response, I moan around his stiff shaft.

He goes rigid under my hands, swells on my tongue mere

moments before the first pulse of semen hits the back of my throat. The harsh grunts and the involuntary jerks of his body only intensify the electric hum in my head. When the tension ebbs from his body, leaving him loose limbed against the door, I let him slip from my mouth and look up at him. My eyes are wet.

His fingers possessively caress my jaw before his thumb applies a slight pressure to my lower lip, then slips inside. I lick the pad of his thumb, listen to his breathing slow and soften.

"Very nice," he says. "Get on the bed."

I step out of my shoes, the uninspiring furnishings nothing but background chatter as I watch him yank the comforter and top sheet completely from the bed to create a wide playground of soft white cotton over a firm mattress. He points, and as the air conditioner emits its low hum, I stretch out on my side to watch him undress, a process that takes less than five seconds. Loafers kicked off, unbuckled belt and jeans shoved down, along with underwear, and he is naked before me.

Each time I see his body, all lean lines sculpted not by heavy muscles but rather by sinews under a thin layer of skin, I am reminded of how unnecessary physical size is to establish male power. I have yet to meet a man with Jack's presence, the commanding aura compelling and seductive. Until tonight, the air of command he radiates has been implicit, humming under the surface of our hotel liaisons. I've gone on my knees for him before, but never with such explicitly dominant overtones. Tonight, as the lingering musk on my tongue reminds me, I serviced him.

According to him, this means I've earned…something. Whatever he decides to give me. A savvier woman would have negotiated on her way down, but I'm not savvy. I'm a stained-glass artist, among other things. Besides, I know Jack won't disappoint me. That would be cutting his nose off to spite his face. Jack's here for the satisfaction of an orgasm, yes, but also for the darker pleasure of watching me shudder, helpless under him.

His warm hand grips my shoulder and rolls me to my back, then he shifts to lie beside me, a heavy thigh over mine to keep me where he wants me. For a long moment he stares into my eyes, and his orgasm has softened his features only slightly. Need roils under his skin. I know this, but it doesn't show in his face. He has a great poker face. Trial lawyers often do.

I, however, am unable to hide even the slightest emotion, especially when I'm alone with him, so I imagine that what I feel is what he can see in my expression. Desire. A hint of embarrassment, perhaps, in the heated flush on my cheeks and neck. Anticipation and uncertainty; those, too, flash through me and therefore across my face. But slowly the heat of his body against mine, the promise in his semierect cock, the weight of his leg pinning me to the bed, work their magic. Without thinking about it I wet my lower lip with my tongue. He watches, then looks down at my lace-covered breasts. My nipples harden under his scrutiny. Only then does he lift his hand from my lower belly, trail the tips of his fingers up over one breast and along the sensitive underside of my arm to lift and press my palm into the headboard.

He repeats the movement with my other arm, then kisses me. "Leave them there," he whispers. "They move, I stop."

In the moments between rising from the floor and now, the colors had begun to muddy again as reality retook my mind. It was a slow invasion, just a mental note to add an appointment to my to-do list, a brief moment when I tried to remember if I'd locked my car before entering the hotel. His words slammed the door on the mundane again, and I notice the yellow tint of the cream wallpaper, the burgundy glow of the drapes backlit by the sun.

I arch my back, testing my body in this position. My elbows are slightly bent, giving me leverage to push against his thigh, but then he straddles me, his weight braced on his elbows on either side of my shoulders, his thighs to the outside of mine. I moan at the demonic move. In this position, trapped under him, I can squeeze my thighs together and shimmy a little, but he knows that's not what I want. I want to spread my legs and rub against him like a cat in heat.

I'm not going to get that. What I do get is the weight of his body on mine as he kisses me, staking his claim on my mouth the way he will on my body, when he decides to. He draws my lower lip into his mouth, nibbles on the fullest part, kisses and licks his way over to the sensitive corner before detouring over my cheekbone to my ear. I am panting, mouth open, tongue flickering out to taste him on my lips. He comes back for another teasing bout, this time lapping at the edge of my lower lip, then the fullness of my upper lip, dodging my tongue.

When I lift my head and slant my mouth across his in an effort to get the full tongue kiss I am now desperate for, he laughs.

"No, baby." Shocking that his voice and words should be so intimate when he's denying me. Controlling me. "Not until I'm inside you."

"Anytime," I gasp.

"You're not ready," he whispers as he licks a trail down my throat to the pulse throbbing at the base of my neck.

I have soaked the crotch of my red lace panties and my clit is buzzing for contact: finger, tongue, pubic bone, his thigh, I don't care.

"I'm ready!"

"Baby, you're lukewarm right now. When you hit a rolling boil, I'll fuck you."

His words make me groan and lift against him, but he just laughs the way he never does outside this hotel room, hard and short, and lifts himself up on one hand to flick open the front clasp of my bra. Beginning at my breastbone, he presses open-mouthed kisses, full-tongue, the bastard, to every inch of my breast until he reaches the scalloped edge of my bra, drawn back almost to my nipple. He nudges the fabric back and I feel cool air, his heated gaze, then his teeth scrape over the tight bud. He laps at the underside of my nipple, then nips the swollen tip. I let out a high-pitched, shuddering gasp and he stiffens.

I open my eyes, ready to tell him he hasn't hurt me, but his concentration is elsewhere. A moment later conversation registers in my consciousness, the tone slightly shocked as it moves down the hallway.

They heard me. They heard that sound escape my throat, one that could only be construed as wanton, lascivious, and a part of me is horrified. My eyes meet Jack's heavy-lidded gaze, all masculine amusement.

"Don't make me gag you," he says, and suddenly silence becomes not a polite necessity, but a dark demand. His words crawl like molten lava through my brain and down my body. I might not be savvy, but I am strong and capable, and a bit ashamed by how well this works.

He returns his attentions to the eager peak. He is slow, methodical and relentless, without a care in the world as I clamp my lips together in submission. As he turns to my other breast, the first nipple swells and throbs in the cool air. I keep my hands pressed against the headboard, trying to breathe through my nose when I want to part my lips and gasp for air. Part my legs and beg for mercy.

He spreads his knees and rubs his now erect cock over my mound, the pressure tantalizingly seductive and maddeningly ineffectual. The rhythmic rasp of lace against skin and hair becomes a slow counterpoint to his infuriatingly even breathing and my own stifled whimpers.

I want to roll him and ride him, part my thighs so he can pound me into the mattress. I want to push his face between my legs and fist my hands in his hair to hold him in place. I want to *come*. And the wanting, the burning ache, grows without check as he pushes my breasts together and licks, then blows on, the superheated nipples. Back and forth, back and forth, coupled with a soul-destroying slide of erect cock and tight balls against my clenched thighs as he lengthens his thrusts over my mound. Need expands inside me, like the flutter of hundreds of hummingbird wings under my skin, with no release. I can't squirm. I can't touch him. I can't spread my legs or writhe, can't do anything except lie under him and take it. In silence.

Just when I think I'm going to lose my mind and scream for him to *do anything, please, fuck me now*, he sits back on his heels and works my panties down my thighs and off. He parts my legs and settles between them as if he has all the time in the world, while I hover on a plateau, the razor's edge of my orgasm just out of my reach. I'm unable to stop the low moan that wafts out of me as he spreads my legs wide. He strokes my inner thighs, lays a big palm on my trembling belly, and says, "Shhhhh. Shhhhhhh," over and over again until some of the tension eases from my muscles.

Nothing happens for several vibrating moments, and I lift my head to see him studying my pussy.

He looks up at me, his eyes somehow both feral and know-ing. "Beautiful. So pink and wet."

His breath wafts against my folds, which feel hot and wet, and also swollen. So very swollen. My clit feels three times its normal size. I drop my head back on the pillow and arch to-ward him, careful to keep my hands on the headboard.

He, of course, ignores my mute pleading. "You like this," he says, and I wonder if I can come from the pressure of his breath on my clit.

"Yes, Jack. I really, really like this." An incontrovertible truth, given the state of my cunt.

The reward for my admission is his tongue. He traces the outline of my folds, circles my clit once, then backs off again to lap and lick. The breadth of his shoulders holds me open for him, his hands deviously stroking my belly, my mound, occa-sionally dipping into the top of my sex, but never where I'm desperate for him to touch. My clit. My nipples. I have no idea how I can feel such brutal need when he's barely touching me.

He slides first one index finger, then the other, through my slick heat, and sucks my clit into his mouth at the same mo-ment his fingers, coated in my juices, reach up to pinch my nipples. He rolls the diamond-hard tips between his fingers and I draw tighter and tighter as pleasure streams between my nipples and pussy. I am there, I am so there, I can feel the chasm opening underneath me and I reach for his head because I love nothing more than to push against his mouth while the waves crest. But I can't find purchase in the sweat-dampened layers of his hair. My grasping fingers graze his stubbled cheek as he pulls away and the orgasm retreats.

"Oh, please, Jack...I'm sorry, I'm sorry," I babble, and I slap my hands back to the headboard. I'm ready to promise him anything, another blow job, sex bent over his desk at work, the elaborate chocolate soufflé he loves, whatever he wants, if he will just...

Oh, yes. *Yes.*

His tongue hardened to a point, he draws circles around my clit, the pressure better than nothing, but not enough, not quite enough. One hand leaves my breasts, and at least two fingers, maybe three, glide in and out of my pussy. Oh God, oh God—pinching my nipple and licking my clit and finger-fucking me and I cannot take another second of this, but I do, then another, then another because he demands it.

When he stops again I know it is possible to die from desire.

In one fluid motion he rises between my legs and claps his hand over my mouth to stifle my needy wail. I stiffen in shock at the rough treatment, but in the same movement his cock slides into my cunt. I am wet, but tight, and the measured thrust rasps along tortured nerve endings. I suck in what air there is behind his cupped fingers, then he moves his hand to grind his mouth against mine. When his pubic bone hits my clit, hard, I go rigid in anguished ecstasy. In that long, terrible moment when I am strung out so tightly I don't know if I can come but know I'll die if I don't, I feel every excruciating detail of the head of his cock tugging against my swollen channel as he withdraws, then rams home. His tongue sweeps into my mouth.

I implode. My vision goes black, and the heavy weight of him, the pressure and possession of his cock, focuses every molecule in my being into a whirling vortex between my thighs. In the next moment white-hot, eradicating sensation pulses out from the dark, secret place where we are joined. I shudder, and shudder again, draw breath and scream into his mouth as he strokes through the convulsions.

When I go limp, he is still hard within me. I am nothing

but nerves and skin, swollen breasts and throbbing pussy, and the only thing keeping me from dissolving through the sheet, into the mattress, is the rigid length of his cock and the purely feminine urge to cling to his hard body.

Jack finds a gentlemanly impulse somewhere and lets me rest for a minute, but the scrape of his teeth along the sensitive tendon in my neck lets me know we are not done.

"I can't," I whisper in protest, my voice a raspy husk in the cool room. Sunlight streams through the window, a weak imitation of the light and heat radiating from our bodies.

"Feel that?" he asks, and thrusts again.

My legs found their way around the small of his back when he entered me. I let them down, the muscles trembling sporadically. I have no answer. I'm open and under him, completely at his command. Of course I can feel it.

He slides his palm along the back of my thigh and lifts it to press into his hip. Another slow stroke as he growls, "You're gonna take care of that."

In a move that looks like denial but is simply another stage in the surrender he demands, I turn my head to the side. He responds by blowing gently into the shell of my ear, nuzzling my neck, then licking and nibbling at the sensitive, delicate juncture of neck and shoulder. He doesn't move, doesn't use my body, which is thoroughly his right now, simply takes his weight onto his elbows, and makes love to my collarbone.

I breathe in slow, deep inhales redolent of sweat, Jack's own unique scent, the musky tang of sex, my delicate perfume, a faint hint of Heineken. The smells are seduction in their own right, even without his deft ability to find and exploit every nerve. He could be banging away; God knows he's hard and thick, ready to drive nails. Instead, he acts with the self-control of a man with a purpose.

There is another session coming. I can feel that in the air as surely as I feel the soreness in my thighs, so I take the respite he's giving me. I breathe deeply, soften a little from the heat and weight of his body, stroke my hands over his curve of his ass. I rest in the colors flowing in discrete streams through my empty mind.

Moments pass, minutes or an hour, I cannot tell. But eventually he has marked the skin over my shoulders and the base of my neck with nips, soothed it with licks, and the weight of his pelvis against mine rekindles the heat in my pussy. His mouth settles over mine for long, languid open-mouthed kisses, the ones I wanted so intensely before he went down on me. I arch into him, feel our damp skin sliding as we shift. In this room, kissing like that means a lengthy fucking; when this is over, I will feel the ache in my thighs for days. Jack doesn't hesitate to use me hard.

He slides one arm under the small of my back, lifts me with him as he sits upright and swings his legs over the foot of the bed to place his feet flat on the floor. I straddle him, my hair hanging in sweaty strands in my face, and grip his forearms as I orient myself.

"I like this," he says. "You do all the work, and I watch." He looks over my shoulder as he says this, cupping my bottom in his hands and moving me up and down on his cock. I risk a quick glance over my shoulder and see we're visible in the mirror above the low dresser. His hands are dark, curved around the pale cheeks of my ass marked by my bikini tan line just below the twin dimples at the base of my spine. He moves me again, and his cock, flushed a deep red and slick with my juices, appears as I rise on my knees, and disappears as I take him inside me, deeper than before. The sensitive skin of my lower cheeks brushes his balls.

The sight makes me moan. I turn back to face him, mightily embarrassed. Experience has taught me Jack can last a good long time in this position, without the primitive thrill of pounding into me. His hips still under my movements mean I'll get the penetration I crave, the repeated action of his cock spreading open my pussy to seat itself deep inside me, without him losing control. And he'll talk to me, that wicked, wicked voice ordering me to move to please him. He'll watch my breasts bounce, my cleft spread wide to take him again and again and again.

I smooth my hands up his arms, feel a surprising quiver in his biceps before coming to rest on his shoulders, for balance. I'm entirely open to him, my breasts, belly, clit, and ass available. Vulnerable. The same slashing excuse for a smile flashes in his face as he cups my breasts, then slides his hands down over my hips.

My eyes flutter closed as I focus on how he wants me to move. The rhythm is slow, a little pause at the top so I can feel the head of his cock caress my pussy lips, then back down to seat him fully inside me. His hard abdomen grinds against my clit on each down stroke. As I catch on, his hands lose their proprietary grip on my hips and begin to roam. I look down to see his tanned fingers, the hair dusting the backs of his knuckles bleached a pale blonde, stroke over my breasts, along my ribs, over the swell of my hips and ass, then reverse course and move back. He loves the softness of my body, and when I am with him like this, I feel truly beautiful.

I'm watching him, but his eyes are focused on the mirror. The image of my pale skin against his darker body, the sheer eroticism of what I'm doing, is burned into my memory so

I don't need to look over my shoulder again. I do anyway, catch his eyes in the mirror, my darker hair falling in tousled waves over my face. A hot red flush stains his cheekbones. His hands clench on my bottom, and I feel him throb inside me.

"Fuck. The look in your eyes."

I don't recognize myself. The body is mine. I see my hair, the shape of my shoulders, the nip of my waist, but the woman I usually see when I look in the mirror is gone. In her place is a succubus, her eyes incandescent with lust. When our eyes meet Jack shifts a little under me, groans and clenches his fingers into my ass, lifts his hips to get a little closer, a little deeper. My breasts chafe against his chest and the tug of my nipples against his skin makes me ripple around him.

Each slow thrust is now torture for both of us.

With every prolonged withdrawal and penetration the burn heightens, grows, pushes everything else aside. Jack is thick, so thick, inside me. I rest my forehead on his, my breath easing from me in soft little pants. His tongue flickers over mine, retreats, then returns. All worries about appearing needy or clingy disappear and I slant my open mouth across his.

He groans again and tightens one arm around my hips. Because I love the restraint I resist this, fighting to rise to the top of his cock. As I rise he struggles to force me back down onto his cock, but I have his number now. When he would keep me snugged up against his pelvis, I force myself back up, rising despite the iron strength of his arm, merely clasping the tip of his cock when he would have me hot and slick around his aching shaft. His legs spread wider and he pushes off with his powerful thighs. His tongue is dancing in my mouth, harsh grunts ripping from his throat as I tease him. I have brought him to the point of orgasm, and the heady power makes me laugh.

His hands grip my hips to pull me down hard against him, so deep inside his balls press against my ass. I expect to feel his release pulse into me, marking me. I'm hovering on the edge of my own orgasm and I twitch in anticipation of the moment his hands relax, intending to sneak a couple of thrusts, heighten his release and send myself over the edge. But his fingers remain firmly clamped around my hips, and I let out a soft groan as I swivel on him, trying to rub my clit against him. When I find I cannot move, I open my eyes.

"Did you think that would work, baby?"

I go utterly still at his smile-that-isn't-a-smile, the dark power in his eyes, the sweat gleaming on his chest and darkening his hair at his temples. I tried to play him, but he won. My cunt spasms around his cock. I don't answer, but he doesn't push. He knows.

"Take your claws out of my shoulders and hand me that case." He nods behind me.

Oh, God. I've actually embedded my short, blunt nails into smooth skin and hard muscle. When I lift my fingers he shrugs then rolls his head on his neck, and I realize he's used the mild sting to focus on holding back...the better to torture me. Slightly off-balance I look over my shoulder again and for the first time notice a black leather shaving kit, the one he uses when he travels, on the low dresser.

I have a fairly good idea what's in it.

I brace one hand on his knee and reach for the kit with the other. The movement seats him even more deeply inside me and I gasp as my outstretched fingers grab the kit. He slides one hand up my back to help me upright again, and I offer him the case.

As casually as if we were seated at a table in a fancy restaurant, not naked and sweating and engaged in a power play in an anonymous hotel room, he sets the black bag between our stomachs and unzips it. He removes lube and a dildo, not nearly his girth but big enough to my widening eyes.

We've played those games before, but only with fingers, never with toys, and certainly not with these dark undercurrents ebbing and flowing in the room. While I'm much the same person in this room and outside of it, he's different here. Harder. Less likely to give quarter. Over the past few months he's taken me places I hadn't acknowledged I wanted to go. I never asked him to orchestrate elaborate evenings at an expensive hotel. Somehow he knew, just as he knew this lay in the back of my clouded mind.

But that's why I'm here. The colors coalesce for one brilliant, shattering moment.

"Jack?" I barely hear the word, almost inaudible over the hum of the air conditioner.

He looks me straight in the eye. I've always loved that about him; he doesn't dissemble or cajole or shy away from his demands. He makes me stand toe to toe with him and either face my own desires, or back down.

"You can take this."

As he says the blunt words, he's looking in my eyes; I don't know what he sees there because I don't have words for whatever I'm feeling. Colors, perhaps, a deep, intense violet swirled with velvety chocolate-brown. A blue the hue of twilight. When I don't protest, don't even respond, he matter-of-factly works the lube into my pucker, smears a bit more on the dildo, then positions it, his eyes intent on our reflection in the mirror.

Heat flashes through my aching pussy.

"Spread, baby," he says, but he's not asking and that makes me even hotter. He widens his legs. My bent knees rest beside his hips, the tops of my feet braced on his thighs, my nails once again digging into his shoulders. He cannot sink any deeper into my swollen channel and I'm now totally vulnerable to him.

He's still looking at my face, unapologetic, and there is no hint of quarter in his dark eyes. If I can't handle his demands I am the one who must halt our play. My implicit, unquestioned trust in Jack stems from the fact that from our first time together I've been able to say no, always. I simply don't.

The pressure increases slowly, patiently. Jack never rushes, not even on the night fifteen years ago when he took my virginity in the more conventional sense. The head of the dildo expects entrance to my ass, but without meaning to I'm resisting. His free hand leaves my hip and slides into my damp curls to find my clit. Three liquid strokes, a shocking counterpoint to the insistent push against my ass, and I quiver, sensation leaping through me. I soften, relax and the head slides in, just a bit, just enough to make my eyes widen.

I clench my fingers into his shoulders and while the tip of his finger continues to caress my clit with a feather-light touch, the dildo's progress ceases immediately. Sensation, however, does not, but rather beats under my skin. My heart is thundering in all my pulse points, the rhythm a deep violet, and my nipples are throbbing caps on my breasts. Heavy electricity is collecting in my groin, sparks firing in my clit, in the stretched nerves of my passage and in the tight ring of muscle about to be unquestionably breached for the first time. Between the rhythmic stroke of his finger, the unceasing demand of his thick cock in my pussy and the heated promise of the dildo, tendrils of pleasure are weaving a net, dragging me into a whirlpool of desire.

I want this. He's given me a taste. Now I want it all.

"Please," I say, and while he makes no noise, I see his lips form the word *fuck*. Jack is eloquent. Fluent in Latin and French. My surrender has reduced him to single syllables of Anglo-Saxon origin.

The pressure against my pucker is now a demand, and I wince as the head pops past the ring of muscle. At the same time, however, my cunt spasms from his wickedly knowledgeable attentions to my clit, and the line between pleasure and pain blurs, then disappears. I arch into his finger, inadvertently clasping the dildo, and oh, it feels so good. He works it in and out, shallow, easy thrusts that glide over astonished nerve endings and send pleasure expanding through me. And while his cock is stationary in my pussy, the dildo creates a heightened sense of fullness, each stroke contracting me around his shaft.

"Look," he says, his normally smooth, even voice a harsh rasp. "Look in the mirror."

I peer over my shoulder to watch him fuck me in the ass with a sex toy. My dark hair hangs in sweaty tangles around my flushed face, and the length of my spine reminds me of a string of pearls. The curves of my ass, round and even and perfectly matched are far less pure than pearls, though, as is the carnal image of the lifelike shaft working me over. I stare in shock, then my eyes meet Jack's in the mirror. Connection arcs electric and visceral between us and suddenly need sears me. I can't keep still anymore. I rise and fall, impaling myself on both his hard flesh and the dildo.

He's got one hand on my clit and the other on the toy; I'm balanced on his lap but using the strength in his shoulders to keep myself upright as I gyrate under his fierce gaze, back arched, reaching for it. The ache balloons, bursts, then collapses in on itself. I come in a wild surge of colors so sharp and jagged I envision only the shattering of an intricate, sunlit window.

"Fucking amazing," he growls when my shudders cease. "So goddamn tight. The friction…"

Heated images explode in my mind—of the dildo stroking my forbidden passage but also of his cock. It's too much; I sag against his chest as he seats the dildo firmly in my ass, then grips my upper arms. In a tumble of light and color I find myself on my back, arms flung over my head, legs spread and shaking from the strain as Jack looms over me. He hooks my knees over his elbows and leans forward, bracing his hands by my ribs. Before I can catch my breath, even anchor myself in the world, I feel the blunt tip of his shaft against my slit. He pushes in, stopping when I quiver, whimper.

"Look at me."

My eyes fly open to find him looming over me, fierce need etched in the lines of his face. I see anguished lust, aching desire, and find the ground I need to take this, to take the fucking he has been promising me from the moment he called. My body softens as I reach that ultimate surrender. There isn't a particle of resistance left in me. He groans as he plunges in, all the way to the hilt.

The dildo forces his cock against the top wall of my pussy, and with each stroke he rasps over my G-spot in a way that lights me up from within. In moments I'm surging under him, writhing as bolt after bolt of sensation sizzles along nerves already raw and vulnerable. I dig my nails into his biceps and lift my hips for more. His control is tenuous, edgy as he pounds into me. I feel his cock swell, his rhythm grow erratic, but to my utter disbelief I am there, I am there. I sink my teeth into his shoulder as all color, all noise disappears from my head. All that remains is white light and silence as I shatter. Vanish.

★ ★ ★

When I re-form, return to the hotel room, he is poised above me, teeth bared in a fierce grimace as he fights his own release while thrusting strongly because he knows the strokes prolong mine. Our eyes meet, and now I'm not the only one naked and surrendering. As he balances on the razor's edge of pleasure and pain, I lay my palms against his cheeks and pull his mouth down to mine. His lips tremble, open and wet, as he drives deep into my body, each thrust strong enough to make the flesh of my breasts quiver with the impact. I take them, one after the other, whispering into his mouth what he knows, has always known.

"I love you. I love you. I love you."

A hoarse groan rumbles out of him as he braces himself on his palms and jets into me. His head drops forward. Sweat drips onto my cheek and collarbone as he jerks, gives a shallow thrust, shudders again. With a softer groan he eases down onto his elbows. After a long, long while his breathing evens out.

My mind is a flawless pane of glass through which streams brilliant, pure white light as I lie underneath him, our breathing slowly coming together, his exhales wafting over my ear, mine softer, quicker against his shoulder. A minute passes, perhaps two, then he shifts his weight to the right. His fingers tremble as they trail down my belly; the muscles jump under my skin at his touch, then I gasp as he slides his hand between my legs to remove the dildo. I feel empty, yet replete.

Without a word he slides off the bed, scrubs his hands through his sweat-dampened hair, then begins to dress. Underwear, jeans, the sweater he retrieves from beside the door, then in a gesture so familiar it makes my heart turn over, he pushes his sleeves to his elbows while he scuffs into his shoes. His hands on his hips, he surveys me for a long moment and I cannot help but think of the respectable woman who walked into the Embassy Suites bar two hours earlier. I am boneless, flushed and quivering, coated in sweat (his and mine), juices (his and mine), and I couldn't stand if my life depended on it. A smile too masculine to be smug flashes across his face. He bends over, braces his hands on the bed and drops a quick kiss on my lips.

"I'll call you," he says. The door opens, then closes behind him.

Ten minutes later I've recovered enough to think about a shower when the door opens to admit Jack, an overnight case in one hand, the key in the other. As he tosses the key on the dresser he offers me a sweet smile, the one that makes his ordinary face magical in my eyes. I prop myself up on one elbow and smile back.

"Your mother texted. The kids are in bed. She'll take them to early services tomorrow and we can pick them up after brunch."

With the trip to his car my dark, demanding lover has disappeared and my husband is back. I don't mind. The rasp of the cotton against my tender nipples is a delicious, sufficient reminder of my night with a stranger.

"Mmmmm…I can sleep in," I purr as he sets the case down on the luggage stand.

"Not too late," he replies, his voice gone hard again despite the smile. The incongruence makes me giggle.

When Jack first took our children to spend the night at my mother's and called me from the Embassy Suites bar, I was so sure someone had the wrong number I had to double check the caller ID on my cell phone. Eleven years into our marriage, the demands of his job coupled with the day-to-day tedium of stay-at-home motherhood had left me fractured and irritable. I wasn't working in my studio, but I was picking fights. Frequently.

One night, after a particularly bitter argument over something I can't remember but which was probably stupid, like dirty socks on the floor, he asked me in a weary tone what I wanted. Equally weary, I told him that I wanted to stop thinking for a while. I wanted to forget the laundry, doctor's appointments, meals, where his badge or keys or glasses were, whether I'd bought enough fish crackers for snack at Katie's preschool, the dog's incomprehensible urge to vomit only on the new living room carpet, all of it. I wanted to stop being responsible for just a couple of hours, and I really, really wanted to fuck more frequently than every few weeks.

He sits on the bed and strokes my damp hair. "Thinking already?"

I smile up at him. "No."

Trial attorneys are often very good actors, and Jack reads unspoken, barely acknowledged cues with experience honed in improv theater and the courtroom. He read what was underneath my impossible demands, because we both knew his eighty-hour-a-week schedule left no room for laundry or snack duties. I didn't want help around the house. I wanted to be transported to another dimension, if only for a few hours. He couldn't buy Goldfish crackers, but he could restore brilliance to hues and shut off my mind. I have no idea what it was about the unique, incessant demands of motherhood that made me crave surrendering to him in bed, and I have no idea how he knew what I barely knew myself, but when he gets this hotel room and strips me of the last shred of my control, I light up like a summer thunderstorm. The lashing, explosive releases give me what I need to go back to the routine, and back into the studio. For days after we meet, images flow through my mind and into the glass. My work is subtly changing. That artistic growth brings me almost as much pleasure as those moments when I become nothing but white light and his cock inside me.

"Want to shower together?" he asks.

I nod.

"Go start the water. I'll call room service."

Still unusually pliant, I nod but lay my left hand on his jeans-clad thigh, my bare ring finger a gentle reminder. His cheeks crease into a smile as he winks at me, then he digs in his front pocket and extends his palm. Gold and diamonds flash as the rings tumble and tink against each other. I select his wedding band and slide it onto his left ring finger. The remaining three rings are mine. My wedding band goes on first, the one Jack put on my finger eleven years before and I take off only while I'm in my studio. Next is the tiny engagement ring he could afford at nineteen, then the sizable diamond eternity band he gave me for our tenth anniversary. We have forged a life together, and without these rings I feel unsettled, like I have left the oven on or forgotten to lock the door on the way to the airport. Being without them heightens the reality of the experience. I am not his wife, not the mother of his children. I am simply *his*.

Married sex is the best sex. Married sex is the thrill of meeting for a hookup or a one-night stand in a hotel, but without any of the risk. It's finding your sexual being again after two kids, a mortgage and payments on cars that smell of stale French fries. Tomorrow morning, before we pick up our children, we will make love in this room as Mr. and Mrs. John Underwood, and it will be good.

In a few weeks the colors in my head will begin to dull, to

clash with one another. Jack will know. One Saturday he'll half bully, half cajole me into the studio then disappear with the kids. My rings will be in his pocket. He'll call when I least expect it. I will likely be grasping for clarity through muddy colors and sloppy lines when my cell phone chirps.

"Meet me at the Embassy Suites bar in an hour," he'll say, his familiar voice not quite his own.

And I will.

★ ★ ★ ★ ★

VEGAS HEAT
LISA RENEE JONES

CHAPTER ONE

Thick raven hair. Intelligent chocolate-brown eyes. Perfectly honed body accented by a well-tailored, outrageously expensive suit. Dante Ricci, the thirty-four-year-old heir to the Ricci Fashion empire, dripped sex and money. A fantasy for women, an idol for most men. And he'd chosen her. Sonya Miller. A choice that had delivered to her the task of discovering what pleased him, of ensuring his satisfaction.

Attorney Sonya Miller sat across from him now, her hands primly folded on the shiny mahogany conference table of one of Vegas's top law firms, not nearly as unaffected by Dante as she would have liked to be. But then, she was quickly learning he had a way of looking at a woman few other men did. A way of casting an attentive inspection that seeped through one's pores, a way of listening that seemed to drink in every word spoken. The man just plain refused to go unnoticed. Not even by her, a woman who kept her professional and personal desires devoutly divided. A woman who never mixed business with pleasure.

And this wasn't about pleasure, not one bit. No matter how

much he made her want it to be. This was about him, a high-profile potential client, requesting her as counsel, not one of the senior partners. At twenty-eight, only three years out of law school, this was more than a compliment. It was a much-needed feather in her cap. The one that might finally earn her the "partner" title she'd fought so diligently to achieve. That her seventy-hour workweeks and a recent win against the city that had earned a client a cool three million hadn't done the job was a bitter pill to swallow.

Regardless of the reward Dante's interest might offer, Sonya listened to his business needs with genuine interest that extended beyond any gain, enthralled by his plans. She clung to his every word as he explained his intention to expand the Ricci name through the heart of Vegas, branding it with his mark, his claim to fame.

Sonya kept her tone as prim and professional as her long blond hair, which was pinned conservatively at the back of her head, despite her excitement over this new project of Dante's. "Acquiring three major casino properties and then re-creating them is a high stakes venture, Mr. Ricci." Her voice lifted despite her best efforts to contain the eagerness she felt to earn this challenge. "But it's also an exciting venture I'd love to sink my teeth into." She enjoyed corporate law, the negotiations, the edge of knowing the right play at the right time. "I sincerely hope you'll do more than consider us as counsel. We won't let you down."

Sonya's boss, Michael Roberson, sat by her side, gaze fixed on Dante with his own form of lusty inspection—the kind born of dollar signs. "We're confident we can deliver results," he assured Dante, his diamond-studded cuff link catching in the lights above. His dark hair was cut short and neatly styled, his face smooth-shaven. "No other firm in this city has the diversity of skill that we do. Anything that can be thrown our way, we can handle."

Dante offered him a cool reply. "Frankly," he said, his stare direct as he spoke to Michael, "I rarely choose a large firm. Too many chances to be handed off in the midst of miscommunication. My confidence is not in this firm, though I'm aware of your respectable reputation." Dante's gaze shifted to Sonya. A gaze so warm, so rich with inspection, she felt as if he could see every intimate detail covered by her conservative light blue blazer. "It's in Ms. Miller." His lips lifted ever so slightly. "I saw you on the news a few nights ago. Quite a victorious courtroom showing."

"Thank you," she said, proud of her win, proud of the tears and sweat she'd put into achieving success, but unsettled by the flutter of ridiculous awareness in her stomach, the heat in his eyes becoming hard to ignore. Why, she didn't know. Arrogant, rich men were plentiful enough in her profession to give her perspective enough to know they were trouble. Arrogant, attractive rich men, like Dante Ricci, were bigger trouble. Without hesitation, Sonya left those types of men for other women to fawn over and please. Except this man, she thought. She couldn't leave him for others to please. He'd become hers for now, hers to please, and trying to block out the sultry images that idea produced, she delicately cleared her throat and added, "It was an exciting accomplishment." She met and held his gaze, never wavering despite the intimate way the contact stroked her inside out, the way she felt the connection in every inch of her body.

"We're quite proud of Sonya," Michael commented.

"You should be," Dante said, flicking Michael what appeared to Sonya to be an irritated look, as he added, "Because mark my word, she's why I'm here. She's hungry for success."

He shifted his attention back to her, his eyes warm with re-gard. "Exactly what I'm looking for. Understand that I'll need a great deal of services. There will be contracts to negotiate on many levels once the properties are secure. There will be a local management operation to set up as well. All the more reason for me to be clear. If I sign a retainer with your firm it will be under the condition that she and I can come to terms that place her as my lead counsel." His cell phone buzzed, shaking on top of the table where he'd set it. He reached for it and punched a button, eyed a text message and sighed. "I'm afraid I must depart." Regret laced his tone as he glanced at her. "Sonya." He said her name softly, a silky play along her nerve endings that stroked her into attention. Damn it, the man got to her when he should not! He continued, "Do you know Parr's Restaurant inside Bell's Hotel and Casino?"

"No," she said, her throat thick, deciding her lack of inter-est in the casino scene might be best left unspoken. "I'm a bit of a workaholic. I don't get out much."

His gaze narrowed ever so slightly. "We'll have to fix that," he said, again his voice low, his words spoken to her as if Mi-chael wasn't present. "Parr's personifies the concept I intend to embrace with this new venture."

"Which is what concept exactly?" she asked, knowing it was the expected reply and that the answer was going to be a loaded one.

"Divine pleasure," he drawled. "Every desire made possible, if only for a few days a year while on vacation." His words, his eyes, his very presence seemed a warm caress with those words. "The atmosphere at Parr's is elegant, the dishes served like art masterpieces. It is an exploration of the senses—taste, touch, smell. That is what I want each of my casinos to offer."

Sonya felt her lips part, felt the ache of awareness in every

single inch of her body. There was something about this man
that reached right inside her and made her melt. She ached
with awareness that defied her professional role. She squeezed
her legs together and willed the feeling to ease, to no avail.
"It sounds like a success waiting to be found."

He pushed to his feet and Michael instantly followed. Sonya
stood as well, smoothing her hand down the slim-cut skirt of
her light blue suit. "I'd like to finish this conversation over
dinner at Parr's," Dante said, clearly speaking to Sonya. He
was tall, broad, more dominant than ever, his very demeanor
saying he wouldn't take no for an answer, as he added, "Perhaps by morning we can have this contracted."

Sonya inhaled slowly, a warning going off in her head.
Alone with this man in a place he defined as "divine pleasure"
did not seem like a smart move. The look in his eyes, the heat
lancing her from their depths, said she better set limits and do
it fast—and not just for Dante...for herself, too. "It's Wednes-
day. If it's possible, I'd like to clear my desk and finish up a
case. I could be ready by Monday and devote myself to your
needs." The minute she said those words, she knew they were
wrong, and only practiced cool kept her from flushing red.

His eyes danced with mischief. "As appealing as your devo-
tion to my needs is, Sonya, I think we still have a few things
to discuss before I'm confident I can put my vision in your
hands."

"Don't worry about your desk," Michael said. "Any help
you need will be offered. Focus on Mr. Ricci's plans and the
rest can be diverted to another attorney."

Dante arched a brow at Sonya, an obvious challenge that
said he knew she was sidestepping being alone with him.
"What time should I be there?" she asked, her tone cool and
collected when she felt anything but.

He smiled his approval and rounded the conference table. "I'll have a car pick you up at seven." His hand extended to hers.

Sonya steeled herself for the impact of his touch before sliding her palm against his. "Seven sounds excellent," she said, her voice softer than she intended, the heat of his fingers closing around hers, stealing her breath.

Seconds passed that felt like hours, his hand over hers, their eyes locked. "Bring your contract," he said. "Perhaps before the night is over, we can toast to a signed agreement."

She believed his reasons for choosing her for counsel. No smart business person, and Dante was that and more, chose an attorney based on attraction. She wanted to toast a signed agreement. This agreement, this man, held the key that could finally lead her to her goals. Years of working two jobs to get through college, of piles of bills that had built up while her mother had recovered from a brutal car accident, came down to Dante Ricci. A man who was the only client that had ever made her want more than a contract. But it didn't matter what she wanted. The temptation he represented, no matter how alluring, was a forbidden one, a path to career suicide. Dante Ricci was off-limits outside pure business.

And that judgment was final.

CHAPTER TWO

It was seven o'clock on the dot when the limo Dante's secretary had set up in advance pulled to the curb of Sonya's office building. She shoved open the door and exited into the hot July night, not about to give the uncharacteristic nerves fluttering in her stomach a chance to take root. Nerves that she was all too aware were a product of hours of inappropriate, but oh-so-delicious fantasies about what "divine pleasure" might be with a man like Dante Ricci. She needed to prove to herself, and perhaps to Dante, that this was business and nothing more. She was pretty sure it was time to get a social life. Heck, the closest thing she'd had to a date in a year was her friend/neighbor/sometimes bedroom buddy that had taken a job in New York and left.

The driver, a gray-haired slender man she guessed to be in his fifties, quickly rounded the hood of the vehicle to help her with the door. "I hope we didn't keep you waiting too long, Ms. Miller," he said, sounding quite formal.

"Sonya," she said, noting that he either logically guessed her identity, or Dante was inside the car and had told him.

The tingling heat sliding down her spine said it was the latter. "And I just arrived moments before you pulled up."

He inclined his head. "Jeffrey," he said and pulled open the door. "The ride is short but if you need anything at all, I'm at your service."

"Thank you," she said, thinking the only thing she needed was for Dante to suddenly become a rude jerk, and therefore unappealing. Since she doubted Jeffrey had such a skill in his arsenal of services, she discreetly drew a calming breath and let it out, willing to bet that she was about to be in a highly intimate space with her highly appealing new client.

She slipped her briefcase/purse combination over her shoulder and did her best to hold her skirt in place as she slid inside. The scent of leather and spicy masculine cologne teased her senses even before she brought Dante into focus.

"Mr. Ricci," she said as she maneuvered a bit to tug her skirt down to about midthigh and squeezed her knees primly together. To Dante's credit, he was a gentleman and kept his eyes on her face, while she, on the other hand, couldn't help but notice his jacket was missing and his chest and shoulders flexed impressively beneath his finely tailored button-down shirt. "I wasn't sure you'd be here or if you were meeting me at the restaurant."

"Call me Dante," he said.

"Dante," she repeated. "And please, call me Sonya."

Jeffrey shut the door, sealing them in the small space that was every bit as intimate as she'd expected it to be. Seconds ticked by in silence, the air crackling with the kind of instant electricity that only happened when two people shared wicked hot, inescapable chemistry.

"Sonya," he repeated finally in a voice as rich and sultry as Godiva dark chocolate. And she liked her Godiva dark chocolate way too much for her own good, just like this man. "And I came along for the ride," he continued, "in case you needed further persuasion to join me for the evening."

She narrowed her gaze on him, reading the message beneath his words. "You thought I was going to back out?"

"You hesitated to accept my invitation," he said, his brown eyes as rich with intelligence as his voice was with sensuality. "It seemed a good bet that you might decide to cancel."

"My boss would have had a conniption fit."

"Otherwise you might have?"

"I'm not beyond admitting that I considered calling you and asking you to reconsider tonight's meeting."

Surprise at her frankness flickered across his handsome, chiseled features. "Because you don't want my business?"

"I do want your business," she said. "Very much. And I'm both flattered and thrilled that you would believe in me enough to ask for me as your lead counsel."

"Then why would you cancel this dinner?"

She opened her mouth and then shut it, before saying, "I'm not completely sure I know the answer to that."

"Try."

Try. She should have seen that one coming. "You have to know that your account could make, or break, my career. You said we needed to discuss some points before you signed with me."

"I'd think that would make you eager for this meeting."

"I know what to expect in an office or courtroom setting. I don't know what to expect in a Vegas hotel where you intend to show me your version of 'divine pleasure.'"

He studied her a long moment without a word, or so much as a twitch. "Do you have the contract I reviewed earlier today with you?"

"Yes, of course," she said. "You want to see it now?"

"Yes."

She quickly retrieved a file from her briefcase she'd set on the seat beside her and offered it to him.

"And a pen?" he asked.

"You're going to sign now?"

"You have a problem with that?"

"Not at all." She offered him her pen and watched as he signed every spot indicated and then removed a checkbook and wrote out a check before asking, "I thought you needed to talk to me about some particulars before you did this?"

He offered her the pen back. "I do, so let's talk. Several conditions apply to this agreement being final. Number one, I don't deal with Michael. I don't trust the man and you better watch your back with him. I've already told him this, but I need you to know this as well."

"You told Michael you don't trust him?"

"Yes. And I told him that you will be responsible for co-ordinating everything for these acquisitions, no matter how big or small, period. The end."

She bit her lip, trying not to smile. She liked Dante more every second. Michael *was* such an arrogant, mean person, with more of a god complex than her mother's surgeon, whom she'd mistakenly dated for all of one week. "I can only imagine how he must have reacted."

"By silently cursing me and actually believing I couldn't see it all over his face." He held out the file with the check on top. "Back to you and me. If we're in agreement with my terms then it's official. You're my counsel."

"Thank you," she said, meaning it. Not only had he given her the opportunity of a lifetime, but he also hadn't made her walk on eggshells all evening. "I meant what I said earlier today. I won't let you down." She reached for the file.

He covered her hand with his, his brown eyes darkening to nearly black. "I hope this means you can enjoy tonight without worry."

Her heart skipped a beat at the words, at the idea of spending hours with this man, being tempted by him. She could have sworn fire slid up her arm and across her breasts. "Yes. Absolutely. Not many clients would do that, either. They'd leave me hanging and on edge."

"I hope I surprised you in a good way then," he said, and leaned back in his seat before knocking on the glass behind him. The car began to move immediately. He punched a button that opened a folding compartment in the floor between them that had an ice bucket and open bottle of champagne on top. "You, by the way, surprise me, and that's not something that happens all that often." He filled one of the two flutes sitting on the tray.

"I surprise you? How?"

He leaned forward to offer her a flute, and she accepted it, her fingers brushing his and sending a shiver of pure awareness down her spine. "You don't tell me what I want to hear," he said. "When I asked if you almost backed out tonight, you didn't pretend otherwise. That kind of frank honesty isn't common in business." He reached for the other flute and touched it to hers. "Let's toast to new beginnings."

She swallowed hard. "I have a confession."

One dark brow arched. "A confession." He leaned back slightly, studying her. "Already?"

"It's important," she said. "For both our protection."

"I'm listening."

"I'm a lightweight when it comes to drinking and I haven't

eaten all day. So if I drink this then one of two things is going to happen. The best-case scenario is that I remember nothing about tonight and most likely make a fool of myself. Worst-case, you'll have to pick me up off the floorboard because I pass out."

His lips twitched. "That's your confession?"

She nodded. "Afraid so."

His smile was instant and it was a sexy smile. Everything about the man was sexy. "While I wouldn't hesitate to pick you up if you fell," he said, "we'll postpone our toast until after dinner." He set both flutes aside. "Because I most definitely want you to remember tonight."

CHAPTER THREE

The ride to the Bell's Hotel and Casino, which was one of the most elegant understated properties in the city, was a short ten minutes by highway. Exactly the reason that Sonya wasn't surprised to find Parr's restaurant to be dimly lit, with a large seating area visible from the entryway and fine art decorating the walls. The floor was an expensive bamboo wood covered with even more expensive oriental rugs. It was just another fancy Vegas hotspot, aside from one unique feature. There were six equally spaced, winding black steel staircases on either side of the sitting area.

The hostess, a pretty brunette in a long black dress that might have been conservative if not for the way it hugged every curve she owned, which were many, greeted Dante by name.

"Mr. Ricci," she said with a smile. "So nice to have you back with us tonight." She glanced at her book sitting on top of the hostess stand and then back at Dante. "You're in 'gold' tonight I see, and since I know you know your way around, I'll let Nicholas know you've arrived."

"Excellent," he said and slid his hand to Sonya's back, splaying his fingers over her spine, branding her with intimacy that felt far more personal than it did professional. He motioned her forward. "Shall we?"

"What did she mean by 'gold'?" she asked.

"Each VIP staircase is color-coded. Silver, gold and platinum—one for each side of the room."

"I see," she responded, and started walking the path he'd indicated, just around and behind the seating area, until they were at the farthest staircase.

Dante motioned her upward. "Ladies first."

Sonya opened her mouth to tell him she'd follow, only to have her growling stomach drown her out.

Dante smiled. "Perhaps you should hurry. Your situation is starting to sound rather critical."

Heat rushed to her cheeks. "I think you're probably right," she said, stepping forward and thinking she hadn't been this nervous since the bar exam.

The path was narrow and Dante followed her, his hand settling on her waist this time, steadying her, and somehow she had the feeling he was testing her reaction to his silent touch. Now was the time she should set boundaries, as she would with any other client. Somehow, too, she knew Dante would respect them, if only she would establish them. If only she could make herself move away from his touch. Instead she was fighting the urge to lean into it. And what if he meant nothing by the touch? Maybe Italians were just more flirty and touchy-feely than Americans. That was probably it, and she should be relieved instead of disappointed.

She rushed up the last two steps, eager to get Dante's hand off of her before she melted into a puddle of wanting woman right there on the steps. She paused at a door and Dante leaned into her, his hand sliding around her waist to her stomach, as if to steady her, before he pulled it back. Every nerve ending in her body tingled with awareness, with the need to lean farther into him, to feel him closer. Which was exactly why she quickly darted away from him and into the room before her. Her gaze swept around the private room, and she noticed the horseshoe-shaped booth in the corner with some sort of sheer curtains tied back on either side. Candles flickered from wall fixtures, scenting the room with vanilla and cinnamon. It was a room that screamed intimacy and romance.

She turned to find the door shut and Dante closer than she thought, towering over her. "I've never been to a restaurant that had private rooms quite like this one."

"Good," he said softly. "This is just one of the many 'firsts' I hope to show you tonight." He motioned to the table. "Let's sit and get you some food."

"Yes, please." She followed him to the booth and rather than entering from the opposite side of her, he waited for her to slide into position.

"What are you five favorite foods?" he asked as he scooted in beside her.

"I'm not sure you want to hear the answer to that question," she said, laughing, glad for something to talk about. "They aren't exactly fine dining, I can promise you."

"Most of mine aren't, either."

"Then you go first."

"All right," he said. "A good hamburger and great French fries any day of the week. Pizza is a distant second. Chocolate cake. And of course, the perfect meatball. I have to have something Italian on the list or my mother will have a heart attack. She already thinks I'm too Americanized."

She smiled, intrigued by the simplicity of his list. "And here I thought you'd be a caviar kind of guy."

"There's a lot about me that I imagine isn't what you would expect," he said. "Your turn. Name your top five."

"My list would be all my favorite junk foods that I don't allow myself to eat on a daily basis. Chocolate cake and pretty much chocolate anything make my list as well. Macaroni and cheese. Love it. French fries but you can keep the burger. And then Starbucks white mochas—and yes, they count as a food group. They got me through law school."

"Even if I count the coffee, that was only four."

"Pizza. Cheese. From a little place down the street from my house."

"Well then, let's order." He punched a button on the table and ordered everything from both of the lists, before explaining, "In the private dining rooms you can use the menu or simply order whatever you want."

"Really? They'll custom-make whatever the guests want? And it's good when it arrives?"

"The food is always exceptional. Anything you want, however you want it, and cooked to perfection. All you have to do at Parr's is ask for what you want and it's yours."

You, she thought. *I want you, naked and on top of me, and without the recourse of a morning after that destroys my career.* "If only life were that simple."

"If it were," he said, "then the idea of an escape to Sin City wouldn't be nearly as appealing and I wouldn't be banking on this investment. Vegas is an adult playground and I intend to take that concept further than anyone else."

"Meaning what?"

"There was an old show called *Fantasy Island.* Did you ever see it?"

"I remember the reruns. The little guy in the white suit screamed, 'The plane! The plane!' at the opening of every show and I swear everyone went around imitating that."

"That's the one," he said. "And the premise of the show—a fantasy granted to each guest—is the premise I intend for one of the Ricci properties. This hotel, if we can make an acquisition happen. It's underperforming and I think we can get it for a steal and make it a success."

"I'm not completely understanding the *Fantasy Island* premise. How are you going to grant people's wishes, which was really what the show was about, right?"

"We're going to give guests more than absolute luxury. We're going to give them the freedom to explore pleasure in ways they never dare at home. That freedom will come from our written confidentiality agreement, which I'll want you to draft, and the old adage of 'what happens in Vegas, stays in Vegas.'"

She swallowed hard. "Are we talking *erotic* fantasies?"

"Erotic fantasies," he agreed. "A place where couples can spice up their love life, or singles can explore who they are before they ever become a part of a couple. For those who have never dared erotic play, they will have a gentle introduction to a new world. For those who are experienced and seek a new level of play, they, too, will find we can meet their needs."

A buzzer sounded and Sonya's gaze jerked to her right, to where one of the two doors she hadn't even noticed before now opened, and a man in a tuxedo wheeled a cart out toward them. "You're about to have fantasy-worthy junk food."

Fantasy-worthy. He was the fantasy and she wasn't a fool. She could see where this was headed. To Fantasy Island, where she'd have him naked and enjoy every second of it...if she dared.

CHAPTER FOUR

The waiter set a cheese tray on the table and then began filling champagne glasses, all the while talking to Dante in a familiar way.

Job complete, the waiter gave a short bow. "The rest of the food will be ready shortly."

Dante immediately scooted closer to her, so close she could smell the spicy woodsy scent of his cologne. So close she could almost feel his body heat and she wanted to. She wanted to so badly that she ached with need. He lifted his glass. "Let's try that toast again."

"I still haven't eaten."

"I'll catch you if you fall."

"What about the forgetting everything and making a fool of myself?"

"You can't make a fool of yourself with me tonight," he said. "And anything you forget we'll do again."

She was suddenly pretty sure she was having a hot flash at a far too young age. "Dante—"

"I thought you said the contract would allow you to enjoy tonight?"

"I guess I'm not good at relaxing."

"I'll help you."

"I'm not sure that's a good idea."

He considered her a moment and then reached for a silver box the waiter had apparently left on the table. He set it in between them and then reached for two note cards and pens. He placed one card and pen in front of himself and one in front of her.

"What's this?" she asked.

"The inspiration for my premise," he said. "This is how Parr's VIP rooms work. You write down your fantasy before dinner and I write down mine. We both place them in the box and give them to the waiter. The fantasy is then arranged for dessert. Neither of us knows what the other person writes down."

Sonya stared at him, digesting what he had just told her, and then reached for his glass and downed the contents.

He arched a brow as she set it down. "You forgot the toast," he reminded her.

She ignored the comment. "I can't do this. I'm your attorney."

"I dated the contracts for tomorrow. And what happens in Parr's, stays in Parr's, *bella*."

Bella. Beautiful. The casual endearment didn't mean anything, but yet, it did. And so did the offer he'd just given her, the fantasy, the escape, that she not only wanted, but also needed. The pressure to succeed, to support her mother while she was recovering, and pay her bills, was weighing heavily on her, and it had been for months now.

The buzzer sounded and she knew the waiter was about to join them. She reached for her drink since she'd drunk his already.

"Oh, no," Dante said, covering her hand with his. "You drank that entire glass of champagne in thirty seconds. You need to eat."

"You wanted me to drink it."

"A sip," he said softly as the waiter wheeled the cart in their direction. "Instead, you tried to find liquid courage."

She grimaced. "I did not."

His lips curved upward. "Yes. You did. And you aren't going to blame alcohol for tonight in the morning. You either stay or you go, but you decide, not the champagne."

"Dinner is served," the waiter said, arriving at the table and beginning to unload his tray.

Dante arched a brow. She grimaced. "Don't do that brow thing. It's arrogant and I don't like arrogant men."

He laughed. "I'll try to remember that."

"No, you won't," she said and grabbed the card and pen. "I assume the ink is so I can't change my mind?"

"That would be the idea."

She drew a breath and started to write on the card. *I want to have wild, wicked sex with Dante and not have it impact my career. And chains and a whip to make him pay for surprising me like this would be okay, too, if you happen to have some.* She laughed and looked at him before dropping the card in the box. "Your turn." She'd committed to this now. She wasn't going to be a wimp. She would hold her own with Dante, somehow, someway, and with the risk this represented for her career, she was darn sure going to enjoy every second, too.

His lips twitched, his eyes twinkling with mischief, before he began writing…for quite a long time. He used the front and the back of the card, then dropped it in the box.

"That was a lot of writing," she said.

"I've been thinking about what I want since I met you at your offices today."

She reached for the box. He shackled her hand and laughed.

"After dinner."

How was she possibly going to eat while wondering what was on that card?

CHAPTER FIVE

Dante slid the silver box to the edge of the table and the waiter reached for it. Sonya quickly averted her gaze by snatching one of the four varieties of French fries on the table. Her taste buds and stomach quickly shouted in joy and any thought of not eating flew out the proverbial window. "Oh, God. This is so good and I'm so very hungry."

"I'll need to test that myself," Dante said, grabbing a fry for himself and then nodding in agreement. "Excellent, but we need salt and ketchup." He quickly took care of both issues.

Sonya sighed as she stared at not one, not two, but three varieties of macaroni and cheese, relieved that the waiter had disappeared out of the room. She took a bite of macaroni and then another before coming to a conclusion. "I see a flaw in your dinner-and-erotic-dessert premise."

"What flaw is that?" he asked, his eyes twinkling with both surprise and interest, at her direct reference to the fantasies, she assumed. But the champagne had made her brave, or maybe she was on the verge of a panic attack for actually writing down what she had on that card.

"A number of flaws actually. For instance, I, for one, am going to be so full that I'll need a nap when I'm done." She took another bite of macaroni and cheese to make a point, and then pointed with her fork to her plate. "This is the best macaroni and cheese I've ever had. I could eat every bite and ask for more, which brings me to flaw number two. Women really don't want to pig out and then be naked. You should really do the silver box at check-in or something like that."

He started laughing. "Just don't pig out."

"I never splurge on calories and food but you put my favorite foods in front of me, and if I was a customer it would be my vacation, and you'd you expect me not to eat them? Where is the escape and fantasy of that?" She set her fork down. "That's just cruel."

Dante reached for her, pulling her into his arms, the heat of his touch searing her instantly, the warmth of his body setting her on fire. One of her hands flattened on his impressively hard chest, which would soon be impressively hard and shirtless. She inhaled the spicy male scent of him, and discarded any thought of him being her client. What would be, would be. It was too late to turn back.

His mouth lowered, dangerously, wonderfully, close to hers. He was going to kiss her. "Your dinner-before-dessert concern sounds like a lame excuse to leave to me."

"I've said what was on my mind up until this point, per your own declaration," she said. "If I wanted to leave, I'd say so. As long as I'm granted the fantasies exactly as I wrote on my card, you can bet money I'm not going anywhere."

He gave her a probing stare. "And what would these fantasies be?"

"You'll find out what I wrote down when I find out what you wrote down. Which would be what, by the way?"

"If I told you, then you *would run*. And then I'd have to chase you." His mouth came down on hers, hot and demanding, and delicious in a way nothing on the table began to touch.

She moaned and sunk into the kiss, her tongue meeting his, her hunger for him, not the food. He unbuttoned her jacket, sliding his hand to her waist. "Do you know why dinner before play works?" he asked when he tore his mouth from hers.

She tried not to pant but that kiss had her burning for another. "Because no one finishes the food?"

His lips curved wickedly. "Because living out a fantasy requires energy, and I can promise you, you're going to need yours." His fingers traveled to her side, barely brushing the bottom of her breast. "So eat before I don't let you and we'll both end up sorry you don't have more energy later." His lips brushed hers an instant before he slid away from her, but not too far.

A flutter of panic overcame her. She was on unfamiliar territory. She didn't know how to do anything beyond talking. She was good at that, at playing a certain tone or mood, because that's what she did when negotiating, when working a case. She glanced at Dante, who was staring at her, his eyes as wicked as his body, and she was pretty darn sure that he was thinking about the after-party, not about making conversation. She was way out of her league, and it both excited her, and terrified her. "What are you thinking?" he asked.

How much I want you. "Why this hotel for your Fantasy Island?" she asked. "And will the other two be anything like this one?"

"Each property will be completely unique," he said. "I'd like to buy older hotels and demolish them to build from the ground up. One of the properties will be an Italian theme and

created by some of the most talented Italian architects and artists in the world. The second will have a fashion concept with
some of the most exclusive shops in the world inside. And the
third, the smallest, will be Fantasy Island."

"I can easily see the idea of Italy and fashion tying to the
Ricci name, but the Fantasy Island concept? How does that
connect?"

"In Italy there's a highly exclusive private club that caters
to executives who have, shall we say, exotic tastes. There are
a number of fantasy components to its operation."

"And you're a member?" she asked.

"Yes, *bella*," he confirmed. "I'm a member and while Sin
City plays up the visual appeal of sex, there's nothing like
that club here."

"I'm sure there have to be kink clubs in Vegas."

"Would you go to one?" he asked, as she finished her mac
'n' cheese and pushed her plate aside.

"No," she said, sipping her water. "Of course not."

"And that's the exact reaction of the average American,"
he said. "But secretly many people are enticed by the idea of
sexual exploration and when given a private, confidential and
controlled experience, they are willing to climb out of their
comfort zones."

"Then I don't think you want to have them come here, to
a restaurant," she said, glad the effects of the champagne had
worn off with food. "It feels too public and I wonder who is
watching."

"No one is watching us," he assured her. "There are no
cameras in the dining areas but there are in the private rooms
we'll go to next. You can choose to turn them on, or leave
them off, when you enter."

"Off," she said quickly.

He inclined his head. "Then we'll turn them off."

She nodded. "Thank you."

A buzzer sounded, different from the one that had gone off when the waiter had entered the room, and Sonya's gaze jerked nervously toward the sound, not sure what to expect. The second door that had been closed this entire time was now cracked open.

"Speaking of silver boxes," he said. "It's time to go find out what's in ours."

Her heart skipped a beat and she decided the champagne brain wasn't so bad after all. She had no idea what Dante's version of "kink" would be and her sexual experiences had been fairly vanilla to this point. She reached for her glass and downed it. This time Dante didn't stop her. She glanced at him. "Liquid courage. I admit it."

"We do nothing that makes you feel uncomfortable, *bella,*" he promised softly. "You have my word."

She searched his handsome face and saw the heat and hunger of his desire, but there was also that honesty he valued so much. He meant what he'd said. He wouldn't push her to go places she wasn't comfortable going. And while she didn't kid herself into thinking she mattered beyond tonight to Dante, not personally, she knew she would feel like she mattered tonight. And that was all that concerned her right now. She was ready to embrace the escape, the fantasy that had so quickly become Dante.

CHAPTER SIX

Sonya accepted Dante's hand as she slid out of the booth. "Ready?" he asked.

"Unless you want to pour us some more champagne?"

"Let's save it for later," he suggested, pulling her close, his lips caressing hers, before he rested his forehead against hers.

"Right," she said, feeling herself relax into him, remarkably comfortable considering she'd only just met him. "That's probably a good idea."

He laced the fingers on one hand with hers and motioned to the door. Habit made her turn to grab her purse only to realize that it was still in the car, and they weren't going back there anytime soon. "I'd really like to get my purse first."

"It's in the room," he said. "I had it brought up before my driver left for the night."

"So you knew we were staying?"

"Didn't you?"

"No." She hesitated. "Maybe. Not consciously."

Approval flashed across his face at the admission and she wondered what made him so surprised by honesty. She let him lead her to the door. He pushed it open and motioned for her to exit first. Sonya peered through the opening, expecting a hallway, and finding what looked like an entryway to a room with a wall that blocked the rest of the suite from her sight. The lighting was dim, shadows dancing on the walls and ceiling. Somewhere in the distance candles burned vanilla and spice.

In front of the wall was a round entry table that might have held flowers in another suite, but in this case there was the little silver box sitting on top...open and empty.

Dante's hands settled onto her shoulders, his powerful body framing hers. He nuzzled her neck. "I can take you home now or at any time."

"I'm staying," she said, stepping forward, her high heels sinking into plush carpet. She was going to have her hot night with Dante. And it was too late to turn back anyway. The dynamic between her and Dante had been changed forever anyway.

The door shut behind her almost immediately but she didn't turn around. She stayed focused on the box and a large yellow envelope resting beside it.

Dante joined her to stand in front of the table. "Let's find out what's in it," he said, reaching for the envelope.

Sonya's gaze jerked to his. "You don't know?"

"Only that it has something to do with what we put in the box."

Nerves fluttered in her stomach, but there was excitement there too, a thrill at doing something daring, something she would never have done before meeting Dante. And also a need, a feminine burn that she'd been suppressing without realizing it, one that he had awakened.

She wet her lips and waited as he opened the clasp on the

envelope and pulled out a piece of paper, as well as a pen. He began to read. "This contract specifies that nothing that occurs from 'blank time' to 'blank time'…we're to fill in the times—" he glanced at her, then his attention returned to the paper "—will have any negative effect on Sonya Miller's working relationship with Ricci Properties. If such damage should occur, Dante Ricci will compensate her by way of—" He glanced at her again. "Another blank for us to fill in."

Sonya's stomach knotted. The contract read like bribery, like a threat, which was exactly what she didn't want to happen. She wasn't going to flip things and do that to him. She grabbed the paper from him and tore it up, letting it float to the ground. "That's not what I wanted." She whirled around and headed for the door, reaching for the knob at the same moment that Dante gently shackled her arm and pulled her around to face him.

"Don't go," he said softly, no demand in his voice, just gentle persuasion. "Not like this. Not if you really want to be here."

"I don't like that contract," she said. "I don't like how it feels. I regret ever writing anything on that card. This isn't what I wanted."

"What did you want?"

"I don't know but not that."

"I know what I want," he said, pressing his hand to the wall by her head, his expression etched with something so raw, so animalistic, it stole her breath. "I want you and I want you in every possible way." He leaned in, his mouth a whisper away from hers, lingering and teasing, then denying her the kiss she longed for. She all but gasped as he moved, his mouth pressing to her ear, his hand sliding under her jacket. "You have no idea of all the things I want to do to you, and with you, but you will." His fingers traced her rib cage, his knuckles brushing her breasts, her nipples puckering with anticipation of his touch, before he added, "Right after I get you to relax."

"I'm not sure that's possible," she whispered, biting her lip as his hand covered her breast, his thumb caressing her nipple through the thin silk of her blouse.

"I'll take that challenge," he murmured a moment before his mouth came down on hers, his tongue pushing into her mouth, hot, hard and demanding. It was a kiss that wiped away her doubts and left her with nothing but need and hunger and... He turned her to face the wall.

"What are you doing?" she asked, her hands pressed to the door.

He pulled the clip from her hair, ran his hands through it and buried his face in her neck. "Relaxing you." His fingers tugged down her skirt, sliding her zipper down.

Her heart beat so hard she thought it might escape from her chest. "It's not working."

"It will," he assured her, tugging her jacket back off of her shoulders and tossing it aside. His hands explored her body, his thick erection settling against her backside, and somehow her shirt was unbuttoned and gone, her bra with it, replaced by his hands. He wasn't gentle, kneading her breasts then pinching her nipples.

She moaned as sensations rolled over her, near pain that splintered into absolute pleasure. She leaned back into him, fighting the urge to cover his hands with hers, to capture him so he wouldn't stop. "Does it feel good, *bella?*"

"Yes," she gasped. "Yes."

"You're not convincing me." He shoved her skirt down and it fell to her ankles, leaving her in heels, thigh-highs and a thong. He lifted her slightly, seeming impatient to get rid of the skirt, and kicked it aside. He caressed her backside and she could feel his heated inspection burning her inside and out.

She tried to turn, suddenly feeling out of control, and she didn't do out of control well. His hand slid to her stomach, holding her in place. His teeth gently grazed her shoulder, as his hand inched downward, pressing between her thighs. He shoved aside the silk of her panties, before he teased her clit and then expertly, and oh so deftly, teased the swollen, sensitive core of her body.

She bit her lip, burning for more, wanting to know what he would feel like inside her, and instinctively widened her stance.

"That's right," he approved. "Open for me." He pressed his mouth to her ear. "I'm going to lick you until you come and then I'll do it all over again." He turned her around and kissed her, devouring her with long, demanding strokes of his tongue before tearing his mouth from hers and going down on his knees. She gasped as he ripped off her panties and lifted her leg to his shoulder.

The gasp quickly faded into a moan as one long finger, and then another, penetrated her. His mouth followed, closing down on her clit. Pleasure rushed through her, hot lava spilling over her skin, igniting every nerve ending she owned. She arched into his mouth, flattening her palms against the door, her head with them. He suckled her and licked her and pumped his fingers into her. She wanted more, she wanted to come. The burn of an orgasm threatened and she tried to hold it off, but it was there—the pleasure, the man controlling it— and it took her, conquering her resistance. Her breath lodged in her throat an instant before the spasms jerked through her body and then she grabbed at his fingers. Everything went black. There was nothing but sensation after sensation, rolling through her with such intensity that she found herself panting with completion, her knees rubbery and weak.

Dante eased her leg down and feathered kisses over her stomach before pushing to his feet. "If you're relaxed now," he said, "we can get started." He didn't wait for an answer. He scooped her up and started carrying her away from the door.

CHAPTER SEVEN

The haze of orgasm fell away from Sonya as Dante carried her around the wall of the foyer area that had separated them from the rest of the suite, bringing a half-moon-shaped room into her view. To her left and her right were sheer curtains covering a space that she couldn't make out. She wondered what kind of kink they concealed, and if she was about to find out.

Instead, their destination was directly behind the wall where a giant mahogany bed was set on top of a pedestal, candles flickering on the nightstands and in fancy fixtures on the walls. Antique-looking hooks were part of the headboard design and so were the chains and wrist cuffs hanging from them. But it was the sight of the walls on either side of the bed that set her heart racing. Each wall held a huge display rack displaying whips, vibrators, cuffs and other items she'd never even seen before. She was crazy to think she could keep up with a man who apparently made sex a hobby. She was out of her league, so very out of her league. This wasn't her world, she wasn't the kind of woman he was used to, and it was intimidating.

Dante set her on top of the pedestal facing the bed, where she found a leather whip and handcuffs laid out. "I assume you requested those?" he asked, his hands on her hips. "Just so you know, that's not going to happen."

"I thought this was my fantasy," she argued because despite her complete relief at his words, the premise of this experience was choosing a fantasy. That and she could think of plenty to do to Dante once she chained him to the headboard.

He turned her to face him, his hands on her shoulders. His gaze raked hungrily over her body before lifting. "Have you ever had a BDSM experience?"

"No, but—"

"And you think I want you to try it with whips that you use on me?"

"Well, I don't want you to use them on me," she protested.

A low rumble of laughter rolled from his lips and he kissed her, one hand settling possessively on her bare backside. "You do know how to surprise me. You don't dive into BSDM hardcore, *bella*, so why don't we rethink your fantasy?"

She wet her lips. "I'd be okay with that."

"Good," he said. "Then give me control. Just let go of everything and do what I say. You will be shocked at how much you will like putting your pleasure in someone else's hands. No thinking. No positioning yourself like you have to in business. Just pleasure."

"I'm not good at giving away control."

"I'll help you."

"You keep saying that."

"Because I mean it, and look at it this way. My sole purpose will be pleasing you."

"What's in it for you then?"

"My fantasy was—is—your submission. I'd like it to be yours, as well."

"That's what you wrote on that card?"

"I told them to get your purse."

She gaped. "You told them to get my purse and I wrote about sex?"

"I can handle my own fantasies. The question is—can you handle your fantasies?" He ran his fingers down a strand of her hair. "Give me control. I'll be gentle."

She squeezed her thighs together against the growing ache there. She couldn't stand there much longer, naked, without him touching her. "What if I don't want to do something?"

"Tell me. Communicate. But when you say 'no' it's 'no,' so be sure you mean it."

Why was the idea of him in control far more arousing than she ever believed possible? "Yes. Okay."

"Yes what?"

"I agree."

"You know what I want you to say."

She inhaled and let it out. "You're in charge."

Satisfaction darkened his stare. "And if you don't want to do something?"

"I say 'no.'"

"Good," he said, roughly twining his fingers into her hair and piercing her with a possessive stare. "Then you're mine for the night." His mouth closed down on hers, a fierce claiming that echoed his words and tore through her like lightning.

She was panting when he pulled back. "Tomorrow morning—"

"Doesn't exist," he said. "Stop thinking." His gaze dropped to her chest, his hand caressing her. "You have beautiful breasts, beautiful plump red nipples."

She was starting to feel weak in the knees again.

"Do you like to have them licked?" he asked.

"Dante—"

"Answer."

She swallowed hard. "Yes."

"And do you want me to touch them?"

She nodded, then whispered. "Yes."

"Show me how you want me to do it." He pressed her hands to her breasts, his over hers. "Show me." He kneaded her breasts with their hands, leaning in to kiss her neck, and trailed his mouth, his teeth, along the sensitive flesh until he whispered in her ear, "You smell almost as good as you taste." He eased her down onto the bed, going down to a knee in front of her, and licked the nipple her parted fingers exposed. She moaned at the wet warm friction and he kissed her, swallowing the sound before murmuring, "Show me how you like to be touched and fucked, but don't come. I'm the only one who gets to make you come." He stood up and stepped off the podium, toeing off his shoes.

She stiffened. "You want me to—"

"Yes."

"I—"

"Spread your legs for me," he said, unbuttoning his shirt. "Let me see that sweet little pussy."

Her reaction was instantaneous. She crossed her arms in front of herself and squeezed her legs together. No man had ever talked to her like that, and it freaked her out to realize she liked it. It freaked her out, this part of her she didn't recognize.

He was in front of her in a second, his finger sliding under her chin, forcing her gaze to his. "There are rules, Sonya. I tell you what to do and you do them. You tell me 'no' and I stop. So say 'no' or do as I say." He softened his tone and ran his hand through her hair. "Stop thinking and just let go." He stroked her bottom lip with his finger. "Trust me."

CHAPTER EIGHT

Trust. The word replayed in Sonya's head, the word that she'd already come to know was so important to him. He wanted her trust. She wanted his. She softened at his voice. "I do. I trust you." And strangely, in that moment, having only just met him, she knew she meant it.

He studied her a long moment and then stepped back, shrugging out of his shirt as he did. His body was all the inspiration she needed. He was rippling muscle, broad and defined, well-honed with hard work.

"Squeeze your breasts together and pinch your nipples."

She did as he said, squeezing herself and rubbing, feeling the inhibition beginning to fade just from the lone simple act.

"Now your pussy. Get it ready for me."

She pressed her hand between her legs and watched as dark desire slid over his features. It aroused her, seeing him react that way, that it pleased him. She didn't remember ever wanting to please a man as she did this stranger. She pressed her fingers into the wet heat of her body, spreading the wetness, thinking of his cock inside her.

He said something in Italian, low and guttural, but her gaze locked on the sexy dark line of hair running from his navel to— He shoved his pants and underwear down and completed her sentence. The line went straight to his cock. His very large, very thick cock. The man was gorgeous and hard and all hers.

He pointed to the floor in front of him. "Here."

She kicked off her shoes and wasted no time complying. She walked toward him, aware that his eyes followed her bouncing breasts. She would have dropped to her knees, but he captured her hand and suckled her fingers into his mouth. Her pussy clenched with the memory of him licking her and tasting her.

He pressed her to her knees and she went gladly, wrapping her hand around the thickness of his erection. Pearly liquid pooled at the tip of his shaft. "Lick it off."

She glanced up at him and snaked her tongue out, stealing the salty wetness and moaning with the intimate taste of him. The pure lust in his expression made her want to shove him down and ride him. She ran her tongue around him and moaned with how much she wanted him.

"Take me in your mouth," he ordered. "Suck me."

She closed her lips around him, drew him in. His hand went to the back of her head, urging her to take him all. She tightened her hand around him and started a slow glide up and down his shaft. He pulsed in her mouth, his hips moving with her.

"That's it." His voice was low, guttural. "Harder. Suck me harder." He pumped faster, his hand twining in her hair, the urgency in him pounding through her, until he stiffened and shook.

She slowly eased the pressure on his cock, adjusting her pace, suckling him dry until he completely stilled. She leaned back on her heels and he pulled her to her feet, picked her up and carried her to the bed, where he set her down on the end of the mattress. He reached into a drawer at the foot of the bed and pulled out a velvet bag.

"What is it?" she asked.

He dumped a piece of gold jewelry onto his palm. "Your introduction into a new kind of pleasure. It's a nipple-and-clit clamp and the only jewelry you'll ever want to wear again."

"I bet you try to tell all the girls that," she said, more than a little curious, and aroused, by this new turn of events.

"The proof is in your reaction," he assured her. "Lean back on your hands."

She did as he said, no longer feeling even slightly self-conscious about her breasts being thrust into the air. He tossed the empty bag on the bed and uncurled the long strands of gold chain before going down on a knee again in front of her. He pressed her knees apart, and trailed the chain up one of her thighs, until it dangled in the V of her body.

"Is it going to hurt?"

"No," he said, stroking the wet silk of her body, and a dull throb of need began to form. "It's like the pressure from a deep massage. You want it to stop but you're so glad when it doesn't." He leaned in and gave her clit a long lick, tricking her into relaxing, and then immediately replaced his tongue with the snap of the clamp.

She gasped at the pressure. He tugged the chain, and her muscle clenched. She sucked in air. "Oh, that is… I don't know."

His lips lifted evilly, sexily. "You'll get used to it."

He dragged the other half of the chain up her stomach, leaving chill bumps in its wake, but when he was about to attach a clamp to one of her nipples, she had a moment of panic.

Sonya sat up and covered her breast. "It's going to hurt."

He moved her hand and cupped her breast, then tugged on her nipple and the chain at the same time.

"That's—" She lost the sentence, no idea what she'd been about to say because he pinched both of her nipples, twisting them, tugging on that chain. Her lashes fluttered, delicious sensation rolling through her.

"Does that hurt?" he asked, licking one of the hard peaks.

She panted. "In a good way."

He slid his hand into her hair, brushed his mouth over hers. "The clamp will be similar. A pinch that turns to pleasure. And I won't put it on too tight."

"Okay."

He closed one of the clamps down on her nipple, and at first it wasn't bad, but then he adjusted it, tightened it, and she didn't like it. "Dante—" His mouth closed down on her other nipple, stealing her objection as he suckled her deeply, pulling roughly on the swollen peak, until she was moaning, all pain forgotten. Only then did he clamp that nipple, and this time, tightening it felt good. A pinch and then pleasure.

His hand slid back to her face and he kissed her, a gentle kiss that defied the bite of the clamps, his tongue making love to her, caressing her. She moaned and wrapped her arms around his neck, needing him now. He deepened the kiss, that primal male side of him she found so hot, seeping into it, until he was outright claiming her again as she wanted to be. He tugged on the chain and she gasped with the pain splintering through her nipples, and her pussy clenched.

"Oh, God," she moaned. "I've never felt anything like this."

"Turn onto your knees. That's the best way to feel the tug of the clamps when I'm inside you." He didn't wait for her reply. He stood and turned her himself, pressing her knees to the mattress. She went down on her hands, even as he lifted her ass high in the air. She heard the tear of the condom package only seconds before his hands were on her hips, and his cock, his blessed cock she'd been waiting for, finally pressed between her legs.

He ran his shaft through the slick wet heat of her body over and over, driving her wild with anticipation. She turned to look at him over her shoulder. "Please. Dante."

He laughed, a low, deep, sexy sound she could get used to hearing often. It was a random thought, lost when he entered her, taking his time to sink deep, until he was buried to the hilt.

His first pump was a slow in-and-out, but her breasts swayed with the action, the clamps tugging on her. She gasped and then moaned as Dante slammed into her and began to pump. Sensations rolled through her and it was then that she gave Dante exactly what he'd asked for. She forgot to think and gave herself to the pleasure and to him.

CHAPTER NINE

The room was dark when Sonya woke, but she was pretty sure it was morning because the suite had no windows for light, and it had been somewhere around four when she had collapsed from exhaustion. She was on her stomach, her body sweetly aching all over, and she smiled when she realized that Dante's arm was across her waist. Sleeping with him somehow felt more intimate than the many intensely erotic things they'd done the night before, though they'd been as intimate as it was possible to be, that was for sure. She sighed and let her eyes start to drift closed when she suddenly realized today was Thursday, and a workday.

Work. Oh, God. She pressed upward on her hands, trying to see the clock she thought was by Dante's bedside, but she was trapped under his big body. For once, that wasn't a good thing.

He lifted his head, his hair mussed up and sexy, his dark eyes laden with sleep. "What's wrong?"

"I can't see the clock. I think I might be late to work."

"You're not," he said, and laid his head down. "Go back to sleep."

"Dante," she said, shoving his arm. "What time is it?"

He sighed and lifted his head toward the clock before turning back to her. "Ten."

"No! Tell me it's not." She tried to get up but he was still holding her down with his leg. "Move. Move. I have to get up. I need a phone. I—"

Dante turned her to her back, and pulled her underneath him. "It's ten in the morning. Panic will not change that."

She shoved on his big, broad, unmoving chest. He was naked and she could feel his erection pressing her leg. "I have to get up," she said not sounding nearly as convincing as she thought she would.

"No, you don't," he said. "I woke up early and had the contract, along with the retainer, delivered to your office. I also included a message that you were attending an early morning meeting with me. Problem solved."

A moment of stunned disbelief quickly transformed into anger. "You should have asked me before you did that. Dante, this is not a bedroom game. This is my career and when you're gone, when this project with you is over, I don't want my job to be as well."

"I'll take care of that SOB Michael. I'll take care of you. Nothing bad is going to happen."

"I don't want to be taken care of. I take care of myself. And that SOB is my boss at one of the best firms in the city, in the whole United States. Don't do this. Don't make last night impact today. You said it wouldn't impact today."

He studied her a long moment. "You're pissed."

"Yes. I'm pissed."

"You're *really pissed*."

"Yes!"

His brows dipped. "I didn't expect that."

"Well you should have because—"

He kissed her, his tongue pressing past her teeth, his mouth slanting over hers, possessive and hot with demand. She tried to resist, she even tried to press on that unmoving chest of his, but her body betrayed her, and her arms wrapped his neck, her tongue tangling with his.

"I have a confession," he said, when he tore his mouth from hers.

"I'm not sure I want to know what it is."

"I never mix business with pleasure. As in, ever. It's dangerous and a disaster ready to happen."

Those words slammed into her with the implication but she tried to act unaffected. Tried t*o be* unaffected. "Is this where I point out that I am naked and so are you?"

"That's the point," he said. "I walked into that conference room yesterday expecting to hire a killer shark for an attorney. The minute you looked at me, I saw something beyond beauty and skill, something wild and passionate, and different. Something I had to experience for a night, which brings me to another confession. I don't stay the night with a woman, I don't wake up next to her."

Her chest tightened. He'd gotten out of bed and come back to bed with her and that realization had her shaking inside, confused, aroused, angry, and there was something else, something unfamiliar, something she didn't want to feel for this man. She rejected all of these feelings, and reached for some kind of control. "Ever?"

"Not for a very long time."

Their eyes locked and held, and her hand heated where it rested on his chest. He wasn't what she'd expected. This wasn't what she expected. "What are we doing, Dante?"

"I say we figure that out in the shower, and if that doesn't work, we'll try over lunch. And if that doesn't work, we'll just have to get creative." Before she knew his intent, he'd scooped her up and was carrying her again. She told herself right then, to enjoy the sex, enjoy the moment, but not to fall for Dante, not to get distracted from her career, and the security she was building for her and her mother. That was her plan. This time she was sticking to it.

Several minutes later, she was standing in the hot stream of water pouring from the gold showerhead with Dante, who was hard and hot and so very perfectly male, pressing her against the wall, and she was absolutely enjoying the sex, the man, the moment. She was going to make this plan work, one lick and touch, and taste, at a time.

After a very long, very enjoyable shower, Sonya stood in the bathroom with a hotel robe wrapped around her, and finished drying her hair. Dante had dressed before her to join a conference call he'd scheduled days before. She opened her purse, and quickly applied makeup, listening to the muffled sound of Dante speaking in Italian somewhere in the suite. Her stomach growled and she exited the bathroom that led directly into the bedroom where they'd slept, to find several dresses lying on the bed and a few bags beside them.

Sonya's stomach clenched, and she walked toward them, to grab the note on top.

> *Bella—I wanted you to have a change of clothes and wasn't sure what you liked so I had the hotel boutique bring you a variety.*

Emotion rushed over Sonya, emotions she tried to avoid, tried never to deal with. But they were there, balled up in her chest and stomach, created by memories of her elitist Harvard professor father, who resented every dime he'd ever paid in child support for a daughter he never wanted. And her mother, who'd foolishly let him in and out of her bed, like that would change things. Sonya dropped the note and walked to the phone, punching a button and arranging to have the clothes returned.

Ten minutes later, she could still hear Dante talking in what she thought was a small office area off the suite while she searched for her shoes, and decided to try the blankets on the bed, no matter how illogical it seemed. She was out of options. A knock sounded at the door and she struggled to toss the heavy comforter out of her way. She managed to get to the door right as Dante shut the door and turned to her.

His dark gaze, a striking contrast to his navy blue dress shirt, swept over her wrinkled clothes and back to her face. "Why would you return my gifts?"

"I like my things," she said. "My clothes. I don't want you to spend money on me."

"Money isn't an issue."

"Not to you," she said, curling her arms in front of her. "But it is to me. I make my money. I spend my money. I don't spend yours."

He walked to her, pure male elegance with a primal edge, as if he were stalking his prey and that prey was her. He stopped in front of her, close, so close. So tall that he towered over her. "I was going to ask you what drives you, what motivates you to work so hard, but I think I have my answer. You depended on someone who let you down."

That he saw through her surprised her, and she instantly deflected it. "And someone you trusted let you down."

"More than one," he said. "But yes. There was someone who opened my eyes. I was young and thought I was in love.

We were going to be married and I caught her in bed with an employee. She wanted my money, not me."

She was shocked, not as much by the content of the story, but that he'd told her.

"Your turn," he said softly.

"My father," she said. "He's a Harvard law professor."

"And you graduated from Brown."

"That would be why. He resented every dime he ever spent on me. My mom struggled, she still does. I don't plan to let her for much longer."

"I'm surprised you went to law school considering who he is."

She laughed, but not with humor. "I think a part of me wanted to show him up. It's that old saying—'those who can do and those who can't teach.'"

They were still standing there in the middle of the suite, not touching, not moving. He reached for her, his fingers lacing with hers. "Come here."

There was such understanding and tenderness in his voice that she melted into him, needing him even when she'd just denied needing anyone.

He wrapped her in his strong arms, and ran his hand down her hair. "I understand why you don't want the clothes but—" She started to object but pressed his fingers to her lips. "Consider this a gift to me. I'm starving. Pick what you want and we'll return the rest if you want and then let's go eat. Afterward, I'll take you to my home office and show you the architectural models for the properties." He smiled. "Maybe after that, we can talk through how to improve the silver box concept."

This was when she should just say "no," where her plan dictated that be her answer. But standing there, in Dante's arms, she felt something she'd never felt and everything inside her told her to gamble on him. She drew a breath and before logic could defeat her, she rose on her toes and kissed him before saying, "Yes."

CHAPTER TEN

Three weeks later, Sonya sat at her kitchen table for the first time since meeting Dante, pouring over a counteroffer they'd received on the Bell's property. Missing him. She missed Dante. She didn't want to miss him and that was why she'd made an excuse about going into her office for some meeting and then staying at her house, instead of his. She'd tried to pretend it wasn't because he was headed back to Italy for a month, but it was. The news had hit her hard after letting herself say yes to his bed, to his life, to his leather cuffs and sex games, and even to his plea that they try to recreate his mother's meatball recipe. She laughed at that memory. They'd made a mess of his sparkling white kitchen and ended up ordering pizza.

She sighed and settled her hand on her chin. She'd spent every second with him since she met him and she'd kidded herself into thinking it was something more than a fling. She'd fallen in love. And now, to make matters worse, she'd failed him professionally. She had to tell him this Bell's deal just wasn't going to happen.

A knock sounded on the door, and she pushed to her feet, running her hands down the front of her jeans and stretching. A glance at the clock explained her stiffness. She'd been sitting there at that table for two hours. That meant her guest was her mother, who'd promised to bring her dinner so they could catch up.

Sonya padded over her tiled floor in her tennis shoes, and opened the front door. Dante stood there, looking every bit as sexy in jeans and a biker jacket as he did in his business attire. He held up a Starbucks cup. "White mocha, nonfat, no whip with an extra shot."

She swallowed against the sudden dryness in her throat. "What are you doing here?"

He pretended not to notice her strain, and dangled a shaving bag from his finger. "I packed my things. We're staying here tonight, right?"

She leaned against the door frame. "You don't want to stay at my place. It's not exactly a five-star luxury place like your mansion in the hills."

He stepped forward, crowding her into backing up and letting him in. He then tossed his bag on the floor to free his hand and pulled her close. "You're here. That's all that matters."

Already her body ached for him, but this time her heart did, too. She couldn't do this. "I need some time at home, Dante. Alone. I need time alone." She was against the wall now, his hand pressed to the wall by her head, her coffee on the glass entry table.

He studied her, those dark eyes probing and all too knowing. "This is about me going to Italy, isn't it?"

She squeezed her eyes shut. "I just need some time."

He slid his fingers under her chin, silently willing her to look at him. "I'll be back."

"Right. I know. You have the hotels and we need to talk about the contract—"

"I don't give a damn about the contract," he said, his voice low, rough, determined. "We need to talk about us."

"Hello, hello!" came a female voice that made Sonya cringe. Her mother had arrived.

Two hours later, Sonya's mother had roped Dante into a game of chess, her new obsession since she'd joined a chess club. To her surprise, Dante had not only accepted, but they'd also been at it for an hour. The two of them seemed to get along well, and both were busy asking probing questions, neither bothering to be subtle.

Sonya grabbed the coffeepot from the kitchen at her mother's request and was about to head back to the living room to fill her cup, when she heard her mother say, "You know, I'd almost convinced myself you weren't one of those rich, arrogant impossible types until you went and did that."

Sonya gaped at the outrageous, out-of-character statement by her mother, panicked at what might be taking place. She rounded the corner. "Mother!"

Dante laughed. "I knew I shouldn't have told her you thought I was rich, arrogant and impossible," he said, repeating a joke Sonya had made on numerous occasions, before glancing at her mother. "I'll never live it down." He glanced at her mother. "And you can't expect me to let you win just because you're her mother."

"Yes, I can," her mother declared, crossing her arms and then laughing. "Okay. No, I can't but I want a rematch." She pushed to her feet. "I better head out. I have to open my store early tomorrow."

Dante followed her to her feet. "Very nice to meet you and I'll happily give you a rematch when I return to the States."

"That's a deal, son." Sonya's mother turned to Sonya. "Why don't you walk me to my car?"

Sonya glanced at Dante, who winked and then reached for his cell phone that she assumed was vibrating. He motioned to her patio to let her know he was going to take it outside.

Fifteen minutes later, Sonya had heard her mother's praises of Dante and dodged all of her questions about where things were headed with him. She was in knots when she entered the house, feeling like Dante was more a part of her life than ever, but yet he was leaving. It confused her.

She scanned the living room and didn't see him, but the patio door was still open. She strained to hear his conversation but there wasn't one to hear. She headed toward the door and pulled back the curtain. Dante was standing with his back to her, his hands on the railing, tension radiating off of him.

"Dante?"

He turned to look at her, the dim light capturing the shadows in his eyes. "What's wrong?" she asked gently.

He pressed his hands back to the rail behind him and looked up at the sky a moment, but she knew he wasn't really seeing it. Her stomach knotted in response. Whatever was bothering him, it wasn't good.

Finally, he looked at her. "That was my father," he said. "Whom you know I don't talk about much."

No. He talked about his mother and dodged questions about his father.

"He wants me to drop the casino project so he can retire," he explained.

"I see," Sonya said, feeling like she'd been punched in the gut.

"No," he said. "You don't. I told him no. It's a power play. I've been down this path with him before. He says he wants to retire but then finds a reason not to hand over control to me. This casino project was my way of just stepping away from that game he plays and creating diversity for the company. So he forced my return. That's why I'm headed home. He called a board meeting to discuss his replacement."

"Oh," she said, her gaze dropping to the ground, her mind processing the implications. Dante would be staying in Italy.

"You don't want to come with me."

Her eyes collided with his. "I didn't ask to come."

"He'll try to tear you apart and send you home. I don't want you in the line of fire."

"Why would he do that?"

"Because the one woman I ever let inside my family circle burned me badly. The relationship ended on a nasty note. We broke up and she went to the tabloids and sold them some intimate details about my personal habits—and you can guess what they were. I didn't give a shit but my father did. He said it tarnished our image."

And now she knew why trust was such an issue. "I... I'd never do anything like that."

"I know." He pushed off the railing and went to her, pressing his hand on the wall beside the door, over her head. "I don't want to let him hurt you, hurt us. I'm coming back."

She traced the line of his jaw, emotion welling inside her. This man had touched her life so quickly, so completely, that it was frightening. "I hope you do."

He kissed her fingers. "I will."

"I need you, Sonya. I need you tonight."

Tonight. He needed her tonight. She didn't want to think about the limits to those words, to his actions, by not wanting her to weather the storm of his father. But he pulled her into his arms and kissed her and her worry faded into passion.

Long minutes later they were on her couch, her straddling him, him buried deep inside her. And there were no games, no power plays, or toys, but somehow it was the most intimate moment they'd ever shared. It was raw and laden with emotion, with unspoken words that she couldn't help but read as a goodbye.

The next morning Sonya dropped off Dante at the airport. A day after that she walked out of Bell's with an agreement she knew Dante would be pleased with, and dialed his cell. He didn't answer. She knew he'd had a meeting with his father and the corporate attorneys that day, but it was killing her to not be able to share the good news. Hours later, she was at home, and he still hadn't returned her call. The next morning, still nothing.

Finally, three days later, in knots over his silence, she sat at her kitchen table and dialed Ricci's Italian offices. Minutes later, she hung up, stunned by the news that his father had died, and praying that he'd return her call. She started to cry. She knew what he was going through and she wanted to be there for him. She didn't understand why he hadn't reached out to her. She dialed his cell phone several times over the next few hours, leaving numerous messages. Time brought only silence. *He'd shut her out.*

CHAPTER ELEVEN

Two weeks after Dante had gone silent, Sonya had returned to work. Her boss, still a fat, happy cat over Dante's retainer, continued to be as nice as could be to her.

Another week passed and there was no word from Dante, but Sonya had pulled her head out of the sand. She rode the elevator to the garage level, loaded down with files for several new cases. The doors opened and her heart skipped a beat at the sight of a limo sitting in front of the door. She could almost feel herself shaking inside.

The door opened and Dante stepped outside the car. "Come. Let's talk."

"No," she said, shaking her head. She started walking.

"Wait." He rushed to her and stepped in front of her, towering over her, his hands settling on her shoulders, sending a rush of awareness through her she didn't want to feel. He looked good, masculine and sexy, in black jeans and a tee, and she didn't want to notice that, either.

"I can't do this, Dante."

"Please just get in and hear me out. If you don't like what I have to say, we'll keep it business. You have my word."

She inhaled, feeling trapped, feeling like she wanted to run. "Okay. But we stay here. We don't drive anywhere."

"Agreed," he said, reaching for her briefcase.

Sonya let him take her bag and slid inside the car before him, tugging at her skirt and realizing it was ironically the same light blue outfit she'd been wearing that first night with him.

He joined her and sat across from her, their eyes colliding. It was then that she noticed the strain in his face, the tiredness and stress. "You look good," he said, a rasp to his voice. "I missed you."

"Don't," she said, pressing her hands onto the seat, her spine stiff. "Don't say that."

"Sonya—"

"You didn't even call me when your father died," she said. "I would have been there for you but you didn't need me or want me or... I don't know. I just know that it hurt and I feel shallow for saying that when you were grieving but I can't help it. People who care about each other don't shut each other out."

"I know," he said. "I screwed up."

She reached for the door. He shackled her arm. "He walked out of a meeting with me and dropped dead of a heart attack."

"What?" She turned away from the door and faced him. "Oh, God, Dante. I don't even know what to say."

"Don't say anything. Just hear me out." She covered his hands with hers and nodded, and he quickly continued, as if he feared she'd change her mind. "My mother blamed me. She's never lashed out at me like she did. The board voted me into control and...I wasn't even sure I wanted the job. I was messed up, Sonya. I didn't want to tell you I'd fought with him before he died. I didn't think I could deal with the distance between us when I told you. I didn't know if I could tell you at all. I fought with him and he died. That is heavy. It's going to eat me alive for the rest of my life."

She pressed her hands to his face and kissed him. "You didn't cause his death and you can't let this destroy you. And, damn it, you should have called me and let me be there for you. You shouldn't have shut me out."

"I know, and if I could turn back time I would. You have no idea how much I want to." He reached for his jacket on the seat and pulled out a velvet box. "But I hope you will give me a lifetime to make it up to you. Sonya, being without you only made me more certain that I don't want to be without you ever again. I need you in my life. I need you in ways I've never needed anyone." He opened the lid and a gorgeous white diamond stone sparkled from the center of white silk. "I love you, Sonya. I have from the instant I met you. Marry me. Come to Italy with me and bring your mother. You'll never want for anything again and neither will your mother."

"I don't want your money," she said, her chest tightening with the impact of his words, and the reasons behind them. "And you're coming off a loss and…"

He pulled her into his arms and kissed her, a long, deep passionate kiss. "I *love you*. I need you. You can practice law, like I could stop you if I wanted to. You will have your life. I just want you to share it with me. Marry me."

Her eyes prickled with tears. "I love you, too. I do. I didn't want to, but I do."

He thumbed away tears. "And you'll marry me?"

"On one condition," she said.

"Name your price."

"That you trust me enough to let me cuff you."

His lips curved in a smile. "As long as you know I'll return every lick of pleasure ten times over."

"Promises, promises," she teased, and then let him slip the ring on her finger.

★ ★ ★ ★ ★

A VERY
PERSONAL ASSISTANT
PORTIA DA COSTA

"Thank God that's over!"

Miranda Austin tossed her leather document binder onto her blotter, threw herself down into her chair and kicked off her shoes beneath her broad leathertopped desk. How was it that sometimes after these high-level meetings, she felt as if she'd been put through a mangle when she returned from the boardroom? Closing her eyes, she tried to claw back her usual calm and poise and center herself.

"Tough gig?" enquired her personal assistant, Patrick Dove, as he crossed the office toward her.

"I'll say..." She breathed in deep, finding it hard to settle. "But I got my way in the end, even though it took some doing with those idiots from Overseas Assets."

"You always get your way." Patrick's tone was smooth and quiet—not false praise, but a simple observation. "Would you like some coffee, boss?"

Patrick made perfect coffee, but right now, Miranda felt too wired and too wound up to appreciate it. Eyes still closed, she shook her head.

"Is there something else I can do for you?" He paused, and the room seemed unnaturally quiet, almost as if neither of them were even breathing. "Some other way I can help you instead?"

Patrick said words like that a hundred times a week at least. Both to her and to the many clients and colleagues he had to deal with on her behalf. But this time Miranda knew he really meant them. Not that he didn't mean them when he was answering her calls, of course. It was just that today his soft, suave, charming voice sounded different somehow, weighted and full of strange intent as if he were trying to manipulate her in a benign yet subtle manner.

Miranda's eyes snapped open. She frowned. Was she imagining things? Probably. She was just tired, a bit burnt-out and weary of deals and wrangling. She loved that she was the highest-ranked woman in the company, and generally she relished even the most confrontational meetings, but sometimes, like now, it all drained her. What she needed was a lift, a boost, and seeing Patrick studying her so intently with those beautiful, sexy, compassionate eyes of his, she suddenly found herself saying, "I don't know.... But I do need *something*.... Maybe you should whisk me off my feet and take me away from all this?"

"Okay then. I will." His voice sounded different in a new way now. Brisk. Decisive. In charge. His gentle eyes somehow weren't quite as gentle anymore, either, but they twinkled with a light of daring and challenge. "You don't have any meetings this afternoon. Let's go for a drive, get out of town, play hooky for a few hours."

Heart shuddering inside her, she felt nervous, excited. As if something wonderful were about to happen, but she didn't quite know what. Leaving the office for the afternoon was absurd, out of the question. She had little enough time to catch up these days. But something in Patrick's smile, and the almost cocky way he was studying her, made her think of a box of chocolates or a heady, potent cocktail. A treat, indulgent but irresistible. And when he flicked his tongue over his lower lip, her body surged, rousing suddenly and hard.

"I've got too much work to do." Her voice sounded odd, too, light and feathery when usually she was so cool, contained and on top of everything.

"Well, you said you wanted to get away from it all." His eyes narrowed, still teasing, still tempting.

"No, I didn't, not really...you know I didn't mean it."

"Ah, but I'm psychic. I can tell you really *did* mean it."

Was he arguing with her? He didn't usually do that, but this time it seemed he was, and as his challenging smile broadened, the mad, insane, totally inappropriate fluttering in her nether regions intensified. She'd always mildly fancied Patrick in a rather disciplined, disconnected way, but her feelings had never broken through or taken control like this.

"No, you're not psychic. There're no such thing as psychic powers. You're just an uncannily efficient personal assistant who mostly anticipates his boss's needs, but who's way off in this case."

"So you say." He tilted his head to one side, his sandy blond hair glinting beneath the strip lighting. It was a bit curly and wayward, giving him the look of an angel from a painting or a fresco. A very naughty, playful angel, with all the earthly foibles of a man. "But I still think a few hours out of the office would do you good." He winked at her, no angel now, but more like the very devil. "Give you what you need."

The fluttering turned to a pounding, and enveloped her entire body. Heart, brain, sex. She felt as if she were standing on a precipice, or before a secret door, or at the edge of some narrow rickety bridge, leading...leading somewhere.

"All right then. But just an hour or so, no more. I'll order the car." Shoving her feet back into her shoes, she sat up and reached out toward the keypad on her phone. "Where shall we go?"

Before she could actually depress the button, a warm hand fastened about her wrist, immobilizing her. Normally she would have shaken off the unsolicited grip of any man, even Patrick, but a delicious honeyed sensation made her yield. Dear God, he was actually making her feel weak!

"No need for a car. I'll drive." His voice was quiet but powerful. "Just do what you need to do and then meet me down in the car park."

His hand tightened on her wrist, just for one moment, then he released her, winked again, and strode purposefully from the room.

This is crazy. I'm his boss and he's my personal assistant, for heaven's sake. We shouldn't be doing this.

Well, if that were the case, why had she primped and preened and fluttered in the cloakroom? Why was she smelling rather more than usual of Shalimar?

Her rational self told her it was just an hour or two out of the office, a change of scene, maybe a drink or a coffee somewhere. Patrick was a good conversationalist, with smart opinions on politics, current affairs and the media. It was always fun and mentally stimulating to chat with him, however briefly.

But her irrational self said this jaunt was all about sex.

Score one for my irrational self.

Especially when she turned the corner, reaching the car park, and her pussy literally rippled at the sight of Patrick.

He didn't look all that different, leaning against his powder-blue vintage Citroën in the sunlight. In fact he looked exactly the same as he usually did, in his sharp, but very traditional three-piece suit that fit his body so beautifully. The only perceptible change was the absence of his tie, and the opening of his collar—but in other ways, it was as if a magic prince had suddenly appeared and the relaxed energy in his lithe, athletic body seemed to promise that anything, in fact *everything*, was possible.

"Er...hi!" The slight squeak in her voice when she called out made her sound like a nervous teenage girl on her first date rather than a confident, powerful woman in her thirties and a senior partner in the firm.

"Hi, yourself," replied Patrick, pushing himself off the car with a smooth powerful shove, then opening the door for her.

The Citroën was low, and Miranda was acutely conscious of the frisky slide of her skirt as she half flung herself into the passenger seat. Patrick's smile broadened and seemed to twinkle as if it'd been animated by Pixar, while their eyes acknowledged the wedge of dark lace stocking top she'd just flashed at him. "Nice," he murmured, leaving her so flabbergasted at his cheek that she couldn't answer.

Clipping the buckle of her seat belt, she expected him to ask, *Where to?* But instead, he just set the car in motion, drove out of the car park and headed off confidently without reference to her or her preferences.

"Where are we going?"

Miranda swallowed, nerves and maniac butterflies fluttering in her chest. She'd been in cars with Patrick before, en route to away meetings and functions, but even though they'd been just as physically close in these instances as they were now, it'd never seemed so intimate, so intense. Senses she couldn't quantify were seeing him in perfect detail even while she affected a nonchalant interest in where they were heading.

"Oh, nowhere you know…just a little place. Off the beaten track. You'll like it."

"But where is it?"

Waiting at a set of lights, he was able to turn to her. His expression was arch, amused, completely in charge. Miranda felt as if the Citroën had become a parallel world where Patrick was the boss, and she the subordinate. And yet even as she thought that, she realized that she'd only ever been his superior in a nominal sense. Even when she'd been giving him instructions and doling out tasks, on some level he'd been oh so subtly controlling her instead.

Oh, God…what am I into here? What are we into?

"It's a secret. Why spoil the fun?" he said mildly, putting his foot down as the lights changed. They were taking a road out of town, and already greenery and sunlight were all around them. "You asked me to take you away from it all, and that's what I'm doing…. I'm taking you away from being in charge."

Oh, God…oh, God…

Miranda trembled. The phrase "a whole new ball game" had never really meant a lot to her, but now, she understood it completely. The door into the new world slammed shut behind her, the thud of it rushing through her body like a hot tsunami that crested deliciously in the pit of her belly and her sex.

As if he'd observed the phenomenon with X-ray vision, Patrick flashed her a quick glance. He barely took his eyes off the road for a second, and yet Miranda knew he'd seen everything, both hidden and unhidden.

"Let's play a game." He waggled his expressive blond eyebrows.

"What kind of a game?"

"Oh, just a little something to loosen you up. To relax you."

Strangely, despite the pounding of sexual excitement, Miranda realized she did feel relaxed. And safe, in an odd way. Which didn't make sense because she also knew, finally and with certainty, that Patrick was dangerous. Very dangerous.

She shook her head and tried to order the mismatched thoughts.

"Okay?" he said immediately.

"Yes…fine. I think."

"Well, in that case, take off your knickers and give them to me."

Miranda's jaw dropped, the breath knocked out of her. It wasn't as if she wasn't partly expecting something like this, but to hear it, in Patrick's soft, mellifluous tones, was like being tackled from the side by a twenty-stone wrestler.

"I beg your pardon?"

Again, that sly, mischievous look from the corner of his eye. "Oh, go on…it's just a bit of fun. Something different to take you out of yourself." His wicked pink tongue peeped out again. "Just for the hell of it."

She was about to protest, but the crazy friskiness of the idea was so seductive. What would they think at the firm, eh? If they knew… No-nonsense, corporate high-flyer Miranda Austin playing silly sex games with her discreetly urbane personal assistant. Her *very* personal assistant, right at this moment.

"All right then! Just for the hell of it!" She snorted with laughter, and beside her, Patrick's smile broadened, and became creamy and smug in a sweet, boyish way. He didn't take his eyes off the road, but she could feel his elation and triumph.

And strangely, it didn't annoy her one bit.

Hitching herself about in the seat, she managed to get a hand up her skirt and snag her knickers without flashing him.

He'd asked her to take her panties off, but she was still in charge, in a little way. She wasn't giving him extras, at least not yet. With a lot of wriggling and tugging and wrangling with her skirt, her underwear and even the seat belt, she eventually achieved her goal and hauled her cream lace-trimmed knickers down to her ankles.

Blood rushed into her face. She was blushing a little already, but when she caught sight of her panties, she felt a huge rush of heat. The crotch of them was drenched and sticky. She'd known she was aroused, turned on by this new, risqué Patrick, but as swimmingly as this? Good God! And she was odorous, too. A rich waft of woman-smell rose from the pale fabric, the perfume of her desire, haunting yet pungent.

"Now what?" she demanded, wadding them into a ball, trying to hide the incriminating evidence, but knowing that even as she did, he was probably fully aware of her state. After all, it was exactly what he'd been hoping to induce, she supposed.

"Throw them out of the window."

"What? Are you mad?" Her heart thudded. She almost wanted to do it, but they were still on a fairly busy road. "There are other cars…and also, they're part of a fairly expensive set that I happen to be rather fond of."

Patrick chuckled and, feeling goaded, Miranda reached for the window button.

"No! Don't do that. On second thought, it'd be a shame to lose them. They're very pretty—" he paused, as if for effect "—and they *smell* amazing!"

Miranda gasped. She couldn't help herself. The heat in her face blossomed, and much the same thing happened between her legs, in her pussy. Which felt all the more breathtaking for her precarious lack of underwear.

"So, why don't you slip them into my pocket, for safekeeping?" he asked, his voice light, deceptively casual.

Why not indeed? Men and their quirks. Somehow she'd not thought of Patrick in those terms...well, not consciously. But he was a man, all the same. Very, very much so. As she reached across, and rather clumsily stuffed the panties into the pocket of his suit jacket, the cloth slipped to one side, giving her a clearer view of his hips and thighs and crotch.

It didn't surprise her that he had a very pronounced and respectably sized erection. He winked again when she glanced back up again. The devil. He'd observed her checking him out, the smug bastard!

"Look, what's all this about?" she demanded, feeling off balance.

"Like I said, it's therapy...symbolic. I wanted you to throw your knickers away as a representation of you discarding your worries and the stress of work."

"And there's nothing in it for you, then, knowing I've got no panties on." She glanced very pointedly at his groin, and her heart thudded. Was he even bigger?

"Of course there's something in it for me," he said softly, his voice more intense and not quite as serene and controlled as before. "The thought of your naked sex is giving me an enormous horn. Do you think I don't think about you that way?" He snuck her another fleeting glance, then concentrated on a right turn, down a smaller road. "Hell, I think about your pussy all the time, Miranda. And your breasts and your bottom and your thighs and every other bit of you. I'm a man, and you're a beautiful woman. I can't help myself. Why wouldn't I think about your body?"

"So, no real interest in my mind at this time, then? I'm just a sex object to you?" she snapped out, covering her shock.

The mock-chastened expression he assumed was utterly adorable. Both sweet and wolfishly sexy at the same time. Miranda's heart pounded harder, and if she hadn't been securely buckled in, and he hadn't been at the wheel of a swiftly moving vehicle, she would have launched herself at him to kiss him, and a lot more.

"Oh, I'm in awe of your mind, boss. Really I am. Why else would I so enjoy working for a woman? With anyone less smart than you, it'd be irritating...and against my nature."

Frowning, Miranda tried to absorb what he was saying.

"You're a dominant?"

His smile was slow now, and narrow. Not threatening, but certainly possessed of power.

"Of course."

He worked for her. He took her orders. Yet all the time, his natural inclination was to give *her* orders. What an irony. What a performance. He never showed it, nor any sign of irritation. What a tour de force.

Miranda fell silent for a while, as Patrick negotiated what was becoming an increasingly twisty lane. They were out in the country now, in the wilds, and he controlled the car with only the lightest touch, effortlessly and economically.

Just the way he was completely controlling her.

"So what do you want me to do now?"

He changed gear before he answered, rounding a bend.

"How about showing me your pussy?" He didn't look at her, but he smiled, how he smiled.

There weren't many vehicles about around here, but occasionally they passed the odd one. Miranda realized her alarm must have shown on her face, because Patrick spoke again, almost immediately.

"Okay, that's a bit too extreme, for now.... So how about

just the tops of those delicious stockings you wear. Mmm, lace…I love it."

"How do you know I wear lace-topped hold-ups?"

He laughed again, a free, happy sound. A little like the way Miranda was starting to feel.

"A man can sometimes catch a sly glimpse when a lady is reaching for something." He tapped a finger on the wheel. "And then there're the couple of spare pairs you keep in the filing cabinet…I've dreamed about them."

Along with my pussy, and my breasts, it seems.

She didn't speak, but she edged the hem of her skirt up her thighs, inch by inch. He'd told her to, after all, and even if a passing motorist got an eyeful, it could be attributed to inadvertent creep of the fabric, not a deliberate act.

Patrick scored a quick glance, then bit his lip, looking pleased as punch with her.

Again, they drove on for a while, in companionable yet dynamic silence. Miranda had never felt this excited and needy in her life before, even after hours of diligent foreplay by previous lovers. It was a state of peaceful desperation. High lust, but almost restful, too.

He's going to fuck me. And touch me. And do things to me. It'll make things hellishly complicated and awkward back at work, but I don't care, I don't care, I don't care!

Eventually, they pulled up in front of a timber-built cottage, the last one in a small row, built alongside a lazy, leafy canal bank. They were clearly holiday homes, but Miranda could see no sign of life in any of them. Maybe they were weekend occupancy, and stood empty in the middle of the working week?

"It belongs to my gran. She likes to come here for little

breaks, and she lends it to anyone in the family who wants a few days' peace and quiet," said Patrick conversationally, nodding toward the blue painted door of the quaint little structure. "No one's here now, though…it's all ours. We have total privacy."

Total privacy. What did that mean? Miranda shuddered, not afraid, more excited.

"Come on. Let's go inside."

She nodded, her heart racing as he leapt out of the Citroën. Shoving at her skirt, she caught the top of one of her stockings and it slithered down her thigh. She was still hitching at it when the passenger door swung open.

"Let me…"

The contact of Patrick's fingers on her bare skin was like a jolt of sweet energy barreling through her. Kneeling beside the seat, he smoothed the lace up her thigh again, deftly righting it, then slid his hand beneath the hem of her skirt for just a moment, touching the soft hair at her crotch and brushing his thumb over it.

Miranda moaned. His touch was fleeting, barely there, and yet her clitoris leapt and her sex rippled as if he'd been fondling and fondling her and almost brought her to the point of orgasm. Maybe he *had* brought her to it, just with words, with his glances, and with his presence.

And then he was standing up, reaching for her hand, helping her out of the low car and onto her feet. Her bag tumbled to the path and he swooped it up and handed it to her, the perfect personal assistant. It was all completely normal and polite, and yet he'd just touched her sex—well, nearly—and her panties were nestled in his jacket pocket.

He led her to the cottage and let her in, the soul of courtesy. It was almost the way he was with her at work when he let her in and allowed her to precede him.

"Well, here we are." The genial host, he pulled out a chair for her, one of several set around a small kitchen table covered with an old-fashioned wipe-down cover.

Miranda slid onto the seat, her skirt rising a bit. He was looking at her with that sweet devil-imp smile again, teasing her. Not telling her what to do, yet not exactly subservient.

"What happens now?" She hung her bag over the back of the chair, still feeling off-kilter. "Do you spank me or fuck me, or what?"

"We can do either, or both, or neither.... But I really would like to see your pussy now." Eyes on her all the time, he shrugged out of his jacket and tossed it over the back of a nearby armchair. "I've been wondering what it looks like since I first came to work for you."

"Really...it never occurred to me that you were interested," she lied. Subliminally, it *had* occurred to her. Subliminally, *she'd* thought about it all the time. too.

Patrick took his seat, too, stretching out his long legs in front of him. His pose was elegant and relaxed, one elbow on the table, his other hand resting on his thigh, and yet everything about him suggested quiet power and readiness.

For what?

"Of course, I'm interested, Miranda," he purred, tilting his head on one side. He'd ruffled his hair somewhere along the line, and his blond curls looked even more boyish and angelic. His eyes looked like Lucifer's, sharp and blue. "But you wouldn't think much of me as P.A. if I perved you all the time, would you?"

"I suppose not." She placed one hand on the table, mirroring his, fingertips just inches away from his.

"Well, then…now we're on neutral ground. Why don't you put me out of my misery and show me the goods?"

Her heart thudded, leaping in her chest while sweat popped out all over her body. She'd had plenty of sex in her time, even a little kink now and again, but this was different…strange, ridiculously thrilling and forbidden. Feeling as if she wanted to gasp for breath, she hooked the hem of her suit skirt with the fingertips of her right hand and edged it up again. Patrick's eyes followed every movement, unwaveringly, even though his body was still and quiet. She loved the look of him in his classy waistcoat, with his shirt open at the neck, a tantalizing combination of the formal and the casual. As the edge of her skirt reached her groin, he took in a breath.

She hesitated. He smiled. She bit her lip. He shook his head, as if despairing of her. In a rough, impatient gesture she hauled up the hem, showing him the triangle of dark hair covering her sex and rumpling her skirt in a bunch at her waist.

"So now what?" she demanded, edging around a bit on the chair. She felt as if she had an engine running in her sex, creating a build-up of energy. She wanted to make wild movements, do extreme things. The urge to part her legs wide and push her pelvis forward, opening to him, was a rampaging hunger.

Patrick didn't speak. He just quirked his blond eyebrows at her, his eyes flicking to her pussy, then to her lips, and then back to her eyes again. His smile widened.

He's got me right where he wants me. He doesn't even have to touch me and he's driving me crazy.

"Well?" she persisted. She was worked up, wound up, and wanted action.

"Feeling horny, are we?" Patrick just stared at her, his fingertip moving in a tiny circle on the smooth, shiny surface of the tablecloth, so close to hers. The action was suggestive beyond belief, and his next words came as no surprise. "Why don't you masturbate?"

Her first thought was, *I can't!* But she knew she could. She knew she wanted to, desperately. There was nothing she wanted more, other than to have Patrick fuck her, right now, across the table. She glanced at the space between them, and the movement of his long elegant fingers, the slow circles that incited her to touch herself.

"All right. I will!"

Shuffling her legs wider, she thrust her hand between them, diving straight in with two fingers, searching and finding her clit. She'd wanted to put on a show for him, a grand performance, but she couldn't wait. She couldn't prevaricate. She needed to come.

"Oh!"

The jolt of immediate pleasure took her breath away. Her clit pulsed, fluttered, right on the edge. She backed straight off and began to slick around her folds. Patrick tilted his head to the side, as if assessing her performance.

"You want to come," he stated, "so why don't you? Why hold back?"

"I…I don't know…. It's what I usually do—I make it last… well, I try to."

Those blue eyes narrowed a little, looked more dangerous.

"Well, I don't want you to make it last. I want to see you come now." Reaching out, he placed his right hand over her left one, on the table, sliding his thumb to her wrist and settling it lightly over the pulse point there.

It was like being linked to him, blood to blood, the tiny contact as intimate in its own way as cock in cunt. Her heartbeat, and its racing rhythm, cried out to him.

With another little gasp, she went for her clit and began to rub, fast and hard, working herself without finesse or real accuracy, just pounding away at the sensitive center.

Barely seconds passed. Her body surged, clenching fiercely on empty air, rippling, grasping for Patrick's as yet unseen cock, the flesh she so longed for.

Moaning, she closed her eyes, as she always did, but he cried out, "No! Look into my eyes! Keep it here!" He passed his hand in a circle before his face, like a hypnotist. "Continue! Come again! You can do it!"

Sinking into a world of blue, of deep, glittering blue, she rotated her fingertip more lightly this time, with more delicacy. Her consciousness was balanced between three points: her clit, his eyes, the touch of his thumb. Silvery messages darted between the three nodes, circling and building up like some arcane power source. Pleasure rose again, buoyed up the circuit, the movement of Patrick's thumb as arousing as that of her finger, and the light in his eyes more incendiary than both.

"Come, Miranda, come!"

Pleasure swelled again, wild and ascending, her sex pulsating as she pitched forward in the hard old chair, breaking the magic triangle as she curved over her own rubbing fingertips. Patrick caught her shoulder with his free hand, supporting her, guiding her head toward his. As she came and came, their foreheads were pressed against one another's.

"That's it baby...that's it," he softly chanted, his breath as warm as a zephyr against her cheeks.

How weird. How odd. I've never come like this before....

The thoughts flitted through her mind as she came back to earth, and finally straightened up, Patrick's warm hand slipping to the nape of her neck and down her arm as she did so. She withdrew her hand from her crotch, and he clasped it and squeezed it, almost as if he were praising her somehow. And all the time he smiled and his eyes glowed with a strange, magical triumph.

"Phew! That was really something." She sounded breathless, even to her own ears, like an innocent after sex for the first time. "And different...not what I was expecting."

"What were you expecting?" Patrick drew her hands together, folding both into his own, vaguely like a therapist focusing the attention of his patient. Miranda was aware that her skirt was still around her waist, but it didn't seem to matter.

"I...I don't know.... A fuck, I suppose."

"A fuck would be nice," replied Patrick roundly, his tongue touching the center of his lower lip for a moment, naughty and enticing.

It would be nice, yes indeed. And suddenly she wanted it furiously. Even despite the orgasms she'd already had. Maybe because of them? Her engine was well and truly primed, and the curiosity that had simmered beneath the surface since she'd first engaged Patrick to work for her rose and bubbled, like water starting to boil.

"Is there a bed here?" She started to rise, glancing around as she felt her skirt slide on its lining and cover her again. She'd not really taken much notice of their surroundings, she'd been so bewitched by her companion, but now she saw two doors leading off the main kitchen and living area of the cottage. Both stood ajar, and in one she saw the side of what looked like a chest of drawers, and the other revealed the white gleam of an old-fashioned wash basin.

"There is...if you want it?" On his feet again, he looked, and sounded, strangely devious, as if he were plotting something. Miranda felt irritated. What was up with him? Didn't he want to fuck her? She glanced down at his crotch, and saw that he did. His erection was prodigious.

"What do you mean? If I want it?"

Still holding her hands, he inclined forward, running his mouth, lips slightly parted, over her cheek and her jaw.

Oh, God, he's never even kissed me yet.

As she realized that deficit, it was rectified. Patrick's lips settled on hers in a strangely chaste kiss, very soft, very tentative, utterly velvety. They moved very lightly, teasing, pressing a little, dragging a little. Then his mouth opened and he gently licked her lips with the tip of his tongue.

"There's something else I rather fancied," he whispered, his breath mingling with hers. "Maybe you'll indulge me?"

"Indulge you in what?"

Patrick's hands moved to her waist, spanning it. She was decent again now, but bizarrely, she wished she were naked so she could press her bare breasts and crotch against him, grinding against the fine, conservative suiting of his waistcoat and his trousers. Without thinking she let her hands drop to her skirt, ready to raise it again.

His smile provocative, he said, "Pretend the table is your desk." He nodded to the shiny surface of the tablecloth. "I'd like to fuck you across it…. It's my fantasy. Has been since the first day I walked into your office."

"But, couldn't we just have done it there anyway? There's a lock on my office door, you know."

"Yes, I do know that…and don't you think I haven't imagined you behind it, taking off your clothes to get changed when you're going out in the evening, straight from work. Putting on sexy underwear for some fortunate guy who gets to fuck you later on?"

She wanted to tell him that there had been no fortunate

guys recently. Nobody of significance since he'd come into her employment.

"So?" she challenged.

"No, it's too complicated, actually fucking in the office. It'd muddle the parameters of our excellent working relationship." She opened her mouth to protest, but he pressed his warm fingers over it. "Here, we're on neutral ground. It's just fantasy. It doesn't screw up how we act together back there."

She wanted to tell him that it might do that very thing for her, but as if he'd sensed her objections, he squelched them with another kiss. Something a bit more proactive and precocious this time. His tongue pushed into her mouth, licking, exploring, tasting, darting about. Subduing her. He was going to get his own way…across the table, whether it was substituting for her desk or not. She moaned into his mouth as he cupped her buttocks through her skirt.

"Come on, boss, over you go," he said eventually when she was about to crumple under the force of her own desire.

Even though she was still fully dressed apart from her knickers, he manhandled her facedown over the tablecloth, pressing her across it until her hot cheek was against the cloth, summarily pushing up her skirt.

Miranda closed her eyes, imagining her pale buttocks displayed to him, rounded and tempting. She had a nice arse, she knew that. She hoped he appreciated it.

When his warm hands gripped her and began to manipulate her, she knew he did. His palms cupped the rounds of her bottom and moved in slow circles, the rude handling tugging and pulling on her sex. Going with the flow, she moved in sync and with a hitch this way, and hitch the other, she managed to position her clit against the hard edge of the table.

"Ah, that's a good girl…work yourself…work it, babe… you can do it."

A hot rush of lust sluiced through her. He sounded like the director of a sleazy porno movie, praising his even sleazier star. She circled her hips, gasping at the pleasure it gave her from the friction against her clit and listening to the wicked sound of Patrick's laughter.

"And you can do it, too!" she growled after a moment, impatient for him. "Stop shilly-shallying about and fuck me, will you?"

"Of course, Ms. Austin," he intoned in his most neutral office voice, and then both of them were laughing, even though Miranda was perilously close to orgasm.

Which was a miracle, really. Sometimes she didn't come all that quickly. She hadn't even stopped to think about that particular phenomenon this afternoon, though. It seemed that with Patrick pleasure was easy, always available.

His zipper slid down, a tiny sound, but she heard it like a clarion call announcing the main act in a drama. Then rustling. Him rummaging in a pocket. Ah, the sneaky devil had condoms on his person. He'd certainly intended to get lucky, not that *she* minded. The luckier he got, the luckier *she* got, too. How could he be anything else but a lover par excellence, given what he could do to her with just his voice and his laughing blue eyes?

I wonder what your cock looks like, Mr. Paragon of All Good Things?

Twisting around, looking across the globes of her naked bottom, she checked him out.

Oh, nice.

He was a good size. A very good size. Jutting from above his pushed-down underwear, he was high and hard and pointing in her general direction, veins pronounced and crown rosy, even through the latex.

"Does it meet with your approval, ma'am?" he murmured in a debonair impression of a butler offering her a choice entrée rather than a man showing her his cock poking out of his fly, along with his underwear and shirttail.

"It'll do."

"Cheeky cow," he returned cheerfully, reaching for her thighs and edging them apart, firmly and with no nonsense. And she liked how he had no qualms about touching himself, guiding himself to exactly the right spot. No macho performance games, trying to push in, no hands, and poking around wildly until he found the entrance more by luck than judgment. "Hold still," he instructed her when she started to push toward him. "Let me do the work...you don't have to do anything."

"But what if I want to?"

"Ack, always have to be the boss, don't you," he observed, pushing himself now. His cock was definitely a bit bigger than it'd looked from such an awkward over-the-shoulder angle. He felt huge as he forged in, making her yield. "I thought this afternoon was all about you relaxing and not trying to control everything for a change." With a jerk of his hips, he was in to the hilt, making her gasp.

The urge to push again, to work herself against him, was uncontrollable. She grabbed at the edge of the table, for purchase, and shook her hips.

"Now, what did I say?" he reprimanded with a chuckle, steadying her with a strong hand on the small of her back. "Stay still...keep it here." He pushed very slowly, pressing her against the edge of the table, then staying there, keeping her pinned.

"But I like to move…when I'm fucking."

His fingers were firm on her back. Unyielding. His cock felt huge inside her, also unyielding.

"Try something different, Miranda…a change. That's why we're here." He leaned over her, and she felt the brush of cloth against her skin, and a tiny discomfort from the teeth of his zipper pressing, too. Inclining over her back, his body felt strong and protective, familiar and yet new and exciting. His breath was warm against her hair and the back of her neck as he nuzzled her lightly with nose and closed mouth, like a cat.

His immobility was dynamic. His cock a hot bar lodged in her sex. She stilled, savoring the feel of him, within. In the midst of crazy sex, she found serenity in his quiet, solid presence, over and inside her.

"Miranda," he whispered, his voice vague, almost bemused. On the surface of the table one hand found hers and laced her fingers with his. The other hand skated along her hip and thigh, then slithered beneath her, searching for her center. Quickly finding it…

Patrick's hands were manly, but deft. She'd always admired the grace of his gestures, the swift, efficient way he typed or gathered papers, even just set down a cup. The tips of his fingers were square, firm, steady. Deadly accurate as they settled on her, on her clit.

His touch was light, angled, teasing. The erotic engine inside her revved up and she began to hitch about again, desperate to release pent-up energy and pleasure.

"Hush," he breathed, still touching, still rocking that beautiful workmanlike fingertip at the very focus of erotic sensation. "If you want to move, move inside, sweetheart…grip me. Caress me with your cunt."

Permission. She'd been granted permission. For a microsecond, every feminist particle of her rebelled, then just as quickly realized the truth. There was strength in giving in, it was her choice, what *she* wanted at this moment. With his big cock in her sex, and his powerful body over hers, pressing her to the table, he was still serving her, giving her precisely the sensations that pleased her.

The scent of his cologne filled her head and made her smile with delight. He, too, it seemed, had topped up just as she had. His woodsy fragrance was always low-key and discreet around the office, but now its sensual notes were strong and spicy.

"You smell good," she said, panting with effort and concentration as she contracted her inner muscles, grabbing at him. It was hard going not to come almost immediately, but now he'd asked for this, she would give it to him—he deserved it.

Within seconds, she wasn't the only one who was panting.

"Oh, hell," he gasped. "That's good...that's fucking amazing."

And still he didn't move. Still he lay over her, deep inside her, rock-hard and unwavering. But his heartfelt gasps and muttered oaths told her she was getting to him. Even his fingertip wasn't moving now. It just rested against her.

But as his mouth opened against the side of her throat, and he kissed her hard there, her control splintered. Silver sensations rippled like electricity around his cock.

"I...I'm going to come.... I can't help it...." Her words sounded choppy and weird. Had she uttered them, or was it Patrick?

"Fuck... Me, too..." That *was* him.

His whole body tensed over her, and as her sex seemed to shimmer and gather itself, she half expected him to start thrusting furiously, as her previous lovers has mostly done at the point of no return.

But still Patrick was different, and himself. He shoved hard, but short. Little jerks, contained power, mastering his own hips even when he shouldn't have been able to keep control of anything. He massaged her sensitive entrance with the girth of his cock, even as his finger circled roughly on her clitoris.

"Come *now*, love," he growled as he did just the same.

With a keening wail of pleasure, she met and matched him.

Later, they set themselves to rights, and drank tea. Miranda could scarcely believe how ordinary everything seemed. Not ordinary in a mundane way, but in a quiet, calm, comfortable way that soothed her and made her feel refreshed. All the sense of being drained and burnt-out that she'd been plagued with just a couple of hours ago seemed to have been erased by the spiritual fire of orgasm.

And her strangely serene relationship with Patrick was unaltered and yet at the same time better somehow. The sex didn't complicate things. It just seemed as if the memories of it were bedded in a deep quiet place that she could draw on when she needed revivification.

It was clear that the dynamics of their working association were going to remain unruffled, too. The cottage was a special place—neither work, nor home. Time out of time. And they returned to it several times in the next few busy weeks. Always after a taxing time, when Miranda had had to grapple with curmudgeonly opponents at high-powered meetings. She'd return to the office, swearing and cursing even if she'd achieved her objective—and she'd see that sweet knowing twinkle in Patrick's eyes.

At home, she thought of him sometimes, perhaps more than she cared to admit, but life was busy. Work took most of her energy, and what little social life she had was with an established group of friends of both sexes. No dating.

A few times, she'd thought about ringing Patrick, asking him out, but the specter of workplace complications hung over the question. She'd seen people get too involved and crash and burn in ridiculously farcical flames.

One day, after a bitch of a morning, grappling with a delegation from the firm's new Swiss partnership—a set of tough negotiators for all their superficially polite amenability—she was at the end of her tether. For once, when she returned from the meeting, Patrick wasn't there, and that absence infuriated her.

She flung her binder across the room and it knocked a tower of document baskets and a potted plant all over the floor.

Patrick wasn't chained to his desk, she knew that. There were plenty of legitimate reasons why he could be elsewhere, and she'd even asked him to get some old documents from the file room....

Yet still, she raged, "Where are you, you fuck! Just when I need you, you go AWOL...you and those bloody Swiss bastards. Men, you're all the fucking same!"

It was nonsense, and ridiculous, and she knew it, but she wanted to knock everything off his desk, and send it flying, and smash all the other plants on the shelves around the office, too.

"Fuck!" she growled again, stomping across the room and swooping down to pick up papers.

"Well, if that's what you want, boss, I guess another long lunch is in order."

Her heart leapt at the sound of his voice, in a most alarming way. It wasn't a sex thing somehow, just relief, huge relief, that he was here.

314 *Portia Da Costa*

"Yes, it fucking well is!" she countered, still down, a sheaf of muddled paper in her hand. Of course they'd all had to slide out of the folders, hadn't they?

Teetering in a crouch, on her smart heels, she glowered over her shoulder at him, then suddenly overbalanced, landing on the carpet on her bottom. Another howl of rage rose to her lips, but within an instant, Patrick was at her side, helping her to rise, and the anger seemed to steam away like morning mist and she found herself laughing along with him as his strong arm brought her back up onto her feet.

"Another rough meeting, I guess?" he said, reaching out and tucking her hair behind her ears in an easy natural gesture.

Miranda's heart did another wild lurch. He never touched her in the office. It was part of their unspoken ground rules. A code they'd somehow formulated without ever once discussing it. She should have been even angrier with him for breaching it, but instead the tiny contact felt exquisite. And she ached for more of it, even as his hand withdrew.

"Absolute shit. Those bastards from the Swiss partnership are the most devious and conniving operators on the face of the planet. They project this nice, reasonable facade but it's a total sham. They're all sharks." She fussed with her hair herself, to cover the way she was shaking. Not with rage but with a sweet trembling at the proximity of Patrick.

"But you aced the meeting all the same?" It wasn't really a question.

"Yeah, how did you know?"

You know me so well, don't you? You can see right through the tantrums to the heart of what happened.

The revelation was alarming, yet wonderful. As was the way his beautiful cologne was tantalizing her, making her feel dizzy with lust and a whole lot more.

"Lucky guess," he replied with a puckish smile. "Look, let me tidy up here. Won't take a second. Get your things and I'll meet you in the car park in ten minutes, eh?" For a moment, he looked slightly unsure of himself, in a way she rarely saw, and a twist of strange yearning made her shudder. "That is, if you still want to?"

"What do you think?" she answered, wanting to reach down and ruffle his gilded hair as he sank into a crouch and began to field errant papers. Either that, or sigh at the way the action tightened his dark trousers around his haunches and his arse, revealing their strong, muscular shape. Instead, she darted away, snatched up her bag, then hurried past him while he was still scooping up documents.

"See you in ten…maybe fifteen, but no longer, eh?" Not looking back, she headed for the car park, via the cloakroom.

Fifteen minutes later and he was walking toward her, jingling his keys, his suit jacket slung over his shoulder and the sleeves of his blue Sea Island cotton shirt rolled up. She liked the look of his smooth forearms. They were powerful, and had a capable quality. Patrick was wonderful with his arms and hands. Well, every part of himself really. She knew his body was fabulous, even though she had yet to see him absolutely and completely naked. Their couplings had so far all been partially clothed affairs, even though not always hurried.

Without speaking, he let her into passenger seat, holding open the door for her, then strode around to his side, sliding in and slinging his jacket on the backseat. He gave her a placid, reassuring smile that seemed to negate even the need for words, and still in silence, they set off, heading for their secret world of sex.

About half way to the chalet, Patrick spoke up though.

Miranda was half expecting him to ask her to remove her knickers, which he sometimes—but not always—requested, but instead, he said, "They're hard on you, these division level meetings, aren't they?" He glanced at her quickly, out of the corner of his eye, his expression compassionate. "I can tell, even when I haven't been to one."

It was as if he'd released a pressure valve. It felt like a huge relief as she smiled back at him and said, "Hell, yes! I do enjoy them in a way…and I pretty much always get what I want out of them. But it's difficult, even in the twenty-first century, to dominate a gathering of men that way. Division heads, part-ners…execs. They take some bloody mastering, I can tell you." She took a long breath, sinking into the Citroën's squashy, comfy seat. "But it really takes it out of me, angling for con-trol all the time…you know?"

"Yes…I know."

Three words, but they seemed to hum with a deep, almost psychic wisdom.

"I know you do…and that's why I like our…um…" What to call them? "Our little get-togethers. I like them because I don't have to be in charge. I can just…just…"

"Submit?"

"Yes…with you, I don't have to decide things or control things or take responsibility. I can just *be*."

It was easy to say it. But complex, scary and wonderful to feel it. She had a sense that in admitting to that particu-lar word—*submit*—she'd stepped through yet another veil, moved onto another level, and her pussy tensed suddenly at the thought of it.

The last time they'd been together, Patrick had landed a single teasing slap on her bottom when they'd been fooling around together, tussling on the small settee in the cottage.

And she'd been stunned how much of a turn-on that had been. She'd immediately wanted him again, and got him, even though time had been short.

But now time wasn't short. She had no meetings for the rest of the day.

They passed the rest of the journey in silence, each mulling over their thoughts. At least Miranda was. For all his amiability and his sensitivity to her needs, Patrick was still very much an enigma. Were her needs his needs, too? Who could tell? She still knew virtually nothing about him outside of work and their time together at the cottage.

As he let her into the small holiday home, he took her bag from her and set it on the sideboard by the door. With a touch to the small of her back, he propelled her into the center of the room, then circled around until he was standing facing her, his eyes fixed on hers.

"You need to let go, Miranda." His hand settled on her cheek, long fingers curving and inviting her to turn her face and kiss his palm. "Remember what you said...just *be*."

A delicious lightness of spirit sluiced through her body, washing away stress and angst. Her concerns about work, her life, even her occasional wistful ponderings about Patrick himself and what she really meant to him. His touch seemed to cleanse her of all that. Especially when he leaned forward and kissed her lips lightly.

"Now remove your clothes."

Clamor in her chest, wild excitement, something new, something new. Immediately, between her legs, she felt hot and wet, silky with desire. An urge to move her hips, rub her thighs together, touch herself even, was like a crackling wildfire surging in her belly.

But Patrick's level blue gaze forbade those things completely.

Dragging in a breath, Miranda shrugged out of her jacket. For a moment, she was at a loss what to do with it, but Patrick took it from her and laid it quite neatly over the back of a chair. Next, her simple silk shell top. She unfastened the little button at the back of the neck, then wriggled out of it, pulling it off over her head. Patrick reached for that, too, but not before smoothing her hair back into place. Then he set her top with her jacket, and returned his gaze to her, appraisingly.

Her bra was white lace, very luxe and pretty. She'd taken to wearing her nicer undies to work—La Perla, Janet Reger, other upscale brands—simply on the off chance that it might be a day when she and Patrick fled the rat race to the cottage. More often than not, her silk-and-lace finery went unseen and unappreciated by his gaze, but there was always a frisson of excitement in wearing it anyway, fantasizing about moments like this. Moments when he smiled archly, his eyes zeroing in on her nipples that showed so darkly through the pale lace and protruded like ripe, tempting berries. Nodding infinitesimally, he swept his tongue over his lips as if anticipating the taste of such luscious fruit.

Her fingers fumbling with the hooks and eyes, Miranda struggled to free herself. The tiny fastenings defied her, turned into impenetrable micropuzzles by her lust and frustration, but just as she was on the point of ripping and tearing like a madwoman, Patrick stepped forward, reached around her and unhooked her in a smooth easy action. For a moment, he left the bra hanging loose, via its straps, then he slid his two hands around to the front of her body and cupped her breasts. A second later, after just a little squeeze, he lifted away the white lace and bared her. The brassiere went with her jacket and blouse across the back of the hard chair.

Bare from the waist up, Miranda experienced an irrational urge to cover herself. Her sense of vulnerability was a sweet taste upon her tongue, a nectar in her blood. Light-headed, she pushed back her shoulders, acting completely on instinct. The nakedness of her breasts was Patrick's by right, she must offer herself. Not resist, or fight, just be his.

"You're very beautiful...very, very beautiful. Those Swiss bastards should have been on their hands and knees, kissing your shoes, and grateful for the chance to humble themselves before you."

She laughed. What a thought. Even in the midst of sex and heat he could entertain her.

"Uh-oh," he said softly, placing a finger over her lips, light as thistledown, to silence her. She might be a goddess, to be worshipped and groveled to by the Swiss execs, but Patrick was *her* god, to be obeyed. "Now, behave yourself and get on with the task in hand."

Miranda experienced a pang of loss when the finger left her lips. She'd wanted to kiss it, draw it into her mouth and suck on it hungrily. Just the tiniest touch and contact excited her out of all proportion. She felt as if she were losing her mind for this man, but in a joyous, exciting way.

The hook and zip on her skirt weren't the barrier her bra hooks had been and in a flash, she was stepping out of it, balancing on her smart, business heels, terrified she'd trip on the hem and tumble. Not because she might bump herself, but because she didn't want to disappoint Patrick. She didn't want to be anything less than perfect and elegant and obedient for him.

Where had this submissiveness come from? It seemed both bizarre and alien, and yet it was like a comforting cloak, slipping over her, suiting her perfectly. She found herself lowering her eyes, respectfully, even though a part of her wanted to gorge on the handsome sight of him. His elegant athletic body in his dark waistcoat and trousers, and the way his white shirt, open at the neck, made him look like a golden laughing prince.

Nervous, she stepped out of her shoes, and then peeled down her hold-up stockings, tossing them aside. Just her panties remained, trim and lacy, the last barrier. She hooked her thumbs in the waistband, but Patrick shook his head. Her hands fell to her sides, as if they had no purpose, and she had no will.

Not sure whether she should, she lifted her head and looked him in the eye. He smiled, beautiful and benign, yet still steely somehow. Keeping his gaze locked on her face he stepped forward until their bodies were almost contiguous, then looked down on her. He wasn't all that much taller than she, but just enough to reinforce his supremacy. His hands dropped to her hips and he pulled her close until expanses of her bare skin were pressed close to the length of his clothed body. The brush of cloth against her breasts and abdomen and thighs was tantalizing and perverse, as was the taste of his mouth as he kissed her deeply again, thrusting his tongue between her lips, exploring her teeth, her palate, the inside of her cheeks.

It was a thorough kiss, a controlling kiss, and that quality compelled her stillness. As he devoured her, she knew she wasn't allowed to touch him in return. Her hands hung motionless at her sides, held there by his will.

He kissed her for a long time thus, one hand on her bottom, pressing her to him, one hand in her hair, securing her head. The power of his mouth was almost cruel, it made her jaw ache, but she rejoiced in it, feeding on his lust.

Finally he drew back, and said, "I'm going to spank you

now. I'm going to spank you hard, and you're going to enjoy it, even if you don't think you will."

His voice was hypnotic, even, gentle. All power in his soft words.

But I know *I'll enjoy it.*

That one casual spank he'd bestowed on her had made her sex flutter and desire gather. More she knew would be wonderful, despite the pain. Years ago, she and an old boyfriend had tried a bit of BDSM play, and that, too, had set a fire in her sex. The man had lost interest, and that hadn't bothered her at the time, but now she knew she would have liked to continue and experiment.

This time it would be different, greater, more wonderful. Because it was Patrick. Looking into his eyes, she knew this wasn't his chief kink. It was just something he liked to do, and wanted to do now, but that was enough for her. With him, she could try everything, do everything.

"Come," he said, taking her by the hand and leading her across the room to the little old settee, which was dun-colored, the worse for years and irregularly stuffed. Still holding her hand he sank down onto it and set his thighs strongly braced. Ready. "Right, Miranda…let's be having you."

Not quite sure how he wanted her, she followed the tug of his fingers and after a bit of hitching and adjustment, found herself face down across Patrick's lap, balanced in a state of both precariousness and safety. Her body and her face flamed, blushing furiously at both her vulnerable condition and the sensation of his solid, frisky erection digging into the side of her belly.

His next words surprised her.

"You can still change your mind, love. If you think this

isn't what you want, we can do something else...even turn the tables."

Her heart pounded. He'd do that for her? It was against his preference, she was sure of it. But for her, he'd go against his natural desires. What did *that* mean?

"Miranda?" he prompted.

"I don't want to change my mind. I want *this!*"

"Good girl...good girl..."

He began to caress her bottom, smoothing the tips of his fingers over her toned flesh through the flimsy fabric of her knickers. She worked hard at the gym three times a week, and she ate a good diet. She was in great shape and her bum was one of her best and sexiest features.

His touch was light, but aroused her exponentially. She felt again that urge she often got with him. The compulsion to move, to jiggle about, to rub against him, working off the electrical energy of desire that he roused in her. She felt as if she were bursting with it, whenever he was near. When she was at the office, she channeled it into work and ambition and the pursuit of excellence. When they were alone, it roiled inside, ever growing and boiling until an orgasm released it.

When she began to move, he said, "Tut-tut," and pressed down on the small of her back, to steady her. She obeyed instantly, and once she was still he peeled down her panties to the tops of her thighs, baring her bottom.

"Beautiful," he murmured...and then spanked her. Hard. Two fiery slaps, one on the crown of each buttock.

Miranda yelped as if she'd been electrocuted. This was nothing like that play slap the other time, and nothing like the meek and mild spanking her former lover had given her. This was powerful, determined, efficient, and just those two blows, and then a couple more, set her bottom and her pussy wildly aflame.

"Oh, God! Oh, God!" she chanted, unable *not* to wriggle now. Her entire sex was throbbing as well as her rear end, glowing and pulsating, just a hair away from climax.

Patrick spanked on, coating the entire surface of her bottom in burning heat, making it feel swollen and as if it were a simmering fluorescent crimson. Maybe it was? She didn't care. She couldn't think. She was desperate for the end of the awful, beautiful pain, but in the gaps between the strikes, she wanted to cry out *more, please, hurry!* By now she was lifting her hips to meet each hit, matching his action with her reaction.

"I want to come!" she wailed suddenly, unable to stop herself.

"Then why don't you?" observed Patrick, still spanking as he laughed fondly.

Hitching around on his lap, and rubbing herself lasciviously against his cock as she did so, Miranda reached around underneath herself to find her clit. She barely needed to touch it. Just one stroke and she came hard, desperately hard, the first pulsations fluttering in time to a couple of Patrick's spanks.

"Oh...ooh...oh, God," she gasped, pleasure cresting and surging, her legs kicking crazily as he ceased the punishment and slid two fingers into her channel from behind. Her pussy grabbed at him, hungrily, welcoming the intrusion as his thumb and his free fingers stirred the redness on the underhang of her bottom. His other hand was on her back, soft and light.

The orgasm seemed to go on a long time, a jerking, pulsing jumble of pain and bliss. Out of her head, Miranda was a castaway washed up on the living rock of Patrick. He was her refuge, and she clung on, sobbing and thanking him.

Eventually, she fell back into herself, intensely aware of his erection boring into her. It was like a knot of oak against her, hot through his trousers. She could feel it glowing, almost pulsing, calling to her, the heat of it echoing her own. Without stopping to ask, she slid off his knee and pressed his thighs apart with her hands. Shaking, fumbling, she unfastened his trousers and rummaged amongst his shirttail and underwear to draw him out into the light and air, an angry reddened column of primal desire.

Before he could speak, she slid her lips over his crown and started sucking hard and not too skillfully, as if her life depended on it.

"Oh, you beauty," shouted Patrick, half purr, half snarl, all desperation and long withheld need. His clever hands sank into her hair, gripping her head, directing her efforts, making her take more of him. "Use your tongue more, love…agh… yes…that's what I like."

She licked and sucked and swirled her tongue all around his glans and every bit of his shaft she could reach. He tasted both foxy and delicious, salty and fine, and he vocalized as she mouthed him, just as she'd cried and shouted when he'd spanked her and then thrust his fingers into her.

When he tensed and went rigid, she reached out and gripped him around the waist, hugging him for dearest life, so he couldn't withdraw. As he started to jerk, she sucked harder, flicking him sinuously beneath his glans, stabbing and probing like a guileful serpent intent on his pleasure.

A harsh oath echoed around the little room as he filled her mouth. Then came another and another, lurid, agonized utterances so unlike his usual easy amenable tones that it might have been another person entirely ejaculating onto her stroking tongue.

I love you.

The words echoed in her head, just as Patrick's profane cries of pleasure rang in the room. Even as he climaxed, and she gloried in it, the revelation terrified her. And confused her. She wasn't even sure if she'd thought it, heard it, or whether it had been the product of her mind or his.

She only knew that wherever the thought had originated, it had been the truth. She certainly loved him whether he loved her or whether he didn't. Letting him slip from between her lips, she looked up at him, half hoping he was still insensible with ecstasy, eyes closed, out of it.

But he wasn't. His blue eyes were as stormy and confused as her feelings, although perfectly lucid. He stared back down at her, intent, astonished...afraid? Then he frowned, made a sound like the growl of a wounded beast and lunged forward, grabbing her by the shoulders and urging her back almost roughly on the rug in front of the settee. In a muddle of her limbs and his, Miranda found herself on her back, her sore bottom pressed against the rough texture of the cheap carpeting. She hissed through her teeth at the surge of pain even as she reached for him, trying to pull him over her.

"No!" he hissed back at her, shaking off her grip, and instead of mounting her, slithering down onto his knees and crouching between her legs. She howled when he grabbed her hard by the buttocks and lifted her, wrenching her panties right off, then opening her up to him like a fruit and plunging his ravenous mouth down between her thighs to feast on her sex.

"Patrick! Patrick!" she shouted as he plagued her with lips and tongue—just as she'd done him—and sucked hard on her tender clit with ruthless intent.

Before she could hardly draw breath again, a fierce, hard,

painful orgasm wrenched at her. Agonizing in the intensity of pleasure and the way Patrick's fingers dug deep into the punished muscles of the bottom he'd spanked.

Somewhere in the furor, she seemed to feel his voice against her throbbing pussy.

"I love you," she sobbed.

Had she echoed what he'd said? Or simply what she'd wished for?

Everything was the same. Everything was different.

The next day, Miranda didn't know how to feel or act or look at Patrick. She'd ruined everything by blurting out her feelings, she knew that. Not that he showed his discomfiture or acted in any way out of his normal, serene efficient mode. But she could tell he was as shaken up as she was.

I can't go on like this. I need him. I love him. I want to talk about it but he doesn't seem to want to.

Work was tough. Two morning meetings were grueling. She managed to get through, and Patrick was still the perfect personal assistant. But when lunchtime came, he asked for the afternoon off. Miranda's heart leapt, hoping he'd suggest a trip to the cottage, but instead, he left alone, and she found herself staring out of the window, watching the Citroën pull away from the car park.

She couldn't blame him. For any number of reasons.

She'd broken the unspoken rules of their relationship.

Office liaisons were severely frowned upon.

She was the one who'd complicated something that was stunning and perfect in its simplicity.

Sex, in a special place, as no-strings therapy. Probably as much for him as it was for her.

The afternoon dragged abominably. She couldn't go on

like this. She couldn't face the weekend brooding and fretting, so she went online, looking for a short break, at a spa, a last-minute deal. Nothing took her fancy, though, so she decided to check email one last time then go home, via an off-license on the way.

Her heart dropped like a yo-yo when she saw a message from Patrick. And when she opened and read the attachment, she felt sick, adrift, shipwrecked.

He'd sent her a formal letter of resignation, a very plain, simple request. A serrated dagger through her heart.

Racing through the building to the car park, she didn't know and didn't care if she'd shut down her computer properly, locked her office, got all her things. She just had to get to Patrick's place. A phone call or a text just wouldn't do. She couldn't find the words, despite her usual executive eloquence, and she had to see him at home as she'd never seen him there before. Their lives had never intersected apart from the office and the cottage, but they were going to now, whether he wanted it or not.

She'd have an explanation, and one last fuck, even if it killed her, or him, in the process.

He lived in a nice building, not modern, but full of character, and built from mellow old stone. It was quirky, like him and his vintage Citroën and his sharply cut but ever so slightly old-fashioned three-piece suits. Miranda stabbed the speakerphone button beside the big black door, under the porch, without waiting and allowing herself to falter. When he answered, after a long wait, she was about on the point of fainting.

"It's me" was all she could say.

"You'd better come up," he answered without even having to ask who it was, despite the tinny quality of the speaker, that no doubt made her voice sound just as odd as his did.

On his landing, she hammered on the door, not caring a jot if neighbors on his landing heard her bashing away. She had to get in. She had to see him. She had to touch him. The door swung open after just a second, revealing him to her.

As she'd never seen him before.

In their trysts, she was reminded again now, he'd never actually taken all his clothes off. It had always been hurried rummaging amongst his linen, his beautiful cock standing proud from his fly, then after a few seconds, plunging into her sex or her mouth.

But now, here he was, obviously fresh from the shower, wearing a short blue silky robe in a paisley pattern. It left his feet and his lower legs completely bare, along with a slice of honey-tanned chest, peppered with a shadowy smattering of wiry sandy hair.

"I can't lose you!" she cried, surging into the little hallway of his flat, forcing him to back up. "I just can't! I couldn't bear it!"

Heat and confusion flared in his blue eyes. Was he shocked that she was here? Was he horrified? For a moment the floor seemed to shift beneath her, then she gritted her teeth and threw her bag down, launching herself at him and not giving either of them chance to think.

She pushed him against the wall, cramming her body against his, reaching up for his head, to bring his mouth down to hers. His blond curls were wet and awry, and she dug her fingers into them as she kissed him, demanding with the pressure of her mouth what she was too desperate to ask for in spoken words.

Joy, even if only temporary, poured through her when he responded, and his arms snaked around her, holding her as hard as she was holding him.

Between their bodies, his cock was hard, a knot of instant, rocklike readiness. He worked it against her, knocking his hips against hers as he kissed her back as furiously as she was kissing him.

Tongues and lips dueled, speaking volumes in gasping silence. Miranda tried to struggle and wrestle with her jacket, but he grabbed hold of her upper arms and immobilized her, his mouth cruel against hers, almost punishing her.

When they were both gasping for air, he let her free a moment, staring, almost glaring down into her eyes. Was he angry? It was hard to tell, but his expression was like a furnace of violent emotion, his face all aglow. Even as she finally managed to catch her breath, he grabbed her again and swung her around until she was the one pressed up against the wall. Then, in a fluid, elegant move, almost like a supermodel shedding a layer on the catwalk, he shucked off his robe and then lunged forward again, pressing his naked, muscular body against her body, still in its clothes and all.

Her hands flew to his back, his buttocks, embracing, exploring and savoring all she'd previously been denied. The notion of skin like silk was a cliché, especially for a man. It sounded like something that should only be a quality of an unattainably perfect romantic hero…but it was true in Patrick's case, deliciously and wonderfully true.

Just running her hands over him was a pleasure in itself, and between her legs, her pussy clenched, wet and needy. This was the final treat she'd been longing for—a naked, unhidden Patrick, free of the mask of his corporate, sartorial elegance.

He kept kissing her, imposing himself on her, his hands sliding beneath her skirt and running up and down her thighs, flicking over her stocking tops. "I can't lose you, either," he growled, before plunging in with hungry kisses again and again.

Miranda was floating, out of it, and only into him. But as her eyes flicked open, and across the little hallway, she realized that the door was still wide open, offering anyone on the landing a prime view of Patrick's fine arse.

But she didn't care, and it seemed he didn't, either. Even when he bunched up her skirt so he could touch her, there wasn't a fiber of her that was bothered by the possibility of exposure. His hand slipped into her panties and all was right in the world.

"I won't take it back," she hissed as he touched her, finding her clitoris with his supernatural touch. "I love you. I can't help it. Deal with it."

"I will," he replied, swirling in her slippery sex, working her. "And I'll deal with you...but first I've got to fuck you." He kissed her, quick, rough, deep. "Now. Immediately. I can't wait." He rubbed her clit in tight little circles. "Got a condom in that bag?" He nodded in the direction of her shoulder-bag, lying on the carpet runner.

She nodded furiously, so close to coming that she literally couldn't speak. All she could do was watch as Patrick swooped down, small, detailed muscles working his back as he rummaged efficiently in the bag and pulled out a familiar foil package. It was hard to stay upright. His body was so amazing that just looking at it made her shake all over, but she laughed out loud as he back-heeled the door shut, then advanced on her, ripping open the foil and rolling the contraceptive onto his mighty erection as he approached.

"Brace yourself, woman," he growled, grabbing her again. "You'll need to help me...knickers off, then guide me into you and hang on for dear life."

She obeyed, loving it. He was in charge here, just as he'd always been during their trips to the cottage. And he was hard as iron just as he'd been there, too.

But still, this was tricky. How were they going to achieve this. It was all very well in movies doing the up-against-the-wall knee-trembler, but she'd always believed it was impossible in real life, with actual people. No previous lover of hers had even attempted it.

"We'll fall," she protested, even as he flexed his strong legs and positioned the head of his cock against her entrance, lifting one of her thighs to get at her better.

"No, we won't, woman. Don't fuss," he said gruffly, working with his hips, already in a little way. "It's a trust exercise. We'll be fine. Believe me. Now help."

So she did, hooking her thigh around his narrow hips, and then bracing against the wall with one hand while she reached down and tangled fingers with his, aiding his entry into her. Luckily she was slippery, running with arousal, soft and yielding.

With a hard shove, his buttocks tensing, he thrust home and hard.

"Lock your thighs around me," he commanded. "Right around... I want to be deeper."

It felt so precarious, yet also wonderful, this trust exercise. She'd never felt so filled before, but she wanted to be more filled. Only Patrick could do this. Only he could reach places inside her that no man ever had. And on many levels that were nothing to do with his cock.

"I'll never let you fall, love," he gasped, looking directly into her eyes, his own intent, dark as night, focused on sex, yet on her, too. "Believe me, I'll never let you down."

She hooked around him, completely suspended from him,

her sex jammed up against his, her arms locked around his neck, holding him as if she'd never let him go.

I never will let you go! Never! I don't care what happens! she cried silently to him and he began to thrust and thrust with his hips, one hand under her buttocks to guide her, the other flat and steady against the wall. Every time he rocked against her, the force, the angle, the weight of his athletic body, and the whole of his heart and soul seemed to knock against her clitoris, shooting jolts of pleasure up her spine and around her body.

Holding him with her thighs and arms, she jerked against him reciprocally, attempting to give as much as she was getting, and pleasure him. He muttered, "Yes, love! Yes!" and that told her she was achieving her objective.

The fucking, the closeness, it was all too much for her. Even though she was clothed and he was nude, she felt as if every part of her was pressed to every part of him. Her suit, her blouse, her bra, everything was insubstantial but her flesh against his flesh. And it was that connection, the one that was so magical and hard to define, that brought her off as much as the action of his cock and the rhythmic tugging action on her clit.

"Oh, hell! Oh, God! Patrick!" she howled as orgasm claimed her completely and her pussy rippled and gripped and gripped and gripped him.

"Oh, baby," he muttered vaguely, holding her to him. "I love you...I love you..." His broad chest heaved against her. "But if I climax here, I *will* drop you.... You feel too good!"

Giddy with pleasure, Miranda thought, *What? How?*

"Hold on, love. Hold on really, really tight." Both of his hands slid under her bottom, gripping her firmly.

Hardly able to believe what he was up to, she still trusted him, and hiccupped with laughter when he swung her away from the wall, and began to carry her, still on the prow of his erection, down the little hallway and into a room at the end. Ever so gently, he used her to nudge the door wider, then strode into what was revealed to be his bedroom, heading for the bed.

Miranda didn't notice much about the room, except that it was decorated in blues, and appeared incredibly tidy, but what she did see was that spread right beneath where he clearly intended to deposit her, was a freshly pressed suit laid out, along with shirt, underwear and socks.

"Where were you going?" she asked, the question purely automatic and female. Despite the fact that his cock was inside her, she felt fear and uncertainty for the first time since she'd walked into the flat. What if he had a girlfriend? Someone he had a real relationship with, not just a weird out-of-office sex thing?

"Don't worry, sweetheart…it was all for you," he said as he set her down, inclining over her. He slipped out of her then, and let rip a lurid curse, but a moment later, he'd rearranged her body and his and he thrust inside her again, this time with the stable surface of the bed beneath her back.

"Good" was all Miranda could gasp, as he began to plough her in even deeper strokes than before.

Despite the fact that they were fucking in comfort now, she felt giddy, whirling, almost hysterical. The sensations doubled, tripled, went off the scale, enhanced and illuminated by subconscious realizations and hopes and dreams. He cared, he loved her, and something even greater and more wonderful than just this sublime physical experience lay ahead.

But she was going to have to live through this, and have an orgasm again first. Or several orgasms…

★ ★ ★

Afterward, naked, and following several passionate join-ings, they dozed. Or at least, Patrick did.

Typical man.

But Miranda smiled fondly at his beautiful fallen angel profile, and his tousled blond curls. He was adorable, and she did adore him and love him. And how dumb was she not to comprehend this a lot, lot sooner.

I should never have given you a job. I should just have asked you for a date.

It would have been much, much simpler from a work and relationship perspective. Who knew where they'd be by now? Far further along their path together…maybe?

As if he'd sensed her troubled thoughts, he stirred and turned toward her, his face alight with that sunny smile she loved so much.

"Well, fancy you being here," he said, stroking her face. "I've fantasized about you being here, and wanked so often while imagining you here, that I can't believe that it's really actually happened."

The idea of him touching himself and pleasuring himself made Miranda's skin tingle, and impossibly, given the amount of climaxes she'd enjoyed, her pussy rippled with fresh desire. But there were issues to be settled, plans to be made, and even in this quiet, special, love-filled room, the businesswoman, the organizer in her, rallied.

"Please tell me you're going to withdraw your notice now." It was going to be awkward working together and maintain-ing a relationship, but if they were discreet and sensible there was no reason why they couldn't manage it.

"No, I'm not," he said, his eyes steady. "I can't come back to the company."

A great, empty hole seemed to yawn inside her, the prospect of not seeing him every day, not talking with him, laughing with him. It wasn't even the sex. It was him, with her, that she'd missed. He was the one constant in her life, the daily necessity, and now she could admit how little she'd looked forward to weekends since he'd become her assistant.

"I can't come back because relationships between staff members are frowned upon. I'd rather see you all the rest of the time, and just get another job." His thumb moved slowly over her skin, brushing her lower lip, that was a little bruised from all the kissing they'd done. "I've been offered a share in a recruitment agency, helping busy execs like you find 'treasures' like me. I think I'll enjoy the work."

See you the rest of the time....

"What do you mean, see me the rest of the time?"

She knew, actually, and her heart was pounding. This was it, oh, God, the thing she'd never thought she'd find.

"I think you know, my love." He waggled his sandy-gold eyebrows at her. "I'm not usually wrong about anticipating what you want...at least I think I'm not wrong." A tiny shadow of doubt flashed across his face, and as if to banish it, he leaned over and kissed her. "I'm not wrong, am I?"

"No, not wrong at all," she answered when he freed her mouth. She was panting for lack of breath, and because of the sweet shock, the enormity of what they were dancing around. "But...um...we've never even dated or anything."

He gave her an arch look, almost smug, utterly delicious. "We've spent a large part of each working day together for the last six months...and in my book that's plenty of time to find out if we're simpatico, wouldn't you say?" Reaching out, he ran his hand over her naked flank. "And we're certainly compatible in bed…or out of it." He winked. "We're perfectly suited."

"Yes, we are," she whispered, leaning into the caress of his hand, willing it to go further, then purring with bliss when it slid to her breast and cupped it. Part of her wanted to start asking practical questions about time scales and flats and engagement rings, but most of her was happy to wallow in happiness and freshly stirring pleasure.

They would work everything out, as they always did. They'd had enough practice organizing their life together during working hours, and at the cottage, so it'd be easy enough to do the same in all the other hours.

Still, she had to ask one question, though.

"So, if we're not at the office, and you don't work for me anymore…who's going to be the boss in this relationship?"

Patrick gave her a long, long look, an intense fiery expression that made her belly surge like boiling honey and her pussy clench with heavy, delicious longing.

"Oh, you're pretty good at negotiations, my love," he said softly, "and I'm good at knowing exactly what you want and when you want it." He threw a long, muscular thigh across her, and reacquainted her with his seemingly unflagging and unstoppable erection. "So I think we'll work out something between us, don't you?"

Miranda nodded, surging against him, rubbing her softness against his hardness as her soul recognized its perfect mate and match.

Patrick's arms slid right around her, pulling her even closer, as he whispered in her ear, "And if you get too uppity, we've always got the cottage."

Images flooded through her mind, delicious images, sensations and memories. Along with sweet ideas and notions and plans for future trips to their wicked little hideaway.

"Maybe we could go there for our honeymoon?" she suggested, reaching down to touch the cock of the man she loved.

"Indeed, my love. I was just going to suggest the very same thing."

His happy laugh turned to a groan of pleasure as she stroked him.

★ ★ ★ ★ ★

TIED UP & TWISTED

ALISON TYLER

An S&M Love Story

The men in the room are all bent into interesting positions. A big blond stands on his hands, balanced and unmoving. Another dangles from rings. A third is leaning over a polished leather horse. Hadley McCarthy watches the men as she moves past them—imagining that they have been put there for her pleasure, fantasizing that they will never move. Hold still. Stay that way.

She hears the voice of the trainer, and her head turns quickly. *Trainer.* In another world, in *her* other world, the word means something else. There, he'd be Dom. Here, he is Coach.

When she sees him, she feels for a moment as if she can't breathe. He is older than she is by maybe fifteen years, and he's tall: at least six foot three. She's good at approximating—being a journalist has honed her observational skills. The trainer has a thick, solid chest, muscular arms. There's a faded tattoo high up on his biceps. Old-fashioned, Sailor Jerry style. But his physique is not what stops her: it's the power that emanates from him. She's never been so struck by a stranger before. He has a presence that draws out her basest, most animalistic instincts. She wants to fuck him.

He turns and looks her way, but he doesn't seem to see her.

The room is in motion, suddenly—or maybe it was always in motion and she had frozen the players in position with the power of her mind. The men are beautiful—young and lithe. Yet she doesn't see them as points of interest. She sees only the trainer, the way he stands and observes, barks, manipulates. He's the oldest thing in the room, and she only has eyes for him.

Would he talk like that to her if she asked him?

Would he bark commands? Push her around?

Would he punish her?

Hadley remains still for a moment and takes a breath. Then she heads to the front desk to find someone who can help her.

Guy watches through the windows in the office. He runs his hands through his thick dark hair, as he always does when he's nervous. A quick gesture, as if to make sure every carefully mussed piece of hair is still artfully out of place. He touches the buttons on the front of his shirt as if they're talismans, shoots the cuffs of his sleeves. Hadley doesn't notice him, but he follows her intently. She is different from the rest of the girls moving through the gym in their colorful bits of glittery spandex. She's older and poised. The gymnasts are poised, too, but in a different way. *Positioned* is a better term. Always on display.

He walks down the corridor and moves quickly after the woman.

Reed Frost sits in the Parallel Bar—the gym's ultra modern upstairs café—staring at this journalist. He sizes her up quickly, the way he sums up any new athlete walking into his gym: dark hair, deep brown eyes, high cheekbones. Delicate features you want to trace with the tip of your finger. V-neck sweater in charcoal and a matching pencil skirt. Lovely. He appraises her automatically, a mental exercise. As he would a new athlete, he puts her through an imaginary routine. She has balance; she's graceful—he can tell that instantly. It's a skill. He smiles to himself. She has absolutely zero interest in his services. This girl is here to do a piece for the local paper. She's not here to ask about becoming a member. Besides, she's two decades too old.

"Why are you smiling?"

Her voice surprises him. He stops smiling and looks at her, his blue eyes narrowing. His athletes don't talk to him like that. But he reminds himself quickly that she's not one of his athletes. "I'm not often the one being interviewed," he says, voice even.

"Meaning?" She holds her pen above her notebook. He likes that she isn't using a laptop. He notices that her pen is sleek, silver and expensive-looking, and her notebook isn't one of those fancy, useless ones from a craft store. She's writing in a Moleskine. He uses the smaller version to keep his own notes.

"For my standard intakes, I run the prospective athletes through a rigorous questioning session," Frost explains.

"Define 'rigorous.'"

He looks hard at her again. It's obvious to both of them that there's a connection. Yet neither one seems willing to make the first move. "You're the writer." He's mock deferential.

She thinks, *Touché,* but moves on. "How long have you been at the gym?"

"Seventeen years."

"That's a long time."

"Depends on how long you've got," he says matter-of-factly.

"How long have you got?" she asks, and she wishes he could see inside her mind. Every time she looks at him, she visualizes what he'd be like in bed. If they were at a bar, she'd slide her leg against his under the table and let him wonder whether the brush of her skin against his was accidental or on purpose. Right when he decides the move was accidental, she'd do it again. If they were at her favorite club in the city, she'd set up a scenario that would make his cock hard in a second.

She hasn't had a man in seven months.

That's the longest she's ever gone without.

She has no idea that Frost has been solo for seven years.

In another circumstance, Hadley would come clean with him. She'd lean in close and whisper that she doesn't believe in love at first sight or instant karma or screwing on a first date. But if he would come to her apartment tonight, she'd let him tie her to her four-poster bed and whip her.

In her scenario, there are too many *ifs*.

"We need you in the gym," Guy says, coming up from behind Frost. He speaks the words quietly, rather than bursting out screaming the way he wants to. He is having an inner tantrum that feels like a ball of fire in his throat, but what he says is simply: "I'll take over." He looks at Hadley, who sighs when she sees Guy. He's a pretty boy who knows exactly how pretty he is. Chiseled cheekbones, dimpled chin, jaw you could use for a ruler. He might have stepped out of an Abercrombie & Fitch ad instead of stepping out of her past.

She wants to tell him that pretty doesn't work for her. Not anymore. She knows exactly where she stands. She is thirty-three. She weighs 117 pounds. She never lies and says she's thirty. She never fibs and says she's 115. But she guesses that if someone asked this dark-haired Adonis his weight or his age, some part of the truth would be shaved off the top. He dyes his hair to achieve those chestnut highlights. She's certain.

Frost leaves. The fact that he doesn't turn around to say goodbye is one more point in his pro column. She's hooked—and fucked—and she knows it.

"How can I help you, Hadley?" Guy asks her as he takes Frost's seat.

"You can't."

Guy follows her eyes, sees she's staring after Frost and sneers, "He's not your type."

"What do you know about my type?"

"More than you think I should. More than I'd like to." This interaction is not going the way Guy hoped it would.

"You don't know anything about me, Guy." That's not entirely true, so she adds resignedly, "Not anymore."

"I know what your pussy tastes like." He can't help himself. Maybe if he pushes her buttons, she'll give him what he needs. He's got a rise out of her in the past. He knows how to make her react.

People turn to look at them. Hadley feels their eyes and wonders if they can sense the distaste she has for Guy.

"So do a lot of men."

"You say that like you're proud."

She stands and looks down at him. "And you say you know what my pussy tastes like as if you know your way around a girl's clit."

She ought to have anticipated this. When her editor had assigned her to cover the gym, she should have asked who'd suggested the story in the first place. But her mind had been on finding a new apartment, reestablishing old work ties, digging into her storage facility for the nuts and bolts of her old life. She'd moved out of Northern California to get free of Guy. She'd never have expected him to be on the lookout for her return. Their relationship hadn't simply evaporated—the dregs had curdled and soured. A year traveling the country had been for her mental health.

Apparently, Guy had been waiting for her to come back. Getting her to write an article about the place where he works is a creative way of finding her once more.

But fuck Guy. She can't spend her whole life doing the things he wants her to do, being the person he thought she was. If she learned anything while traveling the country for the past twelve months, it's that she has to be true to herself.

Guy slips into the private executive men's room, locks the door, and pushes his strong back against the cool, tiled wall. He's as well built as any of the athletes out there on the floor, but he isn't on a team. His job here is head of the PR department. Right now, he doesn't care about his responsibilities. His top priority is to make himself come. He has his hand on his cock before he can even consider what he's doing.

How many times has he jacked off to images of Hadley over the past twelve months? Too many to count, that's for fucking sure. He was certain the situation would unfold differently when he saw her again. No, he doesn't think life is like a happy movie of the week, but he'd yearned for a happy ending. He thought she'd remember what they had, what they were like—how it felt to have his dick deep inside her.

When she'd let him, that is.

His hand pumps up and down his shaft. He was hard since before she arrived. Simply knowing she was coming to the gym today gave him an erection. Part of him—the guilty part—is certain she can guess what he's doing right now. She had him down pat when they were together; she understood what made him tick.

So many times she forced him to wait for his pleasure. She'd make him go for a week, two, three, with no release, and he loved it. When she was in her cruelest moods, she'd keep a red pen by the calendar. Each day he survived without an orgasm, she'd draw an *X* in the little square. There would be a reward waiting for him if he was good, or sweet punishment if he was bad. He enjoyed both situations equally, if he were to be completely honest with himself.

He'd imagined that this year was simply the longest punishment she'd ever meted out. And he'd behaved. He'd been faithful—if "faithful" includes watching an almost endless stream of BDSM porn. He didn't sink his dick into any other woman. That should count for something, right?

His hand works his cock as he imagines her tying him down to her bed, telling him what a naughty boy he's been, punishing him with her favorite array of X-rated weapons. He hesitates only long enough to fill his palm with the synthetic rose-scented pink soap. He's not thinking clearly. He only craves relief. The liquid soap feels like pure sin on his rod. He fucks his slippery palm while he recalls his past with Hadley. She liked to use a wooden paddle first, heating his ass cheeks until they were deep cherry-red. Then she'd stripe him with her crop, watching as he worked hard not to fuck the mattress in his desire for mercy. Sometimes being bad feels so fucking good. Guy knows all about that.

His favorite time with Hadley occurred right near the end. They were fighting a lot—that is, when they were talking. But one night she came home in a mood. He sensed the shift in the apartment as soon as she walked through the door. The molecules in the air seemed to change. She had him bound with cold steel cuffs, his wrists over his head. She brought out a strap-on that night, and a bottle of lube. She set them both on the bedside table, so he could stare at them and know what was coming.

There was discipline first—Hadley always took care of his

needs, the wicked urges that made his dick hard. And then she whispered to him that she was going to use him for her own pleasure. She got his permission first.

"Let me," she'd said, and he'd nodded.

She'd parted the cheeks of his ass and poured lube between, then worked her thumb into his tight virgin hole. For several moments he'd held his breath, afraid that if he made any sort of move, she might stop. How had she known that he'd always wanted someone to fuck his ass? He'd never confessed this desire, and she'd never broached the subject before.

Somehow, she'd simply known.

After prepping him with lube and that dreamy finger fucking, she'd dangled the strap-on in front of his eyes and made him suck the head. He'd started slowly, his lips stretching over the tip, getting used to the sensation before she fastened the toy to the harness that was in place around her slim hips. His lips around the tool had felt like coming home, and he hadn't wanted her to pull back. But ultimately she moved behind him on the bed, parted his cheeks and stretched him wide.

He'd cried when she fucked him. Not because he didn't like it, but because he did.

He's all twisted. He knows that. She knew that, too, and she accepted him.

He makes himself climax in seconds from the memory, shooting in a jerking motion against the floor of the bathroom. But the release gives him no peace.

When she's in bed that night, Hadley thinks about Reed Frost. She remembers the last time she connected with a lover—a man she met at a bar in Albuquerque. "Lover" is stretching what he was to her. She hadn't expected to meet anyone that night either. She'd been working, writing by candlelight in a corner of the bar, and a drink had been delivered to her table.

Curious.

The glass of good Scotch had been followed by the man, who spent the evening doing things to her that nobody had done before.

Up until then, she'd been a domme.

The stranger searched out her sub.

Frost sits at home in his empty apartment. He thinks of the journalist, and he wonders what she's doing. He can imagine that she has a full social schedule. A girl who looks like that must be asked out every night of the week.

He considers, for the briefest moment, going out himself. Finding a bar. Getting a drink. *Idiot.* He has been alone since his ex left. He decided years ago that some people simply wind up alone. Law of averages, and all that.

If he wants a drink, he doesn't need to go anywhere. He walks barefoot to his kitchen and grabs a beer from the twelve-pack he has in the fridge. Why leave? There's steak and mushrooms in the fridge waiting to be fried up. There's football on TV. He's got everything he needs right here.

Doesn't he?

When Hadley meets Frost again—superficially for the interview—she knows exactly what she has to say. He appears disinterested from the moment he sits down. He's not rude, but he's not giving her anything to hold on to. She senses he's built an invisible wall around himself since their first meeting. He's mentally prepared; she can tell.

Hadley is grateful that she dressed professionally. She has on her favorite skirt suit over a crimson silk shirt, and she knows she looks urban and refined. She asks him all of the questions she needs the answers to in order to write her article. Even when she's in lust, she doesn't put aside her hardworking nature. That drive defines her. When she's finished, he pushes his chair back, wood scraping floor. He's ready to leave, but she has to stop him.

"I want you to train me," she tells him. Her voice has changed from when she'd asked him the final question, moments before. There is a hush to her tone now. She is offering him the soft, tender skin of her underbelly. If he were a wolf, he'd grip her muzzle in his jaws in an alpha sign.

The statement works. He settles back into his chair. His silver eyebrows go up. A light in his blue eyes flickers, but she can tell that he thinks she's joking. He actually smiles as he says the words, "You're too old."

She laughs as she lifts her coffee. He's the first man ever to talk to her in this way. She's right; she knows it. He's the one. "No, not too old."

"The ones I train have been putting their time in since kindergarten."

Her chest tightens the same way it does right before she lets a whip land on a submissive's hide. She puts her hand out on the table, imagining being able to slip her fingers under his. What if you could do what you craved, without the constraints of social mores? The world would be a completely different place. People might actually get what they want.

"I want you to train me," she says again, louder this time. He doesn't seem to understand.

All of the nervous gestures she's worked for years to disassemble come back in force. Her head goes down. She looks up at him from under her glossy, dark bangs. She bites her bottom lip, hard, welcoming the immediate spark of pain as a way to clear her head. When she was a top, she was able to bury these glitches—what she has come to consider as the human side of herself—beneath an icy exterior. Somehow, that ability has disappeared. Frost does things to her.

"Don't worry," she says, almost more to herself than to him. She squeezes her thighs together under the table, feels her bare legs touch above the lacy tops of her stockings. She knows, in her mind, what this will be like, what she's asking for. There are men who would snap her up in a heartbeat. She doesn't want those men. Frost doesn't see the treasure she's offering. "Training me won't be so difficult. I'm good. I simply need a little discipline."

He looks at her directly. She feels that appraisal she sensed at their first meeting. "What do you want from me?" His voice is gruff. They're talking for real now.

She can't help herself. "How long do you have?"

He considers what he has to say. The heat between them is palpable, shimmering like hot liquid metal in the air. "I don't think I can do this again."

She's confused, but she sees pain in his eyes, and she wishes she could help him. "We've never done anything before."

"Not you," he says. *"This."* He acknowledges their connection with the slightest gesture of one finger. "It's been too long for me. I'm accustomed to what I've got now."

Everything in her wants him. She visualizes pushing away the table—hearing the coffee cups clattering—and crawling to him on the floor. She knows just what it would be like to undo his fly, suck his cock. If any of those behaviors were socially acceptable, she would be in motion. Or if this was a different type of establishment where the rules are skewered. There are so many places she could go, dark clubs. She knows the way down their shadowy alleys, knows they offer her salvation. She doesn't want that. She wants him. None of this makes sense to her. Love at first sight is a fairy tale, and she no longer believes in fairy tales. But she feels something with this man. The fact that he hasn't walked away gives her hope.

"What have you got now?" She has to ask the question, even though she doesn't think she wants to know the answer. That's the journalist in her, always digging in other people's dirt.

He drains the rest of his coffee. The half-smile on his lips is bitter. "Nothing."

"Good to see you back, Hadley," the ginger-goateed bouncer says as she enters the building. Some habits are more difficult to break than others.

She nods curtly in response, feeling the rush of anticipation build inside her. This is what Hadley does when she's in turmoil. She hits a club. The one she lands in is an old favorite. It's dark inside—they're all dark, but this one, with the rippling black satin on the ceilings and black painted walls, is like stepping into a midnight. Without stars. There are illuminated statements on the walls, artistic quotes bent into curved neon.

She wears all black this evening, as do most of the club's clientele. Her hair is up, tight, shiny and neat, so that the back of her neck is exposed, not a strand loose. She feels cool and ready. The last time she visited, she was a different person. Guy tugged on the end of her leash, and she put him through the motions automatically, almost without thinking.

Now she's different. She scans the room for someone who will play the way she wants to, someone who will exchange power with her for one night. Maybe she can put Mr. Reed Frost out of her head if the pain-and-pleasure mix is perfectly blended. A concoction of the most deliciously decadent sort is on her inner agenda.

As she looks over the rest of the players, a man comes up behind her and slides one hand on her waist. This is a greeting of equals, not a sub seeking her out, not a dom pushing her down so that her knees buckle and hit the floor. She turns and meets his eyes. The man's name is Dean Murphy and he isn't all about show, like Guy. He's a gorgeous, leather-clad master who doesn't give a fuck about the sex of his partners as long as they are willing to submit to his requirements. She's seen him in action a handful of times, and she's always had a colleague's appreciation. Dean's handsome and he's hung, but she's not going to fuck him. They will not be a long-term item: he cannot give her that elusive thing she's looking for. But he can give her what she wants tonight.

And what she wants is discipline.

"You were missed, Hadley."

She's been a dominant for so long the craving for what she wants now feels exciting and new. There's a crackle, like electricity, in her head.

"Dean," she says, in greeting.

He has to press his lips to her ear so she can hear him over the throbbing techno beat. "Which lucky sub are you playing with tonight?" He motions to the figures around them, all those eyes watching hopefully.

"I want to play with you."

He doesn't pick up what she means. Why would a dom need a dom?

She takes his hand and places it on his silver belt buckle. He looks at her. Her heart pounds. She's only been his peer in the past. What is she asking him for? She answers his unspoken query. "Do a scene with me?"

Now he understands. "Are you sure?"

"Yes."

He hesitates only for a second before gripping her wrist. "Back room," she says. He nods, accepting the fact that she's letting him know what she wants. In the past she would have stalked forward, Guy following behind. Now Dean is the one who parts the crowd as he walks, and Hadley feels her cunt respond. She is going to be punished, and she will relish every stroke.

The fact that redemption is so close is flawless, golden foreplay to her. If she were to slide one hand down her skirt, she'd meet instant wetness. She's grateful for Dean because she knows he will give her what she needs. The times she's watched him onstage have told her so.

She's seen him bind down both men and women. She's seen him wield a crop, a quirt, a whip. She knows that he will respect her boundaries, but that he will take her right to the very edge. She wants to tell him that she's ready. God, she is so fucking ready.

Dean is a man who knows his way around a rope. He ties Hadley into place with the artful gestures of a true bondage master. When he's close to her face, he whispers, "Safe word?" and she says, "Angel," naming her favorite rock tune.

Only when Hadley is bound does she finally feel the constant racing of her mind begin to slow. She has never fully understood why bondage works for her, but she accepts that this is her meditation. Her church. Her altar. She used to be the one doing the binding. Being forced to hold still takes her to a whole new level.

Dean lifts a crop. She shuts her eyes for a second, then opens them when he asks her a question: "You're sure you want this?" he says. "You know what I can do." He's checking one last time.

Hadley knows better than to nod. She says, "Yes," and she adds "sir," even though the word feels alien on her lips.

The crop connects with her ass and she sucks in her breath.

Why does she like to play with pain? Why does giving in accentuate the pleasure for her? She used to ask Guy those sorts of questions, late at night, when she was putting him back together after taking him apart. Now she has to come to terms with them herself. But tonight she doesn't ponder the whys—all she does is give in.

Dean whips her quickly, and neatly, lining up the blows. He punishes her through the black leather pants she's wearing, and the fabric mutes the pain. She lasts longer than she thought she might, waiting until he gets in five blows with the crop before saying uncle.

With each stroke, she imagines Frost holding the handle of the weapon.

Guy watches the entire exchange while leaning against a wall and feeling as if he's fallen down a rabbit hole into hell. He can't believe what he's seeing. People change. He knows that. But he doesn't think this is really Hadley. It couldn't be.

Christ. She's back in town. His wish has come true. Who knew that getting what you dreamed of could feel so fucking wrong?

The article runs in the paper, and this gives Hadley the reason to return to the gym. She could mail the piece. But she wants to see Frost. Needs to see him. She stands outside the gym, wavers, returns to her car.

The local mom-and-pop bookstore doesn't carry any porn. (Mom's decision, she thinks snidely to herself. Pop would carry smut.) She can't find the titles she desires. It's a trip to San Francisco before she locates a bookstore that fulfills her requests. She buys him *The Story of O*. She buys him *9½ Weeks*. She puts those along with the article into a brown paper mailer and sends them to his attention at the gym.

Personal and Confidential.

She hopes Guy doesn't get to the mailer first.

That night it is another trip to the club. To take the edge off, she tells herself, like a junkie would. To fill the need. She's always had those needs, the ones that wake her up in the night—or keep her from falling asleep in the first place. Top or bottom, there are urges, cravings. The ones that make her attempt to punish herself when nobody else is available. She's not that capable. She pulls back. Spanking your own ass does nothing—you can't feel the sting. Not the way you can when there's a master on the other end of the whip.

She takes care of her needs in other ways. Dom or sub. No one else would be able to guess. She pushes herself when she works out. When she does anything. She always has to go one step past the finish line, has to cross the line before anyone else.

Guy calls her cell phone as she's arriving at the club. "Come on, Hadley. Don't shut me out."

She won't rehash their final fight. Now that she has distance, she can see that nobody was right and nobody was wrong. They simply don't mesh.

"Frost won't be able to give you what you need."

"You have no idea what I need."

"I used to."

"That and my vibrator will get me off."

She hangs up and shakes her head. Of course, her ex would be working at the same place as the man she desires. That's the kind of luck she has.

Unfortunately, Guy knows her too well. That's her fault. She had him trained to anticipate her desires. She's in a corner of the club when he arrives. He's wearing leather and black, and he moves with the elegance that drew her to him in the first place.

On the surface Guy is everything she ever desired. Scratch the surface and, as she discovered, there isn't much there. Guy is all about his attire, his perfect body, his luxurious hair. He couldn't get to the place she needed to be—couldn't take her there, beyond the shiny exterior, into the slithery mess of her mind.

But that's not entirely fair.

When they were together, she didn't really know what she needed. Now she does.

He spies her, and he starts moving through the crowd. Fuck. Hadley heads quickly in the opposite direction. Her motion halts Guy. That sums up their relationship in the crack of a whip. He sees her approach Dean, and he grimaces.

"Twice in a week," Dean says, and his hand grips the back of her neck. "I must have won the fucking lottery."

Dean is less hesitant this time. He treats her the way he would any other sub. The respect of dom to dom has entirely disappeared. All Dean wants to do is be on top. Hadley is thankful for that. She needs to feel the heat of the pain in her soul. She wants to own every blow.

He uses a slapper this time—two pieces of leather attached together at the handle. The noise is more startling than the pain. She knows all about this particular tool. She's had her own for years, and it was always one of her favorites. Every time the leather connects, her pussy contracts. She can feel that Dean is whipping her carefully, in order to make the scene last. Not too hard, but forcefully. He clearly doesn't want it to be over before they start.

She knows that out there in the crowd, Guy is paying careful attention. She wonders how many times he will stroke his hair while he drinks in the scene.

Watching twists Guy up inside. He was *with* her. He was her sub. What they had together fit for him. He still doesn't understand why she left. He doesn't care about Dean. It's the way Hadley looks at Frost that makes Guy crazy. Guy was the one who brought Hadley into the gym—so that she could see him, so that she could remember what they had together. His plans rarely backfire. He's always been good at setting a web.

What is wrong with her?

Dean switches over to a flogger, and Guy imagines what the tiny tails must feel like to Hadley. He's been on the receiving end of those sorts of weapons so many times before. He loved when Hadley would make him stay in place without any bindings, make him hold his hands over his head while she used a cat-o'-nine-tails on his naked back. That was the most difficult for him—that and when she pegged him with the strap-on.

Now Hadley is the one being punished, and Guy can't comprehend the range of emotions that swell up inside him.

"Twenty," Dean says. "Count them out for me."

Oh, so the dom wants Hadley to keep track. That was one of Hadley's own tricks. Guy would try his best to count for her, but he would always fuck up, and she would start again at one. How many times did she chide him for losing his place? How many nights did she make him stand in the corner, his dick so hard, refusing to give him release because he had been a naughty boy?

Guy mentally counts the blows along with her. At seven, he starts to formulate an idea. He will invite Frost out for a drink to expose Hadley for who she truly is.

But he watches, first. He stares at Dean, seeing the man expertly deliver the pain that finally makes Hadley cry out.

Good, he thinks. Cry.

That doesn't stop him from coming to the image when he gets home. We're all mercurial at some point, he thinks. Desires slip and change, shift and glide. Pain is pain and pleasure is pleasure. For him, and for Hadley, the two sensations are entwined. Does it matter that she needs to be on the receiving end?

Guy uses a bottle of hand lotion this time; the honey-vanilla scent was Hadley's favorite. He likes to smell like her. But as he jacks off, he can't stop himself from envisioning Dean. Dean tying *him* up. Dean flogging *him*. Guy stares at his reflection in the mirror. He tries to make himself fantasize about Hadley whipping him, tries to force that image into his head.

Instead, he sees only Dean.

Frost receives the package at the gym. He laughs to himself when he sees what she's sent him. She's like a child, he thinks, begging so many different ways for a treat. He doesn't know how he should respond, so he does nothing. There's no need to rush.

If she wants something bad enough, she'll tell him in person.

It's been a week. Guy can't function. He's in charge of PR at the gym, and he does his job as if in a dream. Every time he closes his eyes, he sees himself up onstage at the club. Bound in place. Forced to take what he desires, what he deserves.

It's Dean making him count now. Dean instructing him to behave, to be a good boy.

He runs a comb through his thick black hair, a soothing gesture. He tells himself that he still wants Hadley. At the end of the day, as he dials Frost's number, he realizes that he almost believes the lie.

"She's bad news," Guy says to Frost as soon as the older man sits down.

"I haven't even ordered a beer yet."

Guy feels himself talking too fast. His face is hot. He wishes he had asked for ice water instead of vodka while he was waiting for Reed, wishes he hadn't downed the drink so fast. "You should stay clear from her if you don't want to get hurt."

Frost enjoys talking with Guy. The boy is so immature. He's good at his job. Public Relations requires someone slick like Guy. But the kid can't see two weeks in front of him, let alone the rest of his life. Frost is not offended by Guy's words. He finds himself entertained by their interaction. Nothing like this has happened to him for years. So long, he actually forgot what this part of his brain was for. He trains his athletes' core—he'd left his own to decay.

He has no idea what he'll get from the evening. But maybe he'll learn a little more about the girl.

"How could she hurt me?" Frost is genuinely curious. A young waitress in a velvet catsuit delivers his Heineken. He cradles the green bottle in one of his large hands.

"She'll get you all wrapped up, all twisted, and then she'll leave."

"Like she did to you."

"I know her. She's into stuff you won't like." He motions to the bartender for another vodka. He senses he's going to get drunk, but he can't seem to stop himself.

Frost drinks his beer slowly. He wants Guy to try to tell him what he won't like. If Frost chooses to drink more, he can do so at home. His feet up on his coffee table. His apartment, even stark and bare, is a comfort.

"You should look into the club she goes to. You'll find out for yourself what she's into."

"That's not a bad idea."

So Frost is ready when Hadley calls him.

"I want to do another scene."

"We work well together," Dean says, pleased that a woman like Hadley continues to choose him.

"This time is different," Hadley explains. "I want to put on a show for someone else."

She is honest about the whole situation when she explains her desires. Dean is game. He's always up for a performance with a beautiful sub. He'll spank her and humiliate her and make her beg anytime she wants. But they don't have a deeper bond. They go through the motions and everyone gets off, but there's no desire to wrap her arms around him and stay sealed to his body. All she wants afterward is a shower.

What she wants with Reed Frost is forever.

She invites Frost to meet her. She tells him the time. She has no idea if he will do what she requests. There's no worldly reason to believe that he will—except for the connection, except for the fact that when she pictures him, her breathing quickens. When she visualizes his face, her pussy clenches.

She thinks about all those chick flicks she's managed to see over the years. The ones with the cute meets between hero and heroine. The scenes in which one of the players finally realizes he or she has true feelings for the other.

Have any similar meets occurred in a BDSM club? she wonders.

When she meets eyes with Frost this time, she expects him to be ill at ease. He doesn't run this spot. He's not Coach here and he's not Dom. But he doesn't leave.

Dean has her bent over the leather horse. She knows there's a similar piece of furniture at the gym. That one is for vaulting. This is for spanking. Frost stands ten feet away and watches. He has on a scarlet T-shirt, so visible in a sea of black. Don't leave, she thinks. Don't leave. She's begging him with her eyes.

He wouldn't have come if he didn't want to know more.

That gives her a small spark of power. One that lets her last longer than she might otherwise have. Dean stops before she has to give her safe word.

Frost is waiting for her in the parking lot.

He drives an old truck. A beater. What her dad would lovingly have referred to as a hooptie. Hadley grew up with men who drove trucks like this one. Then one day she woke up and found herself in a world of Guys, where men used product and spent more time primping in the bathroom than she did. Maybe she was born into the wrong era. Not only doesn't she want a metrosexual; she doesn't even want to date someone who uses the word.

Frost is leaning against his truck in a pose straight out of a '50s cowboy flick. She knows somehow that he'll use two wires to make the engine catch.

"Do you want to go somewhere and have a drink?" she asks.

"You think you can sit down after being punished like that?"

"I'm tough."

"I'm starting to get that feeling."

"Why did you come?"

"Why did you ask me?"

Oh, fuck, they're so much alike. The only difference is that she's making the moves. Otherwise, they might be lost forever—both wanting, but neither taking the step forward. Topping from below. That's what she's doing. She would smile at the thought that he wouldn't understand what she was talking about—if this felt like a situation in which to smile.

"I asked you," she says, "because you can give me what I need." She wants to tell him more. That if he tried, he could cross her wires and start her engine. She knows this about him. She doesn't know how she does, but she does. Like the man in Albuquerque who slid his wheelchair over by her chair and spoke to her in that low whiskey tone all night. Unraveling her fantasies until she was naked and exposed. He mindfucked her, and it was the best sex she'd had in years.

Reed Frost looks her up and down. She believes he could make her come by looking at her like that. In his eyes is ownership. She would wear his name tattooed on her skin. "Why would you think that?"

"I have a good sense for people."

"Like Guy?"

"I was wrong about Guy."

"Maybe you're wrong about me."

"Am I?"

He puts his hands on her arms and kisses her. The way his lips feel on hers resonates through her entire body. She is demolished by the kiss. He grips her in his arms, and she can feel that he's hard through his Levi's, and this delights her. He got hard watching another man whip her. If he'd been disgusted, he would already have torn out of the parking lot in a squeal of rubber. The throb of his cock through the denim is an unspoken promise. She loves the fact that he wore jeans and a scarlet T-shirt to a BDSM club, when every other player in the building wore black and leather. Through his truck window she can see the striped emerald athletic jacket he wears while coaching.

"Take me home," she says.

He shakes his head. "I can't wait that long."

Oh, God, she thinks, it's going to be good.

He gets her into the truck. They drive to a spot where they can see San Francisco—the whole twinkling fantasy of the city—spread out for them. But neither one has time for the view. Frost has a rough green army blanket in the back of his truck. He lays Hadley on the blanket in the truck bed, and he starts to touch her. His hands are so gentle. She's surprised by the way he makes her feel.

She thinks of the man she met while on the road, the one who talked to her, his voice his instrument, telling her what she needed, getting her off with his words. That was the night she discovered who she really was. She wonders if she can help Frost discover the same thing about himself.

"Take off your clothes," he says.

She unzips her shirt and peels off the shiny PVC. She undoes the three shiny chrome buckles of the skirt, and the fabric falls open. She now has on only a black satin bra and matching panties, thigh-high stockings, and her engineer boots. She'd be cold if not for the heat between the two of them.

"Roll over, baby. I want to see."

Baby.

She does what he tells her, exposing the welts left by Dean's crop on the backs of her thighs. Frost runs his hands over her skin. He pulls her bikinis down to see her ass. She moans as he traces each mark left by the crop. Her hips start to shimmy against the blanket.

"You like what he did to you?"

She looks over her shoulder at Frost and meets his eyes. She nods.

"Tell me why."

"Tell me why you won't be with anyone else."

"I never said that."

"You said you were happy with what you had. And what you had was nothing." How odd to have this conversation while she can feel the rough blanket against her naked sex. He slides one hand under her, and he cups her pussy while they talk. The words flow over her, because she is focused on his fingers on her clit. He plays her magnificently, as if he's always had one hand between her legs, as if he knows exactly how she touches herself when she's all alone in bed.

"I never said I was happy."

"You said you were—" she searches for the word in her mind as his finger strokes her "—accustomed."

"Check your notes. I said I didn't think I could do this again. You've filled in the rest."

"What did you do before?"

His finger splits her nether lips and nestles between them. She feels as if she is balanced on his pointer, as if her whole body is suspended on his single digit. He rubs her clit. She knows she's close.

"I got so tired of the games," he says, and he bends and starts to kiss along her welts, his fingertip still spiraling over her clit. He adds another finger, and she sighs. He's kissing the hot lines of her skin. She's having a difficult time believing this is for real.

"I'm not in this for a game."

"I'm satisfied with what I've got." He licks along the crop marks, and she feels herself teetering right on the edge. He is going to make her come. She wants to ask what he's doing to her, but she's the one who started them on this ride. She's the one who supposedly knows what she's doing. Except she doesn't. This is new to her. Being a sub is like wearing her insides on the outside. She knows only what she wants.

"You haven't got anything."

"*This* doesn't feel like nothing."

He's right. This is something. Something big. If she could paint a picture of what they're doing, she'd put fireworks in the sky. He knows how to take care of her. His fingers play her clit, while his mouth continues to kiss the marks of pain left by Dean. But suddenly she wants more. She wants him inside her. It's bold and demanding, but she says, "Please fuck me."

"Do I have to whip you first?" His fingers stop moving. There's ice in his tone.

She wonders if it was a mistake to let him see another man touch her, see another man hurt her. She tries to be flippant. "Next time. Tonight, just fuck me."

He rolls her over and he presses his mouth to her pussy. She starts to shake. He licks her slowly, using both hands to spread apart her pussy lips. The cool night air on her cunt makes her shiver. His tongue traces circles over and over, and she lifts her hips up and presses against him. She's greedy and she knows it. She wants his cock, but she wants his tongue, and she can't have both at the same time.

"You're pure sweetness," he says, and he sets her back and starts to undo his belt. She can see a time when she'll beg him to use the leather on her. Right now, it's only in the way of getting his pants off. She's desperate to have him inside her. Luckily, he doesn't make her wait any longer.

"I wanted to do this from the first time I saw you," she says.

"I know."

He teases her first, fucking her clit with the head of his cock. She feels as if her clitoris is swelling and expanding. Nobody has ever taunted her like this before. They wouldn't dare withhold pleasure. Reed doesn't seem afraid of her at all. She raises her hips in an attempt to get him to thrust inside her. He refuses to be rushed. Every move she makes, he counters. He simply fucks the wet, slippery length of his cock against her pussy, over and over until she feels the pleasure in every cell of her body. Only when she is on the brink does he thrust inside her. Only when she is begging does he actually start the ride.

"You're so beautiful," he says.

His cock is in her, and she groans at the way he feels. Filling her. Completing her.

"I never had that before. That connection at first sight."
She can't believe she's talking while he's fucking her, but she
wants to explain. She's not a girl who will fuck anyone.

"I know," he says again.

"How do you know?"

He makes sure to slide one hand between them, so he can
continue plucking her clit while he fucks her. "I just do."

She wraps her thighs around him. She is so glad they fit.
His cock is hard and strong, hitting all the right places deep
inside her. She can't wait to suck him, to taste the way their
juices mingle, can't wait to try all the different positions she
loves—doggy-style with him pulling on her hair, reverse cow-
girl so he can grip her hips and work her just right. But right
now, he's on top, drilling her hard, and she knows she's going
to climax.

But then he says, "Why would you let that man whip you?"

There it is. The chilled tone once more. "I wanted to show
you…" She's not sure how to explain. "I wanted you to see."

"But why him…and not me?"

What is he saying to her? The way he's talking is like a
stone-cold dom. She feels a shiver trace along the back of her
neck.

"I didn't think you'd understand."

His eyes are cold. "I don't ever want you to ask someone
else to lay a hand on you when what you really want is me."

The way he says the words makes her come.

Guy stays at the club. There's no reason for him to leave.
She's with Frost, and he has no backup plan. He brought Hadley to the gym so they could have another shot. He told Frost
to steer clear, so he could dance his way back into Hadley's
heart. He isn't a psychopath. She doesn't want him anymore.
He has to accept the fact that she's really gone.

That doesn't make the pain easier to bear. And it's not his first choice of pain.

Dean finds him on a leather bench.

"You were with her for a while?"

"Two years."

Dean puts one hand on Guy's thigh. "I used to watch the two of you do scenes together," he says.

Guy looks at Dean. He leans in close. They share a kiss.

"That's the last time you lead," Dean says. Guy feels as if someone has wrapped a chain around his heart to keep the organ from breaking.

Frost asks, "Don't you ever just want to get a cup of coffee?" They sit in the truck bed together, her legs over his. Their connection feels so natural, as if they've been a couple for years.

"What do you mean?" She's trembling. He reaches through the window of the truck to grab his jacket, and he sets it over her shoulders. The gesture tugs at her. He's a gentleman.

"Twenty-four-seven relationships—like the ones in the books you sent me. Do they make any sense to you?"

So he read the books. "Aren't most relationships 24/7?"

"Smart-ass."

His tone strikes a chord in her stomach. She sits up straighter.

"In the past, have you escaped on the weekends?" she asks him. "Taken a few personal days—got off early for good behavior?"

"I can see how it might feel nice to give you a good, hard spanking."

She lets herself smirk. There's still time. "Do you now?"

He leans back and looks at her. He's told her straight out. He's not someone who plays games. She likes this about him. "I can. I can see exactly what that would feel like, dragging you over my lap, lifting that poor excuse for a skirt up." He nudges her PVC skirt with his foot. "Spanking you on your bare bottom."

He says *bottom*. But she knows she can get him to say *ass*.

"In fact, I can imagine exactly how long I would spank you before you'd cry and beg me to stop. But I wouldn't stop...."

She's getting wet again.

"I'd keep punishing your pretty bottom until I was finished. And that might take me a while. I've got a very firm hand."

She squirms on the blanket. She wishes he'd do exactly what he just described. Even after having been worked by Dean at the club, she's ready for a spanking at Frost's hand.

"But I don't know about having someone waiting for me to tell them what to do."

"That's your fucking job. You tell people what to do all day long."

When she says *fucking*, his eyes harden. "I don't tell them to suck my cock."

He's getting closer. She can almost feel him crossing the line.

"It's not like that."

"Then you tell me what it's like. Stop giving me books and hints and fucking taunts. Tell me exactly what you want from me."

She stares into his eyes. She sees something there. What she saw when she first walked into the gym. "This." She grips his hand. She means the connection.

"I don't get it."

"Take me home. I'll show you."

Frost's apartment looks nothing like Hadley had expected. She'd thought there would be photographs. Medals. Trophies. The walls are white. The furniture is dark. There is nothing else.

He takes her to the bedroom. She sits on the edge of the mattress and looks at him. She's wearing bra, panties and his shiny athletic jacket. "Your house is so empty."

"She took everything."

She.

Hadley doesn't ask who she was. When Frost wants to, if Frost wants to, he'll tell her. He comes close to her and undresses her. Hadley feels like a doll the way he moves her, carefully pulling off the jacket, undoing her bra, slipping her panties down her thighs.

Hadley opens her arms. Frost hesitates before embracing her, gripping her body to his. She's entirely naked, and he has his jeans and shirt on. She likes that.

"You've lived like this for how long?"

"Seven years."

"Seven," she echoes.

"It was easier than doing anything else."

For a moment he simply holds her, his palms under her ass. She feels weightless in his arms. She runs her fingertips along his biceps. She shivers when she feels how strong he is. He sets her down only long enough to strip, himself. Then he carries her across the room and holds her against the wall, pinning her. He'd promised himself that he wouldn't do this again. But he already broke that promise. She's so warm. He feels as if he's melting inside.

Dean hustles Guy into the bathroom. "You're so pretty," Dean says. "I've admired that mouth of yours for so goddamn long."

Guy looks at his reflection in the mirror. His hair is tousled. For once he doesn't move to fix it, even though he has a comb in his back pocket.

Dean traces his fingers over Guy's full lips. "Your mouth was made to suck cock. You know that, don't you?"

Guy thinks of the time with Hadley and the strap-on. He thinks of what made him cry that night, and he nods.

"On your knees, boy."

Guy drops to his knees on the bathroom floor. Dean slides a thumb between Guy's lips. "Suck it," he says. "Show me what you can do."

Guy's cock is a rod in his leather pants. He sucks Dean's thumb, and he stares up at the handsome dom, wanting so badly to suck something else, to drain Dean to the root.

Hadley's thighs are around Frost's waist, her body pressed to his. She knows they're going to fuck again, soon, but she wants him to talk to her first. She needs to know.

"She left," he says, "and I didn't want to try again. I got used to having what I have."

"Nothing."

"Nothing is easy." He laughs, but darkly. "I don't mean it the way that sounds. It was easy growing accustomed to having nothing."

"Sounds Zen."

He shakes his head. "I'm not the type."

"You don't have to be like that anymore."

He slides the head of his cock inside her. She can feel her pussy respond automatically. They are good together. They fit. She has no idea how well.

Frost fucks her against the wall, and Hadley feels the magic of being with someone who knows how to touch you. She has her eyes closed, her head back. Frost is so strong. He balances her easily in his big hands, maneuvers her exactly the way he wants. He has her positioned on his thighs for a moment, and she remembers the first glimpse she had of him as she entered the gym. The power that she felt.

He runs a hand over her clit, and she keens low and sweet under her breath. She feels so real in his hands. He understands suddenly that he has to come clean. He made her bare her soul to him. "I have to tell you something," he says.

He's fucking her as he talks. She can't find the breath to respond.

"I'm not new...not to what you like. What you need."

He has her clit between his thumb and forefinger, and he bears down, giving her too much pressure. No, not too much. *So* much. She feels as if she will explode with the sensation. She's too overwhelmed to unravel what he's telling her. "What do you mean?" She's panting.

He pulls out and carries her to the bed. He spreads her face-down on his mattress and waits for her to turn her head and look at him. Frost has made the decision—he can be honest with her. He presses his mouth to her ear. "Hadley," he says, "You don't have to explain things to me."

"Open wide," Dean says, and Guy parts his lips. Dean has his cock out, and he sets the head on Guy's bottom lip. Guy starts to suck. He doesn't think he will last long. He's sure he will come right in his pants. He wonders what will happen if he does. As if reading his thoughts, Dean says, "Don't you dare get off from sucking my cock, boy."

Guy gazes up at his new dom, hope vibrant in his dark brown eyes.

"If you do, I'll have to take you home and punish that saucy ass of yours. I'll use you in ways you've never even dreamed about." Dean ruffles Guy's hair, and he smiles at his new toy. "But then again, I'll do that either way."

Guy sighs with pleasure. This is a dream come true.

★ ★ ★

Frost can tell that she still doesn't understand. She looks over her shoulder at him, watches as he pulls his belt free from the loops of his discarded jeans. He doubles the leather. Makes the belt snap. She sees the finesse in his movements. She can't believe what he's saying. "I don't get it. Why would you let me go through all that? Why wouldn't you just say..." She pushes herself up on her hands and knees.

He pushes her back down and shrugs as he looks at her. "I was done. Until I met you, that is. I was all finished."

"Yeah, but you said, you told me..." She pushes up again.

"Get back into position, kid. Now."

She glares at him and he lets the belt land against her naked ass cheeks, once, twice. She knows enough not to put a hand back to cover herself. Still, he puts one hand in the small of her back and forces her against the mattress. He licks her with the belt a third again. This time the leather stings. She bucks against the mattress, unable to stop herself. "You said you never had anyone in your power...."

He shakes his head. "You'll have to listen to my words better in the future."

"I'm a good listener." But a bad sub, she thinks. He stripes her again.

"I wanted to hear you tell me what you needed. I wanted you to spell out every desire. I wanted to know why you want what you want. You say you want 24/7. I have to be sure."

It wasn't fair, he thinks. He played her. But she played him, too. There are games, every once in a while, where everyone wins.

"God, I knew," she says. But how had she known? Seeing him like that across the gym had sparked something inside her. She'd sensed his power then; she sees it in action now. He whips her twice more, then opens the closet and shows her what's there. The tools. The weapons. The whips and crops and paddles. Her heart throbs. She sees on the top of the closet a row of books. From the spines she recognizes the ones she sent him—doubles, obviously, of the ones he already has. Plus other classic BDSM titles: *The 120 Days of Sodom. Justine. Gritty. The Punishment of Sleeping Beauty.*

"You want to be with me," he says. It's a statement, but she nods, then says, "Yes, Reed." Has she ever called him by his name before? The name sounds right on her lips.

"You're sure? Because I can't go through this again unless I know."

She looks at him. The connection is more than combustible. She doesn't want to keep her hands off him. "Yes."

"Tell me what you want. I need to hear you say the words."

"You," she says.

"But why?" He grabs a paddle and comes toward her. "You give me a reason, and if I like what you have to say, I'll put you over my lap and spank your ass."

She works to hide the grin. She knew *ass* was in his vocabulary somewhere.

Frost sits on the edge of the mattress and pulls her over his lap. He strokes her bare skin with his palm, and Hadley slides her pussy against his thigh. She thinks about what she wants to say, how she can explain to Frost her desires. Clearly, she doesn't have to unravel the whole mystery of BDSM for him. She only has to come clean about herself.

"You know *9½ Weeks?*"

"Of course," he says. It's like the Bible of their world.

"I've mentally rewritten the ending too many times to count," she says. He lands one blistering blow on her bottom. Then another. She can imagine what her ass looks like. She's been on the "doling out" side of so many punishment sessions. He's not holding back, either. She continues. "Why couldn't they have stayed together? Why did the character have to go crazy?"

He spanks her again, and she grinds her pussy into his leg, getting the contact she craves.

"I always thought that if they kept going, they'd work everything out."

"Optimist," he says.

"Realist. I want a BDSM story with a happy ending...."

He strikes again, catching her sweet spot. She moans, but she doesn't stop talking.

"I want the tenth week. And the eleventh, and the twelfth. Until ultimately I want to lose count of the weeks."

He paddles to the cadence of her words.

"I want to live in a world where everyone gets what they need, and nobody is punished for their desires."

He spanks her again.

"Unless their desire is to be punished."

Frost drops the paddle and pulls her upright. He parts her thighs, splits her pussy lips and sits her down on his cock. She feels how hard he is, how wet she is. They are perfectly joined.

"Baby," Frost says as he kisses her. He's made her work for this. Now comes her reward. "Welcome to the beginning..."

"The beginning?" Her eyes are wet. He kisses her cheeks.

"...the beginning of your happy ending."

★ ★ ★ ★ ★

LETTING GO
SARAH McCARTY

The car pulled up in front of the dark cabin. The white glow of the moon reflecting off newly fallen snow highlighted the isolation of the log home set at the foot of the mountain. It was perfect. Remote. Comfortable. And it was theirs for the weekend. No work. No pets. Nothing to distract them from each other.

The uncharacteristic shyness that had been plaguing her the entire four-hour trip came back in spades as Marc switched off the car's engine. Which was absolutely ridiculous. They'd planned this weekend for a month. Nothing was going to happen here that either of them hadn't eagerly anticipated, but now that it was time for the planning to give birth to fantasy, she was shy to the point of blushing. She, the woman who never blushed, never got embarrassed. Never lost control.

Becky pretended an interest in the scenery as the driver's side door opened. Marc's gaze slid over her like a touch, poking at her insecurities, asking silent questions she didn't want to answer. Anticipation and nerves fluttered in her stomach in a queasy combination. She made her expression blank to hide her discomfort.

Marc sighed. The door creaked open. "We don't have to do this, you know."

She kept her voice just as balanced as her expression. "Yes, we do." Because she was so sick of not being who she wanted to be with him.

"Then why the cold shoulder?"

That got her looking at him. He thought she was brushing him off? She took a subtle steadying breath, inhaling the scent of the outdoors…and Marc. Both were clean, crisp and intangibly tied together in her mind, maybe because they'd met on a weekend kayak excursion, but more than likely because the man was as elemental as the forest around them.

She unclenched fists she didn't know she'd been clenching. Good grief! No wonder he was asking questions. She looked more ready to go into battle than indulge in a romantic weekend. Becky shook her head at her own idiocy, her hair swishing around her shoulders with the movement. She brushed a strand away from her mouth. "Believe it or not, I'm nervous."

"Why?"

He didn't try to make eye contact again, which was good. If she'd looked at him, pride would have demanded she lie. "Because I'm afraid I might not live up to your expectations."

The back of his fingers brushed down the side of her cheek. His low chuckle still sent a shiver down her spine the way it had the first time she'd heard it. Not for the first time she wondered what attracted him to her. He was as sexy and as uninhibited as a man could get, and she had more inhibitions than…well, than anyone needed.

"Baby, we've been married for two years—do you really think I don't know what you're capable of?"

She looked at him then, taking in the amusement and understanding in his gaze. He was so sure this wasn't going to be a disaster. "Neither of us knows that."

His smile was a slow, sexy stretch of the lips she'd seen many times before. Masculine. Knowing. And confident. He was always so confident. "I know."

She clung to that confidence as his hand skimmed her neck, her shoulder, then her thigh. A pat on her knee followed by a quick squeeze and then he was out of the car, leaving her alone with her hopes, fears, and that borrowed bravado. Crisp night air swept in on his exit and she jumped as the door thudded shut.

She shook her head at her own cowardice. They'd devoted this weekend to obliterating the inhibitions between them. Inhibitions neither wanted. Becky slung her purse over her shoulder, watching in the rearview mirror as Marc walked around the back, a tall muscular silhouette cast in moonlight. Cowering in the car wasn't an impressive start on her side.

She yanked the latch and shoved the door open. Snow crunched beneath her feet as she stood and stretched. The night sky expanded before her, a satiny carpet of black speckled with shining stars and dotted with glowing planets. She took a deep breath of the frigid air, shivering as it bit into her lungs.

A cloud wafted across the moonlit sky. She released her breath, watching the frozen vapor rise until it seemed to meld with that wispy traveler, becoming more than what it was, and yet still less than it would be. For a minute more, she watched the cloud skate along, free and unfettered, and then smiled as, with absolute certainty, she knew everything was going to be all right. There was nothing she and he couldn't do. Nothing they couldn't accomplish. Not together. Together, they were like that cloud. More than what they had been before, yet ever growing with boundless potential. She just had to stop being afraid to let go.

Anticipation skittered through her veins as she walked around the back of the car. The view here was as interesting as the night sky, seeing as Marc was stretched forward, retrieving a suitcase. The man had the body of a runner, roped with lean, hard muscle. She slid her hands up the side of his thighs, smiling as taut muscle flexed under her touch, gliding them up over his narrow hips, under his jacket, around his waist.

He jumped at the chill of her hands and then relaxed into her hug, settling his palms over hers, pressing them into his abdomen. As always, he communicated so much with a touch, his thoughts as clear as if he'd spoken. She pressed her cheek against the smooth leather of his jacket.

"I love you, too," she whispered. And because she couldn't resist, added, "And I swear, I'm not going to be like this all weekend."

"Sweetheart, a few nerves aren't going to send me running scared."

"Even if I babble occasionally?"

He turned in her arms, his hands dropping to the hollow of her spine. "I've never seen you babble. Might be cute to witness."

She tilted her head. With a foot difference in their heights, she had to lean back a bit before she could see his expression. "Trust me, it's not a pretty picture."

That half amused, half indulgent smile was still on his face. His head bent. Just before his mouth met hers, he whispered, "I'll chance it."

If there was ever proof that the man got her, it was right there in his kiss. He didn't just take what he wanted like she expected, but rather he seduced, his mouth rubbing against hers in a subtle coaxing that sapped the anxiety right out of her and replaced it with a warm willingness. Willingness to trust him, to do what he wanted, to be what he wanted. What she wanted.

She opened her mouth and stretched up on her toes, accepting the thrust of his tongue, the natural dominance in his hold, tilting her head to give him more, letting him lead her past the point where caution said stop. Spreading her legs for the insertion of his thigh between, she checked her impulse to control the need to rub against him, following her instinct and his lead rather than her head. With her next breath she inhaled his groan of satisfaction.

"That's it. Just let it happen."

His grip moved to her hips, lifting her up against the thrust of his cock, pressing down as she worked her hips in an effort to get closer, to his heat, his cock, to him....

Too soon he was sliding her down his body, setting her feet on the ground, separating their lips.

"Hold that thought."

She didn't want to hold anything but him. The press of his thumb at the corner of her mouth sent a shock wave of need through her. Everything she ever dreaded seeing in a man's eyes was there in Marc's: amusement, satisfaction and, worst of all, a complacent grin that said he knew exactly how weak she was when it came to him. But her inward flinch never got a running start because there was no malice in that grin, just a bone deep satisfaction that was as arousing as it was comforting because it said more than anything else that at least one of them knew what they were doing. And it was completely natural that it was him.

His jacket whispered a protest as she slid her arms free. His hand cupped her cheek in one of those easy touches that reached all the way to her soul, catching her before she could step away. His hazel eyes were dark in the moonlight. She leaned her cheek into his gloved palm and sighed. "I'm an idiot."

His answer was immediate. "Yes, you are, but you're mine, and I kind of like you this way."

She raised her eyebrows. "A neurotic mess?"

His thumb brushed her mouth and a chuckle quirked his lips before his hand dropped away. "Vulnerable."

She held out her hand for her suitcase. "Uh-huh. Well, don't get used to it."

He paused before dragging the cooler out and putting it on the snow-encrusted ground. "I'll try to keep my appreciation limited to the weekend."

She averted her eyes as he settled a brown box on the cooler's white top. "Thank you."

He closed the trunk and hefted the cooler and box. "My pleasure."

Becky followed as Marc led the way down the hill to the cabin, admiring the way his jeans clung to his thighs with each step delineating the strength beneath. She wondered if he was thinking the same things she was. She wondered if his cock was hardening as quickly as her pussy was moistening. God! She wanted him. Wanted this. And, she shifted the suitcase as she hurried to keep up, she was not going to allow anything to stop her from obtaining her goal. She might have more than her fair share of inhibitions, but she also had more than her fair share of determination, and of the two qualities, the second was stronger than the first.

The cabin was cold, the vaulted ceilings and log walls harboring the chill of the outside. She turned up the thermostat on the furnace and set to work on the fire as Marc made the bed and unpacked the food.

From the corner of her eye, she could see the brown box on the coffee table, looking lost in the vastness of the room. The innocent-looking brown box that held all the sex toys they'd selected together. Anything and everything they'd seen that they thought they might use. It had been tough to ignore the expense, but as it seemed the height of ridiculousness to be prudent when pursuing decadence, she'd conquered her caution to the point of maybe going overboard. She battled an unreasonable urge to toss the throw from the couch over it.

As if there was anyone here to see. As if Marc was going to have a problem with anything contained in it. The man had adventure in his bones. She was the one with all the good-girls-don't hang-ups. Heck, judging from his comments as she'd pointed out a few things she'd been interested in and from the confidence with which he'd made his selections, there probably wasn't anything in the box of which he didn't have firsthand knowledge. Just not with her.

And that fast, she added another emotion to the turbulence of the evening. Jealousy that her husband's past lovers had been more adventurous than she.

He came up behind her as she stood by the fire. She shivered as he moved her hair aside, baring her neck. The heat of his breath touched her first, moist and tantalizing, brushing across her sensitive nerve endings in an evocative arc.

"Ready?"

The question whispered against her neck. Goose bumps sprang up in a silent "Hell, yes," she couldn't get past her throat. She tilted her head, inviting a kiss instead, shuddering when he gave it to her. His cock pressed against her buttocks, rock hard and eager while his hands slid down her sleeves until his fingers intertwined with hers.

She gripped his hands in hers. "As I'll ever be."

He laughed into the curve of her shoulder, sending new goose bumps chasing after the last set, the flick of his tongue encouraging their tingling spread to her breast and nipples. His big hands whispered across the front of her coat, taunting both breasts with the promise of a touch she couldn't feel, making her strain for any ghost of sensation. The tension in her limbs gathered in her pussy, throbbing with an eagerness that faintly embarrassed her. As if a woman should consider her attraction to her husband a weakness.

"Having second thoughts?"

"I'm a little stuck in my ways."

He turned her in his arms. "At the risk of repeating myself yet again, I like your ways."

No, he didn't; he couldn't. She didn't even like them. "And that's why you always hold back with me."

"Is that a complaint?"

She wanted to stamp her foot in frustration. "I'm not the one who should be complaining."

Two fingers under her chin brought her gaze up. "The reason you haven't heard me complain is because I don't have any complaints."

"You want a woman who lets go, who can let you be in charge."

His gaze never wavered from hers. "The only woman I want is you."

She dropped her forehead into his chest. The down of his coat cushioned her landing. "I know."

His arms came around her shoulders. "So what's the problem?"

"I want to be that woman, too!"

There, her not-so-secret secret was out.

His coat rustled as his lips touched her temple. "Have I ever told you I think you're a nut?"

She shook her head.

His smile spread against her temple. "I'm fairly sure I have."

"Not today."

"My mistake." This time it was his thumb that propped her chin up. "You know I'll give you anything you want, in or out of the bedroom."

She knew that. He was a very generous lover. She turned her head and cleared her throat. To her dismay, her voice still held a betraying husk of uncertainty. "I know."

"And you want this?"

She wrapped her fingers around his wrist and held on. "The one place I never wanted to be in charge was the bedroom."

And it was the one place where she couldn't seem to let go. His hand stroked her hair, pulling her cheek to his chest, holding her tight. "Ah, baby."

"I know." She closed her eyes. "I'm a nut."

His thumb pressed against her lower lip, bringing her eyes back open. "No, you're my wife."

She angled her head back and wrinkled her nose. "Who's a nut."

"Who's everything I want." His gaze didn't leave hers. "Just the way she is."

That wasn't good enough anymore. At least not for her. "But what if I don't want to be this way?"

"Then we change."

She had so many hang-ups, so many reasons for how she was, none of them worth holding onto. "What if I can't?"

"Then we keep trying."

She took a breath and released his wrist, clutching his coat sleeve instead. She sighed. "You make it sound so easy."

"All you've got to do is whatever I tell you. No right, no wrong. No need to think." He arched his eyebrow at her. "How hard can it be?"

Not that hard. At least in theory. "Marc?"

He reached around her and closed the door to the woodstove. "Right here."

"Have I mentioned how much I love you?"

"I'm open to hearing it again."

The familiar response given with that familiar smile took away more of her nervousness. This was Marc. She trusted him with her life. She could certainly trust him with her sexuality. She linked her hands around his neck and snuggled her hips into his, giving him a smile back of her own. "Make it worth my while and I will."

His brow arched. "Is that a challenge?"

She did her best to look demure. "Maybe."

"That sounded like a challenge."

"I would never challenge you."

His smile spread. "Like hell."

"Well," she amended, "not without reason."

His hands cupped her hips, his fingers stretching to the sensitive inside of her thighs. With an easy flex of muscle he lifted her up. Becky wrapped her legs around his hips as he turned. This close she could see the desire darkening the green of his eyes, feel the tension humming under his skin, feel that side of his personality she'd always fought surge. His gaze held hers, the blue more prominent than the green as it always was when he was aroused. "It's risky business challenging a man with my nature."

She feathered her fingers in the hair at the base of his neck.

"Maybe I've just decided it's time to see how much bite there is to your bark."

"Uh-huh. Know what happens to women who play with fire?"

Her hips jostled against his as he walked to the bedroom, the soft cotton of her sweatpants doing nothing to protect her from the pressure against her clit. Desire sparkled through her blood. Excitement shortened her breath. She loved it when he went all macho on her. "Nope."

Marc stopped just inside the bedroom door, his gaze holding hers as he let her slide down his body, the hot length of his cock caressing the inside of her thighs until her toes touched the floor. Her held her there, suspended in his embrace, his cock notched between her legs, pressing against her through his jeans and her pants as he drawled, "Their husbands get to see how hot they can make them burn."

He let her go. She stumbled, caught between the king-size bed behind her and her husband in front, daring and dread rising with equal fervor.

Of course, he saw. He touched her cheek. "What?"

"Don't let me ruin this."

He shook his head, the firm line of his mouth softening. "There's no way you can ruin anything."

But she could fail. She grabbed his hand. "Promise me you'll just do it like we talked about."

He frowned. "I can't promise that. Not if you're not enjoying yourself."

"I might be uncomfortable at first, but I swear I'll enjoy it."

"Let's see."

He took her hand in his, pulling it behind his back, pulling her into his arms. The touch of his lips on hers was firm when she'd expected soft, commanding when she'd expected reassurance, throwing her off balance. While she struggled to find the rhythm in the kiss, he caught both of her hands and moved them behind her back, anchoring them in one of his, keeping her helpless as his mouth took charge of hers. Fire streaked from her breasts, her thighs, her lips, leaping along her nerve endings, the feeling of helplessness feeding the flames.

The zipper of her coat rasped louder than her heartbeat as he slid it down. His palm swallowed the small mound of her breast, bare beneath her shirt because he'd requested it, pressing and massaging, stoking the burning ache, sending it deeper, and all she could do was stand there and take the pleasure he was giving her. The way he wanted. Oh, God. Her knees buckled. It was so good.

He caught her easily, holding her still for more of his touch, his desire. The pinch of his thumb and forefinger on her nipple made her jump, except she couldn't go anywhere, do anything. He was in charge. In complete control. Her lids fluttered open. He was staring down at her, the desire burning so brightly in her mirrored in the tight set of his expression. Along with that realization came another. He liked her like this. The knowledge settled deep, giving her the courage to lower her lids, lick her lips, and ask, "Is that all you've got?"

His laugh was more sensual than amused; the answer he gave short and to the point. "Hardly."

The pressure on her nipple increased to the point of pain. His gaze never left hers as she waited, breath suspended in her chest, womb clenched expectantly, whether in hope or dread, she didn't know. With a small smile, he released her nipple and turned her around. Becky stood there, breath shuddering, adrenaline flowing for three uncomprehending seconds until he said, "Bend over."

And the conflagration started again, her mind racing ahead

of her actions, picturing how she'd look to him, her hands braced on the bed, her rear thrust back in a purely submissive pose.

When she would have shrugged off her coat, Marc caught her shoulders.

"No."

Subtle pressure bent her over. She caught her weight on her hands, feeling awkward and vulnerable and as turned on as she'd ever been as his hand grazed up the inside of her thigh, pressing her leg to the left in a smooth demand before repeating the same caress with the other leg.

His fingertips pressed lightly against her pussy. "I've been thinking about this since morning."

It was a struggle to find her voice. "What exactly is 'this'?"

His shadow fell over her as he stood, making her vividly aware of his size, the need to dominate he'd always kept in check for her. The need she'd asked him to let loose. His hands on the waistband of her sweatpants were cold. She jumped. Her pants and underwear followed the shiver as it snaked down to her toes. "Your ass."

Which told her nothing and suggested everything.

The snap of his fingers against her right cheek had her jumping again. "Push back."

She did.

Another tiny slap, this one so soft it seemed to absorb the sting of the other. In the aftermath, his palm lingered. "You liked that?"

There was no way she could deny it, even if every liberated bone in her body demanded that she do so. Those betraying goose bumps were at it again, telegraphing her delight. The zipper of his jeans rasped loudly in the silence. She swallowed hard; the image of him taking her fully clothed played like

a siren's lure in her mind. Hard, deep, his focus on his pleasure. Oh, yes. She wanted him to take her like that. To use
her for his satisfaction, to let her be nothing more than what
he needed this once. Not having to think, to worry, just being
there to satisfy him would be so good.

His fingers slipped between her thighs, callused and rough,
sliding easily across her shaved labia. His laugh, when he found
her open and wet, held the smile she'd missed earlier.

"Looks like you've been thinking, too."

"Yes." She always thought about him.

"Did you prepare yourself like I ordered?"

He could feel that she had, so he must just want to hear her
say it. "Yes." Admitting that sent another quiver of delight
through her. Took her another step deeper into her fantasy
where her submissive side got free rein.

"Good."

He eased his cock up the crack of her ass. It slid smoothly
on the lubricated skin, making her shudder and push back.
His thumbs rubbed the inside of her cheeks, holding her open
for the next stroke.

The fat head of his cock caught on the edge of her anus.
Hunger, hot and dark, shot inward. Her cry was involuntary.
He didn't move, didn't even seem to breathe for a second—
and then he snuggled the broad head against the tight opening, teasing her with the promise of the forbidden.

"Step out of your pants," he ordered darkly, then stood
still, letting her efforts to follow his order work him up and
down the crease.

As soon as she was free, she resumed her position. He
pushed her ankle with his foot. "Wider."

She complied immediately, feeling completely exposed.
It only increased her excitement. His cock throbbed against

her. The touch of his fingers changed from caressing to possessive as he moved her around, letting the head of his cock probe first her ass and then lower; not entering, just stroking like one might with a finger.

It was pure torment to stand so, bent over, exposed, wondering where he would take her. When? Would he be fast or slow? Would he let her come, or would he leave her hanging, deliciously full of his semen, pulsing with anticipation?

He rubbed his cock over her buttocks. Despite her efforts to stay quiet, a whimper escaped. It felt too good to tolerate in silence. He rubbed some more. She gave up the effort to control her breathing. It came out ragged and loud.

He pulled back and his cock tapped at her anus. "Are you ready for me?"

He had to know she was. He'd told her to keep herself always ready for him and she did though he'd never taken her that way. Mainly because she always froze up. Her "Yes" was a soft moan of expectancy.

He slid a finger in her ass. The tight ring spasmed, clutching him hard.

"Oh, God," she moaned, trying to steady her knees beneath the surge of pleasure.

"I guess you are," he murmured at the smoothness of his entry, probing gently. She moaned again and pushed back, trying to establish a rhythm. He stretched her wider and introduced another finger. For a moment, she balked, tightening against the invasion. He paid her no mind, pulling his fingers out, dragging against her sensitive flesh as he withdrew.

"Relax and push back," he coaxed, easing them back in, spreading her as he did. "You know you love this."

She did. She loved it when he played with her ass, no matter how he took it. Gentle or rough, it turned her on until she could scream just thinking about him eventually claiming it. She took a breath, waited for the next withdrawal and then pushed back.

"That's it," he murmured. "Show me how much you like it."

She didn't have much choice. Her nerves were on fire. Her entire being focused on his fingers and the pace he was setting, slow and easy when she wanted hard and fast, every twist, every scissor of his fingers divine torture. When she was almost screaming with frustration, he pulled free.

His cock tapped her frantically throbbing opening. She jerked up, hips hungrily rearing back, wanting the consummation. Only to be denied again when he stepped back. She dropped her head to the mattress, her pussy aching, ass clenching, feeling so empty she thought she'd die from it.

Marc nudged her foot with his again. She widened her stance. It took two more nudges before she was at the level he wanted, legs wide, tight muscles straining, every sense attuned to him, wanting him. "Perfect."

It was the only warning she had before he pushed his thick cock into her pussy. She bucked and would have collapsed if he hadn't anchored her hips with his hands, holding her steady for the solid penetration.

It wasn't easy taking him like this—he was a big man and her inner muscles struggled to accept his width as he pressed inexorably inward—but it was also arousing as hell. Feeling his cock drive deep, having him pull her hips back into his on the grinding descent; hearing his orders to take him, to fuck him, moaned hoarsely in her ear as his fingers dug into her thighs, giving her no choice but to do as he ordered, to pleasure him as he needed. It was her wildest fantasy, having him use her like she was there for his pleasure only. And it was now coming true.

She pushed back, taking another inch, his curse flowing above her just so much sweet music because she knew she'd drawn it from him against his will. Just as she knew the next thrust wasn't as controlled as the first. Yes, yes, yes! With every hard thrust she opened wider, took him deeper.

She braced her arms on the bed, pushing back further. It wasn't enough. She wanted more. She wanted him to pound that thick cock into her, ride her until he couldn't hold it anymore. She wanted him to claim her, to make her his in a totally primitive way that went far deeper than any woman would consider politically correct. She wanted him to fuck her without finesse, without control. Just him and her and the need she inspired in him. She wiggled her hips. A smart sting on her right cheek halted the movement. "Stay still and take it."

Oh, God! She bit her lip as the sting melded with the heat burning her from the inside out, feeding it. How had he known? In her dreams he said things like that to her, did things like this to her, but she'd never told him, never written it down. How had he known this part of her fantasy she'd never dared to confess?

His cock continued to plunder her pussy, pushing solidly in, catching on sensitive nerve endings as her muscles parted to accommodate his width, dragging and stretching her flesh as he withdrew, every stroke, every heated inch destroying the control she prided herself on. The control she didn't want in bed. Her clit ached and pulsed, needing his touch, her touch, anything. All it would take was the barest stimulation there and she'd go hurtling over the precipice she could sense him approaching.

He didn't give it to her. Just kept filling her with his cock, feeding her need, her desire, building it until she wanted it to go on forever yet she didn't think she could bear it if it did. Continuing until she couldn't think of anything beyond the fact that she was his, and she loved him so.

With a thrust so deep it pierced her soul Marc came, grinding his hips so deeply into hers, his zipper cut into the flesh of her buttocks. She pushed back, begging for more. Becky could feel his cock pulse that brief second before it jerked, tapping against her G-spot, filling her with his hot come, giving her some of what she wanted but not enough. Not enough to come. She clawed at the comforter and clenched again. His dark laugh let her know he knew what she was doing. What he was doing to her.

"You want more?"

She shuddered and admitted the glorious truth. "Yes."

His big hand worked between them, cupping her pussy. "Greedy thing."

She had no defense. She was greedy. She wanted more. Everything he could give her.

His cock jerked within her, touching that spot. His fingers snapped against the pad of her pussy, sharp and hard. She stiffened in shock as wild sensation burned up into her womb. Before she could sort it out, he was doing it again, harder, stronger. Delight cut through shock, a mixture of sweet pain and searing pleasure, to strong to deny, too overwhelming to sort out. Too fucking fantastic to resist.

"Come for me."

Low, deep and intent, the order didn't leave her any choice. On the next slap she did, bucking and arching her hips for more of whatever he wanted to give her, open to the pleasure, the pain or a combination of the two. Just open....

★ ★ ★

He was holding her, his arms wrapped around her while his big body covered her. With every breath she took, she absorbed his scent, hers, theirs.

His cock flexed within her. They were still joined. Becky opened her hands on the mattress, bracing herself—for what, she didn't know, just whatever was going to happen to destroy this moment.

His lips skimmed her temple, her cheek, soft gentle caresses that melted into her soul.

"Can you feel my seed in you?" he asked, pulling his still-hard cock almost all the way out before sliding back in, his voice as quiet and as deep as the night around them.

"Yes."

"It makes you hot, doesn't it?"

"Yes."

"Tell me."

The order wasn't unexpected. The surge of lust at hearing it, at contemplating obeying it, was. She dug her nails into the sheet, holding on as the quiver shook her from head to toe. Her voice, when she found it, was husky and raw, as if all the screams she'd suppressed over the years had left their mark. "When you fill me with your seed, it makes me crazy."

He stroked her again, slow and lazy. "How crazy?"

"I can't get enough of it," she admitted breathlessly. "Of you."

She surged back, almost there, but he stepped away.

She was suddenly, devastatingly empty. She groaned a protest.

A brush of flesh on flesh, and then there was only the lingering warmth of his seed inside her, keeping her achingly aroused. She knew she'd stay that way until she could no longer feel his essence.

"Take off your clothes," he instructed quietly. "And then climb into bed and close your eyes."

A light slap on her rear had her hurrying to comply. The sheets were chilly. She lay there on her back, shivering with cold and anticipation until the heat from the fire seeped through and then it was just anticipation shaking her from head to toe.

It took her a minute to realize Marc had left the room. With her eyes closed, every other sense seemed to magnify, especially her sense of hearing. She could hear him in the bathroom washing up, track his move to the living room, and then back. He stopped just inside the bedroom door.

She pushed the covers down, the smooth cotton gliding sensuously across her stomach and thighs. The catch of his breath was audible. She smiled, drew up her knee and arched her back, giving him a view of everything that was his.

"Still playing with fire, sweetheart?"

"Mmm." She spread her legs wide, imagining how she looked to him, wanton and eager. His shirt dropped to the floor in a soft rustle. His wallet hit the bureau with a heavy thud. The change in pocket of his jeans jingled as they slid down his legs. The mattress dipped under his weight.

It dipped again as he moved closer. His arm brushed her shoulder. The heat of his body covered her as light as a touch. His scent enveloped her in a familiar hug.

She sensed his lips before she felt them pressing against hers. His whispered,"I love you" wove around her in a protective spell. She whispered it back, letting the vow follow her breath into his mouth, envisioning it blending with his until the two were hopelessly intertwined. His hand curved around her head in a gentle vise, holding her still for his kiss. Her arms wrapped around his shoulders, keeping him still for hers.

Marc separated his mouth a scant inch from hers. "Don't open your eyes."

"Okay."

His finger traced her lip. "No matter what."

Anticipation nudged her pulse up a notch. "No matter what."

His fingers fanned over the side of her face. He eased her lower lip away from her teeth with his thumb. "I like your mouth."

She didn't know what to say to that, so she settled for a "Thank you."

"I want it on me."

She touched the fleshy pad of his thumb with her tongue. "Now?"

"Yeah. Now."

When she would have slid down his body, he tightened his grip on her head. "Turn around first."

The covers wrapped around her as she shifted, then were tugged away, leaving her with only smooth cotton and smooth skin to guide her. She fumbled a little without the use of sight, relying on his hand for guidance. The tendons in her inner thighs strained as she straddled his chest. He was a big man all over. Built strong, inside and out. Solid. Someone she could depend on always. She kissed her way down his stomach, going with the rise and fall of his abs, counting the ridges. One, two, three.

Her lips dipped into the well of his navel, explored and then moved below, following the thin line of hair beneath. His hand tangled in her hair. Ignoring the silent demand she worked lower, not stopping until she found the soft sac of his balls. It came as naturally as breathing to kiss them. His breath hissed in only to be released immediately, sighing, "That's good."

Marc widened his thighs. She nuzzled them gently, sucking softly on the delicate flesh, before kissing them again. Against her cheek, his cock stirred. Because she loved to feel him quicken with life, she snuggled his semi-soft penis against her tongue, cherishing this brief time when she could hold him in his entirety.

With a tug on her thigh, he drew her across his torso until she was covering him like a living blanket. That was fine with her. Having him like this, relaxed beneath her while the echoes of their previous pleasure wrapped them in an intimate cocoon was a pleasure unto itself. She scooted back as his cock grew too big to hold in her mouth, letting her lips slide up his length until only the mushroom-shaped head rested inside the taut circle. She twirled her tongue around the firm tip, compressing with her lips before sucking lightly, the spike of his hips a hot incentive to do it again.

He moaned and shoved the blankets clear. The hand on her head pushed down even as he pushed his hips up. Becky took what she could, giving him as much as she could, wanting to please him this way, too. A bead of pre-come spilled into her mouth, salty, spiced with that flavor that was uniquely Marc, seeping into her desire in a lazy intoxicating wave that gathered momentum as another deep, masculine moan flowed into the darkness around her.

God! She loved the taste of him. The feel. She grasped the base of his shaft in her hand, angling him back. She kept up a lazy rhythm, her senses focusing on the moment and everything surrounding it: the heat of his cock, the throb of his pulse, the stretch in her thighs, the ache in her core, the weight of his palm. In her pussy, she still felt the hot weight of his seed like a loving promise yet to be fulfilled.

Beneath her, Marc shifted. His chest muscles rippled along the inside of her thighs as he reached for something. In her hypersensitive state, she could feel every ridge of muscle, every expansion of breath.

"Are your eyes closed?"

His voice was husky. Deep. Intent. On nothing more than the nuances contained in the question, her womb clenched. She slid her mouth free of his cock. "Yes."

"Keep them that way."

The order didn't require a response. She gave it to him anyway in a slow breath that wafted across the head of his cock in a whispery tease. The hard shaft jerked in her grip. She followed the airy caress with her tongue, flattening it across the broad head, holding it there, holding him there for a heartbeat before wiggling her tongue in the tiny slit at the center, then doing it again when his big body jerked in response, fucking it in tiny pulses that had his breath hissing in between his teeth. Oh, yes, she liked him like this.

She laughed, taking him deep, letting him share in the reverberations of her pleasure. He pushed high with his hips, getting her to take a fraction more, reestablishing the power between them, reinforcing who would give and who would take. While she struggled to accept his cock, something cool and smooth pressed against her anus.

"Umph?"

The answer to her incoherent question was an increase in pressure against the tight ring of her ass. She froze. He had been in the toy box. Her ass twitched in apprehension while her pussy wept with need. She pushed up on her arms. The move pressed her harder against the would-be intruder. "Stay still."

It was a no-nonsense order followed by a no-nonsense push against her butt. Whatever he had chosen felt huge. She remembered some of the toys they had selected. They *were* huge. Her muscles tensed in an agony of indecision. He pushed the fake penis against her butt again. She moved forward to his balls to postpone the inevitable penetration. She made an involuntary move to close her legs, but only succeeded in clamping her thighs around his ribs. His chest hair abraded her clit, making her gasp and twist.

He laughed, a low, husky, distracted sound. His palm cupped her rear holding her to the pleasurable friction while with unrelenting pressure against her anus he forced her body's acceptance. "Relax, Becky."

She tried, but it wasn't easy. He didn't desist.

"You can take this. Just relax and push back."

He didn't give her any choice. Untried muscles gave up on the unequal battle. She panted through the foreign sensation, a combination of pleasure and pain.

More pressure, this time at the back of her head, keeping her mouth full of his cock as he slowly breached her ass with the thick toy.

She breathed through her nose, struggling to relax, torn between wanting him to stop and needing the dark consummation to continue. The slow penetration finally stopped. The rough calluses of his fingers grazed the hypersensitive skin of her rear as he asked, "Okay?"

She took a breath, stilling the panic to try to find an answer. The dildo stretched her past comfortable but not fully into pain, creating contrary signals that her desire absorbed and translated into something darker, something deeper, something intriguingly different. She nodded yes.

"Good. Now, I want you to use your mouth and show me how you want to be loved."

He was allowing her some control, letting her set the pace for her seduction. She was intrigued. Tempted and intrigued. Indecision held her immobile for a timeless, breathless second. She felt too…stretched for anything vigorous.

With the slightest of hesitations, she took just the tip of his penis into her mouth. He throbbed against the inside of her lips. She eased her head gently up and down. The dildo moved with the same shallow motion, forcing her tight muscles wider and the burn higher, the joy higher still.

She could handle that, she decided, repeating the move. It still wasn't exactly pleasurable. There were too many conflicting emotions inside for her to sort out the pleasure from the other, newer sensations, but she could sense it waiting, just beyond her grasp. She forgot to caress his cock, and he stopped.

Darn. She squeezed her eyes tighter and resumed her movements.

"You want it like that for a while?" he asked.

Feeling vulnerable and exposed, she nodded her head.

"Okay. Rest your cheek on my hip and we'll try this for a while."

At first, she couldn't relax, but the steady massage of the penetration soon eased the tension from her muscles. The motion became smoother and easier as she relaxed into the play. She loved the feeling of being penetrated almost more than she loved to come, and the sensation was even more intense, more satisfying this way. And now, with Marc's permission, she was able to fully focus on the stroke of the toy over her most sensitive nerves, to wallow for as long as she wanted in the pure bliss. She lifted her hips facilitating the easy rhythm.

Her ass began to throb and twitch, and the easy screwing became more irritating than satisfying. Rooting with her lips, she found his cock and engulfed him in one deep swallow. The dildo echoed her efficiency.

Her satisfied groan danced down his shaft.

It felt good. So damn good.

She took him again, deeply. Her ass relished the same treatment. Marc caught the rhythm, slow and deep, hovering on the retreat before plunging back in to linger on the push. Unlike a cock, the dildo didn't get too excited and put an end to the sensation. She was free to enjoy it as long as she could, letting the burn become an ache that sharpened to a high-pitched need that spread outward, building in a wave. She yanked her mouth off his cock, sinking her teeth into his thigh, biting down as she took more, her ass clenching down hard, holding tight....

She felt his laugh more than heard it. "Feels that good, huh?"

Again, all she could do was nod.

"Imagine how good it's going to feel when it's my cock instead of a toy."

She closed her eyes, imagining it, wanting it. "Oh, yes."

She shifted up and caught the tip of his penis in her mouth. Just the tip. She closed her lips tightly around it and slid it in and out, flirting with the idea of penetration, making him relive over and over the thrill of possession.

"Oh, God," she moaned as he forced her ass open again and again with the same piercing motion. "Don't stop. Please."

"I wasn't planning on it." Desire roughened his voice to a hoarse parody of his low drawl and any doubt she had that he was enjoying this as much as her died a quick death. "But I think it's time to change things up."

His cock slid impossibly deep, hitting the back of her throat, holding there while she struggled not to gag. The dildo plumbed her ass with the same erotic efficiency over and over again, taking her higher but not giving her that extra something she needed to relieve the screaming demand ripping along her nerve endings. The hot, burning need to come. She twisted in his grip, sucking his cock harder, taking it deeper, faster, needing him to come so she could.

"Son of a bitch." Hard hands fastened on her shoulders,

pulling her up with the same wildness beating inside her. "Come up here."

She did, kissing her way frantically up his chest, nibbling on his flat brown nipples, savoring the jerk of his chest until he pulled her away.

"Tease," Marc murmured without heat, flipping her onto her back.

She rested her palms on his shoulders, sinking her nails into the thick pad of muscle, anchoring the wildness inside. "Can I open my eyes now?"

"Yes."

His big hands slid down the back of her thighs. He lifted first one and then the other over his arms with deliberate slowness, walking his hands up the side of her torso with that same determination until he had her wide open and exposed.

She didn't understand when Marc reached between them, holding her gaze with his until, with a twist, her ass came alive with powerful pulsing throbs. Her eyes flew wide. The dildo was also a vibrator.

"I always wanted to know what one of those vibrating beds felt like," he murmured.

"Oh, God!" She dug her nails into his shoulder, her teeth into her lip as he nudged her with his cock. He tucked it into the small slit, forcing her tight pussy open with the same inexorable pressure with which he'd opened her ass. It was too much. The over-stretching, the throbbing...Becky closed her eyes and struggled to adjust.

Marc didn't give her time, just threw them both into the chaotic well of need with a slow, steady push. And she took him, all of him—muscles straining, quivering, parting, struggling with the near painful tightness caused by the dildo, nerve endings singing as his groin pressed into hers. And still he pushed, as if as close as they were, it wasn't close enough. She closed her eyes, savoring the feeling. It would never be enough.

She had to move, needed to move, but there was no give in his hold, no leeway in his possession. All she could do was clench around him and beg. "Please, please, please!"

The words filled her head, the room. She was begging aloud and she didn't care. She needed him, needed this.

"I've got you, baby."

And he did, in every way that mattered. She opened her eyes, loving the passion in his face, the lust, the pleasure, knowing that she was giving this to him even as he was giving it to her. Ten more strokes and he came violently, slamming hard against her, holding himself high inside her pussy, his cock jerking with spurt after spurt of hot come.

The power of his release triggered her own, sending her surging up against his chest, twisting violently in his arms as overcharged nerves screamed for a reprieve. He gave her none, forcing her to ride every wave, holding her still when she would have ripped free, nipping her breasts when she swore she couldn't take anymore, sending her into another orgasm as if to prove her wrong.

In the aftermath, when everything had subsided to a quivering ache, he lowered her legs back to her sides, and suckled her breasts more gently as he whispered over and over, "I love you."

Inside her, she felt his softening penis and the hot warmth of his seed. Her pussy clung to both, the pulsing arousal inspired by the latter rivaling the toy. With a soft sigh, he eased out of her, still loving her breasts.

As always, she protested the loss. He'd come in her not once, but twice. She'd be achingly aroused all night unless she cleansed away his seed. She was reluctant to do so, especially when he patted her affectionately between the legs on the way down to turn off the vibrator.

"That was so good," she sighed.

His smile was a tightening of his lips against her nipple. "Glad you enjoyed it."

Her nipple sprang into the cold air with a soft pop as he released it and said, "Why don't you turn over? You know you can't sleep on your back."

She turned over onto her stomach, facing him. Resting her cheek on her forearm, she asked, "Aren't you forgetting something?"

His big hand smoothed down her back. His fingers flirted with the crease of her buttocks before dipping between. With a delicate push, he reseated the toy. Her oversensitive body made more of the movement than she'd expected, quivering and tightening. His fingers lingered almost contemplatively.

"Nope."

She cracked an eyelid and noted his speculative expression as he played with the dildo. "Is there a problem?"

"Not a one." He eased down beside her, patting her rear in a sweet caress before encompassing the curve. "I was just thinking—"

"What?"

His lips brushed her shoulder. The sheets rustled as his chest half shifted over her back, covering her with his heat and strength. His cock thrust against her hip as he drawled in her ear, "There are a lot more toys in that box…"

★ ★ ★ ★ ★

FORBIDDEN RITUAL
SASKIA WALKER

First he took off her jacket, then he unzipped her fitted dress, peeling away the outward signs of her everyday life. "This is what I want," Giles stated as he undressed her, "the real woman beneath the high-powered persona you adopt for work." Humor and passion glinted in his eyes. "It's pretty hard to get past it, you know."

"Giles, please," Imogen murmured, embarrassed by what she knew to be the truth. He had a way of exposing her in ways she hadn't considered possible. "I need you."

He paused and smiled. Slowly, he shrugged off his jacket and undid his silk tie, then traced his finger around her erect nipple.

Even through the sheer fabric of her black lace bra the touch was electrifying. Imogen's legs trembled, her body hot with anticipation as Giles toyed with her. He squeezed the sensitive nub firmly between thumb and forefinger, looking deep into her eyes while he lit her right through with that deliberately provocative touch. Imogen leaned toward him, her lips parting with the need to have his mouth covering hers while he touched her.

But Giles continued to take charge. He undid her bra, dropped it to the floor and then went for the handcuffs that he had left on the nearby dining table. Capturing her wrists in one hand, he clicked the cool metal into place, making his claim on her. Then he stepped away.

She swayed unsteadily on her high heels, uncertainty swamping her.

He strode to a nearby chair, undoing and abandoning his shirt as he went, then sat down. "Tell me something, Imogen."

She eyed his bared, muscular chest, and swallowed, hard. "Anything."

He kicked off his shoes and socks, each action like a deliberate stall. "We've been doing this for what…five, maybe six months now?"

Was he bored with her? She clutched at the chain that held her handcuffed wrists together, needing to feel the galvanized steel links between her fingers to hold her emotions steady. "Six months and ten days."

He watched her every move.

"How well do you think I know you?" He rested his elbows on his knees and observed her closely as he asked the question.

She felt completely naked, even though she still wore her high heels, stockings and her black lace panties. Giles had teased her to distraction once he'd got her to his Thames-side apartment, and now she longed to feel the palm of his hand on her backside before he filled her. Had she become too focused on that, she wondered. It was always a possibility. His eyes glittered with anticipation as he awaited her response. It was significant because he knew how hard it was for her to verbalize her needs and to admit her fears.

Her lips parted, and she ran her tongue over her lower lip before she spoke. "You know me well enough."

It came out in a whisper, because it pained her to admit even that much. There was a fierce and stubborn streak in her that she managed to quell when they were together like this, but it rose quickly to the surface if she had to think too deeply about what she was doing, what she was giving away about herself when she submitted to Giles sexually—a younger man, her junior and a talented spin doctor. There was a lot at stake.

"Do I?" There was a confrontational tone to his question. "We have sex, but you leave my bed when I'd rather keep you in it. How can I know you when you don't let me in to your private thoughts?"

Somehow the sudden change in approach made her even more desperate for him to resume his attentions to their mutual physical needs. Between her thighs she throbbed with need. Her core tightened, aching to be filled—preferably while her bottom burned from the punishing slap of his palm as he worked her to climax. She tossed back her hair, forcing herself to breathe.

Her lover had made her wait until her anticipation had built to fever pitch, as he so often did, but the nature of the question indicated how important the answer was to him. Giles always made her beg for it—which turned her on immensely, much to her initial surprise—but he'd never walked away from her before, and he'd never quizzed her like this when he'd already begun to undress and prepare her. Normally he'd stay close, his hands on her constantly, staying her urge to flee or to deny her need to be under his control. Why now, when she was so keyed up, was he examining her need to be independent after she submitted to him?

Giles lounged back in his chair, somehow regal even though he was stripped to the waist and barefoot, his tailored trousers almost incongruous, given how easy this man was in his own skin, a quality she not only admired, but craved. His firm, sensuous mouth made her ache for him. Only he could do this to her, and it made her feel so vulnerable. His chiseled cheek-bones and hard jawline seemed to be visual symbols of the inner strength that called to her. Here in his sparse bachelor apartment he'd revealed just how easily he could take charge of her, a woman who never gave in under normal circumstances.

She braced herself. "You know I have to be this way. Your question is too…personal."

"I mean to be personal with you, on every level." There was no hesitation in his comeback.

Again she swayed. His provocative stare had her skin prickling.

One corner of his mouth lifted.

Erotic suggestion hung in the atmosphere between them. "Please, Giles. You've got me in a state." She tripped on her words, her rising objection making her speak before thinking. "I can't think straight because I want you so much."

When he lifted an eyebrow knowingly, she looked at the floor.

"I want you too," he replied, "but the better I know you, the better this will be."

"It's already too good," she blurted, then bit her lip, realizing what she'd said. She was afraid of getting too deep, afraid that one day she would submit to him and lose herself totally.

"It is good." The hungry look in his eyes as he glanced over her body made her shiver. "But you deserve better than a quick shag at the end of your workday, and I want to give it to you."

What they did was hardly a quick shag, but it was true that their time together was something she engaged in between work and sleep, and that's how she kept it compartmentalized in her life, just like everything else.

He shifted in his seat, resting one ankle on the opposite knee as if they were having a casual chat about business and no more. "Now, tell me how well I know you."

Despite the directness of his comment, his commanding tone made her melt.

Up until that moment she could have turned away, asked him to unlock the cuffs and let her leave. Not now. Not after he'd asked her again, and said it with such deliberate inquiry. It made something inside her begin to buckle. The truth of it was she didn't want to leave, she wanted him too much. She thought they'd found a plateau in their relationship, one that they were both happy with. Obviously not. His dominant nature and her need for an edge of pain to heighten her pleasure seemed to slide nicely along each other. Now he was pushing her beyond her comfort zone. How did he do that to her, she wondered. She'd been lured by his dominant nature, even though it was so far from what she really wanted out of life. To be an independent woman who didn't need a man, that was her goal.

"I'm not even sure how well I know myself," she whispered. It felt like a confession. She stared at his chest, broad and hard and dusted with fine dark hair that tapered into a thinner line leading her gaze from his breastbone to the button on his fly. What she knew without any shadow of a doubt was that when he claimed her, he owned her. In the throes of passion she was his willing submissive, and it was this edgy feeling before she gave in to it, this tight, breathless anticipation he caused in her that made every encounter so darkly delicious. She couldn't risk falling, though.

Giles seemed to sense her hesitance. "Your feminine

strength fascinates me," he stated. "You go after everything you want but you always move on, fast, and that concerns me."

She felt her face heating. That was how she worked, but he wasn't just talking about work, that was quite obvious. By day she was a high-ranking government minister, and Giles was a press officer who had broken through her self-imposed isolation. She'd devoted herself to her job. The intense encounters he offered had become the only ripple in her orderly life, a treasured hour-long reprieve from being proper, formal and dignified. "I'm highly motivated, I have to be, but what's your point?"

"My point is that even powerful people can grow by challenging themselves." He clasped his fingers together, his hands drawing her attention, her skin aching for the touch of them. "You might benefit from more...restraint."

The way he said that indicated he'd thought it through. A darkly suggestive glance flitted through his eyes, and his handsome mouth pursed slightly as he considered her.

Her sex swelled. The nape of her neck felt damp. "You're suggesting more than the cuffs?"

He nodded.

"But we agreed, the cuffs for...what I want." *The flat of his hand on her backside before and during sex.*

"Yup, we agree. Simple as that. A trade, a nice neat business transaction where everyone gets a fair deal." He smiled at her knowingly. "But now I want you to let me tip your scales."

Heat flared at her center, but she shook her head. "I can't."

Giving him total control over her was something she couldn't allow to happen. She began to twist her wrists in the cuffs, wanting them off. The idea of finding her clothes and ending this was tempting, because it was easy. Then she let her gaze wander over his body. Even when fully dressed his expensive clothing barely concealed his obvious strength. Half-naked, the very look of him was enough to dampen her panties. Bulky with muscle, he made her feel supple as a rag doll in his hands during sex, melding her to his body, bringing her to orgasm time and time again.

Giles shook his head, allowing her to feel his scrutiny. "You're an inspiring woman, but even when you come it's as if you're always holding something back."

Breathing had become difficult. His words struck a note with her and she recognized herself in what he said. *Lord, he does know me.* He was right. She held back because she didn't dare do otherwise. This man was her junior, and eight years younger than her.

"Seeing you on the edge of losing control is such a turn on for me," he added. "I enjoy bringing you to that point." He smiled, and it was filled with dangerous charm. "I'm enjoying watching you now. Your eyes are dilated, and your skin is flushed. Your nipples are diamond-hard." He moved his fingers, gesturing at her upright form while he sat in the chair, observing her. "You're racked with sexual tension. It makes me want to break it apart from inside you."

The way he described her sent her aching sex into overdrive.

Then he rested one hand over his belt, a casual gesture but one that made her glance at his groin, where he was hard beneath his zipper. Frustration bit into her. How could he be so in control? He was younger than her and a testosterone-fuelled man, and yet he obviously enjoyed working her to fever pitch before giving her what they both wanted. Subtle confidence oozed from his every pore. It was what had drawn her to him in the first place. The sense of presence he created in a meeting was profound, even when he was quiet and watchful.

"I'd put money on your underwear being very damp," he added.

Her skin raced with sensation, the thrill of his words touching her everywhere, inside and out. She wanted him to fuck her. But he was making her listen, controlling her with his intimate, knowing words.

He looked at her hands. Her fingers were meshed, the cuffs chinking as she fidgeted fretfully, her hands hovering close to the surface of her panties where her clit was swollen and pounding. He didn't miss a thing. "How wet are you?"

She didn't need to think about it. Her underwear clung to the groove of her pussy. The fabric would need to be peeled away from her aroused folds. She shifted her weight from one heel to the other, her eyes closing as she replied. "Very wet."

Tension filled the air between them. She wanted him badly, wanted him inside her where her body was begging to be filled. She took a step toward him.

He shook his head, drawing her to a sudden halt, then gestured at a chair to her left. "Put one foot on that chair, open your legs and show me how wet you are."

His commanding tone left no room for maneuver, but action meant reaction. They were getting closer to what she needed, what they both needed. Swearing under her breath, she followed his instruction. As she lifted her foot and planted the stacked heel on the surface of the chair, she drew her cuffed wrists close against her lower abdomen and saw the way his eyes darkened as she exposed her panties.

"Oh, yes, you are wet." His lips remained apart as he stared at her. "Touch yourself."

She rested her hand over her pussy, rubbed one of the metal cuffs over her mound, and groaned aloud. Her clit leapt when the pressure of the metal rolled over the fabric covering it.

When he rose to his feet, her level of expectation shot higher still, leaving her breathless, dizzy and swaying. He padded across the floor, bare feet silent. When he stepped close against her, her heart thudded so hard she thought she might crack. Her sense of balance was quickly lost and she shifted her raised foot back to the floor, her heel slamming down hard.

"Easy now," he said, then rested his thumbs in the band on her panties. His breath was warm on her face and her back arched, her hips gravitating toward his on instinct.

He squatted in front of her and rolled her underwear down over her hipbones, growling quietly when her pussy was exposed. She stepped out of the panties. When he stood, he kissed her fiercely, his tongue claiming her mouth. Meanwhile he stroked her pussy, squeezing it in his hand, sending her clit wild. She whimpered, entirely locked to his actions.

He moved his right hand to cup her buttock, squeezing the flesh in his hand.

Her skin prickled with anxiety. She inhaled deeply.

"Bend over the table." He grasped her by the shoulders and turned her round, bending her over the dining table and pressing her down onto it, his hands roaming over her exposed buttocks as if he couldn't get enough of them.

She slumped gratefully over the table, her bottom lifting. As soon as she was in position he delivered a sound slap to her buttock. The sting and the suddenness of it made her shudder. He kissed one shoulder, a fleeting anchor that made her glance back at him. When she met his stare, he gave her a wicked grin and spanked her again. Each sting fuelled the need for more physical contact. Heat speared from the points of contact, as if each strike connected with the pounding pulse that had been raging inside her.

"Giles!"

"Yes, you love it, don't you?" He traced his fingers across the sensitive niche at the top of her thighs, making brief, maddening contact with her pussy. Then he pushed her legs farther apart with a demanding knee. "Let me see you."

Pleasure, pain and shame quickly engulfed her, swamping her with another wave of desire. He ran a knowing thumb back and forth over her clit. Her body was so wired that she reached orgasm moments later, crying out with relief. She was still shuddering when she heard the sound of the condom wrapper being torn open. He opened her up with two fingers and eased his cock inside her, capturing her as she ebbed back from the edge, quickly sending her back to it again.

"Giles, so good," she whispered in relief, suddenly filled with him, her innards melting with pleasure and clasping him gratefully. When he brushed against her buttocks it sent shock waves through her. Her body was singing. She grasped at the table for anchorage, her cuffs rattling against the wood surface.

He kneaded her flesh, hauling her buttocks apart, his cock nudging deeper into her swollen pussy. He groaned with pleasure as he bent over her back, sliding in and out, filling her to the hilt.

"Oh, yes." She shuddered with sensation, her hands clawing for the far edge of the table.

"Good?" he murmured against her back. When she moaned agreement, he thrust again. "Is this just a game to you, a bit of rough play, or does it mean more?"

He stroked her hair back, encouraging her to turn her head.

"Giles...please." She put her cheek to the bare wood of the table, giving herself over to him.

"Do you trust me?"

"Yes." Her hips lifted and she pushed back, offering herself, but Giles rested his hand on the small of her back, stilling her and keeping her under his control.

The slow deep thrusts hypnotized all of her senses, leading her into ecstasy.

He breathed close against her ear, his thrusts slowing. "What do you see, over there on the floor?"

She was so close to coming, but he ran his knuckles along her jaw then pointed. She blinked and focused. A black lacquered box stood against the wall, and a length of rope spilled out of it onto the floor. She hadn't even noticed it before, so focused was she on him, her lover. Now she saw it, and she knew what he'd been leading her to. "Oh, God."

The crown of his cock massaged her deeply at her center, as if his arousal grew in response when she looked at his offering. She moaned loudly, unable to hold back.

"Rope bondage—*shibari*. It's the ultimate ritual. If you offer me yourself completely and allow me to bind you, you would be showing me how much you trust me."

"I can't," she blurted. Even as she said it, she wanted to know what it would be like. Images of being totally bound filled her mind. She thrust her cuffed wrists right across the table, and her core clamped hard on his shaft, her hips rolling back into his.

"Oh, yes, you're interested. Your body always gives you away, my dear."

He'd set it up to test and tempt her, to introduce her to the idea.

She shook her head.

His cock reached. His hand on the small of her back exerted more pressure. That only made her buck against him all the more. Desperate for release, she writhed against the hard surface of the table, her body needling all over as she hovered on the brink of release.

"You want to feel that rope against your skin, don't you?" The immense amount of self-control he was using was palpable in the atmosphere. He was holding back in order to tease her with this suggestion.

Imogen couldn't take it anymore. "Maybe. Not yet."

He kissed the back of her neck. "How well do I know you?"

There was humor in his tone now, and she bucked against him, edgy with conflicting emotions.

He chuckled darkly and eased his cock out, leaving her bereft. "How well…?"

She cried aloud. "All right, yes!" She blurted out the acknowledgement, her frustration spilling over. "You do know me…damn you, you know me better than I know myself!"

Blinking back tears of frustration, she whimpered, hiding in her hair as it fell across her face, thankful he didn't respond verbally.

Instead he locked his hands on her hips and began to drive and thrust with real purpose, speeding them both toward the peak. As she blossomed into climax, her body awash with relief, she stared across at the rope all the while, wondering, wanting, and yet afraid of what it meant about her—what it meant about them both.

Two days later, Andrea—Imogen's personal assistant—deposited a stack of files on her desk. "I have those documents you requested."

"Thank you."

"There's also a package for you. Anything else you need before I head off?"

The package lay on the top and was marked for her attention only. Imogen recognized the handwriting, it was from Giles. Her pulse tripped. She smiled at Andrea and shook her head. "No, we're done for the day, thanks."

Once she was alone she picked up the package. She was due a set of press release statements about changes in the department, but the envelope was bigger than she'd expected. When she opened it she found the paperwork, together with a plain black box marked for her attention only. She turned it over in her hands, savoring the thought that he'd handled it, that he'd sent it to her. That was how much she wanted contact with him, and that alone made her sigh with longing. Just two days without that connection made her feel slightly unreal and disjointed. It was as if he'd become an anchor to her. How had that happened?

When she was sure she wouldn't be interrupted, she removed the tape that sealed the box. A note rested on top of the tissue paper inside.

> *I know you are curious, I saw the way you looked at it. I didn't want you to be afraid, so I'm sending you this sample. Feel how soft it is, how malleable. I had it made especially for you. It's the same color as your eyes when you reach climax.*
>
> *If it doesn't appeal to you, that's fine. I just want you to consider it, because my feeling is that this will be a gift of freedom for you and I want to give you that gift, and so much more. Yours, Giles.*

Imogen put the box down on her desk and stared at it.

After a long moment she teased the tissue aside with a trembling finger, and looked at the skein of electric-blue rope lying in the box. Just looking at it made her go hot all over. She crossed her legs, attempting to quell the interest in her groin as she imagined him naked with the rope in his hands, standing over her as if she were a creature to be tamed. Ironically, he said it was her spirit he wanted to unleash, the unfettered side she only showed when she abandoned herself to sex, to him. Bondage did do that to her. She thought it was just the edge that spanking added to her experience, but he'd been right. Handing over control took her further into abandonment, heightening her pleasure.

He *was* taking a big risk though, because he was exploring her boundaries and both of them knew she wasn't sure how much further she wanted to go. Risks, wasn't that what life was about? Imogen stared at the box and smiled wryly to herself. Her job was all about risk and making judgments about policy, and yet she was so much more cautious when it came to exposing herself to this man. Why? *Because I care about him.* As hard as it was to admit, there was more to it. If she gave herself completely, she might get hurt.

When she'd been preparing to leave after their previous encounter, he'd cupped her face in his hands. "I'm taking a risk here."

He smiled quickly. It's what he'd said to her the first time he indicated he was interested in a relationship outside of the office. "Let me know if you're ready to let me introduce you to *shibari*," he continued. "I promise you won't regret it."

Curious thoughts had plagued her ever since, even though she tried to keep her mind off it, and now he'd sent her this, something she could touch and hold against her skin. She stared at the snake-like coil and pictured the rope stretched taut between his hands. She trailed her fingertips along the edge of the box and allowed herself to consider what he would do with it. It was more than her wrists that he would bind, she supposed. She would be powerless, completely at his whim.

As that thought occurred to her, she had to rest her back against her chair. Every ounce of strength left her body when she considered the effect that might have on her. Giles was already her master, when she allowed it. Could she let herself acknowledge it more than she already had?

She closed her eyes and recalled the thrill she'd experienced when he'd first approached her. The attraction between them had existed from their first introduction. Then one day he'd spoken to her privately as he'd been leaving her office, and he'd reached for her hand and lifted it to his mouth, brushing it with his lips before releasing it. Before she'd had a chance to react or to speak, he looked into her eyes. "I'm here for you. If you want me, just let me know."

She'd been shocked, and undeniably aroused. His hand touched her back briefly. It made her skin sizzle and the pit of her stomach fluttered eagerly. She'd longed for his hand at her back more firmly. Then he'd smiled and turned away, leaving her breathless and clinging to her door handle—awash with physical and emotional feelings that she'd thought long buried.

For a whole three days she'd resisted, debating whether it was right or wrong, while her body heated as she imagined what it might be like to be with a man like him, one who seemed so confident and knowing. She'd been single for ages, after being married young to a man who didn't respect her choice of career. They'd split after three years of disagreeing about what her role in his life should be. After that she'd grown a thicker hide and vowed herself to her job. It was lonely, and sometimes she'd had a fling. Never with anyone she worked with though, and never for very long. And now Giles said he wanted to keep her in his bed, overnight. A younger man with a taste for exotic sex.

Imogen sighed deeply and stared out of her office window,

trying to ignore the corridors of power that surrounded her and her obligation to all of that. She had to keep her head— she couldn't afford to mess up playing with a colleague. What had been a friendly arrangement about sex had morphed into something else. The kinky sex made her think he played the field and it was going to burn out in due course. Now she wasn't sure what to think, especially because it was he who was asking the heavy questions. She turned back to her desk.

"Is it just a game?" he'd asked her.

No, it meant more, a lot more. She'd fallen for him, but she wasn't ready to say that yet. It was too hard. Reaching into the box, she pulled out the sample. Was this the next step, would this bring her closer to freedom?

Running the slender hemp rope through her fingers, she let her imagination run with images of ritualized erotic sex, characterized by domination and submission. Pleasure was what he gave her. Giles was the best lover she'd ever had. Only fear was stopping her from discovering what it would be like to give him that level of control during lovemaking. That was what this was about. He'd offered her sex and she'd gone after it. Risk assessment? He just wanted to play. Her lover was a thirty-two-year-old man and she, at forty, just had to enjoy the hot sex while it lasted. She would regret it if she never tried what he was offering. She could stand the thought of being alone, but not with regrets. *Hell, at least I'll have the sexy memories.*

The sample was less than three feet long, but long enough for her to hold and turn in her hands. The rope was soft to the touch but when pulled taut it became firm and strong. With one heel on the floor she shifted her seat from side to side, edgy with arousal as she considered it. Then she put the rope against the hemline of her knee-length skirt, and pulled the skirt up with the rope. Her sex ached, desire flaring wildly, taking her over. She rode the string up as far as her stocking tops, to the place where the tops of her thighs were bare. The rope made her skin tingle wildly, and her clit throbbed.

The need to touch herself became urgent.

With her hand inside her panties she squeezed and rubbed her clit, the rope Giles had sent her clenched inside her palm. *What am I doing?* she wondered, feeling dangerously out of control. She had her hand under her skirt and she was touching herself, in her office. She'd never done that before, but Giles had driven her to it. As she brought herself to climax, the rub of the rope across her tender flash seemed to mock her for her earlier resistance.

What would Giles do with the rope?

I have to know.

By the time she arrived on his doorstep she could scarcely keep her breathing level. She'd wanted to run straight over to his place, but she'd ordered herself an hour to cool off. In the end she'd managed to wait all of thirty-five minutes, but it was an important time, time to get her thoughts in order. Or as much in order as possible, given the circumstances. Her emotions still swung wildly and she was torn between the desperate need to be there and see it through, and the urge to take flight. She rapped on the door before she could change her mind. *All I have to do is enjoy the sex.*

After a few moments the door swung open and Giles stood there. "You came."

"Yes. I came." *Now show me.*

His mouth lifted at one corner and he nodded. Not smugly though. It was just an acknowledgement, for which she was grateful. He leaned one shoulder up against the door frame.

His hair was wet and he wore jeans and a casual T-shirt that clung to his chest as if he'd just got out of the shower and his skin was still damp. To all intents and purposes he was totally chilled, but the glint in his eye as he assessed her was both predatory and stimulating.

One hand tightened on the strap of her shoulder bag, the other went to the button on her jacket, locking onto it. He watched her every movement, as if each and every thing she did was important to him. Nervous butterflies gathered in her stomach. It wasn't just that he was attractive and powerful-looking. He had that elusive quality of a man in control. It made her self-aware. Mostly she forgot herself in her daily duties. Giles did not allow her to forget she was a woman, one with needs. And yet he looked as if nothing would ruffle him. Ultimate control—how could she not admire that?

He closed on her. Arousal pulled heavily inside her, heating her body through, making her skin sizzle and her fingertips twitch. He held her gaze, not allowing her to look away. Tension filled the air, clinging around them like static. He was reading her. He knew she'd opened the box and that she'd come here willingly. She felt it, and it set loose a wild fluttering at her center. The recognition was there in his expression. She saw desire there too. It was blatant, raw and incredibly powerful. He wanted her, and he was glad she'd come to him.

"You're ready to take this to the next level?" His voice was low.

She nodded.

He put one finger under her chin, looking deep into her eyes. In that one touch he conveyed his authority. It made her wet. "You're going to have to get used to me looking at you if there's going to be rope involved." Then he moved closer still, so close she could feel his breath on her face, and he ran the backs of his knuckles down the front of her throat, stroking her skin as if he were admiring her. "You're going to look so good adorned in rope."

She shifted from one foot to the other, the touch of his hand making her nerve endings go crazy. A muted gasp escaped her lips, and he caught her stare, holding it. They were on a precipice, she could feel it.

Giles shifted his shoulders, rolling them as if he was limbering up. His rising passion was palpable in the air around them. That made her realize that he'd been holding something of himself back, just as she had. Her legs went weak under her as she considered that he hadn't even begun with her. "Giles, please...I confess that I'm a little afraid."

"Don't be." His eyes shone darkly, as if he relished her confession.

It made her pussy tighten with anticipation.

"I'm here to look after you. I think I know what you need, but if I ever do anything you don't want, just tell me."

Imogen swallowed then nodded. She knew his sense of justice wouldn't let him take advantage of her, not unless it was what she wanted. Then his fingers moved beneath her hair, and he pulled her in against him, kissing her hungrily.

She heard the thud of her bag as it fell to the floor. Her hands locked around his head as she gave herself over to him. With urgent fingers he hitched up her skirt, grasping her bottom in his hands, pushing aside the flimsy fabric of her panties so that he could touch her skin. Mercifully she heard the door click shut. He lifted her from her feet, pressing her back against the wall as he held her easily. She grappled with one hand for the skirt, hitching it higher still so that she could wrap her legs around his hips. As she did, he ducked his head to kiss her throat. Her head fell back against the wall and she circled her hips, making contact with the bulky erection inside his jeans. His teeth grazed her throat before he shifted and arranged her in his arms. She clung to him gratefully as he carried her into the bedroom.

"I want you so much," she murmured against the hard column of his neck. She felt delirious as she said it.

He put her down at his bedside.

The curtains were closed, but the windows beyond were open and the curtains lifted on a warm breeze, making odd patterns of light shift through the darkened room. When light moved over the bed, she saw several piles of slender blue ropes, each neatly arranged in a figure of eight. They rested on the black linen sheets as if he'd known she would come for them.

She nodded at the bed. "I see you were expecting my arrival."

"I like to be prepared." Walking around the bed, he observed her from several feet away, studying her intently.

"That's why you do so well in your work." She meant it. Part of his talent was anticipating what might be needed. But for a moment he seemed to take her comment wrongly.

"Imogen, I wasn't sure you'd come, but I hoped." The serious look in his eyes assured her he hadn't taken it for granted. It was as if they each mirrored the resistance, the fear, in each other.

That made her want to reassure him. She undid her watch and put it down on his bedside table. "I'm here because you made me want to know."

He nodded. "Show me how much."

Something about the way he was hanging back, watching and waiting, made her want to ask him to do what he had to do to show her the way. She felt like the novice here, even though she was older. *But he always makes me beg.* Yes. Perhaps she wasn't so gauche after all. They were both learning each other. That's what it was all about. Kicking off her heels she took off her jacket and unzipped her skirt. *Calm down*, she told herself. The truth of the matter was she couldn't get her clothes off quickly enough. After she'd given way to her doubts and overcome them, she had to know what it would be like.

She was down to her stockings when he lifted the first rope from the bed, unfurling it as he did so. He ran the rope through his hands as he watched her undressing. It snaked across the floor between them with one twitch of his arm. She paused in the act of rolling down her stockings, then pushed them off even more hurriedly. His brows were drawn low over his eyes in concentration and his mouth was set firm. Everything about his posture showed that he was pacing himself.

He is going to tie me up and then fuck me, and it will be good. The words kept going back and forth in her mind, like a mantra. It was meant to calm her, but it did nothing of the sort. Here in his room where she had climaxed time and time again and the scent of his aftershave swamped her senses, everything conspired to make her more eager. By the time she was fully naked, she was trembling.

"I'm ready," she whispered.

"What is it that you want?"

"That." She nodded down at the rope, then at the bulge of his cock inside his jeans, "and you, inside me." Her hand moved to her pussy, and she slid one finger into her wet groove, resting it over her clit, pressing and squeezing.

He watched her fingers moving.

She stared at him, almost panting with need.

He pulled his T-shirt over his head and off, abandoning it. The hard muscles of his chest and abdomen gleamed when the light caught them. "Show me how much you want it."

For one moment she teetered on the edge. Then, on instinct, she dropped to her hands and knees. Lifting her chin, she looked up at him. There were six, maybe seven feet apart, and he towered over her. In this position, with her breasts dangling and her bottom lifted, she felt vulnerable and exposed, and she knew that's what he wanted to see.

The rope still moved through his hands, then he patted his thigh with one hand, beckoning to her. That simple gesture made a tremulous wave of relief and anticipation pass from her chest to her pussy, and she made her way over to him on her hands and knees, until she was right in front of him. Kneeling at his feet, she rested her forehead against his thigh. The rope was a hair's breadth from her face and as she clung to him, he moved it, lifting it and looping it around her so that it slid down around her back. He had her entrapped.

When she looked up at him, she was startled by the captivated look in his eyes. It did arouse him to have her lassoed that way. Simple, symbolic and yet so deeply meaningful. She had offered herself, and now she was his.

She leaned back against the rope. The muscles in his arms went taut as he measured and balanced her, responding to her action. She was allowing him to tip the scales, and boy, was it good. Plucking at the button on his fly, she undid his jeans. The soft black cotton briefs beneath bulged as she folded the denim down. When she latched her fingers over the waistband of his briefs, she looked at him for permission. He nodded, and the rope tightened against her back.

Dragging the fabric down, she sighed with longing when his cock bounced free. She licked the length of his shaft, savoring his flavor, adoring the heat and potency of him— the part of him that joined them together. His eyes gleamed with pleasure, his lips parted. She took the swollen head into her mouth, riding it against the roof of her mouth. When he groaned, she took him deeper, sucking him hard.

"Enough." His voice was hoarse. "Stand up."

As she rose to her feet, he pulled his jeans and shorts into place. He cupped her breasts and dipped his head in order to suckle her nipples, first one and then the other. The rope was crushed against the sensitive flesh of her breasts and he rubbed it there with his palms, making her feel it. She moaned aloud, shifting from foot to foot, tension looping from her nipples to her pussy and back, making her unbearably hot. When she swayed back, the rope tightened around her back.

Every inch of her was aware—aware of the containment at her back, the dense smell of their mutual arousal in the room, and most of all she was aware of his attention.

"It is the ritual that makes it so special," he whispered. "It will take me a while to make sure you are properly secured."

As he spoke, keeping her informed of his actions, he lifted her arms at the elbow, indicating she should keep them raised and away from her body. He began to loop the rope under her arms, backwards and forwards across her chest and then beneath her breasts. The flexibility only just distracted her from the fact it would be tight against her skin soon and only he could release her.

Occasionally he would stop and bring another length of rope into play, knotting it into place. That created pressure points on her body—key points, the base of her neck, and along the edge of her rib cage.

"Good?"

She nodded.

"This makes me feel as if you really want to be in my bed." His smile was wicked. He was right though. Each intricate knot he made bound her to him, and she became mesmerized by the caring attention he showed her. It truly was a ritual for him, and it was fast becoming that for her.

It didn't feel overly tight at first, not until she took a deep, ragged breath and then she felt it. Her chest was constricted, breasts squeezed tight and nipples poking through the arrangement of slender ropes. A heady rush hit her. Never had she been so ready to be fucked, never had he made her wait quite so long.

"I'm going to put you on the bed now." He lifted her into his arms and she rolled against his body, the bindings making her want to be right against him where she was safe.

When he laid her down she put her arms flat against the surface. He drew one hand and then the other into one of his, moving them against the decorative metal posts of the headboard. With a length of rope he secured them, tying them together against a single strut, then he looped that length of rope down and around one at her lower rib cage.

He stepped away and stood at the end of the bed looking down at her. The weight of his gaze was almost too much. She was strung out, raw, and dying for him to take her. When she tugged with her wrists it pulled the rope latticed over her chest. The restraint forced her into a different zone. It made something give way inside her and she rolled her head on the pillow, her pulse racing and her breathing shallow and erratic.

"Open your legs."

She did as instructed. The cool air on her inflamed pussy maddened her swollen clit. She wriggled, desperate to be touched there.

He moved her legs further apart—spread-eagling her, making her gasp aloud—then lifted another length of the rope. Again he ran it through his hands, readying it. His biceps flexed and caught the light as he did so. With the rope taut in his hands, he moved it to her inner thigh, resting it in the crease of her groin. He looped the rope around the top of one thigh, weaving it into the latticework over her chest, before bringing it down the other side and around the top of the other thigh. Imogen shut her eyes and inhaled deeply. Every action heightened her senses, while her splayed pussy felt increasingly vulnerable and exposed.

He loomed over her, his expression intense while he watched her every reaction, noting every move she made, every whisper of sound that escaped her.

The rope around her rib cage felt gloriously restrictive, the pressure above and below her breasts and around the tops of her thighs making her more horny than she'd ever been, and when she glanced down at her totem-like nipples between the electric-blue hemp it looked so lewd and lusty that her head rolled against pillows.

After he checked that she was secure, he lay at her side, one hand on the pillow next to her head, the other stroking her left nipple. When he pinched it and she cried out in ecstasy, he watched her face. "Are you comfortable?"

She nodded. It was true, because she felt naked and raw but incredibly safe, because he had secured her. "It's good," she whispered.

Moving his hand around her right breast, he cupped it, squeezing it before placing his fingers around the nipple. Through his jeans she could feel his erection solid against her hip, but still he took his time. She squirmed, her sex throbbing, desperate for him. Each touch set free a burning sensation that traveled to her core, where it stoked the fire there.

Moving over her body, he ran one finger beneath the rope, as if checking it. Then his hands trailed over her abdomen to the plump flesh of her exposed pussy. He stroked her engorged clit then squeezed it between his thumb and forefinger. Needles of sensation shot through her groin. She felt as if the skin on her chest and neck was burning, her stomach tight in response to the delicious provocation. When he pinched, she almost came.

"You know why I'm doing this now, don't you?"

A breathy laugh escaped her. "To drive me insane."

Still he brushed his fingertips over her exposed pussy, tantalizing her swollen folds with the briefest of strokes. The rope around her inner thighs seemed to tighten as her body blossomed under his touch, the restriction making her gasp in delight.

"Because I adore you, and to have you like this is the closest I can get to making you let go and enjoy it completely."

Imogen blinked, her ability to focus on his words fading in and out.

"I want more than you've given me," he added.

"I've given you everything," she gasped, her body tight with the need for release. "You've got me here, like this…please, Giles. Please fuck me."

"Oh, I will, but that's not the only thing I want."

Sweat broke out on her skin. "What do you mean?"

"I want us out, as a couple. I want us to be together, officially."

Her throat tightened and her eyes smarted. There was no escape from hearing this and having to respond. On instinct, she shook her head. That need to run was ingrained in her, despite the state she was in.

He eased one finger inside her sex. Her body clamped, grateful for the hard intrusion, her hips rising as much as they could from the surface of the bed.

"There's no reason not to. Unless you're ashamed of having me, a younger man, your junior, in your bed?" He withdrew his finger.

"God, no!" She blurted out her response, but when she met his gaze she saw the humor there and she cursed softly. "Damn you. It's not that at all... It's just hard for me to..." The words wouldn't come.

"What... Hand over your stubborn independence in exchange for a good relationship?" He rose to his feet and looked down at her while he unzipped his jeans, then ran his fist up and down the length of his erection as he considered her.

Imogen didn't think she could get any more needy, but she was wrong.

"I think you've underestimated me. The rope isn't just about the thrill, if that's what you thought." He gestured at her. "This, *shibari,* is about the next level for me. It's a sign of ultimate commitment and trust."

Battling down a rising sense of panic, she met his gaze. When she did, he put his hand back between her legs, and she had to blink back the wave of pleasure that shot through her groin when he stroked one finger over her clit and down the groove of her pussy.

"You're so aroused, so swollen."

Her face flushed. She could feel her hair sticking to the damp skin on her neck. Mumbling incoherently, she pressed her face against her tethered arm.

"You want to come, don't you?"

She nodded.

"How badly?" He squeezed her clit, locking it between two fingers and rocking his hand.

"Oh, God." She half sat, her wrists jolting against the rope at the headboard. Staring at him, she saw how still he was, how watchful. Her back arched against the bed, the tension in her hips and chest intensifying. Hot liquid ran down between her buttocks.

"So wet." He ducked down between her legs, his mouth closing over her clit.

"Giles, please."

He sucked her, took another lick, his tongue moving from her entrance up to her clit. Breathing over it, he sighed.

"Fuck me," she cried out, "please!"

He moved his hands away from her pussy. "Are you agreeing to my terms?"

Oh, God! What were his terms? "Yes, Giles. Please, please fuck me."

He stood up. Reaching into his pocket, he pulled out a condom packet.

Shoving off his black briefs he let them fall to the floor. His cock bounced free, slapping against his belly as he tore open the condom packet. The pulse in her groin beat wildly as he rolled the rubber sheath over his upright shaft. Then he climbed over her and moved into position. He rested a kiss on her breast over her caged heart, and then she felt the head of his cock at her opening. He filled her in one smooth lunge, pressing to her very center.

The room spun. Her eyes clamped shut and she bellowed aloud. Her wrists tugged this way and that as another liberating climax hit her.

He urged her on, rising up onto his arms, thrusting deep and rhythmically, his eyes shining with determination as he watched her. She was lost to it, her core clenching and unclenching around his cock, setting off another rolling wave of pleasure as it did it so. She was so wide open, and he was so deep. Her entire groin burned with pleasure, deliciously edgy with raw sensitivity and almost too much to bear.

She moaned, begged for mercy.

Still he pushed her on, his breath hot on her face as he arched over her.

He was getting closer and his skin shone damp in the half light, the occasional grunt escaping him as he worked himself into her. She knew he was giving her everything he had.

"Oh, God, Giles, yes."

He nodded, growing still, and his head went back, the muscles in his neck standing out as he let rip and roared. One last thrust, deep and hard, and she felt as if she'd been doused with liquid fire as his cock jerked inside her, over and again.

Afterward, he brought her iced water and held the glass to her lips as she drank. When he put the glass aside, he began to undo the rope. He started at her groin and left her wrists until last. She gazed at him through the haze of her afterglow as he worked. Each knot was undone with care, and he rubbed her skin gently and checked on her.

"You really enjoy this, don't you?"

He flashed her a grin. "Kinky sex?"

She laughed softly. "No, I meant this…."

"Ah, looking after you?"

She nodded. "Why?"

"Because I love you."

Imogen was stunned. The way he'd said it, so matter-of-factly, while he continued to undo the rope that bound her to him made her think she'd imagined it. She stared at him in disbelief until he suddenly looked at her, catching her, and her face heated. She tried to look away, but he drew her back to him with one finger beneath her chin.

"Don't be so surprised. You are lovable, much as you hate to admit it."

She was floored—not only by what he said, but by the easy way he spoke to her now, after the intensity of what had gone before.

He looked at her expectantly. "This is the bit where you tell me how you feel," he added.

She rolled her eyes. "You know how I feel or I wouldn't be here, allowing myself to be exposed this way."

He flashed her a challenging glance.

"Okay, I love you. Damn it, Giles. I fell in love with you ages ago, but I was scared."

"No need." The simple comment was an understatement, but it meant so much. Unbinding her hands, he drew them to his mouth and kissed the tender skin inside her wrists. "I was serious about sharing breakfast too. Starting tomorrow morning. You'll have breakfast here with me."

"But I don't have a change of..."

He put his finger over her lips. "And I want us to spend our evenings together. We can even talk about work sometimes, if you insist."

The final resistance she clung to began to dissolve. He really did know her. She chuckled at the idea of it. "But we might end up arguing over policy in our own time."

"That's what couples who work together do."

"Couples..?" She felt dizzy even though she was on her back.

"Yes, Imogen, couples. That's what we're talking about here."

Before she could even think of objecting, he kissed her, halting her words.

Her emotions soared and for the first time Imogen allowed herself to sink into the moment completely, her arms wrapped around him—the only man who could anchor her, the only man who knew how.

★ ★ ★ ★ ★